Nicky marveled at ju the moonlight. She was woman he had ever know with the sound of gentle waves hitting the sand in the background.

"It's time, Nicky." She stood up and faced him so that her back was to the last of the moonlight shimmering over the waves. Slowly, she took off her leather jacket and tossed it to the side. Taking her time, but not as if she were performing, Didi peeled her tank top off and dropped that too on her jacket. Didi hesitated because she felt petrified that he would reject her. She gazed into his eyes, desperate for confirmation, and saw him smile. She reached behind her and unclasped her bra and watched his eyes as she slipped it off and tossed it away.

Her sensual beauty transfixed Nicky. Her nipples resembled stiff bullets resting atop beautifully rounded breasts. She stood still, and he knew she was watching to see if he approved. *My God, isn't she beautiful?* was the only thought that rocketed around in his head.

Didi liked that she saw a hunger in his eyes. She took a deep breath, then bent at the waist and peeled her panties down her smooth legs and off, kicking them away to land near the rest of her clothes. For the first time in a very long time, she liked that a man could see her nude.

"Come on, Nicky. Let's go skinny-dipping!"

Praise for Stephen B King

"Being a new author with a famous name, I was a bit unsure. Then I got pulled in… I found the story to be quite beautiful, centering around a complex relationship. The love story is believable, made more heartfelt with Nicky's relationship with Didi's small daughter. To be honest, I cried; it reminded me of meeting my stepdad for the first time, one of the best days in my family's life. The crime story is fast paced, exciting, and shows the complexity of the people behind the crime as well as the badge. I thoroughly enjoyed this book, and look forward to reading the others."

~ Antionette Westley

"What an amazing book. Have never looked at a killer like that before. A must read for anyone who loves a good crime novel. Can't wait to read more books by this author."

~ Sara Charles

The Vigilante and the Dancer

by

Stephen B King

The Vigilante and the Dancer

Cover Art by *Kim Mendoza*

The Wild Rose Press, Inc.
PO Box 708
Adams Basin, NY 14410-0708
Visit us at www.thewildrosepress.com

Publishing History
First Edition, 2023
Trade Paperback ISBN 978-1-5092-4344-0
Digital ISBN 978-1-5092-4345-7

Published in the United States of America

Dedication

For my mother, Greta, who loved her five children unconditionally, I miss you, mum.

Didi's Song

For love burns like a candle bright
To remind us in our loneliest night,
That even though we bear the pain,
Memories will keep us from loving again

Chapter 1

Just Another Night in Northbridge

His fingers pressed deeply into her arm, leaving circular bruises as she walked and was half dragged along the footpath on Lake Street. It was just after three in the morning, and the rain tumbled down, though it had eased while they had been inside the nightclub. The gutters were like mini rivers with rapids made from cigarette butts, broken glass, and kebab wrappers, highlighted in the flashing neon lights from the gaudy signs that adorned the buildings.

Rebecca Mallory sobbed, hurting from the earlier punch in the stomach her husband had delivered and the bruises which were forming on her arm. She knew worse was to come later; it always did when he had been drinking. Her mascara ran from a combination of tears and raindrops, and she had a ladder in one stocking.

Desmond Mallory forced her to cross the road toward the taxi rank while she stumbled in her stiletto heels and tight pencil skirt, which made it difficult for her to keep pace. He was tall and built like a heavyweight boxer, so he dragged her easily. Rebecca was twenty-eight years old, blonde, tall, and slim. They had been married for five years. She knew, in her sinking heart, that Des had enough alcohol that night to make him mean. In such a mood, it was inevitable he would hit her, probably on several occasions during the rest of the night. He would force her to have sex with him. Rather than stop the violence, that usually made it worse. Things would escalate and make him abuse her more, as the alcohol would inhibit his ability to perform, and that would be one more thing he would blame her for.

It was times like this Rebecca hated her life, and him in particular. She wanted to leave but knew it was impossible. If she ran, he would find her, and then she would know the true meaning of suffering. More likely, he would kill her. Des wasn't cruel when he stayed away from alcohol; he was a good family man most of the time. Rebecca had hoped because tonight was a special occasion, he would watch how much he drank. Sadly, she had been wrong.

They had been at Mimi's Bar, with a hundred or more others, to help celebrate his big brother Jimmy's birthday. Jimmy Mallory was one of the more colorful local underworld figures with a reputation for using violence to keep control of his territory. He dealt in cocaine, heroin, and meth through one of the local biker gangs. Des wanted nothing to do with his brother's criminal empire; he loved violence, yes, but he drew the line at drug dealing, at least that was what he told Rebecca, and she fervently hoped it was true.

Usually, Des did his best not to drink during the week at home because he knew he had a problem. Those times he could be kind, considerate, and generous, the complete opposite to when he was drunk. For Rebecca, it was like living with a Jekyll and Hyde. He would sometimes bring home gifts or flowers and be gentle and romantic. Then he resembled the man she had fallen in love with years before. But even when Des tried hard, usually every three to four weeks, he would slide back into his old habit and drink to excess, what she had heard some people call a bender. When Des had one too many and reached his point of no return, he would find anything she did not only wrong but offensive. When annoyed with her, there was usually only one outcome; he wanted to hurt her and enjoyed seeing her in pain and subjugated.

The next day, following a beating, he would be contrite and promise he would never do it again, and every time she so wanted to believe him. But inevitably, a month or so later, it would be another broken promise he hadn't remembered making. Sometimes Des agreed to alcohol counseling or to see someone about his violent behavior, but those promises never came to fruition. When Rebecca made appointments for him, at the very last minute, he would be too busy at work, or something, anything, would come up, which meant he couldn't go. It was as if, while he knew he had issues, he couldn't, or wouldn't, face solving them.

Des dragged her toward the cab as the rain fell. "I'm going to teach you a lesson once and for all," he told her, his voice trembling with rage.

The night had started well enough when Des picked out what he wanted her to wear. He chose a crimson-red short-and-revealing outfit, which showed off her large breasts. Of course, he forbade her to wear a bra. He liked it when other men ogled her, but she was forbidden to flirt back. Even a glance could mean a Vesuvius-like outburst of violence toward her, the man she was deemed to have flirted with, or usually both.

While Des orchestrated the dress and flimsy, see-through panties she was to wear, he made it clear she was to make him proud and ensure that everyone there envied him. But she knew it was a fine line between being desirable and being seen by Des to appear unfaithful. She shuddered to think what would happen if she ever actually slept with another man. His jealous rage would know no limits. She was sure he would murder her without a second thought.

He began the night with orange juice and good intentions, feigning that he had to work the next day as an excuse to stay off alcohol. But the inevitable pressure from his brother and peers ensured that the first glass of juice was the only one he finished. Once the first bourbon was thrust into his hand, in a tall glass with ice and cola, though considerably more ice than cola, Rebecca knew she was in trouble.

Rebecca tried to stay happy and jovial so as not to incur his wrath by appearing not to be enjoying the occasion. Spoiling Des's night out would be a surefire way of making him irate. Des, like his brother, had a well-known reputation for letting his fists speak for him, and most of his so-called friends feared him. Even if they chose to take Des on, they knew that if they won the fight, they would lose the battle. His brother Jimmy would have them beaten up by a couple of burly biker types with baseball bats. Worse, they could be discovered battered and broken and floating dead in the river. It would be far better to take to hiding from Des than risk angering Jimmy.

Des dragged her across the road, but Rebecca tripped on a pothole and twisted her ankle. The stilettoes he picked out for her were too high for the pace he was setting. Rebecca would have fallen if he did not have such a firm hold of her arm, and he yanked her upright. But that didn't slow him down. He seemed determined to get her home as quickly as possible to begin her punishment.

Des clamped his fingers and thumb into the fleshy part of her upper arm even harder. In the morning, she would have five very prominent, ugly blue marks, along with whatever other bruises he would decide to inflict on the rest of her body. He rarely hit her in the face, thankfully, other than slaps. It was never a guarantee that he wouldn't, but in the past, he preferred to hurt her in places that didn't show. Generally, punches to her breasts, stomach, and arms were his favored means of ensuring her obedience. Keeled over in pain, crouched in fear, she quickly learned how to show him the proper respect he believed he was due when drunk.

Des yanked open the rear door of the cab at the head of the queue and pushed her in. But he was too quick for her as his force thrust her forward before she could duck low enough. Rebecca saw stars as her head hit the top of the doorframe, but that didn't slow him from trying to cram her onto the back seat. She knew he was beyond caring about showing any niceties and seemed to enjoy the cracking sound her head made against metal.

She fell, sprawling into the cab, trying to rub the circulation back into the wounded area of her head while Des shoved her roughly across the bench seat, and she cried out in pain. Her skirt rucked up, showing off the thong she wore, and Des slapped her rump hard, telling her to hurry up.

The cabbie turned in his seat with a concerned look on his face. "Are you all right, love?" he asked.

Rebecca was stunned, not only from the blow to the head she had received but also to hear a cab driver show any concern at that time of the night without a heavy accent. Australian, Caucasian cab drivers on the night shift were rare indeed. Most of them appeared to be from anywhere rather than her home country these days.

"Shut your mouth and take us to twenty-two Towsten Street, Redcliffe. The bitch is fine. Don't worry about her," Des replied in a raised voice, bristling with barely suppressed rage and malice.

Rebecca noticed the driver didn't seem to be scared, as most normal people were when they came face-to-face with her husband. But then she realized this man had no idea who Des was, or more importantly, who his brother was. The cabbie stared back insolently and didn't reply. He turned his gaze to her with a raised eyebrow. She dared not say a word but pleaded with her eyes and nodded for him to drive.

Eventually, Des broke the silence. "The bitch is going to cop it anyway, whether you drive us there or not, pal. So, the only difference is whether I punch your fucking lights out first, and we take another cab, or you mind your own fucking business and hit the road, *pal*."

But the cabbie was in no hurry and raised his eyebrows again in her direction. He nodded encouragingly, completely ignoring Des, and Rebecca knew she had to avoid the impending orgy of violence. "Twenty-two, Towsten Street, just drive, please. This is my husband, and I'm fine."

The cab driver turned around slowly and drove off,

and Des punched her in the side, just below her ribs. The blow took her breath away, and the pain was sudden and excruciating. Rebecca bent over, gasped loudly as the breath was forced from her lungs, and she very nearly vomited.

The cab slowed, and Des, in his most menacing voice, said, "Pal, it's your fault I hit her. That was for sticking your fucking nose into my business. If you stop the cab, I will hurt her some more and then you. It's your call. Pull over, I fucking dare you." He sneered, then taunted him further, "I own this bitch. She's been a fucking tramp tonight, and she is going to get it, *real bad*. So you can make it easy or hard for her. It's your choice. I don't give a fuck, either way, *pal*." The cab sped up again, the driver shook his head but stayed silent, and Des sat back into the seat.

The traffic was thin, and the bright neon nightlife slipped past as they left Northbridge to head onto the Graham Farmer Freeway toward Redcliffe. Rebecca noticed the driver tilted his rearview mirror up, no doubt so he couldn't see what else happened in the back seat, but she saw what looked like smoldering hatred in his eyes before they disappeared from her view. For the rest of the journey, there were only sounds of wipers sloshing rain from the windscreen, and Rebecca's sobbing moans, as she held her side and tried to get her breath back.

****

Nicky Pantella kept to the speed limit, gripping the steering wheel more tightly than he needed, a rage coursing through his body. He was conscious of the time, and a glance at his watch told him he had plenty. He wanted to get back into Northbridge to pick up the only cab fare that made his whole nightshift worthwhile, and he didn't want to be late.

Didi, short for Deirdre, was his friend. She finished her shift as a lap dancer at four in the morning, and it had become his habit to take her home. He looked forward to once more trying to make her smile because she was the saddest person he had ever known in his life. On the rare occasions when he could make her laugh, her face lit up the cab, and her big brown eyes sparkled. She was stunningly beautiful, but he knew she didn't know it, or if she did, for some reason, she'd stopped caring.

Eight minutes later, Nicky pulled up in the driveway in Towsten Street and said the first words since he had asked if she was okay. "Twenty-eight sixty."

Des slowly opened his wallet and took out a fifty-dollar note. He spat into the middle of the bill, screwed it up in his hand, and threw it onto the floor of the front passenger side of the cab. "Keep the change, *pal*."

He jerked the door open, got out of the cab, and dragged the woman with him. Nicky watched as she stumbled in the rain toward their front door. But as they got there, he saw the man slap her face, which rocked her head violently to the side. *He's going to kill her,* Nicky thought and shook his head.

He reached a decision, then backed the cab out of the driveway, turned, and headed back the way he had come. He glanced at the dash clock and confirmed he had enough time to pick up Didi, so long as he didn't stop for longer than ten minutes, which he didn't intend to do.

****

Rebecca fumbled in her bag for the keys, not wanting another slap for being too slow. With trembling hands, she got the key into the lock and turned it. Des grabbed her neck in his large hand and shoved her head into the door as he used her face to push it open. She fell through the doorway onto the floor, and he kicked her legs out of the way so he could close it behind them.

"Please, Des, I didn't do anything wrong. I only did what you told me to do." She whimpered.

"Is that right? You did what I told you to, did you?" He kicked her just under the ribs, the same side he had punched earlier, then leaned down and grabbed her hair. He yanked her back up to her feet, almost pulling long clumps from her head. Then he pushed her, screaming, into the bedroom, where he threw her onto the bed.

"Did I tell you to act like a whore, did I? Did I tell you to let that guy Gordy keep putting his fucking hands all over you, did I? You liked him touching you, didn't you, you slut? I saw you. And what is it with the fucking cab driver? What, you think I couldn't handle him? I gotta have you help me out with a fucking cab driver?"

"Desi, Gordy works for your brother, and I was friendly like you told me to. It's you I love, not him," she pleaded.

He bent down and, with his left hand, grabbed the front of her dress and yanked it away from her body, tearing it until her breasts spilled free as he lifted her upper body from the bed. With his right hand, he slapped her face, which split the inside of her lip against her teeth, and she tasted blood. She howled, knowing the night ahead would be long, miserable, and painful.

"I didn't tell you to let him think he could treat you like a slut, did I?" He dropped her back on the bed, and she crawled into a fetal position, her head buried in her hands, crying.

Through her fingers, she watched Des look down and smile. It was clear he loved to see her cower in fear. She couldn't help it; when he was like this, he terrified her. He took his jacket off and tossed it on the floor, and then he began to unbutton his shirt. *Oh, God, it's time for him to fuck his bitch. That's how he sees me, his bitch*, she thought as the doorbell rang.

"That must be one of our nosy neighbors, coming to check up on the sniveling noise you've been making. Why does everyone in the world want to stick their nose into my affairs tonight? Well, I'm just in the mood to punch some bastard's lights out," he roared.

Des slammed the bedroom door closed behind him and stormed to the front door in a red veil of rage. He threw it open so hard it banged into the wall, intending to shout a string of obscenities before swinging his first punch at whoever dared to ring his bell at three o'clock in the morning. He would follow it up with a roundhouse punch he was famous for or a kick if the interloper went down from the first blow. Instead, he saw the gaping barrel of a silenced pistol pointing at him.

"Hey, *pal*," the quiet voice of the cab driver whispered as he pulled the trigger three times in quick succession: *phut, phut, phut*. The three nine-millimeter hollow-point bullets hit Des in the chest at point-blank range. He stumbled backward from the hammer blows, a look of shock and horror on his face as he came up against the opposite hallway wall. He slowly slid down until he was sitting on the floor, the light and life fading from his shocked and disbelieving eyes.

****

Nicky tucked the gun into the front pocket of his black hooded jacket and calmly picked up the ejected shells from the carpet. The soft-nosed bullets would have mushroomed and changed direction inside his chest. Nicky knew they would have caused massive internal damage and bleeding, from which no one could survive.

He heard the faint sounds of Rebecca crying alone on her bed, and he smiled; she was still alive. She hadn't heard anything, and even if she had, Nicky's reading of the situation told him that she dared not investigate. She would think her husband would handle whoever it was that had come calling and return to her when finished. Nicky silently closed the door with his right hand encased in a black latex glove so as not to leave fingerprints.

Back at the cab, he unlocked the door and silently drove away with his for-hire light turned off. He wanted to pick up Didi, and he wasn't going to risk getting a passenger who wanted him to go in the wrong direction and make him late for her, or worse, miss her altogether if she got fed up waiting and caught another taxi.

He felt nothing but contempt for the man he had just killed. He was only one more piece of crap in a sea of floating scum so far as Nicky was concerned. On any given night in the city, he saw all sorts of mayhem, more so in the early hours of the morning. He'd seen fighting, people vomiting in gutters, muggings, robberies, or gangs of thugs threatening innocent people who were out for nothing more than a good night in the city. He'd witnessed all that and worse on a sickeningly regular basis.

On many streets in Northbridge, you didn't have to walk too far to see old, fading bloodstains. Sometimes just droplets, other times where puddles had pooled and dried on the pavements. Sirens sounded with monotonous regularity between ten at night and six in the morning; it was not much more than a rat race. Nicky blamed the escalating violence he witnessed almost nightly on the rising tide of drugs and alcohol. No matter what the reason was, Nicky believed things were getting worse. As far as he was concerned, the goody-goody bleeding heart liberals could make all the excuses they liked about the misfortunate upbringing or lack of opportunity for youth. But they weren't out at three in the morning driving a cab and seeing the horror people could inflict upon each other.

It seemed to Nicky that a fight was never just a fight between two people. It was a surprise hit from behind without warning to knock someone to the ground. Once defenseless, the real beating would start. Or several thugs would surround and attack one vulnerable victim. It wasn't about knocking someone unconscious; it was about disfiguring or maiming. The extent of physical damage attackers caused seemed to be a badge of honor, like a fun night wasn't complete without seriously injuring an innocent victim.

Nicky had reasons other than monetary gain for patrolling the streets in the taxi at night. He lived in the hope of seeing the men he was hunting, perhaps walking between restaurants or crossing a road. His highest hope was that one would hail his cab by chance. If they did, Nicky would not hesitate; he would execute them and not lose one minute of sleep afterward.

Occasionally, the police would try to curb street hooliganism by flooding the area with uniformed officers, sometimes on horseback, to provide a visible deterrent. They came up with catchy names, called it operation this or that, and they would pat themselves on the back publicly for the number of arrests made or the reduction in crime statistics for that weekend. Unfortunately, when those operations finished, it would return to normal. The thing with statistics, Nicky believed, was that most people didn't report assaults unless they were hospitalized. Victims might wake up with their phone, wallet, or purse missing and decide it wasn't worth the hassle of reporting it to the police as their injuries were minimal. So a temporary drop in crime statistics didn't mean too much so far as Nicky was concerned. It was rather like trying to hold back rising floodwaters with sandbags, he thought. Eventually, the deluge was going to break the levy; it was just a question of when.

The increased availability and affordability of drugs like methamphetamine, ice, cocaine, and crack cocaine was, in his opinion, the real culprit. He saw deals occurring on street corners, in shop doorways with monotonous regularity. If he could see it, Nicky wondered why the police couldn't unless they were being paid not to. Northbridge was awash in illicit recreational drugs and had been for a long time.

Nicholas *Nicky* Pantella shook his head to clear his mind of thoughts about the rising crime wave; it depressed him, and he wanted to be cheerful when Didi sat alongside him. He realized the rain had stopped as he crossed the Windan Bridge, and the air was thick and muggy. Steam rose from the streets, so he rolled the window down, choosing fresh air to air-conditioned. It felt like the day ahead would be a hot one.

Nicky made it back into town with ten minutes to spare and, with the extra time, stopped at Cha Cha's 24-Hour Doughnut House for two large takeaway coffees. One was black for him, the other a caramel-flavored latte, with an artificial sweetener, for her. He then drove to his usual spot to park, with the light turned off, and waited. He slipped his jacket off and straightened his hair, checking his appearance in the rearview mirror. He crammed the coat, gloves, gun, and expelled casings into his backpack, then shoved it underneath the passenger seat so he could grab it quickly if required. Nicky wanted the front seat clear for Didi to sit on when she arrived, never behind him. He liked to look at her profile as he drove her home. Sometimes they stopped for a late-night coffee and cake at a twenty-four-hour café if she was in the mood. She was sometimes less melancholy if the customers hadn't tried to paw her too much during her shift, and she felt willing to stop and chat with him.

The humidity made the cab warm and sticky, but he didn't mind. With the engine switched off, the air conditioning was too, so he turned the radio down low and opened all four windows a few inches using the electric switches on the armrest. Nicky kept the doors locked for security; cabbies were as vulnerable as anyone else.

The man the press had dubbed the *Northbridge Vigilante* leaned back in his seat and let his mind drift back to a time six years before when his life was so much different. Then, he had promise, a bright, cheery future, and a loving family. All that was wiped out in an instant by a drunken driver who had broken up with his girlfriend and was determined to die in a high-speed accident which sadly took Nicky's parents with him.

Chapter 2

Dinner, a Concert, and Two Deaths

Nicky recalled when he had prospects, a future even, and the thing was that through the ensuing years, that fact hurt the most. He could have done something with his life rather than drive a taxi on the night shift for a living, hosing out drunks' vomit, and taking customers' abuse. It hadn't always been like that. Nicky had a stable family, a good childhood, and a younger brother who idolized him. At school, Nicky had been a good student though he didn't excel at studying, but he enjoyed a multitude of friends. He wasn't bullied because he was well-liked by everyone. His report cards and assessments always said he was a pleasure to teach, well mannered, but he could do so much better if he would apply himself harder. It was common knowledge that Nicky would do anything for anyone. His heart was big, and he tended to land on his feet when life tried to trip him up.

Nicky had no idea what he wanted to do for a career as he approached the final year of school. He graduated, but not with high enough grades to go on to further education, though that would have been a waste of money anyway. His family and friends had been more important than studying. Many of his friends went on to university, leaving Nicky behind. Even then,

Nicky didn't begrudge them their successes or bemoan his own lack of it. He was delighted for them and thought that sooner or later, his break would come.

Girls adored him, and they clamored for his attention. Not only was he good-looking and well-built, he also had an air of profound mystery to him, which they found irresistible. There was just something about him that attracted them to him like moths to the flame. They saw him as caring, considerate, and unusual for his age. Nicky liked to listen when they had something to say. He seemed to find girls' thoughts, feelings, and beliefs interesting. He never took advantage when he dated, and inevitably, that meant girls would let him do anything he pleased because he hadn't expected it and showed them respect.

When it came to the school graduation ball in year twelve, all of the unattached girls wanted Nicky to invite them, and they waited for the possibility, declining other offers. In his typically kind-hearted way, Nicky chose Marie, a plain girl who wouldn't have been invited by anyone else because she wasn't part of the *in* crowd. It was Nicky's nature to help others, and his motivation for asking her was so that he could make her feel special on such a momentous night. He didn't want to know that she went to the ball with no date, no one to dance with, and no one to care. That night she glowed, looking as beautiful as if it were her wedding day. She felt so proud to be with the most adored boy in year twelve, even though she knew he didn't want her as a girlfriend; he had his pick of those. But for her, that one night, she *was* his girlfriend.

Such was Nicky's charm that the others, who missed out on a date because they waited for him in vain, didn't hate him for it. Sure, they wished it was them dancing with him and would have permitted sex at the end of the night, but they accepted who he had chosen to take and why, knowing he was a genuine guy with a loyal, caring heart.

Marie was a virgin. She had never even come close to making love, though she did once give a hand job to a guy at a party in hopes he would ask her out afterward. Of course, he hadn't. He'd told his mates what she had done, and they laughed and joked at her expense for the following month. On the night of the ball, she would have gladly given it up for Nicky. She wanted him and always had, and she wanted to show how grateful she was that he had chosen her.

When they left the prom, everyone watched them go, her arm through his. Jealous girls nudged each other, believing that within minutes she would be sans underwear, legs open with him on the back seat of his car parked somewhere dark. Most of the girls wished it could have been them. But instead, Nicky drove into Fremantle for ice cream, and they walked along the fisherman's harbor amid the trawlers and quayside restaurants and talked for two hours. When he took her home, she thanked him for the best night of her life and told him that she understood that he wouldn't be phoning her to take her out again, but she loved him anyway for being so kind. He kissed her on the doorstep, her hands clinging around his neck, knowing she would never forget that kiss for the rest of her life.

End-of-year exams came and went, and he went to Busselton with thirty others for the weeklong end of school celebrations. A party wasn't a party unless he was there. But his first thought was always for his friends. Were the drugs and drinks they were taking safe? And if a fight occurred, he was there, calming tempers and standing between the guys who wanted to punch it out. Because everyone liked Nicky, he was able to calm a situation down and get the protagonists to shake hands and be friends again. He never got too drunk or too high that he couldn't look out for people he cared about. Male or female, friend or lover, he treated everyone with genuine affection and made them feel special.

His parents adored him, and his *everything will be all right* attitude, but by the time the end of school dust had settled, he had not found a full-time job and still had no real idea of what he wanted to do with his life. As much as his parents loved him, they gave him a stern lecture. One thing was for sure, working part-time at the local hamburger shop, as he had since age fourteen, wasn't going to be his career. His father suggested applying for an apprenticeship, but the only trade that held any interest for him was electronics, and try as he might, he wasn't able to get anything in that field.

Finally, in loving exasperation, they knew they had to put their foot down and give him one month to find a decent job or else. They never specified what *or else* meant, but eighteen days later, Nicky announced he was joining the army, much to their chagrin and his brother's horror. The family tried to talk him out of it. After all, they didn't want to see their eldest son live in another state while in training, or worse, fight in a Middle Eastern hot spot. But his mind was made up. The army recruiter had promised he could work in electronics. The papers were signed, and he was going.

Nicky's parents loved him, their perfect son, and though they were devastated, the night before he left, they threw a party for him at their favorite Chinese restaurant. All his friends and family from near and far attended to say farewell, and most of the single girls from school cried. Guys, too, were upset to lose such a great friend, and his younger brother, Simon, was inconsolable. The following day at ten in the morning, Nicky waved goodbye at the airport and flew out for his induction into the army. His father never forgave himself for feeling he had pushed him into a career that moved him five thousand kilometers away.

****

Nicky breezed through basic training, naturally amassing friends along the way, and he excelled as a soldier. He learned about weapons and was a naturally gifted marksman, thanks to his father being a hunter who taught him to shoot at an early age. Nicky enjoyed improving his fitness and became very adept at hand-to-hand combat.

After basic training, Nicky got the chance to apply for the promised apprenticeship in electronics. In particular, he was interested in surveillance, electronic countermeasures, and missile technology, as well as computers, as they related to warfare and strategy. He worked hard to keep up with the guys who were smarter than he. School had always been where he made friends, but now he had to study, and he did well. Going back to the books was tough for someone like Nicky. But because it was something he had dreamed of since childhood, he buckled down and put in the effort to finish in the top three of his class in the first year. Nicky had found his niche in life, and in the second year, there were more practical applications, and he loved his chosen career. He was excited for a future in an ever-growing field of immense and exciting possibilities. At the end of his second year, he was promoted to corporal.

At ten minutes past one, August fourteenth, during the middle of his third year, his lecturer came to his desk and told him to go immediately to the commanding officer's office. He jumped up, saluted, and left the classroom, wondering what he had done to justify such a summons. He shook his head as he ran because Nicky didn't think he'd done anything wrong, but going to the commander's office had to be serious. He loved being in the army and wouldn't do anything to jeopardize his career.

Nancy, the CO's secretary, looked up as he entered and nodded toward the door, directing him to knock and enter. Nick's unease grew significantly. He had been told by those who had gone before him that being summoned to the CO's office would usually mean at least a fifteen-minute wait in the foyer. While waiting, Nancy would frown in a menacing way, so your nerves were jangled by the time you got to see him. Usually, that was to have the riot act read to you for some misdemeanor.

Nicky knocked, entered, and closed the door. He then marched to stand in front of the desk, stood at attention, and saluted before saying, "Corporal Pantella reporting as ordered, sir."

"At ease, Corporal, please take a seat."

Nicky felt petrified. He had never heard of anyone summoned to the inner sanctum and be asked to take a seat unless you were an officer. Nicky had a second shock when he saw his sergeant already seated in one of the two chairs in front of the desk. Silently, he took the other and sat at attention, waiting for an ax to fall.

"Corporal, it is my very unpleasant duty to have to tell you that your parents were involved in a serious car accident last night. Your father died at the scene, and your mother is fighting for her life in hospital."

Nick's world fell apart. He felt dizzy and almost blacked out from shock. He had always been close to his father, and memories came flooding back of them fishing together, hunting, and camping with his little brother, Simon. Those were the best times of his life. Nicky could shoot as well as anyone in the hunting parties he was invited to attend and was considered by the adults to be one of the men. He could kill a wild boar with a single shot at a hundred yards by the age of fourteen and could skin rabbits and kangaroos. He butchered animals to keep the parts worth eating, using his bowie knife, which had been a valued thirteenth birthday present.

Distance hadn't diminished the love Nicky shared with his parents even though they lived in Perth, and he worked at the Defense Force School of Signals in Watsonia, Victoria. Never had a week gone by that he hadn't talked to his mother and father. Many of those talks had been with Simon in the background, chatting about his schooling. Simon told him repeatedly he wanted to join the army, too, to be with his brother as soon as he was old enough, though he preferred the idea of going into the medical corps.

They'd spoken only two days previously, when his mother had been excited because they were going out to dinner, followed by a concert by her lifelong musical idol, James Hendry. Nicky realized the accident must have been before or after that show.

"How...when...why?" was all Nicky could bring himself to say.

"The details I have are pretty scant, Corporal. I'm sorry, but the weather was appalling last night in Perth, I'm told, with heavy rain and strong winds. They were driving home, and a car came through a red light at high speed. The driver of the other car is also in critical condition, but I don't have any more information than that. I'm sorry."

Nicky shook his head, unable to speak further.

"Nancy has arranged a flight back to Perth for you, and I have my driver waiting to take you to the airport shortly. Sgt. Joyet here is going to accompany you to make sure you're okay and to see if he can help once you get there. Take as much leave as you need, Corporal. Here is my card with my mobile number on it so you can let me know if I can help in any way whatsoever. I will also have a liaison officer contact you in Perth to make sure you get all the support you need from us."

Nicky was in such a daze he barely heard the CO's words, but he allowed himself to be ushered out of the office to go and pack his things. The next few hours, he spent in a fugue, as if shell shocked. Nicky got ready to leave without conscious thought and then wondered afterward how he had packed, as he had no recollection of doing so. Time seemed to slow down and drag, while other pockets disappeared entirely.

Nicky was midway through the flight when the first tears of grief hit him; he was inconsolable by the flight attendants and Staff Sgt. Joyet as he wept. When the plane landed, he had recovered sufficiently, but he had reverted to operating on autopilot and was quiet and withdrawn.

The sergeant organized a cab to the hospital, and when they pulled up to the front, he led Nicky to the reception area to inquire where to go. He shook Nicky's hand and wished him well before returning to the taxi. In a fog, Nicky gave his mother's name to a middle-aged matronly looking woman who sat behind the desk. She directed him to intensive care on the third floor via a bank of elevators. Simon, along with their aunt and uncle, was in the hall sitting on plastic chairs and stood when Nicky arrived. Nicky tried to hold in his tears, but seeing his brother so visibly upset, the dam broke, and they hugged each other as they cried unashamedly.

Time dragged by until a haggard-looking doctor ushered them into a room where he delivered the bad news. Their mother's injuries were too severe. They had tried everything to save her, but she had passed away without regaining consciousness. The brothers were parentless, and Simon was only thirteen.

****

Nicky made the decision for his future, and the day before the funerals, he resigned from the army on compassionate grounds. For him, Nicky had no choice; he had to look after his grief-stricken younger brother rather than see him shipped off to other family members and an uncertain future.

It was a tough time, and sometimes Nicky wondered how he would get through it. He had the funerals to arrange and pay for, and Nicky, at twenty-two years old, had to grow up fast. There was no will, or life insurance policies, which brought unwanted complications. They needed a lawyer to help sort things out and get through probate. Financially, Nicky realized they couldn't afford to keep the house with the debt level it had, so it had to go. Selling the family home added to their trauma, but they salvaged what mementos they could of their parents and watched, heartbroken, as it was auctioned and taken by the highest bidder.

When the dust settled, Nicky and Simon lived in a small, three-bedroom stone cottage in South Perth, paid from the remainder after their parents' debts were discharged from the sale of the family home. They had around sixty thousand dollars left to split between them and a manageable mortgage on Nicky's new income as a cab driver. Their lawyer told them there could be a government insurance payout from the accident but that it could take a long time before they would see the money. He offered to pursue it on their behalf pro bono, taking a percentage of the settlement, which Nicky gratefully accepted.

Simon took the deaths harder than Nicky, who had to be his brother's rock. He required counseling twice a week to help battle depression. Nicky was there for him, and they had family support, but his schooling suffered, with missed lessons from illness and headaches. Some days Simon found it impossible to get out of bed. Nicky tried to get a job where he could finish his studies without success. Because the kind of electronics he had been working with only applied to the armed forces, his training didn't help. He stumbled into driving cabs at night as a means to pay the bills and had the added benefit that he was available during the day to help Simon through the worst of his dark, sometimes suicidal, periods of depression.

They became inseparable, sharing their tragedy, with Simon unwilling to leave his older brother's side for the first four months after the accident because of recurrent nightmares he suffered, in which Nicky was taken from him too. No amount of reasoning could assure Simon that he wouldn't be doomed to be alone for life.

Nicky cooked, cleaned, and did the laundry; the discipline of his army training helped enormously. Eventually, Simon rediscovered his balance with the world, and he pitched in and helped as much as he could. They were not only brothers but had become best friends. They shared chores and spent a lot of time together, with Nicky helping out with Simon's homework when he could, even though it had never been his strong suit when he had been at school. Simon tried to make up his lost ground, but that ensured neither of them had a social life outside of each other.

Slowly things improved, and Simon knuckled down to study harder. He realized he owed so much to his brother, who had given up everything for him, and Simon wanted to make Nicky proud, so he worked tirelessly to that end. Two months after his sixteenth birthday, Simon met his first true love, Jenny. With Nicky's blessing, they went out in the evening on date nights to the movies and coffee shops.

Nicky, who had put his own love life on hold, began to live his life vicariously through Simon's eyes. He welcomed Jenny into their home and eventually permitted her to stay over on weekend nights while he worked. Nicky figured they were going to have sex anyway, so they may as well have his blessing; they were in love after all.

Nicky saw that Simon was like he had been himself at that age; he respected people in general, and especially Jenny. Jenny's parents loved Simon too and thought their daughter had met the perfect someone to be her life partner. Simon finished school and graduated as dux, and Nicky never felt prouder than when he was at the graduation ceremony. He shed silent tears as he watched Simon walk on stage to accept his certificate. If only his parents could have been there to share in the experience, Nicky wished. He believed that if there was an afterlife, they would surely be watching from somewhere and would be feeling the pride he felt for his brother.

Nicky took the two lovebirds out to dinner to celebrate their graduations, and they had a fantastic night at that same local Chinese restaurant that the family had frequented for many years. The owner, Alan Chan, poured them each a glass of champagne from the secret supply he kept for *"very special people"* on *"extraordinary occasions."*

There was no way for Nicky to know at the time, but Simon had only twenty-three days left to live.

Chapter 3

Didi and James Hendry

Nicky leaned across the cab onto the passenger side and clicked the door open for a very tired-looking Didi. The time was four sixteen in the morning. As she climbed in, he silently handed her the caramel latte, which she gratefully accepted and managed a crooked smile. Didi wore a blue faux-leather jacket, jeans, and a black tank top. He could tell this would be one of the nights she didn't feel like talking much, so instead, as he drove toward her home, he remembered back to the morning they first met.

He happened to pull the cab into a laneway to do a U-turn around four a.m. when he saw a scuffle occurring in the darkness. He saw moving shadows up against a brick wall and noticed one of the three people was a woman, and she appeared to be in trouble. Nicky stepped out of the cab and grabbed his five-battery, steel-cased torch, which he kept by the side of the driver's seat for times when he needed to defend himself. As he approached, he heard one man say to the other, "Hold her still, Max, I'll take a turn with the little bitch first, and then I'll hold her for you to have a go."

The woman, although she struggled like a demon, couldn't scream, as the burlier of the two had his hand over her mouth from behind.

There was no doubt in Nicky's mind about what was going on. His blood turned to ice water, and a hot mist of rage came over him. Quickly and silently, Nicky approached and, with a full swing of his torch, hit the attacking man on the side of his knee. With a grin of satisfaction, Nicky heard the unmistakable sound of bones breaking. That blow ensured the would-be rapist would take no further part in the fight. He fell in a writhing heap, screaming as he clutched his shattered knee.

The burly one named Max snarled and threw the woman against the wall. She bounced off the brick surface and, with her feet tangled in her shorts, lost her balance and fell. Max began to take up a fighting stance to confront the interloper, but Nicky didn't give him time. Nicky raised the torch and brought it across the man's face. His aim was true, and the one-and-a-half-kilogram light hit squarely on his nose, breaking it instantly. A cascade of crimson squirted out, drenching the front of the man's plaid shirt. He grunted and covered his face in his hands, blood raining down through his fingers. Nicky kicked him in the groin, hard, with near-perfect timing, and watched as he clutched at himself, bent forward, and made an "ouff" sound as he fell face-first onto the cobblestone pavement.

Nicky grinned, his eyes sparkling, high on adrenaline, enraged that such a big man would crush a tiny, defenseless woman while his mate raped her before he took his turn. Nicky brought the torch down again on the back of the man's head, and he ceased moving.

Barely fifteen seconds had passed, and both

attackers lay on the ground, one unconscious, the other screaming in pain, yet Nicky hadn't broken a sweat, though adrenaline coursed through his body, making him pant. Nicky wanted to hurt them more, a lot more. He stood, torch in hand, contemplating murder; he wanted to. The bloodlust and anger created an almost overpowering urge. But he remembered the woman still lying on the cold, paved alley, and he made his way to her, helping her to her feet.

She was angry and crying; her mascara had stained her pale cheeks. Her short, black hair was a mess, she had grazed the side of her face against the wall, and it was bleeding. Nicky took a clean handkerchief from his pocket and held it to her wound. Her shorts and underwear still clung to her ankles, and she almost fell again. Nicky held her by her arms as she steadied herself.

"Are you okay?" he asked gently.

She looked into his eyes, and he tried to convey compassion and genuine interest, which was in complete contrast to the cold rage he had shown the two men. She sniffed back tears and nodded, then bent at the waist and pulled her shorts and panties back up, holding them so they didn't fall again. "I'm okay, I think," she answered coolly, her voice breaking.

Nicky realized she was unsure that he wouldn't take advantage her or at least steal a peek at her exposed pubic area. But he was more interested in looking into her eyes to make sure she wasn't in shock. Her pupils seemed fine, and it looked like she could focus; *no serious damage,* he thought.

He smiled encouragingly. "Just wait one second, and I will take you home, okay?" he said quietly, but she clung to him. She glanced to the men on the pavement, then nodded and let go of his arm. Nicky saw she watched as Nicky squatted down alongside the man with the shattered knee. The man's wallet was poking out of his rear jeans pocket, and Nicky removed it, opened it up, and took out the driver's license, which he tucked into the top pocket of his shirt. Nicky dropped the wallet on the ground and then tapped the man's chest hard, three or four times, with the bloody end of the torch to get his attention.

"Are you listening, dickhead, or shall I break one of your arms?"

"I need an ambulance," he cried.

"Well, let me tell you, dickhead, I'm all cut up about what you need. What about what the girl needed? Maybe you should have thought about that before you attacked her." He bounced the torch on his chest another three times. "Are you listening to me?"

"Yeah, I'm listening," he whined. "We were only having a bit of fun; the bitch teased us, showing us her boobs all night. She wanted it; she told us in the club."

Nicky nodded slowly, still trying hard to stop himself from hitting him in the face with the torch. *So she is a stripper or a lap dancer,* Nicky realized. That explained why she was alone on the street at four o'clock in the morning. Keeping his voice low and quiet, which only made it sound more menacing, he said, "You listen to me, now, you fucking low-life piece of shit. If she wasn't watching, I'd kill you both by caving both your fucking faces in, so think yourself fortunate. I've got your driver's license, so I know who you are and where you live. If you make any trouble or come back and hurt this girl in any way, ever again, I will visit you. If I do that, I will break both your arms, legs, and every bone in your face. Do you believe me, or would you like a demonstration?"

"Yeah, yeah, yeah, I hear you. Now call me an ambulance, please."

"Okay, dickhead, you're an ambulance. One last thing, don't come back into Northbridge for at least a year. If you do, and I see you, you're dead."

Nicky had no intention of calling for an ambulance for two rapists. If there were any justice in the world, they would be picked on by muggers while they lay there, unable to defend themselves. Whether that happened or not, he didn't care. He had the girl to look after, and he needed to make sure she wasn't hurt or in shock.

As he stood up, Nicky couldn't stop himself; he brought the torch down one more time on the man's knee, making sure it was severely damaged and that he wouldn't be walking unaided for a good long while. The man screamed, and Nicky turned and gently took the woman by her upper arm and guided her to the cab. He opened the front passenger door and helped her into the seat. She seemed to be in a daze, and once inside, she didn't move as if she were catatonic. Nicky put her seat belt on for her, being very careful not to touch her inappropriately. Then he got in the driver's side, backed out of the alley, and drove away.

"My name's Nick Pantella. People call me Nicky. You're safe now; you can relax. Are you hurt in any way? I can take you to the hospital if you are, and if not, where would you like me to take you?"

Slowly she came out of her stupor and seemed to realize she was still holding the handkerchief up to her face. She wiped away her tears, further smudging the mascara, and gave one more sniff. She replied softly, "I'm Didi. I share a house in North Beach with a couple of friends. Thank you for coming to my rescue. They came out of nowhere and grabbed me from behind."

She started to cry again, and he didn't press her for more information. After a few seconds, she spoke again, "They just grabbed me and dragged me into that alley. I'm not sure what would have happened if you hadn't come along. I will never be able to thank you enough for helping me. I should have known better. They looked like trouble and had just enough to drink. They had been on at me all night for a freebie, grabbing my bum, trying to feel my tits, and just being drunken obnoxious fucking pigs." She turned to face him, venom in her voice yet pleading with her eyes. "But I don't do that. I dance and let them look; I don't like them to touch."

Nicky felt embarrassed whenever people thanked him. He squirmed in the seat, feeling uncomfortable. He just did what he did and never wanted anything in return. "It's fine, love. No thanks required, and you're safe now. I'm happy to have been there to help. Didi, that's an unusual name. What nationality is it?"

He hoped that changing the subject would steer the conversation away from what had happened and stop his embarrassment from her thanking him some more. She gave a little laugh without smiling, which just came across as sad.

"No, Nicky, it's not foreign. It's short for Deirdre. My mum's an Aussie, and my dad is as English as they come; he's a real fish-and-chips man. I mean, seriously, who would name their child Deirdre other than an

Englishman?"

"It could have been worse; they could have called you Gertrude, or Broomhilda, or Agnes even."

She gave another sad little laugh, but her heart wasn't in it. *She's probably still in shock from the attack*, Nicky thought, so didn't press for any further details. He waited for her to make more conversation or stay silent, whatever she felt comfortable doing. For the first time, he looked at her using his peripheral vision as best as he could in the reflected dash lights and overhead streetlamps as they passed underneath. Didi was stunning. In fact, Nicky realized she could be staggeringly beautiful. With her slightly olive skin, thin, lithe body, and perfectly accentuated figure, he understood why she worked as she did. She looked like she might be in her mid to late twenties or so. It was hard to tell in that light, and he didn't want to be caught ogling.

Didi had several brightly colored tattoos visible; though in the dim light, it was hard to tell what they were, but at first glance, they looked spectacular. She had a tiny diamond pierced through the side of her nose but no other jewelry anywhere on her fingers or around her neck. Her eyes were big, round, and dark with thick eyelashes. *This woman could be stunningly beautiful if she tried*, Nicky thought, but for some reason, he believed, it didn't seem like she wanted to work too hard at it.

"Do you mind if I put some music on, Didi?"

"It's your cab, man. Do what you like." Her voice sounded brittle as if she was trying hard to be tough and not cry.

While some might consider her rude, Nicky didn't

think that at all. He knew she was suffering emotionally from the near-rape experience and the violence that followed his intervention. His plan was to calm her with music. He switched the radio to an auxiliary input, searched for albums on his phone, and pressed play when he found the right one.

"This was my mum's favorite album. She died a few years ago in a pointless car accident, so I try to play this now and again, when it's quiet, to remind me of her."

****

Didi turned in her seat to study him, momentarily able to forget her trauma. He appeared to be no ordinary man with his voice so full of melancholy where before he had alternated between kindness and gentleness with her and a barely controlled violent rage against her attackers. Of all the things she thought a man might say when he put music on to impress her, that was not one of them. In her experience, normal men didn't wade into a fight against two men to save a woman they didn't know, armed only with a torch—they scurried on by.

She saw he was tall and well-built with little or no excess fat. He had dark brown to black curly hair, and it looked like he was half a day overdue for a shave. He wore jeans and a black cotton shirt with a button-down collar. He was, without a doubt, the sort of guy any woman would want to get to know better in other circumstances. She glanced down at his left hand and didn't see a wedding ring or a faded area where it had been recently removed. He seemed to have an air about him, but she couldn't quite put her finger on what it was. He was self-confident, for sure, and very calm, as if he knew how good he was and didn't have to prove it. For a woman who met men several nights a week who just wanted to screw her, she thought that this one might be different. At least, for the moment, he appeared to be, but it wouldn't be the first time she had thought someone was worthwhile only to find out they were just like all the rest and inevitably let her down.

As her thoughts continued to drift, James Hendry began to sing, "You Saved My Life Tonight." Didi remembered the song with fondness and was genuinely surprised he would play it. Didi assumed his tastes would have been more substantial, more modern perhaps. He looked like the kind of guy who was into pounding electric guitars. The song had the effect of lifting her from the self-pity and loathing, which was her normal state.

She quietly spoke to him, "Man, I love this song. Is that why you did it? Saved my life tonight, I mean, because it's your mum's favorite song?"

Nicky laughed, but it sounded hollow. "No, I promise I didn't even give that a thought. At the time, I just reacted to what I saw, and I'm glad I did, but yeah, it does seem kind of prophetic, doesn't it? This song is from my mum's favorite album. When I was growing up, she would play James Hendry all the time, and this one in particular. It's called *Memories.* She went to his concerts whenever he came to Perth, and if she heard the song *You are my Life* on the radio, it just about brought her to tears every single time." After a pause, he added, "It's good to have something to help remember her by."

She stared at him for a while longer, a look of confusion on her face. "Mister, I mean this in a nice way, but I don't get you. You're a good-looking guy, fit and healthy, yet you drive a cab all night and play sad songs to remind you of your mum. You haven't got a wedding ring on, and you saved me from two guys who could have killed you as soon as look at you. Are you gay? Not that it's a problem if you are. A lot of my friends are that way inclined." Again, he laughed, louder this time and with feeling. *He has a nice laugh, too*, she thought.

"No, I'm not gay, and I'm not married either. I don't even have a girlfriend, to be honest. It's hard to have one when you work nights, but I'm most definitely not gay. I'm just too busy driving the cab. I'm trying to save up to buy my own, but it's expensive, and I've got a long way to go before that happens. I'll get there one day, though."

"How old are you?"

"Twenty-seven."

"Twenty-seven, and your only dream is to own your own cab? Are you for real?"

He turned to face her in the low light and said, "And you, Didi, are you going to be a lap dancer the rest of your life?"

"Ouch. *Touché,* you're right. Note to self, shut up with the criticisms when a good-looking man saves your life, Didi. Maybe we deserve each other; we both work nights and are social misfits." She smiled.

****

Nicky noticed her face had lit up, and she possessed one of the most beautiful smiles he had ever seen. They stayed quiet for a while and listened as Hendry sang *Better Dead*. As they got close to North Beach, she gave him directions to the street where she lived. He pulled up in the driveway three minutes later and doused the lights. She unclipped her seat belt and turned to him.

"How much do I owe you?"

"Well, with all the excitement, I forgot to turn on the meter, so this one's on the house. You've had a bad enough day. At least it can end on a high; save your money." He winked at her. "Here, take this. It's my card, and it has my mobile number on it. Call me before you finish work each night, and I will take you home, make sure those two guys don't come back."

She took the offered card and very warily said, "I'm not going to invite you in, and I'm not going to give you a blow job here in the cab."

"Thank God for that. I was worried you might." He winked again and smiled to show he was kidding. "Really, it's fine. I have to get back to work; I have *'Miles to go before I sleep.'*"

Her face lit up for the second time that night, and he realized once more she was a strikingly beautiful woman when she smiled.

"Man, I love that poem; I haven't heard it since my school days when I studied Robert Frost, but I still remember it word for word. You're a different kind of guy, aren't you, Nicky Pantella? Robert Frost poems, James Hendry, and taking on two guys to save a woman from a fate worse than death. But there has to be something wrong somewhere. Don't you like me?"

"I like you just fine, Didi. Why would you think I don't like you?"

"Well, maybe I'm just used to guys who spend all their time trying to screw me. You saved me tonight and don't even want the fare covered. I mean, what's that all about? I'd say that's pretty weird, but then, I don't get to meet any genuine good guys, so how would I know? I think you are a very nice man, and they're a dying breed in my book."

He shook his head, embarrassed once again. For a fleeting second, he wished he had met her under different circumstances, in a different time, when he would have been capable of caring. "Good night, Didi. Stay safe and call me if you want me to pick you up. I work every night, okay?"

She stared back for just a minute longer, and he thought she still expected him to make a move, grab her and force himself on her, but he didn't. She opened the door and was about to get out when she leaned across the seat and kissed his cheek. "Thanks, Nicky. Thanks for everything. I mean that." And with that, she was gone.

****

Just over three months had passed, and he still remembered that kiss on the cheek as if it were yesterday. She hadn't done it again, and he hadn't tried anything untoward either. He was content with her company and thought she felt the same way about him. They slowly built a wary friendship when he picked her up after work after she finished her shift. It was as if while both were interested in the other, neither could let go of their inhibitions or distrust, though they rarely spoke of their pasts. Nicky always played his first choice of music during the drive home, and Didi learned to love it with him.

"Thanks for the latte, Nicky," she said out of the blue. "How come you always know what I want when I've never once told you how I drink my coffee?" she asked at the halfway point to North Beach.

"Oh, you look like a girl who likes a caramel latte. You want it sweet, but you look after your figure, so I guessed you took sweeteners rather than sugar. It's not hard, this deductive reasoning. Don't know what all the fuss is about with that Sherlock Holmes dude."

"Oh, you've seen my figure, have you? You snuck into the club one night and watched me dance?"

He noticed the sudden change in her tone as if she was suddenly angry. "No. I never have and never will. I'm not that guy."

"Why not, Nicky? Don't you like me? All this time you never once made a move on me. Now you're telling me you wouldn't want to see me undressed?" Her voice sounded brittle as if she was looking for an excuse to shout at him.

"You really don't know why, honestly?"

"No, I don't." She was staring at him, and he knew she was serious, so he chose his words carefully. Nicky had long known her self-esteem was at rock bottom; he just didn't know why. Didi had no idea how beautiful she was, and she did what she did not because she wanted to but because, for some reason, she felt she had to. He didn't know what that reason was, but he just knew there had to be one.

"Didi, if I did that, I would be no better than you have always expected me to be. From day one, you've been waiting for me to be like every other deadbeat and disappoint you, and I won't do that. If I were to use my Sherlock Holmes deductive powers again, I'd say you got hurt by a guy once, maybe even more than once, and you've never forgotten or forgiven him for that. Now you believe that all men are the same. You won't let your guard down for another because you don't want to risk getting hurt again. You are a stunningly beautiful woman, and you work at a job where guys get to see your body, and you have to play up to them. Naturally, they want to paw you, and you despise them for it. We're not all like that, Didi. I'm sure there are a lot of guys who would love to know you better, myself included, and that doesn't have to include seeing you naked at work."

"What does that even mean, Nicky? What are you saying? You do or don't want to see my body?" With that, she burst into silent tears. Nicky thought they were either tears of disappointment or frustration, but he couldn't deduce which.

He waited for her crying to stop, knowing she didn't want him to make a fuss about it or give her meaningless platitudes to make her feel better. She grabbed a tissue out of her bag and blew her nose.

"Sorry, it's been a shitty night," she mumbled, but Nicky believed the tears came from the fact that he had hit the nail squarely on the head and not that she had a bad night. He thought she was wondering how could he possibly know all those things about her?

"I'm human, Didi. Of course, I want to see your body. You are an incredibly beautiful and very sexy woman, and yes, you turn me on. But more important to me is the fact that I don't want to lose our friendship. You make my working nights worthwhile. And I figure, if I made a pass at you, you might say yes, you might say no, but either way, you wouldn't want me dropping you off every night anymore if I did. Why? Because you would despise me because I had lived down to the low expectation you have of me and of all men. Then I would lose you from my life, and I don't want that. I like you being a part of my nights. When you're working, I look forward to picking you up. I know you won't believe me, but you are the highlight of my night. And if you want the truth, you're the highlight of my entire life, as it stands these days."

Didi stayed silent for a long while as if digesting what he'd said. It was one of the longest statements he had ever made, she realized and smiled. Nicky had never volunteered anything too personal other than the one conversation about his mother's death. When she had asked about his past, he gave short, curt answers, and he knew she would wonder at times. *How can he know to say the right thing?*

"Can you take an hour off, Nicky? Like right now, there's something I'd like to show you."

"Sure. What did you have in mind?"

"Let's go to the beach. The sun will be up soon, and it's a hot and humid night now that the rain has gone. Let's watch it come up together. Can you find a quiet spot?"

He looked across the cab to her and nodded. "I think so."

Twenty minutes later, he parked in a small car park on top of the dunes behind some trees so that the car couldn't be seen from the road. Didi kicked off her shoes and wriggled out of her jeans, showing her black lacy panties. He couldn't help noticing her legs. It was the first time he looked at her with anything that could resemble hunger, though he was more interested in the colorful serpent tattoo which wound its way along her upper thigh.

"C'mon," she said. "Let's go sit on the sand and

watch the waves."

He locked the cab and turned on the alarm, then followed her down through the dunes, admiring her tight behind as she walked, clad only in black lace. Didi found a spot she liked and sat on the cool, damp sand, stretched out her legs in the moonlight, and felt better than she had in months.

"Do you mind if I smoke?"

"Not at all. Smoke away." Nicky was surprised because she had never mentioned cigarettes in the past.

It was a warm night, still humid, with only a gentle breeze on their faces. Nicky sat next to her and leaned back on his hands, enjoying the view. He stared out at the darkened sea, watching the flashing channel markers in the distance. *God,* he thought, *I haven't been to the beach in years.* He smiled when he heard her light up and smelt the unmistakable aroma of marijuana.

"Do you do that often, Didi?"

"Only when life sucks the big one, so yeah, pretty often. Are you going to lecture me, Nicky?"

"Fuck no. I was going to ask you for a hit."

Didi burst into surprised laughter and shook her head as she exhaled. He always knew how to surprise her. She passed the joint over and watched as he inhaled deeply, then passed it back to her after exhaling.

"Mmm, well, that's one way to swap saliva," he said and then giggled uncontrollably as the grass hit his system. He lay back on the sand, interlaced his fingers under his head, and looked up at the stars.

"How come you like me, Nicky? Tell me the truth. I undress for men most nights, let them stare at me, while the creeps think about using me. And if I can, I give them private teasing lap dances to get them even hornier, so they go home and beat off, thinking about me. Seriously, what do you see in me, and why don't you ever try to hit on me like everyone else does? What would any decent guy see in someone like me?"

He turned on his side, facing her, with his head on his left hand, and replied, "You just answered your own question, Didi. I don't want to be like everyone else. And for your information, taking your clothes off is something you do. It's not who you are. I haven't quite figured out exactly who you are yet, but I'm working on it. I can't judge you because of what you do, only who you are, and I like who you are. I like you a lot."

"Jesus, that's two long strings of words tonight. You're really opening up now, aren't you?"

****

She had instinctively known not to pester him about his past and never asked probing questions. She also sensed, somehow, that he had experienced deep and dark troubles, which had molded him into the man he was. And, while he was very good looking, there was a smoldering hardness to him that somehow made him unattainable and, to her, even more attractive.

Didi wasn't sure what else she saw in him, other than her eternal gratitude for saving her from being raped that night in the alley three months before. Though they never spoke of it afterward, she never forgot how close she came to being brutally assaulted, hurt, and possibly even worse. Perhaps they would have murdered her so that she wouldn't have been able to identify them as her rapists.

She had never known a man quite like Nicky. If

there was silence, he didn't feel the need to fill it with useless bullshit. He was content to stay peaceful. He radiated an inner calm like some Zen Buddhist monk, which was infectious and very desirable. He had this incredible insight as to when to talk, when to listen, and when to stay quiet. He could be humorous but never stupid, sexist, or racist, and the coffee order he surprised her with blew her out of the water. Even that he instinctively knew she was desperate for a caffeine high that particular night, as work had been dreadful, was intoxicating. There had been a big fight in the club between three men and the bouncers, leaving bloodstains and damaged furniture everywhere.

It had been the worst, most violent fistfight she had ever witnessed and had occurred while she had been on stage. Yet when she finished her shift, feeling depressed, there was Nicky with a caramel latte for her, which was a deep, secret love that she had never told him. It was spooky when it happened, and at that moment, she realized that he was quite possibly the single most thoughtful and insightful man in the world. More surprisingly, for some reason that she couldn't fathom, he was interested in her as a person. To him, she was not a mere sex object but a living human being. That was both weird and very frightening to her. Didi had long since given up trying to attract anyone who could be remotely thought of as decent. Being a lap dancer meant she wasn't worthy of that, but her choices for jobs had been limited, and she had been desperate at the time.

Nicky laughed along with her and admitted, "It must be the grass; it's some terrific shit."

Their eyes met. Didi decided it was time she took a

chance. "What if we got to the point where I wanted you to look at me, Nicky? Would that frighten you away? Would you suddenly like me less?"

She passed him the joint again. He took another long pull and then gave it back.

"I think you are gorgeous, Didi, and I've often wondered if you have as many tattoos under your clothes as you do above. And then, tonight, out of the blue, I got to see the snake on your leg, and it is stunning. Good legs, too, by the way, not to mention your bum. There isn't much you could do or say that would frighten me away. I like your company, and I don't want to do anything to lose your friendship. I know men have hurt you, and I don't want to be one of those guys who you think is going to take advantage of you. I'm in no rush, and I'm not going anywhere anytime soon. Does that answer your question?"

Didi nodded and took the last drag from the joint and tossed the butt into the sand. She couldn't figure Nicky out. He was still a mystery. But he liked her; he listened to her and didn't hold her job against her. And with the pot and the calm ocean air mellowing her defenses, she finally admitted to herself that he turned her on like she hadn't felt in years. Didi wanted him. More than that, she wanted him to want her. She silently sat for a moment longer, looking out to sea.

"It's time, Nicky." She stood up and faced him so that her back was to the last of the moonlight shimmering over the waves. Slowly, she took off her leather jacket and tossed it to the side. Taking her time, but not as if she were performing, Didi peeled her tank top off and dropped that too on her jacket.

Didi hesitated because she felt petrified that he

would reject her. She gazed into his eyes, desperate for confirmation, and saw him smile. She reached behind and unclasped her bra and watched his eyes as she slipped it off and tossed it away. She stood still, watching to see if he approved.

"My God, you are so beautiful," he whispered, his voice husky.

Didi liked that she saw a hunger in his eyes. She took a deep breath, then bent at the waist and peeled her panties down her smooth legs and off, kicking them away to land near the rest of her clothes. For the first time in a very long time, she liked that a man could see her nude.

"Come on, Nicky. Let's go skinny-dipping!" she said breathlessly.

She ran off into the shallows, turned, and waited for him, the last of the moonlight shimmering behind her on top of the waves.

****

Nicky had had just enough grass to lower his inhibitions and feel at peace with the world. He had never felt this way about a woman, and he realized he had an erection from watching her take off her clothes. Nicky knew if he stopped to think, he would talk himself out of it, and he didn't want to allow that to happen. He jumped up, stripped off his clothes, and followed her into the water. As he got close, she lowered her gaze and said, "Mmm, I think little Nicky is pleased to see me, too." Then she splashed cold water on him, giggled, and ran farther into the ocean.

He dove after her. They rolled together in the waves, the water chilling and refreshing him. When Nicky came up for air, they were facing each other, arms entwined, her hard nipples pressed into his chest, and his hardness thrust against her tummy. They kissed, long and hard: a kiss that had been three months in the making and needed barriers to lower and trust to build. But in that instant, they both knew it had been worth the wait.

Chapter 4

Jimmy Mallory and the Looming War

Jimmy Mallory and his younger brother Desmond
were born to English parents in the tough Perth
suburban neighborhood of Hollowood, where many
migrants lived at the time. This flocking created a little
England of working-class families who could still argue
over football teams, the lack of decent pork pies, and
why Australia should stay in the Commonwealth so that
the Queen remained the head of the government. People
relocated to Hollowood from places like Liverpool,
Sheffield, Brixton, Portsmouth, and Glasgow, which
created enclaves. For some reason, migrants wanted to
mingle with other UK arrivals from the home country
they wanted to leave.

Hollowood High School was one of the toughest in
Western Australia, and students learned to fight and
fight hard to avoid being one of the ones who were
picked on and bullied. Gangs sprang up like weeds, and
there would be threats made from the likes of the
Liverpool Lads to the Scottish Boys. When such a
challenge was laid down, there could be twenty to thirty
youths fighting on the sports ground surrounding the
school within minutes of the siren heralding the end of
the lessons for the day. The reasons for brawling could
be as trivial as a perceived insult made against one of

the boys or sometimes even looking at someone the wrong way.

The smoldering potpourri of aggression was the training ground of the man who would become the king of the Northbridge underworld and supplier of most of the illicit drugs to Western Australia through his network of clubs and bars in partnership with the biker gang he also headed up, the Devil's Grave.

When he went to school, Jimmy learned very quickly if you weren't on top of the heap, you were crushed underneath it. His father was a massive brute of a man who had been famous for bare-knuckle fights in the shipbuilding yards of the Liverpool docks. Brian Mallory taught his two sons how to fight at an early age and wasn't averse to using his fists on them to punish them if they stepped out of line. From an early age, when either of them got into a fight, they were expected to be victorious. In the eyes of their father, that meant severely hurting the other boy or boys and ensuring the victims visited the school nurse.

Jimmy only ever lost one fight, and that was to three older boys who picked on him after school. When he arrived home, he received two reactions from his father. Firstly, Brian Mallory dragged him to each of the boys' houses, where he beat up their fathers, while Jimmy fought each boy in a one-on-one fight. When they returned home, bruised, bleeding, yet victorious, his father taught Jimmy a lesson he would never forget. He was beaten as punishment for losing in the first place. That last lesson, brutal though it was, ensured that for the rest of his life, no matter what the odds were, Jimmy would always go down fighting to the death if it were necessary. He wouldn't walk away from a brawl and never, ever lay down if wounded. He thought of himself as a tank that would just keep on keeping on until the threat was defeated.

Jimmy and Des were taught that the secret to fighting was to be the first to hit, make it hard, and then don't stop punching or kicking until the opponent can't, or wouldn't, get up. And then kick them some more to give them something to remember. Hollowood High School and his uncompromising father were the perfect training grounds for Jimmy's future of controlling a criminal empire.

Jimmy learned to smoke at ten years old, regularly shoplifted by eleven, and was breaking into homes at twelve. The brothers, even at a young age, would not hesitate to use violence if they were interrupted while committing a robbery to avoid trouble with the police. Whether the boys were disturbed by someone male or female, old or young, fat or thin, it made no difference. They would beat them up enough to scare the homeowner so the police wouldn't be called. Inevitably, at age fourteen, Jimmy was arrested, charged, and found guilty of breaking and entering. He helped Des escape while he faced the police, a debt Des never forgot, and Jimmy was sent to the juvenile home, Longmore Detention Centre in Bentley.

At Longmore, Jimmy had to build a reputation all over again as it was full of other tough kids from different areas and schools. They, too, understood that the only people to respect were those who were more violent than themselves. Jimmy rose to the challenge and, within three months, led one of the most ruthless and violent gangs inside, which ran the black-market cigarettes.

Everyone was afraid of upsetting Jimmy. By the time he got out, even his father was wary of him, as he had filled out and grown to his full six-foot three-inch height. He was fearless and without morals or conscience, though generous and giving to his friends. He had no compunction whatsoever about using anything close to hand as a weapon, and it was only good luck that he hadn't killed anyone before his sixteenth birthday, as he had caused severe injuries to numerous unfortunates.

Everything changed during a gang turf fight in Hollowood Reserve when someone pulled a knife on him. Jimmy had a bike chain and advanced toward the much larger thug. Once Mallory had knocked him to the ground by hitting him with the chain, he disarmed him and stabbed him six times in the abdomen and chest. When another youth came to the fallen one's aid, Jimmy stabbed him too. The Good Samaritan survived the ordeal but lost a kidney in the process.

Perhaps Jimmy's life would have turned out differently if he had gone to prison for that death. But no one would identify him; such was his reputation even at that early age. Nobody dared name him because they knew what would befall them if they did. They realized that if Jimmy were arrested, that would leave his best friend Gordy, or Jimmy's brother Des, or worse, his father. One of them would exact deadly revenge. Gordy and Jimmy were inseparable, and Gordy would kill anyone who dared to give evidence against his best and only friend. Jimmy's father was still a feared man in the neighborhood, and no one wanted a visit from him for ratting on his son. Some dared to think Jimmy and Gordy were gay, because they were so close, but the string of girls they attracted dissuaded them from that line of thinking, and no one was brave enough to ask.

By the time he was nineteen, Jimmy headed up a gang of nine thugs, including Gordy as his number two. They regularly burgled businesses and homes together. When the team broke into places on their own, they always paid Jimmy a percentage of everything stolen, and as a gang, their reputation grew and garnered serious interest from the police, though they could never get enough evidence to arrest them. Jimmy's reputation grew until one day, the owner of a Chinese restaurant in the heart of the city contacted Gordy and asked if he could speak with Jimmy privately and urgently. Jimmy had taken his boys there for dinner often, and Mr. Fong, the owner, invited him to the back courtyard to talk in private.

He explained to Jimmy that he was paying five hundred dollars a week to a biker gang for protection. That sum was manageable, and business was good. However, Mad Dog, the leader, had demanded it to be raised to two thousand dollars. Such an amount would surely send him broke, and Mr. Fong was frightened. Mad Dog had told him, in no uncertain and very colorful terms, that if he didn't pay, his business could be burned to the ground, robbed, burgled, his staff and family attacked, or all the above. Mr. Fong was distraught and pleaded for Jimmy's help. Extortion was a new experience for Jimmy, and he learned a precious life lesson that day; people were willing to pay him for his friendship to avoid harm from others.

Jimmy was well known for his violent side, but that day he also became known for his statesmanship, planning, and strategy. He asked Fong what the most was he could afford to pay to avoid the business being destroyed. No more than a thousand dollars was the reply. Jimmy paused and nodded sagely and told him to leave the problem with him. He would act as an intermediary and get the fees lowered. Jimmy told Mr. Fong that if he were successful, he would expect that he and his friends could eat there for free occasionally. In fact, for a while, it would be necessary for Mad Dog to know that they were eating there, which would help with the deterrent he would provide. Mr. Fong agreed wholeheartedly and promised to cook for him anytime personally.

Later that night, Jimmy and Gordy met Mad Dog, who was a mountain of a man with a completely bald head and thick handlebar mustache, in a bar on William Street. Jimmy politely asked if he might have a quiet word with him on a business matter. Mad Dog agreed and took him to a table. With the highest amount of respect he could muster, Mallory explained that Mr. Fong was a long-standing friend of his family and had asked him to talk to Mad Dog on his behalf. The business, he explained, hadn't been going so well and would have to close its doors if they had to pay two thousand dollars a week. Should such a thing happen, Jimmy pointed out, Mad Dog would be out of pocket from what they were already receiving, and he asked if there might be a compromise. He would consider it a personal favor, which could be redeemed at any time, if he, Jimmy, paid Mad Dog seven hundred dollars per week and let Mr. Fong pay back what he could afford when he could afford it.

At that time, the Devil's Grave was a small biker

gang trying to make its mark and grow. They were so small the more prominent groups like the Coffin Cheaters, Bandidos, and Comancheros allowed them to operate for a small consideration fee. Mad Dog thought about the offer and sized Jimmy up as a man better to have as an ally than an enemy. He felt sure that underneath his polite and respectful words was a very violent undercurrent. In fact, he had heard of Mallory's reputation and agreed to the proposal, not from fear but caution. It made sense to gain an additional two hundred a week rather than lose five.

They had a drink together to seal the deal, which increased to several more. Around three in the morning, the two men decided that perhaps a merger of the two gangs would help them all make a few extra dollars. On that night, the Devil's Grave increased their membership by nine, although none of Jimmy's gang had any interest in motorbikes. Their passion was violence, making money, and having fun.

Within three months, they started selling ecstasy tablets in nightclubs, rave parties, and select street corners in Northbridge. Business was good, and the gang grew in numbers using their violent reputation by dissuading other pushers from working the local streets. Inevitably, they expanded by distributing methamphetamine, cocaine, and heroin.

As Jimmy learned from Mr. Fong, providing protection and mediation services could be profitable, and it provided a steady stream of cash with little or no risk. They looked for similar bars and restaurants in Northbridge that needed protection and convinced the owners that without their guardianship, there could be severe consequences.

Jimmy's method for taking over businesses was quite simple. He offered a partnership at an affordable rate, as he could see no point in making any establishments go broke trying to pay him. He thought it better they pay what they could manage to be under his protection than pay nothing at all. For those stupid enough not to see that this was their future, his retribution was swift, violent, and extremely public. People never got a second chance to be under Jimmy's wing.

In the first year, Jimmy bought into his first nightclub and, within a further six months, had three others in partnership. It didn't take long, and Jimmy convinced his partners it would be better to sell him their interests completely. His reputation grew, and he became known as a formidable opponent who should be avoided at all costs. Those who didn't learn that Jimmy's way was best didn't live to make a second mistake. Murder became a way of life for Jimmy, and with his aura of invincibility, huge profits, and wages he was paying, the other members of the gang would do anything for the boss.

Slowly, Mad Dog realized he was working for Jimmy and not in partnership. The stealthy takeover had happened so slowly he hadn't noticed until it was too late. His gang was doing what Jimmy said and when he said it, including Mad Dog himself. He decided enough was enough.

He spoke to three of his most trusted and long-standing members over a pile of cocaine washed down with bourbon at the clubhouse one late night in December. Together they planned a coup to take place at Mr. Fong's on the night of their third merger anniversary. At precisely eleven o'clock at night, right after the last course of Peking-style spareribs, when the last of the other diners left, the three men stood up and pulled their guns, aiming them at Jimmy.

Mad Dog smiled and said, "Goodbye, Jimmy. It's just business; you've outlived your usefulness." Suddenly, the men turned their guns from Jimmy to Mad Dog and shot him nine times in the chest. Mad Dog's chair tilted back with the first impact, and his body fell to the floor, bullets hitting him all the way down.

After weighing up their options, they knew Jimmy had done more for them and their pockets than Mad Dog ever had, or would, in the future if they permitted him to return to being the boss. They had wisely gone to Jimmy and told him of Mad Dog's treachery the following morning, and together, they hatched the alternate plan.

Jimmy took two thousand in cash from his jacket pocket and handed it to Mr. Fong. He gave him a wink and placed a finger over his lips to ensure that the elderly Chinese man, who had always been grateful, would keep quiet. "Merry Christmas," he extended his hallmark phrase, which filled everyone with dread when he used it at any time other than Christmas. Then the four men left quietly, leaving the owner to phone the police and tell them that three masked men had burst in and shot a man who had been eating by himself.

In Jimmy's opinion, Mad Dog had held the gang back from reaching its true potential, but because he was loyal, he hadn't wanted to act against him without provocation. With Mad Dog out of the way, Jimmy was inundated with offers from other criminals who wanted to align themselves with him rather than risk becoming an enemy. Jimmy's reputation and empire grew exponentially.

In a masterstroke of planning and execution, which became an urban legend, Mallory invited all the smaller individual drug dealers from the inner metropolitan area to one of his clubs for a special party. He provided forty of his best prostitutes to act as hostesses who would do anything asked of them. The guests could indulge in as much alcohol, drugs, and sex as they wanted for free. At the beginning of the festivities, he told them that he had an announcement to make later that night, and no one was to leave until he did. The nightclub was closed to the public, and over a hundred and fifty small to large drug dealers were in attendance. They knew better than to decline such an invitation from Jimmy Mallory.

At midnight, Jimmy stopped the music and took to the microphone, asking the women, who were engaged in various acts with guests throughout the club, to please leave for fifteen minutes while they conducted some business. After they vacated, Jimmy announced that he had negotiated a significant pipeline for drugs into Perth from a Mexican cartel that he had been cultivating for some time. The Mexicans were interested in an alliance for him to supply a stable environment, and Jimmy promised huge profits from his future regular, secure supply lines. All Jimmy had to provide was the distribution, which was where his guests came in.

Jimmy proposed that in the future, all drugs sold in Perth came only through him. He guaranteed that his rates would be better than they were currently paying, and everyone would make significantly more money because all dealers would pay the same price, giving them a monopoly. With one supplier, Jimmy pointed out, the petty wars would stop between them, and they could all work together to their mutual advantage. He said that all he wanted was a clear majority, and anyone who chose to go their own way was free to leave. In fact, a fleet of limos was waiting at the rear exit, ready to take them wherever they wanted to go, with no hard feelings. Those who stayed would find out the details of the partnership and exactly how much they would be making. He promised them it would be at least double what they were currently bringing in, with far less risk, as he would ensure police protection for everyone involved. He also offered his extensive resources to ensure they would be free from any retaliation from their current suppliers.

Fourteen men stood and thanked Jimmy for his hospitality, explaining that for various reasons, they could not, or would not, cease dealing with their existing suppliers. Jimmy was courteous and thanked them for coming and listening. He shook their hands individually and sincerely wished them a *"Merry Christmas,"* though it was April. One by one, they walked to the limousines he had so thoughtfully provided for them.

In what became known as the Easter Massacre, the drug war that was fought, won, and lost in one night, all fourteen men were found dead, riddled with bullet holes, floating in the Swan River in Fremantle the following morning. Overnight, Jimmy controlled the entire drug trade in Perth.

There was some opposition from the previous

suppliers, who were backed by various organizations in the Eastern States. They were staunchly offered two scenarios. The first was an offer for ongoing considerations to be paid to them, from Jimmy, to stay out of Perth. Most wisely saw the merit of being paid to do nothing and not have any risk and accepted his generosity. Those who declined and sent muscle to the west were dealt with swiftly and brutally. Word traveled quickly back to the gangs to leave the remote capital alone, and eventually, they did. The peaceful and profitable business environment lasted for several years until the *Northbridge Vigilante* inadvertently killed Jimmy's only brother and, in doing so, opened Pandora's Box.

Jimmy Mallory did not possess one ounce of kindness or compassion. Some joked behind his back that if you looked up the word sociopath in the dictionary, you would see *Jimmy Mallory* as its definition. Despite Jimmy's absence of scruples, his brutal father had instilled in his sons from a very young age that family was everything. Jimmy and Des had only come to blows once, and that fight was broken up by their father, who beat them viciously for going against each other. When the boys were sufficiently cowed, bloodied, and bruised, he told them never to forget that friends and acquaintances would come in and out of their lives, but family was forever. Jimmy was incapable of feeling *normal* emotions, but he never forgot that lesson. While he would not be able to mourn, miss, or grieve Des, he vowed that he would, by any means possible, avenge his death.

****

When Jimmy was told his brother had been shot

dead at home after leaving his birthday party, Jimmy exploded in an insane rage. He kicked and smashed furniture and punched the man who brought him the news. When he'd calmed down, he gave as close to an apology as he could and helped the man to his unsteady feet while handing him a roll of banknotes in compensation. Jimmy had to blame someone and not only seek revenge but be *seen* to take revenge. Des was his brother, so that alone earned his murderer a death sentence; he could not have it common knowledge that anyone could attack his businesses, drug distribution empire, or family without retaliation. If he let this incident go, it would be bad for business, and people would lose the respect that had taken so many years for him to build. Jimmy had to strike back in such a way that left no doubt in people's minds as to what would happen if they dared attack him again.

His right-hand man, Gordy, was the link between himself and the lieutenants in the biker gang who managed distribution through the nightclubs and street pushers. In a seething, white-hot rage, he screamed at Gordy what he wanted done, who he wanted to have killed, and exactly how to do it. He thought he knew who was responsible, and they would pay dearly.

Business had been good for a long time; everything ran smoothly, and everyone was making more money than ever. The police were being paid off in the right quarters, the bikers were happy, and Jimmy's Mexican supplier was as delighted as a maniacal Mexican drug lord could be. Jimmy was aware that one thing was constant in the drug business, though; nothing stays the same forever. There was always someone wanting to make their mark by stealing parts of Jimmy's territory, and generally, they were taken care of ruthlessly without fuss. Things had been quiet for a long while, though, and Jimmy wondered if it had been too long. Maybe his opponents thought he had gone soft. If so, that would be a misconception he would have to fix in such a way they would never believe it again.

A new biker gang had set up a chapter in Western Australia with Jimmy's knowledge and tacit approval. The Apaches were based in New Zealand but originally hailed from America and had spread their tentacles toward Australia via Auckland. They said they wanted to set up peacefully and not tread on anyone's toes, but rumor had it that their real ambitions were in complete contrast with what they *said* their intentions were. Jimmy met the senior Apaches at one of his clubs some months prior, when they followed the right protocols and asked Jimmy's permission to set up in WA. The five gave assurances that they had no interest in his existing drug trade and that they would not be looking for any trouble with him. They said they were more into organized extortion in suburban businesses and restaurants. They also controlled most of the construction unions in the Eastern States, which also had branches in the west. Jimmy gave them a list of venues that were under his protection, and the gang promised to leave them alone. Predominantly, Jimmy's territory was Northbridge and Perth City, which by anyone's definition was the jewel in the crown of organized crime in Western Australia. Assurances were given that if at any time they chose to move into the drug trade, it would only be in the outer metropolitan areas, and they agreed to source stock from Jimmy. After they left, Jimmy sat with Gordy and made plans so they would not be surprised by a preemptive strike if the Apaches were lying. They agreed that it was best to allow the Apaches to operate but watch closely and be ready for trouble if it occurred. Jimmy would rather have the Apaches on his side than have them try to take over by force when he least expected it.

To date, the alliance had run smoothly, but it was evident to Jimmy that it was probably the Apaches that had launched their first attack on his empire. It seemed to him that they had hoped to blindside him by killing his brother, thinking such a loss would throw him off-kilter. Well, they would have to learn the hard way that he wouldn't take anything lying down, least of all his brother being murdered.

Gordy invited the top three Apaches to one of his bars the next night for a late dinner and drinks. That was how he wanted Gordy to word it: late supper. He also had Gordy promise them some new women he had brought in from Thailand who would be at their disposal in the private VIP area of the club, The Marquis, in the heart of the city on King Street. Three bikers of Maori descent arrived just after eleven, and Gordy and Jimmy welcomed them like long-lost brothers. The topless women served top-shelf bourbon, and there were bowls of ecstasy and cocaine on the tables.

The Apaches were large muscle-bound men who would not be easy to take down in a fistfight, but Jimmy had no intention of there being one; he had an ambush planned. At four a.m., the paying customers left the club, and the band and staff packed up. The men were invited out to the back, where they were promised something special in a more private area with the girls who had gone on ahead to prepare. The unsuspecting men were led by Gordy, who was his usual stone-faced self. The bourbon and drugs had relaxed them, and they laughed and clapped each other on the back. Instead of the expected VIP experience, however, what they found when they got to the storeroom area were four men with sawn-off shotguns holding handcuffs. In their inebriated state, they didn't see the ambush until it was too late.

Initially, the bikers thought it was a joke until they were told to strip naked, and only then realized they were in trouble. Once nude, they were handcuffed, arms raised above their heads, and hooked onto a steel rail that ran across the ceiling to the loading bay. In its past life, the building had been a meat wholesale business specializing in restaurant supply. The rail was for transporting whole beef, pig, and lamb carcasses from vans to the preparation area. Underneath the hanging men were sheets of clear plastic neatly laid out to stop the inevitable blood spillage staining the floor.

In keeping with the theme of the meat wholesale business, Jimmy entered wearing rubber boots and a butcher's apron. He had removed all of his clothes, and in his hand, he held a meat cleaver, which gleamed in the harsh, white lighting. In any other setting, Jimmy would have looked hilarious. He approached the first Apache, named Greg, who held the position of sergeant at arms. Jimmy waved the weapon in front of his face and quite calmly said, "Right, you've drunk my booze, eaten my food, and been sucked off by my girls. Now it's time to pay the piper. I want to know which one of you had my brother killed and why. And you only get one chance to tell me."

The man struggled to get free from the handcuffs, but the hooks on the rail were too big. Jimmy waited patiently for the man to answer.

"Jimmy, we didn't do anything to your brother. Why would we? We came in peace and have enjoyed working with you. We're not against you."

Jimmy swung the cleaver, hitting the Maori in his side just below the rib cage. The blade dug deep into his body and jammed. Jimmy seesawed it out of the flesh while blood spurted out, the crimson reflecting off the metal. Mallory raised the blade again and hit his other side in a backhanded motion. The man screamed in pain and horror as the blood gushed in streaming gouts. Jimmy stayed silent while striking the man on one side, then the other until he hung lifeless from the loss of blood, and his intestines drooped below his knees.

Jimmy waved to Gordy, who threw him a towel so he could wipe his face and hands. Blood and gore had sprayed a considerable distance and covered the front of his apron with rivulets dripping onto his rubber boots. He walked over to the next man, whose eyes were wildly jerking from side to side, looking for any help or escape. "Jimmy, bro," he shouted, "I swear to you we didn't do anything to your brother, man. We didn't even know you had a brother. We don't want a war with you. Why would we?" The Apache second in command, Henry, pleaded with Jimmy, who nodded as if contemplating.

Henry thought he had convinced him until Jimmy smiled, winked, and shook his head. "Don't you like your legs, my son?" he asked with a grin. Jimmy swung the heavy blade again and chopped into Henry's left leg halfway between knee and hip. He didn't stop, just kept hacking seven more times until the leg fell onto the plastic-covered floor. Jimmy looked up, sweating from exertion, to see what Henry had to say for himself, but he had died from shock and blood loss.

The head of the Perth chapter of the Apache Gang, who was known as Jack the Knife, knew he was going to die. It seemed inevitable. But unlike his fellow members, he understood that extreme risk came with the territory. He hadn't gotten to be head of the gang by showing fear, and he wasn't going to start then. He'd had a good run and made a lot of money, which he sent back to his family in Auckland. They would want for nothing now. Philosophically, he presumed that if it was over, it was over. He had knowingly signed up for the lifestyle, after all. What he couldn't understand was why? They hadn't intended to go to war with Jimmy until they were ready, which would probably have been another month or two away when they recruited more local members and reinforcements arrived from Sydney.

Jimmy's ferocity was well known, and they had paid their dues out of respect on arrival, knowing in time when they were ready, they would strike. But that would have been against Jimmy and Gordy, and if someone was stupid enough to kill Jimmy's brother, it certainly wasn't one of them.

"Hey, Jimmy, man, you can kill me; that's your choice, and obviously, you will now. But you've started a war with the Apaches, man. You've fired the first shot, not us. If we wanted to hurt you, we would have attacked you, not your family. Think of this, man; if we had offed your brother, would we have come here tonight as if nothing happened?"

Jimmy was completely covered from head to foot in blood and resembled a character from a horror film. He walked in front of Jack and tilted his head to one side. He could see the man wasn't scared, and now that he thought about it, what he said made sense. *Maybe*, he thought, *it wasn't these bastard Apaches who killed Des after all*. But he had come too far now to stop. He couldn't let this man go; he would lose too much face. "You fucking Kiwi scum came into my city because I allowed it, and now I'm revoking that permission."

He swung the cleaver and buried it in Mack's throat at a forty-five-degree angle, severing his jugular. He quickly stepped back as the arterial spray squirted over a meter in the air. He dropped the weapon on the plastic sheet, shrugged out of the apron, and threw it down too. He beckoned again to Gordy, who tossed him another towel to wipe himself down.

Once he wiped his face, he turned to the four armed men who had been watching the proceedings, who were laughing and pointing at the hanging corpses. "Before you clean up the mess, boys, listen up. I want all of our people on the street. Turn this fucking city over and find out who killed Des. There's a hundred grand reward for whoever gives the bastard up."

The four bikers nodded, murmured in agreement, put down their shotguns, and got to work. They wrapped the bodies in the plastic, using packing tape to seal the gaps and retain the pools of blood inside. They opened the loading dock roller door where the delivery van had been backed up and manhandled the bodies inside. There was a boat on standby at Fremantle harbor, and the corpses would be wrapped in chains and dumped far out at sea for the sharks to find and eat.

Chapter 5

Sam Collins and The Northbridge Vigilante

Detective Sgt. Sam Collins was not happy with his job. On reflection, he decided that downright miserable would be a more accurate way of describing his feelings since his promotion to sergeant. His unhappiness increased since hanging up the phone on the call, which told him he had been summoned to appear before the police commissioner himself, Warren McFarlane.

The commissioner was a rather dour man of little personality and likability. However, what he lacked in character, he made up for in political skills required to run a modern-day police force. He knew how to garner and keep the grudging respect of most of the West Australian police officers as well as his government minister. He was well versed in his media responsibilities, and since his tenure began, there had been very few embarrassments for the department.

Sam considered that since being promoted, he had been cheated, pure and simple, at a time when he felt he should have been rewarded. Sam had waited for his first assignment eagerly after his promotion and was horrified when told he was to find and stop the *Northbridge Vigilante*. Deep down, Sam had grudging respect and applauded the mystery do-gooder. Secretly, he wouldn't mind one little bit if he kept on killing the scum that polluted the streets of the city he loved. The problem with that scenario, which he acknowledged, was that he was a policeman and supposed to be against vigilantism. Though he would never admit it, Sam didn't mind his job being done for him by someone with no compunction about killing repeat violent offenders who gave nothing back to society. But to counterbalance that, by not stopping and catching the vigilante, he jeopardized his career and future advancement. It was a lose-lose situation, and he hated it. No matter how much of a good job the vigilante performed, the question had to be asked; if you permitted him to rule the streets and enforce rules, would it escalate to killing people for dropping a cigarette butt or spitting on the pavement? Who was the referee that made the laws as to who could or couldn't be killed? That was why there were the police and the courts to hand out justice, though it was true to say that sometimes, it seemed, justice was sadly lacking.

Sam had gained his promotion to sergeant and received a bravery commendation for capturing a serial killer on the rooftop of a Como apartment block while he was off duty some months before. The story was to be featured in an upcoming book and possible movie adaptation of the story, and the resultant pre-publication media attention had increased his profile to an unacceptable level in a lot of people's eyes.

He and the police force had enjoyed positive publicity from the capture and ending the killer's reign. The much-anticipated book would show the target of the killer's murderous plot, Dave Barndon, to be the real hero, and Sam was delighted with that. Barndon had risked his life to save the final victim and, in Sam's eyes, was worthy of the recognition. But becoming the center of the attention as Sam had for saving Barndon's life and capturing the killer, his colleagues came up with a range of nicknames for him and never missed an opportunity to make jokes at his expense. He was asked for his autograph regularly and called *"Superstar"* often. Sam was tired of the whole business and just wanted to do his job. He had only ever wanted to help people and catch criminals, and while it might seem like an old-fashioned concept, he aspired to make the city a safer place to live. He did, on occasion, still catch up with Dave Barndon because Sam enjoyed his company. Dave was a down-to-earth guy who, through his poor life decisions, had unleashed a maniacal serial killer who targeted him and any woman he slept with.

Sam was handed the *Vigilante* case after the third shooting, but the investigation went nowhere. He was given more officers when the fourth victim of the vigilante was discovered shot dead when breaking into a restaurant on William Street after midnight. The owner had been viciously beaten, and were it not for the intervention of the vigilante and a phone call he made for an ambulance using the owner's mobile phone, there was no doubt it would have resulted in his death. The restauranteur's injuries had been horrific, and he was lucky to have survived. Ballistics matched the bullets used on his attacker to the earlier criminal victims, and the newspapers again made a hero of the man they dubbed: *The Northbridge Vigilante.*

As Sam drove to the meeting with the commissioner, he went through the facts of the killings so his mind would be clear if asked specific questions.

The first victim, William Papertalk, was an alcoholic who was well-known to police for over a hundred offenses. He registered .287 percent blood alcohol in his postmortem results. He was in the act of bashing his long-suffering partner, Shanae Glover, with a beer bottle in a park on the edge of Northbridge around four a.m. when he had been shot dead. Papertalk had punched and kicked his girlfriend into unconsciousness, and it wasn't the first time he had beaten her. He knelt over her unconscious body and hit her on the forehead with an empty bottle; he wasn't drunk enough to do it with a full one. Investigators believed he intended to keep hitting her until she died, but he was stopped mid-swing by a hail of nine-millimeter bullets from the direction of a car parking rank on the street twenty meters away.

Papertalk's body was found a little later that morning next to his girlfriend by people walking to work. She had suffered internal bleeding, which resulted in being in a coma for ten days, and had no recollection of the incident on waking. There were no witnesses; no one heard gunshots, there was no evidence at the scene of the crime, no shell casings, and police had absolutely nothing to go on. Ballistics couldn't match the recovered bullets to any previous crime, and the police were forced to assume it was a random intervention. Papertalk's family and friends were clueless and hadn't cared much about him. They all feared Willie when he was drunk, and no one mourned his passing. Without evidence, motive, or witnesses, and because of the victim's history and no serious pressure to find his killer, the case dried up and was left open to be looked at again if further information came to light.

The second victim, Russell Gant, was shot dead while he was in the process of beating up a drunken young man, Tim Matheson, who had staggered out of a nightclub. On his way to the nearest taxi rank, he entered an alleyway because he needed to throw up and relieve a full bladder against a brick wall. He was in no fit state to be able to defend himself, so he would have been seen to be an easy target by Gant. Tim was hit from behind without warning, and his face hit the wall before he fell unconscious, his jaw broken in three places. Gant then stomped on his head several times.

The reason for the unprovoked attack was unclear. Police hypothesized it could have been an intended robbery or perhaps an argument that had started inside the nightclub and escalated outside. More likely, though, the attack was carried out by a man whose idea of a fun night out was a violent attack on someone who couldn't fight back. Gant had had three previous convictions for assaults and grievous bodily harm, with the most recent attack causing his victim to spend the rest of his life in a wheelchair. That injury came from a kick to his lower back, which was delivered so hard it smashed two vertebrae.

Again, no one saw or heard the shooting, and there was no evidence at the scene, so police were baffled. Patrons inside the club were interviewed and could shed no light on any fight that included Matheson or Gant. Neither had been ejected for causing trouble, and they appeared not to know each other. There were no CCTV cameras in the alley or its entry that could show images of the victim or the person responsible for the shooting. As in the previous case, the murdered victim was stopped from potentially killing an innocent and had been shot three times in the chest. When the ballistics report matched both killings to the same gun, warning bells sounded that there could be a vigilante who was killing violent offenders. The police tried to withhold the vigilante theory, quoting the need to avoid an anticipated citywide panic, but it leaked regardless because some police officers had no sympathy for the victims.

Four weeks later, the third incidence occurred. Three men attempted to mug a young man and his girlfriend as they left a restaurant. They demanded his wallet, watch, and phone, and the male refused. The twenty-year-old woman, Beth Michaels, was punched and kicked unconscious; she suffered a broken cheekbone, and three teeth were knocked out. Her boyfriend, Thomas Arnold, was stabbed twice in the stomach. The attackers were each shot three times. One died immediately, one later that night from his wounds, while the third recovered. He provided the first description to police of the vigilante; a burly man wearing jeans and a jacket. The description was vague because he had a streetlight behind him, so none of his facial features could be seen. He was described as tall, though he couldn't say how tall, as the victim had been lying wounded, bleeding heavily on the ground at the time. Brandon McLoughlin suffered bullet wounds to the shoulder, hip, and thigh and had been close to unconsciousness from shock at the time.

The bullet casings had been picked up by the gunman, there were no other witnesses, and no forensic evidence was found at the scene of the crime. Investigating officers thought it odd that no one heard the shots though some had heard Beth Michaels scream. Not a single person reporting gunfire at that time of night troubled the investigators, who agreed it made no sense. Nine gunshots would have been loud, and the alley would amplify the sound, so they should have been heard by someone. There was a large apartment block behind the restaurant, and most residents were home at the time of the attack, yet no one admitted to hearing a sound other than one short scream. Detective Whittaker suggested that the vigilante used a silenced pistol, but that theory was kept from the press for a good reason. It couldn't be substantiated, no matter how much sense it made, and silenced pistols were rare due to the strict gun ownership laws in Western Australia.

When it became obvious there was a serial killer vigilante, a small squad of Major Crime officers was assembled, and Sam was ordered to head it up. It was his first case in charge, but rather than be pleased to be in command, he was morose. Sam saw it as an unpopular investigation to be lumbered with, and he thought it almost impossible to solve without the killer making a mistake. Sometimes, Sam wondered if he wasn't given the job as a punishment to bring him back down to earth after his previous high profile and popularity. If that were the case, he thought the tactic had been successful. Sam speculated that one of the reasons there were no willing witnesses was because *The Northbridge Vigilante* was gaining in popularity. The fact that matching bullets had been recovered from similar cases had leaked to the press. The vigilante was applauded in certain circles, as he had singlehandedly lowered the incidents of violent crime in the city. People felt safer going out at night with a protector on the loose, and violent crimes in the area dropped by over fifty percent. Restaurants reported an increase in trade, and people stayed out longer using the bars. The police were embarrassed because it made their previous efforts look ineffectual.

It felt bizarre to Sam that the pressure was increased for him to catch the vigilante so that the crime rate could go back up, which he felt was the most ridiculous thing he'd ever heard. But he also knew in the long term, they could not permit it to continue. There was no doubt that, while the vigilante had taken lives, he'd saved others by doing so. If you asked anyone in the street, as TV crews did repeatedly, they would all agree that the people he killed were worthless compared to the innocent victims they had chosen to rob, beat, or potentially murder and had been saved by the vigilante. That linked to the deterrent effect was a good thing, they argued.

The police had no leads or evidence other than the fragmented soft-nosed bullets recovered from the bodies, which had been fired from a nine-millimeter automatic handgun. But as that caliber was a standard one used by police, army, and the more knowledgeable criminals, that didn't help very much. The best hope was if they recovered the firearm and matched it to the barrel marks on the reconstructed bullets. Suddenly, the media posed the question, was the vigilante a disgruntled policeman? That did not help Sam's cause, and more pressure was brought on him to get a result, and he too wondered if it wasn't a rogue cop cleaning up the streets.

Tracing nine-millimeter ammunition sales was a dead end as they could be purchased easily on the internet. Local gun shops and clubs provided lists of customers who purchased that caliber, but everyone seemed to check out after exhaustive interviews. Because the casings were picked up at each scene by the shooter, Sam believed the killer was a professional hitman or dedicated sport shooter who reloaded his own bullets.

Sam confirmed that the original officers did everything by the book and didn't miss anything procedurally. They door knocked the area, spoke to everyone they could, checked any local CCTV, investigated the victims' past to find any possible enemies or links to each other, and more. Thus far, Sam's team had nothing; the killer was a ghost. TV appeals for help had the lowest response rate ever; even the crazies, as Sam called them, who would usually line up to plead guilty, didn't want to take credit for these crimes. The killer, Sam presumed, had been out on the streets and chanced upon a crime in progress, and he (or she, as a woman could not positively be discounted) shot the offender dead. The murders had occurred on different nights of the week and at different times, though they were all late night or early morning hours. There was no discernible pattern in victims, locations, or types of crime being committed other than they were violent and death or serious injury would have been the outcome. Sam gained authorization to put undercover officers on the street at night to watch and wait, but so far, nothing had come of it other than arrests for minor drug-related crimes or assaults the officers witnessed.

Sam sometimes sought help and counsel from his old sergeant and mentor, Felix Milanski. They often spent an hour over a beer discussing the case in great depth. Felix assured Sam that he was doing everything correctly, and unless he had a lucky break or the killer made a mistake in his next execution, he was uncatchable on scant evidence. Because the vigilante was carrying out truly random killings, it could be days, weeks, or months before the next time he struck.

The murders were welcomed by most business owners in the inner city and Northbridge areas, so they were unhelpful, even sometimes antagonistic to police inquiries because, at times when they previously reported crimes in progress, it took too long for overworked officers to arrive. Sam saw that if the vigilante kept succeeding at lowering the violent offender rate in the city, there wouldn't be many more crimes he would make a mistake while committing. Sam and Felix agreed he might never catch him.

After the successful conclusion to the *Domin8* case, Felix had been promoted to detective inspector and transferred to the Organized Crime Squad, where his uncompromising ethics and rock-solid dependability enabled him to excel and gain a reputation as one of the best police officers in the state. He was as unbribable as he was unflappable. For this, criminals gave him grudging respect. Sam, having been hailed a hero, was now mentioned in police circles as the man who couldn't catch the vigilante. Most days, he wore a perpetual scowl as he sensed others laughing behind his back.

Sam worried about being summoned to appear before the commissioner, and he theorized it could only be bad news. *Maybe today's the day I will be relieved of command of the investigation and transferred back to uniform and traffic,* he thought morosely. But then he tried to assure himself that it would be unusual for someone of the lofty rank of commissioner to intervene in his lowly investigation. On the seventh floor of police headquarters, Sam knocked on Commissioner McFarlane's office door and waited for the command to enter. "Come." The barked reply shouted through the closed door.

Sam entered and was surprised to see Felix sitting in front of the commissioner's desk. He looked at Sam, smiled a welcome, stood, and held out his hand to shake as Sam approached. "Good morning, Commissioner, hello, Felix," Sam said, returning Felix's smile, confused.

"Take a seat, Sergeant," the commissioner said. "I know you two know each other. Something has come up that you need to be aware of, and it directly involves the inspector here. Why don't you get the ball rolling and tell him about it, Felix?"

Felix turned in his chair to face Sam, crossed one leg over the other, and began, "Sam, you've no doubt heard of Jimmy Mallory? He's a nasty piece of work who we've been trying to put away for years, but he does everything at arm's length through his henchmen and the Devil's Grave biker gang. We know he is responsible for most, if not all, of the drugs coming into Perth, but it's impossible to get any evidence against him. It seems like whenever we are going to raid one of his places, he knows about it ahead of time thanks to his wealth of informers."

Sam nodded. Everyone knew of Mallory and the rumors that surrounded him. The papers described him as a colorful underworld figure and known criminal when he was really a drug-dealing hoodlum with a reputation for cruel, violent outbursts at a moment's notice. Sam had seen him one night while dining at an outdoor restaurant in Northbridge when he had been out with a girlfriend. The Mallory gang heads, with their wives and girlfriends, were at a large table, and as he observed the situation, some things struck Sam as morbidly fascinating.

There was a never-ending procession of men who walked past in the street and saw Jimmy eating. Each of them would go over to his table and be welcomed with open arms by the underworld boss, who must have gotten a week's worth of exercise as he stood up and hugged each man like a long-lost brother before offering them a drink and sitting down again. It seemed to Sam that if Jimmy offered you a drink, you weren't supposed to accept it, as each person bowed graciously and politely declined before wishing him well and continuing their way down the street. This showing of *respect* simultaneously angered and amused Sam.

The second thing that surprised Sam was when a huge, well-dressed Asian man, with what looked like two bodyguards in attendance, joined Jimmy's table. They talked and acted like they were old friends. During the conversation, they became business partners in what sounded to Sam like a stock market venture. When the passing traffic was quiet enough, Sam heard Jimmy say that they were going to make millions together in some share-trading deal, but the rest of the details were swallowed up by the background noise that comes with dining at an alfresco restaurant in the heart of the nightlife area.

Milanski continued his briefing. "Jimmy had a brother named Desmond, or Des as everyone called him. Emphasis is on the word *had* because he was shot dead in his home in Redcliffe in the early hours of Sunday morning. Ballistics have matched the bullets used to your vigilante's gun. This is why we've brought you in, Sam. It appears you've got your fifth victim: Jimmy Mallory's brother."

"Jesus Christ, that can't be right."

Before Felix could say another word, the commissioner broke in, "There's no need for that kind of language, Sergeant." Sam remembered that he was a devout man who didn't like his officers using swear words or profane language.

Milanski continued, ignoring the interruption. "At first, we thought it was a gangland attack on Jimmy's empire. We've heard on the grapevine that Mallory believed so too and struck back at who he thought was responsible and killed three of the top men of the Apaches' biker gang. They're a reasonably new chapter set up in Perth, from New Zealand, but their roots are in America. We have reliable information that Mallory thinks they are trying to move in on his territory, with his only brother being the first target in an impending war. Everyone is shitting themselves now as they fear an all-out battle between the two gangs. A lot of pushers are trying to hide until the dust settles, fearing they could be next to get hit, so the next week or two will be interesting."

"Interesting is one way to put it," Sam replied.

"Here's the thing, though, Sam," Felix said as he pointed a finger in Sam's direction. "As soon as Jimmy hears that the same gun was used by your vigilante, he will put two and two together and pull out all the stops to find your man himself. I know you wouldn't want him to do your job for you because he will kill him; that's how Jimmy rolls. With the impending all-out gang war, and Jimmy trying to find your guy, it will be a nightmare out on the streets. Mallory is nothing short of a psychotic sadist who will stop at nothing to avenge his brother's death by torturing and killing anyone he thinks will lead him to the guy who did it. There will be carnage."

Sam nodded thoughtfully; he knew of Mallory's reputation. "So far, our vigilante has only killed people on the streets in the act of committing violence or attempting murder, so this shooting is out of character. Was Des part of the family business?" he asked.

"Not so far as we know. Des owned his own electrical contracting business and was doing all right so far as we can see. He employed a young bloke as an apprentice, had been married for five years, and had no criminal record. He is known to be violent like his brother and has come close to an assault charge or two, but nothing more serious than that because victims were reluctant to press charges. It doesn't make any sense that your vigilante would kill him. He and his wife Rebecca had been out at Jimmy's birthday party and, by all accounts, had only just got home in the early hours. They went home in a cab, and the killer must have been waiting for him to return. We're trying to track down the cab driver who took them home, but we don't hold out a lot of hope that he saw anything, even if we do find him, which is proving difficult. That time of night, cabbies sometimes don't log their fares and take cash."

"Could it be that the gun was lost or stolen and used by someone else, making this just a coincidence? I can't see anything else that makes sense," the commissioner asked.

"Anything is possible, sir," Felix replied. "But it would be a heck of a coincidence, don't you think?"

Sam couldn't help but answer them both. "Yeah, it would, for sure. Stranger things have happened, though, and to date, our guy has been killing people who were doing something violent, so what could Des have been doing in his own home? And even if he was planning something, the change in MO seems strange. How would *the Vigilante* even know about Des?"

"Certainly, Des has not committed a crime that we know of, and there were no drugs found in the house, no weapons, or anything of a criminal nature. The home is nice without being ostentatious, and they aren't living beyond their means. The wife has been under sedation since she found her husband's body, but we think we can talk to her late this afternoon. All we know so far is what she told the initial investigating officer; she was getting ready for bed, and Des was shot in the hallway, having gone to the front door to answer it."

Sam interjected, "So the killer wasn't inside the house? He let them enter, then knocked on the door and shot him when he opened it? That makes no sense, either."

"We agree, Sam. It doesn't add up. If it was a professional hit, and the killer was waiting outside, why let them get inside the house first? And if it was *your vigilante*, how and why would he do it that way, unless it's a case of mistaken identity? We assume Desmond Mallory went to open the front door for someone he knew. Possibly it was an appointment that the wife wasn't privy to, or maybe someone he met earlier at the party and invited them back to his home. That would infer the vigilante is known to the Mallorys because it was his brother's birthday party. The gun must have been silenced, as his wife, Rebecca, didn't hear the gunshots. That ties in with the lack of witnesses who heard any shots at the previous shootings. The neighbors didn't hear anything out of the ordinary, though one of them thought they heard a female scream but said that could have been just two cats fighting. Apparently, loud arguments were not uncommon in the Mallory home, but people knew to leave Des alone because of his reputation. The killer picked up the shell casings, like every other time, which suggests he reloads his ammunition or is smart enough to know we could lift prints or DNA from them. That's about all we have. We are at as much of a dead end as you are with the first four cases. Except, this time, Jimmy has declared World War Three against the Apaches and anyone else who can lead him to the murderer."

Sam leaned back in his chair, running through a summation in his mind. "So Des and his wife go out for the night to the brother's birthday party, they cab it home, she goes to bed, and he goes to meet someone at the front door who shoots him dead. That just about sums it up?"

"Yep." Felix nodded. "That's it in a nutshell. Hopefully, the wife can shed some light on it all when we interview her in about an hour; she was in too much shock at the first interview. We've tried talking to Mallory and others at the party earlier without success. None of his clan want to be seen dead talking to us."

The commissioner spoke up, "I want you two to work together for the moment until we get a clearer idea of what's going on, even though you are in different departments. Is that going to be an issue?"

Both men shook their heads; Sam was delighted to have Felix's help and guidance. McFarlane continued, "I agree it's a baffling case. No one scenario fits all the facts as we have them at the moment. If we get the feeling it's the vigilante, then it's back to your case, Sam. If we determine it's related to the underworld and somehow someone else has access to the gun, it's yours, Felix. I want reports delivered every morning at nine a.m. You are both going to be very busy, and I want you to treat this job with absolute top priority. We do not want a bloodbath on the streets. If you need any extra help, let me know directly. Your jobs are to catch this so-called vigilante and stop Jimmy Mallory from waging war, understood?"

They both nodded. Sam spoke up, "I think, either way, sir, we need to put more undercover officers out on the streets at night watching and listening. We need intel as to what's going on. Northbridge isn't that big an area; if we could put another twenty or so officers out there to be eyes and ears, we might gain some useful intelligence."

"Okay, good thinking, Sam. Leave that to me to organize. I will have uniform work with the drug squad and get twenty more bodies out every single night. Get going, gentlemen, and report back to me in the morning."

Chapter 6

Siobhan and the Crunchy Nut Cornflakes

After Didi and Nicky made love slowly and tenderly in the early morning light on the beach, they talked, wrapped in each other's arms while the sun poked its head from between white clouds above the dunes. Neither had enjoyed a sexual partner for a long time. Nicky didn't have a social life, working seven nights a week as he did, and he didn't have the desire to after Simon's murder. Nicky realized that morning, as he caressed Didi's body, he had been living in a cloud of depression.

For Didi, she couldn't bring herself to trust anyone after the man who had been her whole life mistreated and abandoned her. Didi worked five nights a week, which removed most opportunities for her to socialize. Unwilling and unable as she was to see customers from the club, it left precious little time for dating, even if Didi did meet someone she thought she could trust. But the reality was Didi had never permitted that to happen or placed herself in a situation where it was even possible.

As the sun came up, they dressed. Didi felt a radiant glow through her body, which she hadn't experienced for years. She had developed strong feelings for Nicky without realizing it over the past

85

three months. He had been content to be her friend
when she needed one, and it seemed to Didi her
feelings had blossomed so slowly they had snuck up on
her. Over the years, she had come to believe it was not
possible for someone like her to have a deep and
meaningful relationship. To her great delight, Nicky
had proved her wrong with his patience and
understanding. He somehow knew when to leave her
alone with her thoughts, and she needed a lot of alone
time; that was her way.

As Didi slipped her jacket back on, she suddenly
felt a wave of sadness wash over her; she was about to
learn if he was like all the other men she had ever met.
Didi had to tell him about Siobhan, and then she was
sure he would extricate himself from her; there was no
doubt in her mind he would want to leave then. Also,
now they had sex together; that was when most men
wanted to run away with the chase over and the race
run. She could see no reason why he would want to
hang around now he had gotten what he wanted from
her. Even if by some miracle he did want a second or
third helping, once he learned of Siobhan, there was no
doubt he would head for the hills at a million miles an
hour, so there was no point delaying the inevitable. Didi
consoled herself that it had been the right time to finally
take the gamble and roll the dice, in case, by some
minuscule chance, her fears were groundless. Didi saw
herself as spoiled goods, forever unlovable, and
destined to be lonely. But at least she had felt the
pleasure of being made love to, not fucked, or used, but
softly and gently loved to a series of earth-shattering
climaxes.

Nicky noticed Didi had slipped back into what he

thought of as her melancholy mood. He wrapped his arms around her and gave her a long kiss. When she pulled away, Nicky shared his plans for the day. "I've got to get the cab back to the boss for seven o'clock and pick up my car now, but would you like to meet for breakfast at eight?"

"I can't, I'm sorry; I already have a breakfast date," she replied. She saw his face drop with disappointment.

"Oh my God, I'm so sorry. I had no idea you were seeing someone. Why did you let this happen? I would never come between you and another man, Didi."

"Cool your jets, tiger; it's not what you think." She smirked a little. *Maybe he is one of a kind. He wouldn't sleep with me if I had someone else in my life? What's that all about?* Most men who came to the club were married, and that didn't stop them from trying to screw the girls. They never bothered to find out if the dancers had their own partners because they simply didn't care. She looked down at her bare feet and made little circles in the sand with her right big toe. She was about to give Nicky the perfect reason never to want to see her again. "I have breakfast every morning with my little girl before I help get her ready for preschool. Her name is Siobhan. She is nearly five years old, and she never misses her crunchy nut cornflakes with her mummy."

Nicky sat down hard on the sand, his mouth open wide in amazement. He seemed stunned that after three months of knowing Didi, he had no idea she had a child. That was what she wanted. It was private, so Didi had never spoken of her.

****

Nicky could see in her eyes the love she had for her daughter and finally understood her air of melancholy and total lack of faith in men; it finally clicked into place. Everything about her sadness made sense as he saw through the veneers and barriers she had built up to protect herself from further pain. The father had died or left her to raise her child alone, which was why she had zero trust left and wouldn't let another inside the protective shell she had created. *She is expecting me to dump her, and that's why she is so sad again.*

"Well," he began slowly, "that's a breakfast date I wouldn't ever want you to miss, Didi. I bet she is as gorgeous as you. If you ever trusted me enough, I would love to meet her. And by the way, I quite like crunchy nut cornflakes myself."

"You would?"

"Yeah," he said, nodding as his gaze bored into hers. "I really would. I wish you would stop thinking I am just like every other man who hurt or disappointed you in the past." He reached out and took her hand in his and felt her tremble. "I'm not running away from you, Didi, not now, not ever."

****

Didi felt his hand squeeze hers as she, too, sat back on the sand and put her head on her knees. *Can I really trust him?* She knew nothing about him or his past except that he was kind and understanding. Oh, and brave. She could never forget how he came to her rescue that night with nothing more than a flashlight. He had never made a pass at her, seemingly understanding she had so little self-confidence and belief left in herself. She desperately wanted to trust him but knew in her heart if she let him in, and he dumped her, she would be finished. She couldn't risk it again.

"It's okay." Didi shook her head as a tear trickled down her cheek. "Men don't want a ready-made family; I know that. You'd do far better to find someone who can give you your own children because I can't have any more, Nicky. Siobhan was a parting gift from a man I loved and who I thought loved me." Her voice broke with the sadness of remembering. "He went back to his old single life when I was seven months pregnant because he said—" She gulped and choked back tears. "—he couldn't handle the stress of fatherhood. I had complications in childbirth and almost died, so I learned very quickly about the stress of motherhood. Thankfully, the surgeon saved me, but I can't have any more children, ever. It's okay, Nicky. I wanted to make love with you knowing it would be our one and only time. Honestly, I wanted this for my reasons, and it's fine for you to leave now. Find a woman who can give you children, your own family; I know you will make a great dad one day."

****

"Look at me, Didi, please?"

She slowly lifted her head from her knees and gazed at him from the saddest face he'd ever seen. He saw the tears sparkling like diamonds in her eyes, and his heart went out to her, more so than any other person in his life. "Don't you know I love you, Didi? Can't you see that in me? I think you are an amazing woman, and the fact that you do what you do to support your little girl makes me all the prouder to know you. I'm not leaving you unless you want me gone from your and Siobhan's life. Every night when I've taken you home, I've listened to you, watched you, and every night I've fallen more and more in love with you."

She moved onto her knees and threw her arms around him. Didi buried her head in his shoulder, shaking as she cried, holding him as if not daring to believe he was telling the truth and so scared that he wasn't. "If we start seeing each other, you know, like date each other, you will want me to stop dancing, won't you?" she asked. Nicky thought he knew she already believed what his answer would be; of course, he would.

Nicky took a moment to gather his thoughts, knowing she was still testing him. He wanted to be honest and knew she would be able to tell anything that wasn't the truth. Eventually, he gently pushed her away so they could look into each other's eyes. "Didi, I will never come and watch you work, not because I don't want to see you dance, but because I wouldn't want to watch other men disrespect you. I told you once lap dancing is something you do. It's not who you are. Other men see what you do, but I'm lucky enough now to see who you are, and I love that person. I wouldn't want a relationship with someone I had to change into being what I wanted them to be. My mum used to have a saying she would tell my dad when she got cross with him. 'I am not in this world to live up to your expectations of me,' she would say. I like that saying, and I believe in it with all of my heart."

He smiled and continued, "From the day I first met you, I sensed something in you that was so much more than what you do to earn a living, Didi. You have depth and character that is much more than any other woman I've ever known. I've always suspected you had been hurt, deeply, and now I know you have a little girl who you love to bits and who loves you. It all makes sense. I can see why you work as a dancer and let other men see you when you despise them for it. Whether you dance or not is your decision to make, not mine, and whether you do or don't continue, I want to be a part of your life. I will never ask you to stop being you or doing what you need to do to live the way you want to live. That said, if you ever choose to stop lap dancing, I would be delighted to be the only man who gets to see you without your clothes on."

He felt her tremble throughout her entire body as she couldn't stop the tears of joy from streaming down her cheeks. "I never, ever, thought I would say this to anyone else ever again in my life. Nicky, I love you."

They talked and cuddled for another ten minutes until Nicky told her he had to go. The cab had to be cleaned and handed over for another shift, and it was the worst sin to be overdue for the next driver. Fortunately, the cab wouldn't take much to get it ready, but he would still be late if he didn't get moving straight away. Nicky had never been late before but had seen his boss angry with others who had.

****

Nicky dropped Didi back at her home with the promise to call her later in the day, then almost broke the speed limit to get back to the depot and hand the cab over for the day-shift driver. Once achieved, he drove home in his old coupe, and inside he made himself a black coffee before attending to his chores.

The jacket went into the washing machine, set to the hottest cycle in case it had picked up any microscopic blood spatters or gunshot residue. He ejected the magazine from the Glock and loaded another three bullets from the box in its hiding place in the fireplace. His father had worked for many hours to make a concealed compartment in the highly ornate fire surround, which Nicky had rescued from the old house before being sold. He wanted it as a keepsake, knowing how long his dad had spent to hand carve and install it in the family home.

The door was spring-loaded and only opened by pressing one of the petals on an embossed flower. Once opened, it was large enough to hold the gun, silencer, spare magazines, and three boxes of shells. Nicky also had a container for the empty shells and could one day reload them if and when he began to run short, but he was in no rush to do so. Nicky had inherited all of his father's hunting rifles and equipment and had all of the reloading tools. He had transferred ownership and had the correct papers for all the guns in his possession, except for the pistol. It was an illegal firearm, hence the hiding place where it lived, but it harked back to his father's time, long before, and he could not bring himself to get rid of it.

While he turned the gun over in his hand, watching as the light glimmered off the evil-looking barrel fitted with the bulbous silencer, he thought back to when his reign of being a vigilante had all started.

****

Nicky couldn't remember exactly when he started putting the gun in his backpack and taking it with him to work because it wasn't a conscious decision he'd made to do so. The timing was soon after the court case that had given the inexcusably light sentences to the men who had killed Simon seven months after his funeral.

Nicky supposed, with hindsight through rose-colored glasses, he started having the pistol in the taxi for his protection. An unlucky cab driver had been brutally beaten, stabbed, and robbed one night by three drunken men picked up from a Northbridge pub, and Nicky realized the heavy-duty flashlight he had by the side of the seat might not be enough if someone tried to rob him at knifepoint. He felt comforted to have the pistol with him, but he had made no conscious decision to use it, only to wave it around to scare a would-be attacker away.

The pistol had been his father's, and he knew it was illegal, but he found it hard enough to get rid of many of his parents' possessions after the funerals, and he knew how much the gun had meant to him. Nicky easily got the permits and permission to hunt on three station owners' properties because they knew Nicky from the numerous occasions he had hunted with his dad. Nicky needed the permits to transfer the licenses for the other weapons, but there was no such license for the Glock. It wasn't that Nicky wanted to continue hunting as such, but the rifles were his father's, and he couldn't bring himself to get rid of them. He also thought that if he had a son himself one day, it would be good to take him shooting, as his father had with him and Simon. But Nicky could not remember his dad ever talking about the pistol or where he had acquired it. How his father had come by a Glock nine-millimeter automatic pistol, with a silencer no less, remained a mystery until he asked some of his father's hunting friends about it. They just put a finger to their lips and said, "Shush, top secret," or "Hush, hush," and changed the subject.

Brian Bartholomew, his father's oldest friend and

fellow hunter, later told Nicky that the group bought one each when he went to America on a business trip. The guns were cheap, readily available, and easily concealed in the container of machinery parts he was bringing back to Australia. They decided they wanted silencers; after all, if the guns themselves were more exciting *because* they were illegal, how much more exciting was it to have them silenced? Sometimes on hunting trips, the friends used the pistols on wild pigs, goats, or kangaroos to increase the degree of difficulty, though mostly they used them for target-shooting fun. Brian offered to purchase the pistol from Nicky after the funeral, but at that time, Nicky couldn't bring himself to part with anything belonging to his mother and father that he didn't have to. The gun was perfectly safe in its hiding place, and Nicky felt it was a decision he could make later. When time passed, and he thought of the gun, Nicky wasn't sure what he should do with it. The dilemma was that if he handed it in to the authorities, he would have to explain where it came from, and Nicky had no intention of besmirching his father's name by tainting it with an illegal firearm.

When he'd gone hunting with his dad and his friends as a youth, he remembered the adults all had the same pistol. Sometimes, they would have fun around the campsite, shooting tin cans and the like, and they let Nicky have some lessons with the handgun, which he loved to do. Nicky worried, after the funeral, if he did hand it in to the police, his father's friends could also be in serious trouble, and Nicky couldn't bring himself to do that; after all, he reasoned, they weren't criminals. He decided that, for everyone concerned, it was better to leave it in its hiding place, and one day, he would throw it in the ocean to get rid of it. Deep down, he knew he was fooling himself; he would never be able to bring himself to dispose of anything that meant so much to his father.

Years previously, after a mass shooting, there had been a government-sanctioned amnesty for the public with illegal guns to hand them in to the police and not have to answer questions about their origins. The pardon was a way of reducing the number of illicit weapons in the public's hands, and Nicky always hoped such a plan would be relaunched, but it never was. Around two years after his parents' deaths, Nicky received a letter stating the police were going to call and inspect his weapons and means of storage to ensure he was complying with the rules. The inspection seemed to be cursory at best, and once the officer saw the secure gun safe, he left without searching the house, which for some reason, Nicky thought he might. His fears of being found with the pistol diminished.

Nicky went to the court case for Simon's attackers every day and gave a victim impact statement in tears from the witness stand, explaining how the death had changed his life. He later watched disgustedly as the ones who had been set free on suspended sentences clapped each other on the back, laughing, in front of the courthouse as they left, free. Nicky wondered what the judge would have thought if he saw the look of victory on the faces of the attackers; certainly, they didn't appear to be concerned they had cumulatively murdered his brother. At that moment, Nicky imagined in great Technicolor detail how he would like to kill them. The two who went to jail for such a short term also fueled his murderous fantasies. Nicky dreamed of finding them one by one and taking their miserable lives in long, drawn-out, and painful ways. But they were fantasies, and he never intended to carry them out, though he remained hopeful he might.

Nicky could have stopped driving a cab and found something else to do after Simon's death, but he believed he didn't have much to live for anymore. *Why bother?* he asked himself repeatedly. That was Nicky's mantra that he lived by for months as he fought against his soul-destroying depression. He was living from day to day, surviving, with no goal or dreams to work toward, except the faintest hope of revenge against Simon's killers if he ever happened upon them. It was fortunate that their home addresses had been suppressed at trial, or Nicky would have visited them and beaten them to death.

What sustained him throughout his darkest moments was the dream that some night, one or more of the men who killed his brother might hail his cab, or he would see them on a city street. Nicky knew what they looked like and suspected they would keep going into Northbridge; it was only a matter of time before they ventured back to a place that provided so many opportunities for violence. He wouldn't be able to stop himself from committing murder if that ever happened. Subconsciously, that was the reason Nicky started taking the gun to work, concealed in his backpack, just in case his dream came true. Months passed with Nicky living in a fugue, driving and hoping.

One morning, before dawn, he was driving along Beaufort Street near the Weld Square Park when he saw a large, dark-skinned man beating up a woman just inside the park. She could have been the attacker's wife or a stranger; Nicky had no way to know. They were obviously drunk, and the man was shouting, calling her the filthiest names imaginable. Nicky saw the man punch her in the face repeatedly until she fell unconscious on the grass. Nicky pulled over and watched with growing horror as the man walked to a pile of beer bottles near a rubbish bin and bent to pick one up. It was evident to Nicky he was intent on using it as a weapon on the woman.

Nicky scrambled for his bag and tried to pull the gun out, intending to frighten the man away from the woman. But the pistol snagged on the stitching of the pack. By the time he got it free, the attacker knelt over the woman's prostrate body. Nicky cursed as he watched him hit her on the head with the bottle at full swing and heard the sickening sound it made as it struck. The bottle bounced off her skull, almost as if in a slow-motion movie scene. The man lined up for a second swing, which Nicky knew if it connected, would kill her.

As if in a trance, Nicky lowered the window with the electric switch, raised the gun to aim through the passenger side window, and took careful, steady aim at the attacker's chest. The assailant was a big man, and at that range, Nicky knew he could hit him. As his army instructor had taught him to do years before, he fired three shots in rapid succession. The man fell to one side, dead or alive, Nicky wasn't sure, but he knew he wouldn't hit the woman anymore that night. Nicky woke up from the trance-like state he had been in and realized what he had done. He frantically looked around and fortunately couldn't see anyone who had witnessed the shooting. The silencer had done its job and had not brought people on the run to see what had happened.

Nicky put the gun back in his backpack and drove off without squealing the tires. Once away from the area, he pulled over and picked up the ejected shell casings from the floor and tucked them in his pocket. He had watched enough TV crime shows to know he could get caught from fingerprints on the shells from when he loaded the magazine. Back at home, after his shift finished, he took all of the bullets out and cleaned each one. Then, wearing gloves just in case he ever used the Glock again and did lose a casing, he reloaded the gun. *Better safe than sorry*, he thought. Nicky felt satisfied, the happiest he had felt for a long time, as if he had done something worthwhile. Not that he consciously thought about ever doing it again, but he believed he had done a good thing that night and struck a blow for law-abiding people against the growing, violent culture on the city streets.

Over the next few days, Nicky suffered pangs of guilt at odd times when he thought about the man he'd shot. He worried about spending years in jail if he was caught, but those feelings were tempered by reading in the newspapers that the woman had survived her ordeal. A doctor said in an interview that he believed she would have died if she had been hit with one more blow as forcefully as the first had been. The newspapers called the unknown gunman a Good Samaritan and, in a backhanded way, were complimentary of his act. For a while, rumors emerged that a police officer could have shot the attacker due to his frustration with the judicial system, as the offender was well known to them. Nine-millimeter bullets were police issue, it was pointed out, and it was even hinted the man was such a nuisance that police were reluctant to waste their time arresting him for things like assault as, historically, he had been released almost immediately.

For days, the TV news and papers were asking the question: *Who is the Good Samaritan?* Nicky stopped feeling guilty on day two after the newspapers printed a list of previous offenses on the man's criminal record that included sexual assault, violent assaults, burglaries, car theft, and more. The list, though it wasn't acknowledged how the newspaper came by it, showed that over half of the man's life had been spent in jail. He was never going to have reformed, the papers argued, so was his murder a justifiable homicide? Nicky decided Willie Papertalk was no real loss to society. At the time of the shooting, it was a simple equation; he had to die so the innocent woman could live.

Several weeks later, Nicky had been driving late at night in the cab along William Street when, from the corner of his eye, he saw an obviously drunken man stagger into an alley. A few seconds later, another, more aggressive and very muscular man followed him after glancing around furtively. *He is looking to make sure there are no witnesses,* Nicky thought. Nicky had worked the streets long enough to spot the signs of a robbery or violent mugging that was clearly about to take place. He pulled the car over, grabbed the gun, and hopped out, pulling his jacket and hood over his head as he ran. He knew, as if by some sixth sense, what was going to happen in the alleyway if he didn't stop it. Nicky turned the corner into the near darkness, only to see his worst fears had already been realized. The drunken man was lying unconscious in a puddle of blood, his face a bleeding mess as the attacker lined up another kick to the head. All Nicky could think was how the group of men had kicked his brother to death while no one had been there to help. He was consumed with rage and fired at the assailant's body. The man danced and spun as the nine-millimeter bullets crashed into him before he fell, twitching on the cobbled surface. Nicky calmly bent down and picked up the ejected shells, turned, put the gun into his pocket, and left. The shooting had only taken a few seconds.

This time Nicky felt no guilt whatsoever, and the papers changed from calling him a Samaritan to a vigilante. Everyone had an opinion, but most were talking about *The Northbridge Vigilante* in terms that likened him to the Lone Ranger or Robin Hood. The common view was the man being kicked on the ground could easily have died if not for the intervention. Nicky didn't have strong feelings about his new media notoriety; he was still in the depths of depression, living from day to day with no future or dreams for a better life. He didn't spend too much time thinking about anything, but when he did, Nicky believed that the two men he had killed were both no better than scum. The planet was a better place with them not stealing decent people's oxygen; that was how he preferred to look at what he had done and didn't lose a moment's sleep.

The next occasion Nicky used the gun, he had been taking a break. He was sitting in the cab, slumped down in the seat and resting his eyes, although he was not asleep. He was waiting for Didi to finish her shift so he could take her home when he heard the footsteps of a young couple walking past the cab. A few seconds later, a group of three men followed. Nicky heard one of the three men say to his friends as they were level with the cab that he wanted to "Kill the prick," then "Let's steal the bastard's wallet, watch, and phone." Without hesitating, Nicky grabbed his gun, tucked it into the waistband of his jeans, and pulled the hood up over his head. He silently got out of the car and locked the door behind him.

By the time he caught up with them inside the alley, the woman was lying unconscious in the grime, blood pouring from facial wounds and her skirt up around her waist. The attackers had surrounded her partner while he was propped up against a brick wall and were punching him, while one of them stabbed with a knife. Again, Nicky's blood turned to ice, and he fired a hail of bullets at the three men, hitting them all. He kept firing until the clip was empty, enraged at the mindless violence and for beating the woman with such brutality. Nicky picked up his casings and spent extra time to check on her condition. She looked in a bad way but was breathing.

Nicky moved her into a recovery position so she wouldn't choke and pulled her skirt down to maintain her dignity. He then turned and checked the injured boyfriend, who had fallen to the ground but was still barely conscious. His stomach was awash with blood, and Nicky feared he might not survive. Nicky fumbled in the man's pocket and took out his phone. He dialed the emergency number and hurriedly reported two severely wounded people from a savage mugging before tucking the phone back where he found it after wiping it with his jacket to remove his fingerprints. The man weakly raised a hand in a gesture of thanks, and Nicky waved back, then turned and ran.

Back in the cab, he pulled out into the street and left the area before the screams from the wounded men could bring witnesses. He found another parking spot where he could watch the door Didi exited from and waited for her. When he drove away with Didi alongside him, he smiled as he saw an ambulance arrive with a police car shortly after. He hoped the couple would live but had no such feelings for the men he shot.

Again, the press hailed *the vigilante* as some modern-day anti-hero, very much like the fictional superheroes of comics, who really should be arrested but were doing the job that the police couldn't. The newspapers inferred that until he was arrested, everyone should enjoy the significant drop in crime on the inner-city streets. The headline in the Sunday newspaper two weeks after the shooting glaringly reported that violent crimes were down almost fifty percent, which made Nicky smile. It became clear to Nicky that the police didn't have a clue that they were looking for a cab driver in general and him in particular. He wondered if he had been lucky or whether there was a genuine reluctance among the public to help the police identify him. For a while, Nicky had worried he would receive a visit from the police and possibly he would be arrested. He felt sure someone would have seen the cab drive away, or the man who was being beaten up could have identified him. But weeks passed, and no one knocked on his door, much to his relief.

Nicky pulled into the carpark behind the Lotus Blossom Restaurant after it closed to pick up the owner who had lost his driver's license. Nicky suspected the man had been waiting when attacked, and he saw him lying on the ground. Nicky crouched over him to make sure he was breathing and heard someone inside the building. Sickened by the horrific injuries the burglar had caused to the man with a steel fence stake, which lay alongside his unconscious body, Nicky entered and shot dead the offender. Again, he made an emergency call using the owner's phone because he realized if he didn't, the restaurateur could very easily die. Nicky worried it might already be too late to save him, such were the head injuries so savagely delivered.

The newspapers reported, to Nicky's delight, that he had saved the man's life. They also listed the string of previous convictions of the attacker, a known methamphetamine addict who regularly broke into homes and businesses to get money for his next fix. He had been arrested many times over the years for violent assaults, including one case of manslaughter. When Nicky read the report, he felt exonerated and again ceased to feel any guilt.

Nicky was far from heartless; in truth, he had always been the complete opposite and was not usually a violent person. He believed the positives of his acts far outweighed the negatives of taking lives. The men who had killed Simon hadn't worried about what they had done, so why should he? Nicky thought that if he hadn't taken the decisive action he had, the victims and many more innocent people in the future would have died at the offender's hands. Therefore, if it came to a choice between them and law-abiding people, there was no contest as far as he was concerned.

****

Nicky stared at the gun in his hand and felt the weight of it. Just for a fleeting moment, he wondered if he had done the right thing the night before. Nicky had

no doubt he had dispatched the worst kind of wife
abuser, who, he believed, had every intention of beating
the defenseless woman to a bloody pulp in the one
place she should be able to feel safe: her own home.
Nicky believed that if her husband had not murdered
the woman that night, possibly he would have sooner or
later; abusers often did.

He turned the gun over in his hand, staring at the
ugly beauty of its deathly lines. *Maybe it's time to give
it all up,* he wondered. He'd had an incredible time with
Didi earlier when they made love on the beach. He felt
genuine love for the first time in his life for someone
other than his parents or Simon. Given a choice
between a lifetime in jail and a life with Didi, it was an
easy decision to make, and he wanted the relationship
to grow. *The time has come to retire*, he thought.

Nicky decided to put the gun away for good, or
even the right time had come to throw it in the ocean, as
he had always told himself he would. Finally, with
Didi, possibly he could have a normal life, the kind of
life everyone else had. He could feel the change that
had occurred in him since they made love as if their
very souls had entwined. He wondered if he could now
move on from the loss of Simon, his mother, and his
father; he hoped so.

Once the weapon was stashed inside the hidden
compartment, Nicky made himself a toasted ham and
cheese sandwich and a cup of tea, which he had while
watching the morning news. With stunned fascination,
he learned that the man he had shot the night before
was not only a lowlife wife-beater but was the brother
of an underworld drug dealer. *He must be a criminal
himself,* Nicky believed, so, by anyone's definition,

what Nicky had come to think of as his final kill had been justified. He turned off the TV and went to bed.

When he woke around two in the afternoon to his alarm clock's shrill, he got up and made himself a cup of green tea, which was another reminder of his mother, as that was her preferred drink. Nicky sat on a swinging chair on the back patio to digest his thoughts. Didi had told him she always slept until three, and then she went to pick up Siobhan from preschool and walked home with her. They might stop at a park, where she would watch Siobhan play, and would usually be home by four. Nicky was determined to phone at four on the dot.

His mind drifted back to a happy time when he and his brother spoke about what Simon was going to do with his life.

****

"It's not fair to you, Nicky. You put your life on hold for me when Mum and Dad died. Now it's time for me to get a job and stand on my own two feet, so I can help pay my dues," Simon said firmly.

"Don't be daft," Nicky replied. "You're twice as smart as I ever hoped to be. You go on to university and study medicine. It's what Mum and Dad would have wanted, and you know it's what you want, too. I'm fine, mate, and happy to support you and help you get through it all, and then later, you can support me when you are a rich doctor." He grinned and ruffled his kid brother's hair.

"Nah, it's cool, Nicky. I don't have good enough marks to get into medical school anyway. I think it's time for me to get a job, let you go back to studying electronics, finish your apprenticeship, and get your life back on track, man."

105

Nicky understood Simon and tried to sound resigned. After all the years growing up, he knew how to get around his younger brother. "So you're saying that if you had gotten enough marks, you'd have gone to university like Mum and Dad would have wanted?" Simon nodded. "And the only reason you won't go is that you think you won't get accepted?"

"Yeah, of course, I would have gone, but I didn't make the grade, so let's not worry about it. I can get a job doing something else and start paying my share of the bills."

They were sitting at the breakfast table. It was ten days after the graduation ceremony and dinner at Alan Chan's, and Nicky had just gotten home from work. Simon greeted him and put a steaming hot mug of coffee in front of him and a bacon and egg sandwich on a small plate, with extra sauce, the way Nicky liked it. Nicky got up from the table, went into his room, and came back out, holding an envelope. Without a word, he passed it to his brother.

Simon took out the letter and, with wide eyes, read what Nicky already knew; he had been accepted to study medicine at the University of Notre Dame in Fremantle. "I knew you were never going to get around to making the application," Nicky said quietly. "So I did it for you. It's too late, Simon. I've paid the first semester's fees. Dr. Pantella, you're going to uni."

"But you can't keep supporting me, Nicky. You've got to have a life, too."

"I will. Don't worry about me. You're going to get a part-time job to help with the bills too. That's the deal. Now that that's decided, let's talk about something more important. Your eighteenth birthday is in a few days. What do you want to do?"

Simon had a tear in his eyes as he stared at his big brother, knowing it would be useless to argue. He could never beat Nicky in a debate, and the best way to show his gratitude and love for his brother's gift would be to excel in his studies. "I can never thank you enough for all you've done for me, Nicky," Simon whispered.

"Don't worry about it. You can repay me in my old age by paying for a nice nursing home, not a crappy one. Now, for the birthday, what do you need me to do?"

"Well, if it's still okay with you, there will be about twenty of us here for pre-drinks, then ten of us that are all eighteen are going to chip in and share a stretch limo into Northbridge at about eleven and go to a nightclub."

"Sounds like a great night. Remember to call me when you're ready to come home, and I will pick you and Jenny up. I don't want you hanging around a cab rank that time of night, okay?"

"No worries, Dad."

They laughed for a moment until they both realized how much their dad would have wanted to see Simon turn eighteen.

****

The party went without incident, and the limo was on time to take them into the city. Jenny looked radiant, and Nicky thought that Simon might think about proposing to her sometime soon. Sure, they were young, but they were just so ideally matched. They laughed at the same things, clearly cared deeply for each other, and both were going to the same university to study medicine. It wasn't Nicky's place to judge, of

107

course, but he didn't think his younger brother could do any better.

Nicky had taken the night off work when he got the call that they were ready to come home, and he left in his car to pick them up outside the Lantern nightclub. It was only fifteen minutes from their house in South Perth at that time of night. When Nicky arrived, the area was awash with flashing blue lights and a crowd milling around being held back by uniformed officers. With a sinking heart, Nicky parked illegally and ran over to find his brother, but he was too late. Nicky explained who he was when he noticed Jenny crying. He was led through the cordon and saw Simon on a stretcher and being lifted into the back of an ambulance, an oxygen mask over his broken face. Jenny cried hysterically, and Nicky saw her wringing her hands. Joey was covered in blood and concussed as he kept screaming over and over for Simon to wake up, which he couldn't and never would again.

Nicky found out what had happened from Jenny in the ambulance on the way to the hospital. Always the peacemaker, Simon tried to intervene inside the club when his best mate Joey was picked on by an aggressive man and his friends. They all had way too much to drink, and the guy wanted to fight someone. Joey must have looked vulnerable, and the aggressor selected him to be his victim while his mates urged him on. Simon tried to come between them and pleaded with the much bigger man that it was his birthday and would he please not spoil it by hurting his friend. He even offered to buy them all a drink. Security guards came to the rescue because the gang had a history of trouble inside nightclubs. They were forcibly ejected, leaving the birthday boy and friends to finish their night in peace. When they were ready to leave, Simon called Nicky, while others phoned their parents. Then as a group, they made their way outside to wait for their rides to go home.

After they were ejected from the club, the thugs blamed Simon and his friends for ruining their night. Rather than find somewhere else to drink or go home, they chose to wait outside for the boys and get even. The moment Simon and his friends stepped outside, they were attacked without warning. Joey was surrounded, and a multitude of punches was thrown at him by three men. When Simon saw, he jumped in to help his friend by trying to pull one of the men off. It was at that point Richard Churcher smashed a beer bottle over the back of Simon's head. Simon fell to the ground, where he was surrounded and kicked repeatedly in the head until long after he lost consciousness. Joey was felled too, and it seemed the sight of Simon's blood drove them on to hurt them more, to disfigure, or possibly even kill.

****

The life support system that had been breathing for Simon was turned off four days later. Jenny and Nicky said their goodbyes, spoke a prayer with the hospital chaplain, and then hugged each other. Their feelings of loss were more than they thought they could bear as the beeping from the monitor slowed and then finally stopped.

Over three hundred people attended the funeral. Simon had made a lot of friends, and virtually the entire year from his school turned up in a moving tribute to how much he was loved, admired, and respected. Nicky was in shock and was like a ghost when people spoke to him. He had given up everything for Simon, and in the twinkling of an eye, he was gone. Somehow he got through the funeral, and the next day and the one after that. Nicky kept telling himself, just one more day, *just one more day*. He lived his life as if by remote control, never smiling, rarely eating, and going through the motions of living in a fog.

The six men who took part in the attack were arrested, as CCTV cameras recorded the incident outside the nightclub. Yet the ultimate irony came when no one could be identified as the person who killed Simon. Their lawyers argued that it could have been any one of the twenty or more kicks to the head he received.

Until then, Nicky had always believed in the law and that justice would prevail. But when four of the men were released on suspended sentences because it was their first offense, all Nicky saw was that the justice system had decreed that Simon's life wasn't worth enough to punish those who caused his death. The remaining two men were sentenced to nine months in jail for assault, occasioning bodily harm, or death. With time already spent on remand awaiting trial and allowing for good behavior, they were set to be released in less than three months.

They received a stern talking to by the judge, who called them a pack of sadistic animals and bullies of the worst kind. They had, at their lawyer's suggestion, undertaken *Anger Management* classes as if that made them suddenly human. What it all came down to in Nicky's eyes was that a decent human's life was snuffed out, and the punishment was only three months for two of them and nothing for the others. Nicky believed the judicial system was a joke. He sat in the court that day and made a promise to himself, and Simon's memory, to get even some way, somehow.

Chapter 7

Mr. Banshee

Didi answered the phone on the second ring. While Nicky couldn't wait to phone her, it seemed she hadn't been able to wait either and had been sitting, willing it to ring.

Hesitantly, her voice trembling, she answered, "Hello?"

Trying hard not to show how nervous he felt, he replied, "Hi, beautiful; it's me. How did you sleep?"

Her relief was audible as she let out a sigh. "I slept really well, thank you. For a while anyway, I'm so glad you called. I was worried you might have changed your mind."

He shook his head and smiled. It was going to take a while for her to trust him, and he was aware he needed to tread softy and be patient. "I will never knowingly break my word to you, not ever, Didi. I said I would call at four, and here I am. I slept well for a while, too, but then I woke up and couldn't get back to sleep. I kept thinking of this amazing woman I've fallen for."

He imagined Didi was blushing during the pause but was shocked when she finally spoke. "I have someone here who wants to say hello to you. I've told her all about you, and she has been sitting with me, patiently waiting for you to call. Here she is."

"Hello?" a tiny voice said, and Nicky sat up straight, more nervous than he had ever felt in his life. Instantly, he realized that for her to tell Siobhan about him, she had lowered her barriers to let him in, and that meant so much.

"Hello, Siobhan, you have the prettiest name. My name is Nicky. How are you?"

"I'm good. Will you come and have tea with us before my bedtime?"

"I would love to, Siobhan. Will we have crunchy nut cornflakes? They're my favorite."

He was delighted the hear her giggle outrageously. "No, silly. We only have that for breakfast. They are my mummy's favorite too, but we do have toast sometimes when we runded out of cornflakes."

"Well, what would we have to eat for tea, then? Not snails, I hope. I find snails yucky. Spiders are okay, though."

She rewarded him with another giggle, and he heard Didi laugh too. Then he heard Didi say, in the background, "Go on, you can ask him if you want to."

"My mummy is a hexcellent cook, and we want you to come for tea today before you both go to work. If you come, I can show you Mr. Banshee."

"Wow, how can I refuse that? I'd love to meet Mr. Banshee. So long as Mummy doesn't cook snails, I'll come."

"You won't cook snails, will you, Mummy? I want him to come and meet Mr. Banshee."

"No, baby, I won't cook snails this time. How about lizard livers, though?"

The giggling started up again. Nicky thanked them

and said he would be there in an hour and then hung up to get ready.

His heart raced with excitement, a feeling he hadn't experienced for a very long time. He showered, shaved, washed his hair, deodorized, sprayed cologne, and dressed, then re-dressed again as he didn't like his first choice of clothes when he looked in the mirror. He was out of the door in twenty minutes and heading for North Beach. Within five minutes of driving, he realized he had neglected to take the gun out of its hiding place and take his jacket off the washing line. He shrugged and chose not to worry. There would be no vigilante tonight and, more importantly, probably never again.

He couldn't turn up empty-handed; he knew that, and as they both had to work that night, a bottle of wine wouldn't be appropriate. He stopped at the shopping center and bought a small bunch of flowers, a box of chocolates adorned with a red ribbon, and an outrageously cute, giant stuffed fluffy bunny. Then he fought the rush hour traffic to get to Didi's house.

The door was yanked open immediately to his knock, and a tall, rather angry-looking, but beautiful woman with short blonde hair stepped out to confront him. She pulled the door shut behind her, then stepped off the doorstep and came within inches of him.

"You must be Nick. Look, Nick, this is none of my business, really, and she would kill me if she knew I was saying this, but that woman has been to hell and back. Don't you dare play with her emotions, or you will have me to contend with, and I know some very, very bad people, let me tell you." She folded her arms aggressively and waited for his response, ready, it seemed, to strike out and punch him if he said the wrong thing.

Nicky stood his ground and replied quietly, "I am so madly in love with her. I would kill anyone who hurt her myself." Nicki meant it too.

She stared into his eyes, and Nicky thought she saw his sincerity and believed him. She breathed a sigh of relief and relaxed her shoulders, and then she uncrossed her arms and held out her hand. "I'm Caroline; we have been best friends for years. I'm sorry for the tough act, but she has been through the wringer, and I love her to bits."

"Well, with both of us to look out for her, she should be in safe hands, then. How about a deal? You make sure she is safe at work, and I will make sure she is safe out of it."

"You saved her from being raped. For that, I owe you big time. But emotionally, she is so very fragile. Please be careful with her."

"I will. You have my word."

He juggled the things in his arms and shook her hand firmly. She nodded and pushed the front door open and beckoned him inside, yelling, "Vonnie, your dinner guest is here."

There was the sound of running tiny feet, and Nicky was confronted by a miniature version of Didi, looking up at him. Siobhan wore a black dress with white ruffles. She had the same short black hair, a slight build, and a beautiful face with rosy red cheeks. She stood looking wide-eyed at the stuffed bunny in his arms.

"Is that for me?" she asked, her voice full of wonder, and Nicky squatted down to her height, the scene watched closely by Caroline. He handed the girl the bright-yellow rabbit and said, "He sure is. I found him and said I was coming here for lizard liver dinner, and he asked if he could come too. He said he likes lizards."

She hugged the rabbit tightly, her face lighting up. "What's his name?"

"Well, he doesn't have one yet. That's for you to decide because he belongs to you now."

Didi appeared from the doorway behind her daughter. "I hope you remembered to say thank you, missy."

She raised her eyes comically to him and then said, "Well, I might have forgotten with all the hexcitement. Thank you. Shall I call you Nick?"

"Well, my very special friends call me Nicky."

She nodded deep in thought, and Nicky wondered if she was trying to decide if she was a special friend or not. Finally, she held her hand out for him to hold as they walked down the hallway and said, "Will you please sit next to me for tea, Nicky?"

"I would be delighted to sit next to you, Siobhan, if your mummy doesn't want me to sit somewhere else."

He allowed her to pull him along the passage into the family room area, where another woman was setting the table for dinner. She looked up as he was dragged in and said, "Hi, I'm Bree, Caroline's sister. Oh, thank you, but you shouldn't have got me flowers," she joked.

"Ah, umm, well, lucky I didn't, then." He smiled at Didi and handed her the flowers and chocolates.

Didi took them and stood on her tiptoes to kiss him. She seemed genuinely pleased, as if no one had ever bought her flowers before, and was thrilled to receive them. "Thank you, they are lovely. Let me put them in water. I think we have a vase somewhere. I hope you don't mind the others being here; they wanted to meet you. Sometimes they are more like my two mums than my friends."

"It's been so long since I had a home-cooked meal that I didn't prepare myself. You could have invited the philharmonic orchestra if you wanted. And by the way, I think they are excellent friends to have."

"What's a fillomonic?" a tiny voice asked, still holding his hand and looking up at him.

Nicky looked down at the pretty face, and instantly he was smitten as he felt a tug on his heartstrings. "Well, it's a group of elegant people. The men dress up in suits and ties, and the women wear beautiful ball gowns, and they all play different musical instruments and perform."

She nodded thoughtfully, mulling it over, before asking, "Mummy, can Nicky read Mr. Banshee and me a story?"

"Well, sweetie, why don't you ask Nicky if he minds? But maybe give him a few minutes. He's only just walked in the door. But you can tell him dinner will be in about twenty minutes, and I will be busy in the kitchen, so if he wants to read you a story, he has time."

She looked from her mother to him, her eyes pleading, not willing to ask directly and smart enough to know she didn't have to.

"If we have time, I would love to read you both a story." He still had no idea who Mr. Banshee was.

Without a word, she raced off to find a book, and as soon as she was out of earshot, Didi whispered to him, "Mr. Banshee is the only thing Marcus, her father, ever gave her, and he didn't even do that face-to-face.

He left it on the doorstep." Nicky could see the anger and disgust in her voice. "She hasn't seen him in four years. Siobhan takes Mr. Banshee with her everywhere she goes. She named him herself, and we have no idea how she came up with the name. It took forever to get her to go to school without it. And be warned: she won't allow me to wash him, so he is very grubby. It's her security blanket, and I'm not sure she will ever grow out of it. You grab a seat on the couch, and I will get you a drink. Then I have to go and work my magic in the kitchen. It's been a while since I've cooked for anyone other than the four of us; we usually take it in turns."

"I will love whatever you cook, and it will beat my usual efforts in the kitchen, hands down."

She turned away and then stopped. She turned back and added, "Listen, this is very unusual for Vonnie. She seems to be quite taken with you. She is generally standoffish with people, but men in particular. When I told her about you today, she couldn't wait to meet you. Who knows: maybe she's psychic? I've never brought a man here before, so I've never seen her quite like this. You should feel honored."

"Well, I do feel honored, Didi. She is gorgeous, and you've done an amazing job bringing her up on your own. I hope I'm worthy." He squeezed her arm sincerely.

"So do I, believe me, so do I," she said, with a nervous smile, so softly the other women who were watching from the kitchen didn't hear. She left him to sit on the couch and wait for Siobhan to bring him a book to read. He felt like he was treading water, unsure of what to say and how to act. Nicky knew he was being watched and judged by Caroline and Bree, as well as Didi, and he knew in his heart if Siobhan didn't accept him, Nicky might never see her again. *No pressure...* he told himself.

He desperately wanted it to work so badly because, for the first time in months, he felt something inside him other than a burning rage and hatred for the world. He realized he was capable of caring, loving, and even living again because only a short while before, Nicky didn't care if he lived or died. He let himself daydream while waiting for the cutest little girl he could ever imagine to find the right book for him to read.

****

Nicky didn't start out trying to get to know Didi; far from it. For some reason, he wanted to make sure she got home safe. She seemed so lost he genuinely thought she needed protection when she finished work, in case the two men had friends who would attack her. Beyond that, he didn't stop to think about his feelings for her either way. He had no interest in getting emotionally involved with anyone, and the attraction to her was perhaps subconscious. In any event, he went with the flow of getting her home after her work with no other motive in mind.

Didi phoned him the following night after the attempted rape and, in a very nervous and timid voice, asked him to pick her up after work. She sounded as if it would be an imposition rather than what he did for a living, and that seemed so cute to him. Once she was in the cab, they barely exchanged a word all the way to her home. She stared out of her window as if she was petrified. He knew well enough not to try to talk to her when she didn't want him to. The only time she smiled was when he played James Hendry's *Burn down the Jets,* and Nicky sang along, emphasizing the stuttering lyrics. When he pulled up at Didi's front gate, she said, "Thanks," and paid him. She then got out and then leaned back and gave him a little wave and an extremely nervous smile.

After the simple yet sweet kiss on the cheek the night before, it seemed she had retreated once more into her sad little shell. The following night it was the same, but as she got into the cab, she said "Hi," and smiled at him, but only for a moment. The smile erased quickly, and she didn't look at him again. In that one moment, though, he felt something stir inside himself. He wasn't sure what it was, and as soon as he was aware of it, he pushed any thoughts of her away. After all, he reasoned, she could barely string two words together around him. To her, he was probably just a friendly cab driver and nothing more.

Over the next few days, he found himself thinking about her at odd times, wondering why she seemed so melancholy. That was the perfect word that summed her up: melancholy. Not depressed or angry at the world as he was. No, she was sad, almost terminally so. In the same way, he knew she was down; he also knew she wouldn't want to talk to him about it until she was ready. So he never asked and never expected anything from her. But every night that she worked, she called him. When he sensed she was ready to have a conversation, he asked her about the tattoos she had. She told him about each one. Mostly they had no real significance, except that she thought tattoos were pretty. As she was inherently beautiful in her looks and nature, he agreed that they suited her.

Nicky had never been into tattoos, but on her, they added so much more than they detracted. In part, that was because they were, without a doubt, the most colorful he had ever seen. Previously when Nicky had seen tattoos on women, they were usually ugly and dark blue with some dull coloring, and he thought that women were stupid for disfiguring their bodies. He had no time at all for anyone dumb enough to permanently put a lover's name on their skin as he knew better than most how fleeting people and relationships could be in the real world.

On the fifth night, when she hopped in the cab, he had a coffee waiting for her, and she graced him with a dazzling smile of appreciation for his thoughtfulness. To see that smile was worth the expense of a coffee. And so they continued slowly growing a friendship that was as fragile as it was mysterious, both drawn to each other but neither understanding exactly why. Still, on some nights, she wouldn't speak a word to him, and on those occasions, he could sense it was best to leave her to her thoughts. He realized that some nights were worse than others in the work she did, and only she knew why she did such a job. He would never ask because he knew she was embarrassed and possibly even ashamed of it.

He understood that to earn a living, the men she would have to expose herself to, flirt with, and dance for would often be drunk. They would want to touch her. She was gorgeous, after all, and they would treat her like she was nothing better than a whore, or a piece of meat. He understood why she would be in a bad mood sometimes but tried to calm her with his never-ending supply of his mother's favorite songs. He often wove a little story or background about tunes or why his mother liked particular ones so much, but never with too many details to be boring.

Other nights were better. Didi's employers expressly forbade Didi to date men from the club, and she had told Nicky she never would meet with her customers outside of work even without the ruling. But sometimes, she would let her guard down and talk to someone who didn't treat her like she was a hooker. Sometimes men showed what seemed like a genuine interest in her as a person. On those nights, she was more talkative. She never gave many specifics about her work; mostly, that information was private. Her world was a secret to him, and he knew better than to press her for details. His world was also off-limits to her too. He had no desire to talk about his miserable past. He barely even wanted to think about it, let alone discuss it, and on the rare occasion that she asked a question, he would deflect it to maintain the status quo.

He could see she had fallen in love with his James Hendry songs, and they worked their way through his extensive catalog of music. She had once told him that, at work, she found herself looking forward to what he had chosen for her to listen to on the ride home.

"Truth be told," she admitted, "having something to look forward to helps me get through the nights, especially the bad ones." When she was in her more talkative moods, they would discuss Hendry's incredible lyrics and melodies at great lengths. For Nicky, her song became *Nightlight in the Wind*, which she had never heard before he introduced her to it, and he realized it was her song to a tee. She was just like a candle in the breeze, dancing from side to side and could so easily be blown out.

****

Nicky was jolted out of his reflections by Siobhan standing in front of him, holding out a book with one hand and a very grubby and tired-looking rag doll in the other. She beamed a smile, holding both her arms out to him. He realized that Siobhan wanted to be picked up and sat on his lap, which he did. He gently plonked her down, and she wriggled to get herself comfortable. His heart felt full to bursting as this just felt so right to him, as she snuggled in and waited for him to read to her. Nicky looked up across to the kitchen to see the three women watching him, smiling to see how she had accepted him. He felt as if he had come home, at long, long last. He grinned as Siobhan sat Mr. Banshee on her lap the way she was on Nicky's.

Since the night he found Simon being loaded into the ambulance, battered, bleeding, and dying, his world had been devoid of emotion, bar anger. At that moment, with a little girl sitting waiting for a story, he knew that this was how he wanted to spend the rest of his life. He read her a tale about a marshmallow boy and his friends, making up outrageous voices for the different characters. Siobhan alternated between giggling and looking up in awe. During the tale, the women in the kitchen seemed to marvel at how he seemed to capture Siobhan's heart and her imagination.

Nicky couldn't ever remember having a more beautiful night. The food was simple and delicious, served with iced tea for the adults and orange cordial for Siobhan. Slowly Bree and Caroline seemed to warm to him and included him in conversations about a wide variety of subjects. Occasionally, when he looked across the table to Didi, he found her smiling at him, using her eyes as well as her lips. He knew she was letting him know he had been accepted into their family.

They talked mostly about inconsequential things, including Siobhan in conversations, as she was one little lady who didn't like to be excluded from anything. At one stage, out of the blue, she asked him point-blank if he had any children at his home like her and looked at him expectantly for an answer.

"No, princess. I don't have any children, but if I did, I would like them to be just like you." She seemed very pleased with that answer, as if knowing she wouldn't have to share him with others.

After dinner, he insisted that he wash up the dishes while Didi bathed Siobhan and got her ready for bed. Caroline and Bree dried up and put things away, mainly because he didn't know what went where.

He was tempted to throw soap suds over the women and wondered whether he should dare. By the time they had nearly finished, he couldn't hold back any longer, so he took a handful in each hand and tossed one at Bree, the other at Caroline. They both shrieked at the same time, and while Bree scooped her suds up and threw them back, Caroline rubbed hers in his face. The three of them ended up giggling like school kids and finished with Caroline telling him in a solemn voice that he was, "All right." Nicky felt she had accepted him and bent down to wipe the spilled suds off the floor with a paper towel, smiling to himself.

Didi came into the kitchen just as the frivolity ended. She grinned as she looked at him and said,

"You've made an impression; Miss Muffat would like you to read her a story in bed, which I usually do for her. My own daughter has dumped me." The look on her radiant face showed that she was kidding, though; there wasn't one iota of angst in her words.

Nicky was genuinely pleased that Siobhan would ask that, and he looked at his watch and decided he had time. Even if he didn't, he knew he would have made the time as Nicky didn't think that he could refuse Siobhan anything; he was so taken with her. While Didi stood in the doorway of her daughter's bedroom, leaning against the frame, she watched as Nicky read another story and pointed out the pictures, and delighted Siobhan by doing each character with different voices once again.

****

He's a natural, Didi thought. *Karma must be at work somehow*, she mused to herself. She knew she loved him. Siobhan had taken to him better than she could have ever dared hope, which was all the better because she hadn't pushed for it. It had just happened naturally. They just seemed to like each other and bonded instantly.

He was a mystery to her, a mystery she wanted to solve piece by piece. If there was such a thing as the perfect man, she believed she was looking at him right there: reading a story to her daughter in strange, funny voices to her wonderment and delighted giggles. Didi had heard her laugh more in that one night than she had in the entire month before. *You can't knock a child's instincts*, she told herself and was touched with sincere and sudden gratitude to whomever or whatever force had brought them together. The only decent thing in her life, other than a loving friendship with Caroline and Bree, was Siobhan, and that something so beautiful could be borne from such angst and suffering amazed her.

The story ended, and she watched as Siobhan hugged him good night. He kissed her forehead as sweetly as if he was her father, yet they had known each other only a little over two hours. She realized that was one of his charms; he didn't try to make people like and accept him. He was just…there for them. Siobhan couldn't help but be drawn to his caring nature like a moth to a light in the night.

She walked him to his car with her arm through his until he turned and leaned back against the driver's door. "This has been the best night, the best meal, and the best company I've had in a long, long time. I can't thank you enough for the invite and for the chance to meet the most beautiful little person in the world. You're an incredible woman, Didi. I love you. You do know that, right?"

Didi hugged him tightly, biting her lower lip, her heart soaring. She had never thought she could let anyone in this close ever again. She realized just how much she had missed the closeness and joy of loving and being loved.

"Oh, God, I love you, too. You know that in the last twenty-four hours, you've stolen two hearts, don't you?"

He pushed her gently away from him and gazed into her teary eyes. "I will never hurt you or Siobhan; I would die before that ever happened."

They kissed until reluctantly, he had to leave to go to work. Didi, too, had to get ready herself.

"See you soon. Love you," he said through the window as he backed out of the driveway. She blew him a kiss, waving. Didi stood alone with her happy thoughts long after he had disappeared down the street. In an ideal world, he would have driven her to work, but he had to go and pick up the cab, which meant their starting times didn't mesh.

Chapter 8

The Interview Process (1)

Felix Milanski and Sam Collins arrived at Rebecca Mallory's home and knocked on the door. They surveyed the street and saw several trees planted on the verges and bushes growing in the neighbors' gardens that could easily have concealed someone lying in wait for the Mallorys to come home on the night of the shooting.

Forensics had checked the likely hiding places and could find no footprints, cigarette butts, or anything that would indicate someone had stood around waiting. That was no guarantee it hadn't happened that way though it had rained that night, so footprints would be visible. But more likely, the killer waited in a parked car rather than stand in the rain.

A middle-aged woman opened the door, and the first thought Sam had was: *mutton dressed as lamb*, which conflicted with earlier reports of her being an attractive woman.

"Mrs. Mallory? I'm Detective Inspector Milanski, and this is Detective Sergeant Collins. May we come in?"

She shrugged and opened the door. "Rebecca is in the lounge room. I'm her sister-in-law. Might have known you lot would come sniffing around."

"Ah, Maureen, is it? I've heard so much about you, but we've never met." Felix held his hand out, but she just stared at it and sneered as if she wouldn't be seen dead shaking it.

"Most of it bad, I bet. Go on through. I'm making a cuppa, but I won't make you pigs one, so don't bother asking."

"I wouldn't dream of putting you out, Maureen. You'd probably spit in it anyway, or worse. Don't worry. We'll find our own way." Felix brushed past her, and Sam followed, stifling a grin; he, too, had heard of *the wicked witch of the west,* Maureen Mallory.

They entered through the door she indicated and saw a sad-looking blonde woman sitting in an armchair watching a daytime soap opera on the large flat-screen TV. Rebecca was far more attractive than her sister-in-law, though the bags under her eyes gave her a haggard look. Sam hoped she wouldn't have the same attitude toward them as Maureen.

Felix wasted no time; Sam knew he wanted to get started before Maureen came back because she would dominate the conversation. "Rebecca Mallory? We're the police. I'm Insp. Milanski, and this is Sgt. Collins. We are very sorry for your loss. Do you mind if we ask you some questions about the other night?"

"Sure, I've been waiting for you guys. Sit down. Why has it taken you so long to come and see me? Have you caught the bastard yet?"

"Mrs. Mallory, we stayed away because your sister-in-law told us that you were in shock, too upset to speak, and had been sedated. To answer your question, no, we haven't caught him or her yet. That's why we'd like to talk to you."

They sat on the couch, and Sam took out his book to take notes, as he always had when they worked together previously. Her first words were not very encouraging. "I'm not going to be any help to you. I didn't see or hear a thing."

Felix nodded. "Well, perhaps if you wouldn't mind, would take us back to the night in question? You were at Jimmy's birthday party, I believe, and that was held where?"

"Yeah, it was a good night. We were at Mimi's Bar. A band played, Desi and I danced a bit, and we had a few drinks and finished with tequila shots. I spent some time with Gordy, Jimmy's best mate since school, while Des played pool, and then the two of us caught a cab home."

"Did anything unusual happen at the party?" Felix asked.

"No, not that I know of. What do you mean by unusual?"

"Well, were there any arguments or fights? Did anyone get untidily drunk, make threats, anything like that? Anything at all that seemed out of the ordinary?"

"At one of Jimmy's shows, you're kidding, right?" She shook her head incredulously as if he were mad even to contemplate that. "No one would dare. No, there was nothing unusual at all that I saw. Everyone seemed very friendly and had a good time."

"Okay, thank you, Rebecca. So you caught a cab. Did you call for one or go to the rank?"

"It was raining, but Des wanted to walk. We went to the one farther up the street on the other side of the road. It only took a few minutes to get there, and no one else was waiting, so we got straight into the one at the head of the queue. The rain seemed to have sent everyone home early."

"Did you notice anyone following you or see anything unusual in the street on the way to the cab?"

Rebecca stopped to think, recalling being half dragged by the arm and concentrating on not falling over. She had been incapable of noticing anything, but she didn't want to tell the police that Des was violent toward her. She had been warned by Maureen that if Jimmy heard that she had bad-mouthed his brother's memory, there would be hell to pay.

She shook her head. "No, sorry, I don't remember anything. It was raining, and we had our heads down a bit and hurried to get the cab. I didn't see anyone. I'm sure there were other people about, but I didn't notice them."

"Okay, so you got in the cab, and he took you home. Did you notice anything unusual then, anyone following you, maybe?" Sam noticed the testiness in Felix's voice.

"The only unusual thing was the cab driver himself."

They both sat up to take notice, and she burst out laughing. "No, not unusual in that way. It's just that he was nice and friendly. The strange thing was that he was Australian, and let's be honest, you don't see too many of them anymore, especially late at night. They probably have too much sense and leave it to the foreigners; maybe they're used to it. I didn't notice anyone following us, the drive home was uneventful, and Des gave him a cash tip. He drove off, and we dashed inside because it was still raining."

"Did you see anyone hanging around outside?" There was more than an undercurrent of annoyance creeping into Felix's voice, Sam noticed. It was good to know he hadn't changed; his short fuse of a temper had been a part of his style, which Sam had complimented when they were partners. They had been legendary at the good cop, bad cop routine.

"No, we just hurried to get in because it was wet."

"So what happened next, Rebecca? Think carefully, please?"

"Nothing. We went to bed, and while I was getting undressed, there was someone at the front door. Des went to open it, and because I was just about naked, he closed the bedroom door behind him. He didn't come back right away, and I must have nodded off because, when I woke up later, Des wasn't in bed with me. That was about five o'clock. I went to check where he was and found him...dead." The dam burst. Rebecca buried her face in her hands and cried as she recalled seeing him sitting on the floor, his back against the wall where he had slid down, eyes open and dead, his white shirt drenched in blood.

Milanski shook his head slowly. "You didn't hear any raised voices, an argument, anything at all?"

"Nothing; I must have gone to sleep pretty quickly. It was very late at night, and I had been drinking a lot."

"Rebecca, your husband was shot three times, only a few meters away from where you lay in bed. Surely, you must have heard the gunshots?" Felix said loudly.

At that point, Maureen entered with a mug of tea and angrily joined in. "You pigs are all the same. She told you she didn't hear a thing, but you've got to call her a liar, don't you? Rebecca's the victim here. If she said she didn't hear anything, she didn't hear anything. Maybe they had one of those thingamajig silencer things."

"Well, Maureen, if you are suggesting the murderer used a silenced pistol, that would suggest a professional gangland hit, wouldn't you agree? Perhaps it's something to do with Jimmy's business interests, after all. Thanks for bringing that up."

She instantly became incensed. "Don't you fucking dare try to frame Jimmy for killing his brother. Jimmy is a legitimate club and bar owner and loved his brother to bits. You are fucking mad to suggest otherwise. Are there no depths you will sink to trying to get at Jimmy?"

Things were rapidly spiraling out of control, and Sam tried to calm the situation down. "Maureen, we are not trying to frame anyone. What we *are* doing is trying to find the person who shot Rebecca's husband, your husband's brother, dead. He was shot three times, but Rebecca heard nothing, and *you* suggested a silenced pistol. That would infer it was an underworld hit because silenced guns are not readily available to Mr. Joe Public, and again *you* were the one who brought up a silencer. Help us out here. Who do you think did this?"

"What if she is just a heavy sleeper? They had had a lot to drink. She was probably pissed by the time they got home and didn't hear anything."

Felix shook his head silently and tried to calm down. Antagonizing these women wouldn't achieve anything. "He was shot three times by a nine-millimeter pistol. In a confined space like that hallway, it makes a hell of a noise unless it was, as you suggest, silenced.

But even then, a gun is not silent; the noise is suppressed or reduced. Perhaps Rebecca may have heard it, but in her half-asleep state, she thought it was something else, so what we are asking is, what did she hear? Let me ask you both one more time; can either of you think of anyone who would want to kill Des? One of his work colleagues or a competitor, someone he owed money to or just someone he had fought with; anyone at all we should look at for this?"

Neither answered. Maureen stared back insolently while Rebecca buried her head in her hands and quietly sobbed. Felix stood, and Sam followed suit, knowing there was no more they would learn. Felix took out one of his business cards and placed it on the coffee table. "Rebecca, if you think of anything else at all, please give me a call. My mobile number is on there, and you can get me anytime. Maureen, please tell Jimmy we will be along to see him tomorrow."

"Tell him yourself. I'm not your fucking secretary. You sit tight, love; I'll see these pigs out," Maureen said.

She ushered the two police officers out to the front door. As they left, Sam couldn't help himself. Having been quiet for most of the interview, he had to have a parting shot. "Well, it's been lovely to meet you, Maureen; I must say you've lived down to your reputation."

Her only reply was to slam the door, just missing Sam's backside as he stepped through.

At the car, Sam asked Felix, "Is it worth coming back and talking to her when her guard dog isn't with her?"

"That won't happen anytime soon, Sam. Jimmy

won't allow her to be alone to answer questions in case we get her to talk about his business. We need to find the cab driver, in hopes he saw something, even though it's probably a waste of time. This shooting has all the hallmarks of a professional hit, with her not hearing the shots. The only thing that's a curveball is it's the same gun as your killer used, and so far as we know, Des was not part of Jimmy's world. I guess if there are no more vigilante murders, then we can assume your man got rid of the gun, and someone else is using it. I hate to say it, but at this rate, we will probably never know who killed him unless we find the gun."

****

The Interview Process (2)

Maureen Mallory waited by the front door and watched the cops through the window until they got in their car and drove away. She grinned as the car disappeared, then went back into the lounge room, shut the door, and stood in front of Rebecca until she looked up at her. Maureen slapped Rebecca's face hard, slamming her head to the side and cutting the inside of her mouth. It was the same spot where Des had hit her, and Rebecca howled in pain and surprise.

"Right, you bitch," Maureen said menacingly, "now tell me everything you didn't tell the pigs." She yanked Rebecca back upright on the chair by her hair and proceeded to slap her cheek repeatedly. Rebecca wailed that there wasn't anything extra that she hadn't told them, but that only riled Maureen more. Being an ex-gang member and street fighter, she stopped hitting her face and punched Rebecca in her solar plexus, which stole her breath and made her retch.

Fifteen minutes later, Maureen knew it all. She

listened while Rebecca admitted Des was drunk and in a nasty, foul mood when they left the party and had hit her several times that night because he was jealous of the attention Gordy had paid her.

"Gordy? He tried to fuck you, did he?" Maureen demanded and slapped her again.

Rebecca screamed, "No, he was just nice and friendly."

"Des didn't hit you in the club. We would have known if he had. You're lying, slut."

"*No, he didn't hit me in the club*," Rebecca almost screamed. "He waited till we got outside, and then he hit me again in the cab. He hit me twice."

Maureen stopped to think. *Something is wrong with this picture*, then realized what it was. "Earlier you said the cab driver was nice. What did you mean by that?"

"He just asked me if I was okay. Then Des threatened him and told him to mind his own business, and he took us home. He didn't say another word; he just asked me if I was okay. He didn't seem to be scared of Des, but nothing else happened between them after Des threatened to hurt him and me more if he interfered again."

Maureen couldn't see anything mysterious there and changed her tactic. "Now tell me, really, why didn't you hear the gunshots?"

"I don't know, Maureen. We came in, and Des hit me a couple more times; he cut my lip, see?" Rebecca opened her mouth and used her fingers to pull he lip down. "He even kicked me, and then he threw me on the bed and ripped my dress off. I was crying because he hurt me, and I was scared of what was to come. Then the doorbell rang. Des thought it was a nosy neighbor and slammed the bedroom door and went out, angry, to see who it was. I swear I didn't hear a thing other than some muffled kind of noises. When he didn't come back straight away, I thought it must be some sort of business thing and fell asleep. I swear that's everything."

Maureen wanted to punch her some more, just for fun. She'd never liked the stuck-up, big-titted bitch, but held off for the time being. Maureen was quite pleased with herself. She had learned three things that the police didn't know, and she knew Jimmy would be happy with her and keen to know what she'd found out.

Piecing things together, she learned that Gordy had made a play for her that night. Maybe they were fucking each other, or perhaps something was going on that warranted Jimmy checking out. Maureen also got out of her that the cab driver witnessed Des hitting her and was threatened when he asked if she was all right. She wasn't sure that meant anything because the silenced gun, as the police inferred, suggested a professional hit and not a cab driver getting even. Still, it could be worth tracking him down for a chat. Lastly, Des wasn't expecting the caller. If he were, he wouldn't have been angry when he went to the door to check out who it was.

She spent the next half an hour thinking things over, and the more she did, the more she came back to the most obvious, and that was that Gordy had the hots for Rebecca and had killed, or had someone else kill, his rival so he could have the bitch all to himself. It wouldn't be the first time one competitor killed another over a woman. Maureen went out to the garden for some privacy from the whimpering cow inside. She phoned her husband to report in; Jimmy would want a quiet word with Gordy; of that, she was sure.

Chapter 9

Learning Secrets

The next few days flew by for Didi and Nicky as they fell into a routine that worked for them. Nicky not only picked up Didi after work but arranged with the cab owner to change his start time so he could drive her to the club after having dinner with her and Siobhan. He became incredibly close to Didi's daughter, and bedtime stories became the highlight of both of their days. Nicky sought out new books to read to her, with particular emphasis on interesting characters that he could bring to life with his previously undiscovered talent for making up different voices to enhance each one's traits. He could make her giggle so easily, and he never tired of hearing her laugh. They became best friends, as she quickly found the father she never had, and he found the family he didn't know he needed.

Didi was amazed at how easily he fitted into their lives but also how quickly Siobhan accepted him. Now she would not only seek her mother's approval for something but Nicky's as well. Once she asked Didi a question and wasn't entirely happy with the answer. She folded her arms across her chest and said: "I'm going to ask Nicky instead." Didi almost wet herself with laughter, much to Vonnie's chagrin. On another occasion, Bree went to sit in the dining chair, usually used by Nicky, which of course, was alongside Siobhan. Her face showed complete horror as she called out to her mother that Auntie Bree had stolen Nicky's chair, and it was Bree's turn to laugh as she jumped up to vacate it.

Even Caroline agreed he was a good man, a keeper as her mother would have said. The difference he had made to Didi and Siobhan was nothing short of a miracle. Didi began to sing songs around the house. If she didn't know the words, she would whistle or hum over them. Singing and whistling was something Bree and Caroline were not used to hearing from their housemate. One evening before Nicky arrived, Caroline walked into the kitchen while she was singing, cooking that night's dinner. Caroline stood with her hands on her hips and demanded to know who she was, what she was doing there, and what she had done with Didi. When Didi looked at her quizzically, Caroline explained that the Didi they knew didn't sing around the house. She moped around and looked sad, so the singing cook couldn't possibly be the Didi they knew and loved. Didi blushed, bowed her head, and grinned.

Though she hadn't told Nicky, she had decided to try to change jobs, as she no longer wanted other men to see her nude. She dearly wanted the only man to enjoy her to be Nicky, but the obvious question then was, what would she do for a living? Didi was unskilled and had only worked in a supermarket before she fell pregnant, so she had nothing to fall back on. Didi had also gotten used to working nights, and because Nicky worked those hours too, it suited both of them. If she switched to a day job and he stayed working nights, they would hardly see each other, and that was not going to happen. Now that she found him, she wanted to be with him as much as she possibly could.

She spoke to her boss, Marty, while on a break and asked if she could switch from lap dancing to something else, explaining she had fallen for the right man and wanted to get out of the game. Marty liked Didi and was happy for her and said he would keep his eyes and ears open for an opportunity. He could see she was serious, and he would rather keep her as an employee than lose her altogether. Now that she was in love, he knew it was only a matter of time before she would stop dancing. That was how it went with some of the girls, and he approved, which was one of the reasons he was a great manager to work for; he cared.

Two days later, one of the bar staff quit with a week's notice to go traveling to Queensland, and he phoned Didi to ask if she wanted that job instead, explaining that the money would be significantly lower. That was a given, she realized. The dancers could earn between two to six hundred dollars a night, depending on how well they could flirt with the men and get them to pay for private lap dances. The customers tipped with the fake money which they purchased on entry, and at the end of the night, the girls would cash in their play money for real cash, less the house commission.

Some girls used their assets and flirted to more significant advantages than others and earned a lot of money. Others, who were not much more than prostitutes, used the club and their lap dances to hook up with customers after their shift finished, even though it was expressly forbidden. But not Didi. Marty knew she danced only to support her daughter, and her demeanor was that she always had a melancholy air to her. That sadness was her "*thing*," and some men found it attractive, and they wanted to befriend her or save her. They would tip her because they felt for her, but even if she was getting paid well, Didi always stayed sad and aloof, though friendly.

Didi was an accomplished dancer and had never used her body or the promise of sex to sell private dances. When she did perform them, it was her strict instruction to the customers that there was no touching allowed. She took her clothes off for men, and sometimes women, but would not do it in a sex-starved or vampish way. She got more than enough men to pay her to justify keeping her job. Besides, Marty liked her, and there were plenty of high-money earners he didn't like at all, so he saw it as a balance. It was also the type of job that attracted transients, but Didi had been with them for a long time. She was always reliable, not a drug addict, and honest. In reality, Didi would probably earn more than half as bar staff. She would wear a skimpy but tasteful uniform that was designed to arouse men without showing off their private areas. The fact was that Didi would wear less at the beach in summer, so it wasn't about being nude. It was more about dressing to promise more, and the dancers would provide the nudity.

When Marty explained the difference in pay rates, he took great pains to point out that the bar girls could still earn good money in tips if they worked at it. They had three girls who worked the bar at night, and the tips would be shared equally among them after the house took its cut. The friendlier the girls were at the bar, the more tips they would pick up, therefore the more she would receive.

Didi accepted without hesitation. In the four years she had been a dancer, Didi had saved almost thirty thousand dollars, which was for emergencies and Siobhan's future education. With two paying housemates, her living expenses could handle the reduced income. The most important thing to her was Nicky; she wanted to quit not only for herself and her self-esteem but to show her commitment to him. She knew he would never ask her to cease because it was not his way to impose his will on her. But at the same time, she knew he didn't like drunken men ogling her and trying to grope her. Didi needed the right time to tell him, and it came sooner than she thought.

Nicky arranged to take a rare night shift off to coincide with one of the nights Didi didn't work. He checked with Bree if she wouldn't mind babysitting Vonnie, and when she agreed, he asked Didi if she would like to go out with him like a normal couple that didn't work night shifts. For a moment, Didi showed a confused look on her face and became a little anxious as she had never been out at night and left her daughter on her own if she wasn't working. She had never been out with a man at all since her ex abandoned her. But seeing the look in Nicky's eyes, she agreed. He wanted to be with her, and that knowledge covered her body in goose bumps.

Nicky spent that day cleaning his house, as he intended to bring Didi back after dinner and wanted her to see it tidy and sparkling. He put a bottle of white wine he thought she would like in the fridge and phoned Alan Chan's Chinese restaurant to make sure he could fit them in. When told he would be bringing a woman, Alan was delighted and promised a special meal that he would prepare himself. For years, Alan had been goading Nicky by saying things like, "Why you no have a girl?" or, "When you getting married?" He always made sure the single waitresses he employed worked Nicky's table when he brought his younger brother in for dinner. They used to dine there at least once a week, sometimes twice, and Alan would make sure Nicky knew his waitress was single and available. After Simon was killed, Alan knew Nicky was depressed and had become half the man he was before. Undeterred, he worked tirelessly to match Nicky with one of his waitresses, but to no avail. Now Nicky was bringing a girlfriend to his restaurant for the first time, and no one was happier than Alan.

Just after two o'clock, over the noise his old vacuum cleaner made, Nicky heard the doorbell singing its somewhat dated tune and went to see who it was. He opened the door. There were two unmistakable plainclothes police officers: one male and one female. They introduced themselves as Detectives Jenny Markham and Bryce Johnson while holding out their ID cards and asked if he was Nicholas Pantella. Nicky had been expecting this visit sooner or later and had planned what he would say and how he would act. He thought it would have occurred sooner than it had. "That's me. How can I help?" he asked, smiling.

"It's regarding a fare you picked up from Northbridge around three a.m. on Saturday the fourteenth."

Nicky tried to look blank. He shook his head and raised his shoulders as if to say he didn't remember. "Saturday night? I probably had over forty or fifty fares. What do you want to know?"

"Mr. Pantella, you picked up this couple from the Lake Street cab rank at about three a.m. and took them to a house in Redcliffe. We need you to remember that night, as it is an extremely serious matter."

Nicky paused and looked suitably thoughtful as if trying to recall, though, of course, he remembered it well and had rehearsed his reply. "Hmm, tall, fit-looking guy, blonde woman, well dressed? They weren't drunk, they didn't throw up, and they were fairly quiet during the trip. I seem to remember it was raining that night. He gave me a decent tip, probably for rescuing them from the rain. What else do you need to know?"

"Did anything unusual happen? Did you notice you were being followed, or when you dropped them off, did you notice anyone hanging around their house?" Jenny Markham asked.

"Followed? Why would anyone follow us?" Nicky burst into spontaneous laughter, and both officers looked at him sternly, and he apologized, "Sorry, I just had this mental image of someone hopping in my cab and saying, follow that car."

"Please just answer the question, sir."

"I'm sorry. No, I don't remember that I noticed anything unusual. It was just another fare on a rainy night, so far as I can recall."

"You're sure you didn't notice anyone hanging around when you dropped them off? For your information, the man was shot dead in his house shortly after you dropped them there."

"Jesus Christ, shot dead? Fuck. Oops, sorry. I didn't mean to swear. Good job, he didn't get gunned down in my cab; I might have been shot too. It's

Stephen B King

become a very violent city, hasn't it? I'm sorry. I can't help you. I don't remember seeing anyone hanging around. I'm pretty sure I would have noticed someone with a gun."

"Thanks for your time; this is my card. If you think of anything, please call me directly."

In the car, Jenny Markham phoned Felix and told him the cab driver was a dead end; there was no help forthcoming from him at all, which was precisely what they had expected.

Nicky watched them leave, confident the police had no idea they had been talking to the one who had, shot their victim. Nicky went back to his cleaning chores, believing he wouldn't see the police again. He cranked up the home stereo while he worked, singing along as Hendry sang: *The Bitch Is Dead*.

Nicky had taken the time to speak to Siobhan that morning by phone, before school, and asked her permission if he could take her mummy out for the night. Her response was delightful. "But who will read me a story at bedtime and do the voices?"

"I will, baby. I wouldn't miss that for the world. I will take Mummy out for our dinner only after we put you to bed, and then Auntie Bree and Caroline will be there to look after you," he assured her. There was a long pause while she thought about it, and he could almost hear the little cogs turning in her brain while she considered it from every angle. He had never experienced such pure love as he had developed for Siobhan, amazed that she placed so much trust in him unconditionally. While he understood it was most likely through psychological scarring from her father abandoning her, he didn't care why she cared so much for him so much, only that she did.

"Will you still sit next to me when I eat my tea?"

"Only if you're not eating snails. I hate snails." She giggled as she so quickly did for him, and he knew it was all right for him to take her mother out.

That evening, at story time, with Didi watching as she always did from the doorway, she smiled to see her little girl so happy. When Nicky finished, and they had their good-night hugs and kisses, Didi and Nicky left the room and closed the door quietly. Siobhan suddenly looked so sad as they left that Nicky's heart ached, and he almost decided to go back into her bedroom and tell her he was canceling their night out.

Didi stopped him by holding his arm and shaking her head. She understood what had happened but assured him it wasn't because Siobhan didn't want him taking her out; it was that she couldn't go with them. "She idolizes you, Nicky. You're the dad she never had, and she isn't used to that. She also isn't used to sharing her love for me either. It's a confusing but wonderful time in her life. She will be fine, honestly. Just give her some time, and don't worry; she loves you so much. Her biggest fear is that she will disappoint you, and you will leave us."

He looked as if he had been hit with a cattle prod. "Oh my God, Didi, I could never do that. That little girl is the second most important person in the world to me."

"I know. You've made such a huge difference in her life; you've changed her more than I ever imagined anyone could."

"And yours?"

She nodded, her eyes wide and childlike. "And

mine, most definitely, I love you." They hugged in the passageway outside Siobhan's bedroom door, and he whispered back that he loved her with all of his heart and soul.

On the drive to the restaurant, he chose a James Hendry song which he had decided would be forever, to him, her song. While *Nightlight in the Wind* summed her up before they fell in love, afterward, he realized there was another, an older one that meant so much more. He had saved it especially for this occasion; their first official date. After he told her what the song meant to him and how whenever he heard it, he thought of her, he hit play. The car was filled with the rolling piano riff that heralded the start of *This is Your Song*.

It was a song she had heard on rare occasions as background noise on the radio but had never really paid any attention to it, just like she had never really paid attention to any James Hendry songs before Nicky. She stared at him in wonder as the words began. No one had ever dedicated a song to her, but then no one had ever treated her like he did. Nicky unashamedly sang karaoke-style as he drove, looking at her when a good part came up, smiling and winking as he did. She sat open-mouthed, listening, and stared back with love.

"This is the important bit coming up," he yelled excitedly and put one hand on her thigh as they drove along Beach Road. He sang, in a terribly out-of-tune baritone, how incredible life was; now Didi was part of his world.

Some women might have felt embarrassed to have a man sing to them in a very average voice. Some may even have been angry, but Didi felt such a tug in her heart that she had tears in her eyes and felt more complete than at any other time in her life. Since the moment Nicky played *Memories*, Didi knew that would always be the song that summed up her feelings and thoughts about him. A day never passed without her playing it at least twice. And still, without fail, she would have it on when she went to bed alone so that the last thing she heard, through her earphones, before falling asleep was James Hendry singing Nicky's song.

How typical of Nicky; that he would implant a song in her head about freedom and memories of happier times to come. Because he saved her from a fate worse than death and showed her that good men do exist, she, at the very least, wanted a memento of him. Didi had gone out the day after he saved her and bought the album. The more she played it, the more she came to love it, and the more she thought of Nicky.

When she found the courage to phone him the night following the attack and ask that he take her home, she told herself that it was just because she needed a cab anyway, and nothing else. She also thought he would be too busy or come up with some other excuse so he couldn't pick her up. Even though driving a cab was what he did for a job, surely he couldn't have any interest in her. He was bound to be located at that time in a different area, she believed. Didi had no idea until months later when he told her Nicky had been sitting in his cab half an hour before what he thought was her finishing time, just around the corner with his for-hire light turned off, waiting and hoping she would call. Even if she didn't call him, he'd told her, he wanted to make sure she was safe and that the two men from the night before didn't come back to hurt her.

He sounded happy that she had called, though she could tell he tried not to appear that he was. To her surprise, he said, "Yes," and told her he could be there in two minutes, as he was close. Her next fear was that he would try to take advantage of her; after all, he was just another man, wasn't he? For the entire trip, she sat petrified he would do something to her, though why she thought that, she couldn't fathom. Only when she got inside the safety of her own home did she realize that she was disappointed that not only did he not try anything, he barely even spoke to her. She argued with herself that she didn't exactly talk to him either. She realized he was probably put off by her standoffish attitude, which she knew she displayed to men. She couldn't help it; that was who she was.

The next night there he was again when she phoned, and she was pleased to see him and couldn't help but smile, which she took back immediately with the thought that the gesture might make him think she was giving him the come-on. Still frightened, she stayed silent for the rest of the trip. *Surely this time, he will try something,* she thought. Yet once again, he seemed to respect her silence and kept his distance from her.

At home, Didi played her new album every chance she got. Nicky introduced her to more songs during the drive home over the next few nights, and each time was a revelation. Didi downloaded the words to the songs and was staggered with the beauty and hidden meanings of the lyrics, and even Siobhan loved the song about the butterflies flying free. But Didi felt the music was wearing thin on Caroline and Bree. From then on, when she played her music, she listened through headphones when it wasn't appropriate to play it out loud.

When Nicky sang *This is Your Song* and told her that the song best summed up his feelings for her, she was staggered. That was something that only ever happened in romantic comedy movies, but never to the likes of her: a single mother and a lap dancer at that. When the song finished, he asked her what she thought of it. Didi gushed that she loved it. She couldn't think of a better time to tell him she was giving up lap dancing and was switching to being a skimpily dressed bartender or a *bar bitch* as they were affectionately known in the trade.

He seemed deep in thought when she told him, and he turned into a side street and parked the car. Without turning the engine off, he put the car gear shift into park, turned sideways in his seat, and asked, "Why are you doing this, Didi?"

She stared back and replied carefully, "Because I've fallen in love with you, Nicky. You're the best thing that's ever happened to me, and I don't want to share my body with anyone else, ever again, except you. All I have, all I am, I give to you." She sat with her chin stuck out and a determined look on her face, daring him to challenge her on it.

They gazed into each other's eyes. "You know you don't have to do this for me. I'm not going anywhere; I love you and Siobhan."

She took his hand in hers and held it in her lap. "I know, Nicky, that's one of the fantastic things about you, and that's what I have trouble getting my head around. You are so into me, for me. It's not because of what you want me to be, even though I know I am so not unique and so not worthy of you. I know you'd never ask me to do anything I didn't want to do. Giving up dancing is what I want to do for you, and also for me, because I know, you would never ask me to do that. Since Marcus left me when I was carrying Siobhan, I never thought I would give my heart to anyone ever again; that I could never trust anyone enough. But everything I have, everything I am, is yours if you want me. I want to be the best I can be for you, and that means stopping other men from seeing what I've given to you. I want to do this, Nicky."

Nicky leaned toward her, put both arms around her, and kissed her deeply and lovingly. "Thank you." The two words said everything for both of them. Nicky felt a level of gratitude he couldn't describe, and Didi knew he was happy she had made the decision she had. Life was perfect.

When they walked into Alan Chan's Four Gold Coins Restaurant, Alan greeted them as if he had been waiting for them alone. He was wringing his hands together with glee as he looked at them. "You must be Didi. Welcome to my little place." With that, he bowed to her, and she blushed, unused to such acts of chivalry. Then he turned to Nicky and, in a stern voice, said, "Nicky, why you no tell me she so beautiful. You make sure you bring her back lots of times, and when the time is right, I make for your beautiful wedding food."

Nicky laughed and shook his head, then handed him the bottle of white wine he had brought along in its padded cooler bag. "Do you think you could pour us a drink and bring us some dim sims before you marry us, Alan?"

Alan waggled a finger at Nicky and continued in a mock stern voice, "Nicky, Nicky, Nicky, I see your wine choices before, and they rubbish. This special occasion call for special occasion wine. Trust me, wine already at your table. I put this one in bathroom; maybe someone use it for mouthwash or floor cleaner."

While they laughed at his humor, Alan turned and led them through the main dining room, which busy with people enjoying their food, then down a passage into a small alcove. Didi walked ahead of Nicky when she suddenly stopped, and Nicky walked into her accidentally. He heard her say, "Oh my God, Nicky, what have you done?"

In the alcove was a solitary table, exquisitely set with gleaming silver cutlery on a white-and-pink tablecloth. There were white covers on the chairs to match, and pink rose petals were scattered on the floor and table. In the middle stood twelve beautiful fresh red roses in a crystal glass vase. A beautiful Chinese teenage girl stood in the corner with a bottle of wine, ready to pour. Nicky laughed. "Not guilty, Didi. All this is Alan's work. He's been trying to marry me off for years."

"It okay; you thank me later when you pay bill. Now, Miss Didi, he good man but lousy at choosing wine, let me take your jacket. This is Lulu. She is your waiter tonight. She, my daughter, so she works cheap, we all happy."

Didi turned her back to Alan, who slipped the leather jacket from her shoulders, looking into Nicky's eyes as she did. She had worn a simple, backless, dark-blue mid-thigh dress, which showed off her white skin and dark hair in such a way that she looked stunning. Alan had a sudden intake of breath as he stared at her shoulder blade.

"You have a beautiful tattoo of swimming golden koi. Nicky, you must marry this woman. She is going to enjoy long life, much happiness, wealth, and good luck. The golden koi brings all that for her. Miss Didi, you have any Chinese blood in your family?"

She shook her head, smiling, and said, "No, I don't, not that I am aware, as far as I know."

"I think you should have some, so why you no dump Nicky and marry me."

"Oh, I think Mrs. Chan would have something to say about that."

He nodded with a jokingly fake sad look on his face, and the three laughed. The tone for the night was set. Alan pulled out the chairs for them each in turn, and they sat down while Lulu poured the wine.

An hour and a half later, they were so full it was not possible to eat anymore. Lulu had continually served small, delicate dishes of seafood, meats, dumplings, noodles, and soups. Each course was superbly cooked and presented. Lulu kept their wine glasses topped up with what was a far more excellent wine than Nicky had bought. Alan was correct; Nicky had always been a beer man and didn't know too much about wine. The man in the liquor store had recommended the one he brought, and Nicky had taken his word it would be acceptable.

It was nearly ten when Alan emerged from the kitchen and pulled up a chair to sit between them. Didi and Nicky complimented how good the food was, and Alan nodded, acting blasé, agreeing. *Yes, yes, the food was good; that is a given*, seemed to be his reaction. Alan had cooked it and made it obvious. Nicky asked if he could arrange for the bill to be brought, as it was time for them to go.

"No bill tonight. This my gift to you both."

Nicky protested, and Alan firmly held up one hand to stop him. With the other, he picked up Didi's hand and said, "Nicky, you shush now. I speak to Miss Didi. This man does not know what wine to drink, but he is a good man and has huge heart. He no tell you this, so I tell you. His family comes here for years; many, many years, I know Nicky since this high." Alan held an arm out at table height. "When he goes off to the army, we hold a farewell party in this restaurant for lot of people. His family is good, well-liked. Nicky gone three years, and his family misses him. They all close, very close, they still come in to see Alan once a week, very nice people I miss them a lot. They both killed in a car accident, and Nicky has to give up army life to look after his brother, Simon."

Nicky interrupted him, "That's enough now, Alan. No more, please, not now. Thank you for the beautiful meal."

"Okay, I in trouble now. Talk too much, always my problem, but ask him about brother, and you learn how good a man this is. And you have golden koi with you; perhaps he brings you both happiness and good luck. Thank you for coming to show me Miss Didi, Nicky. I think she may be a good wife for you. Marry her before she swims away like koi."

With that, he stood and put the chair back and was gone. They were silent for a while. Didi wanted to ask him about his brother but could tell he didn't want that. If and when he was ready to talk about it, he would, she knew and didn't think it was the right time, not just yet.

"What a lovely man. I think he wants you as a son.

I can't blame him for that."

Nicky just laughed and shook his head ruefully. "Shall we go? I have a caramel latte waiting at home, made especially for someone I love."

"Mmm, yes, please. I'm dying to see your place." Her eyes sparkled with love as she squeezed his arm.

"Oh, trust me. It's nothing special."

"That's where you're wrong. You live there, so that alone makes it special."

Ten minutes later, they arrived. Nicky opened the front door and led her inside the 1920s-built stone cottage, which had been modernized fifteen years prior. He left her to wander around while he made coffees. When he returned, she was standing in front of his father's ornate wooden fireplace that held with the secret compartment for his gun. The shelf was adorned with family photos, and Nicky thought it was hardly surprising she would be there, looking at the pictures, considering what Alan had spoken of earlier. Nicky knew it was time to tell her the rest.

"That one there is Simon and me horse riding, just before I joined the army. He was about ten at the time, and I was eighteen."

She took the coffee he offered and nodded, knowing he was about to tell her the things he had kept inside for a long time.

"I was twenty-one and studying electronic engineering in the army when Mum and Dad died in a car accident, and I had to come home. Simon was only thirteen, so I became the head of the household overnight. I needed to be able to raise him and make a living to support us, and that's when I started driving cabs on night shifts. I needed to be there for him during the day, before and after school during the week. He struggled for ages and needed all the help he could get. For a long while, I thought he was going to have mental issues; he was so depressed. What with arranging the funeral, selling the house, sorting out the debts, and paying for Simon's grief counseling, I was working all the hours I could get to get him through that time."

Nicky paused to take a long breath and quell the beating of his heart which felt like he was close to a heart attack. "But eventually, he made it out to the other side. It took about a year, but he bounced back and then worked his ass off at school to get his grades back and to make me proud. Believe me: I was so very proud."

"What happened to him, Nicky?"

There was a very long silence as Nicky composed his thoughts. "He, umm, went into Northbridge for his eighteenth birthday, you know, umm, the first time he could go to a nightclub legally, as they do these days. So a bunch of them went in by limo after drinks here. One of his mates got into a fight outside while they were waiting for me to pick them up. Simon, um, oh God, this is so hard. Simon, umm, went to help out his friend because that was the kind of guy he was. Simon wouldn't hurt a fly; in fact, he had just been accepted into medical school; he was going to become a doctor." Nicky paused again.

Didi could see how it was tearing him apart to tell the story, but she also knew he not only wanted to, but he needed to talk about it. She put her coffee down, took his coffee from his hand, and silently put her arms around him and held him tightly.

"There was a pack of them. They smashed a beer bottle over Simon's head, and then, when he went down, they kicked him over and over again. They killed him, Didi. They kicked him to death. And do you know what happened to them? Four were let off with no penalty at all because they were good boys, just misguided, and the other two served only three months. He was worth more than all of them put together and then some, but in the end, all they made them pay was three months each."

"I'm so, so, so very sorry, Nicky. So sorry."

Eventually, they went to bed and made slow, gentle, and passionate love.

Afterward, he cuddled into her. She held him and tickled his back until he fell asleep. She loved him with every fiber of her being and every bone in her body. She felt as if she were a part of him, and he a part of her. No matter what he did, what happened to either of them; this was her man for life, and she knew she would fight to the death for him.

Chapter 10

The Northbridge War of the Roses

Because Jimmy Mallory thought the Apaches had arranged the murder of his brother, he fired the opening salvo by executing the three heads of their gang. That false belief was fueled by his paranoia ever since the Apaches had set up their chapter in Western Australia. He sensed that despite their promises to the contrary, they would one day make a move on his empire. Therefore, when Des was shot dead, it seemed natural for Jimmy to blame them.

After he took his retribution, Mallory reasoned that even if they hadn't done it, it gave him the excuse he needed to put the Apaches back in their place and reinforce that he was no easy mark and ruler of the roost. He still needed to find out who was responsible for the murder of his brother, but so far as the Apache situation was concerned, he considered it a win-win even if they had nothing to do with the execution.

Since they had set up in Western Australia, Jimmy noticed that some of his gang appeared to become disillusioned that he had relented and given permission for the newcomers to operate in Perth. Over the months, he heard disturbing rumors about members being unhappy with his apparent *softness*. The Devil's Grave members' feelings were apparently that they should have gone to war immediately with the Apaches before they got a foothold. They did not understand that Jimmy and Gordy had plans in place for if the day came when they had to retaliate against an attack.

Jimmy also realized that to attack them *before* the Apaches had a foothold would be pointless; without a clubhouse as their headquarters, there was nothing to attack. So while the taking down of the three heads of the opposing gang had been very personal, it was also about restoring faith and trust in his leadership. He further thought that by killing the leaders, the rest would scatter or go back to New Zealand with their tails between their legs.

Jimmy and his men were on high alert for the first few days, which was the prudent and practical thing to do, but there were no retaliatory threats, warnings, fights, Molotov cocktails thrown, or any sign that a war was about to begin. Jimmy lowered his guard, believing that the Apaches didn't realize it was he who killed their men, or they were too scared to retaliate if they did. If that was the case, they deserved no respect from him whatsoever.

When the Apaches did return fire, they did it unforgettably, which showed their resolve, cunning, and almost military precision in planning. When the retaliation came, before his uncontrollable rage took over, Jimmy, just for a moment, thought that maybe he had made a colossal mistake in awakening a sleeping bear by poking it with a stick. The media nicknamed the war that followed *The War of the Roses* because of the cleverness and nature of the Apaches' counterattack.

Maureen reported by phone her suspicions to

Jimmy that his right-hand man Gordy had developed feelings for Rebecca and possibly had him killed so he could have his way with her without repercussion from Des or Jimmy. Jimmy shook his head, not wanting to believe that his best friend since school days would kill his brother so that he could fuck his wife. That was just ridiculous; *only a woman could come up with that scenario*, Jimmy thought.

Jimmy had idly thought since the shooting that he wouldn't mind fucking Rebecca himself now that Des was gone. Before that could happen, he had to find out who killed his brother and take the appropriate action because there was no doubt in his mind; this was a strike against him, but if not the Apaches, he couldn't figure out who would have the balls.

There was no shortage of women Gordy could have if he wanted to, and quite a few of them were considerably better looking than Rebecca. Maureen's conclusion didn't sit right with Jimmy, and he quickly dismissed her theory. He asked her what else she had found out.

Maureen knew Jimmy well enough to know not to argue with him. He would mull it over in his mind and act if he thought he needed to when he was ready. That could take a day or two, but she was sure he would have a chat with Gordy at some point at the very least. She went on to tell him that the cab driver witnessed Des assault Rebecca in the cab, but once Des threatened him, he seemed to accept it. Des had even given him a tip, which she took great pains to point out to Jimmy, so she wasn't sure it meant anything of value. Jimmy agreed but made a mental note to talk to one of the cops on his payroll. He would ask if the police had interviewed the cab driver and what the outcome of that talk was. Jimmy had seven officers of assorted ranks in different areas of the force, to whom he paid a monthly retainer. The bribes were money well spent for information received at critical times, such as when the drug squad were about to raid him.

Maureen next told him that Rebecca had not heard the shots from the bedroom, which was close to the hall where Des was killed. Logically, she thought that meant that it was a silenced gun that had been used. She kept silent, letting Jimmy dwell on the facts, sure that it would slowly take him back to Gordy as it had her. They talked for another half an hour or more, discussing scenarios and possibilities. He told her that he appreciated the superb job she had done with his sister-in-law.

Des had never been a part of Jimmy's *business*, so it was unthinkable that he was shot dead in what looked very much like a professional hit for any reason other than a message to him. Jimmy had to admit, though, that possibly it could have been a murder of passion and that perhaps someone in his organization had the hots for Rebecca, though he could not believe it was Gordy.

****

Jimmy made calls to several of his police *friends* and let them know what he was looking for, promising them a very *Merry Christmas* if they came through for him with any useful information. Meanwhile, he turned his mind to the Gordy situation and knew he had to have a word with him soon if nothing else developed in other areas.

Two days later, Maureen was busy doing the books upstairs at the Lantern Bar. That was where they had offices to do the mundane admin work involved with running the various legitimate bars, restaurants, sex shops, tattoo parlors, and lap dance clubs. Some of those establishments were nothing more than fronts to launder the immense amount of cash that came in from drug sales, while others were profitable. The two police officers who had interviewed Rebecca, Felix Milanski and Sam Collins, arrived to interview Jimmy, but he was out. It was the third time they had tried to speak with him. She called him on his mobile, and he refused to talk to them and told her to tell them to come back only with a warrant or, to use his exact words: "Arrest him or fuck off."

They shrugged and left as if it was no more than they expected. Forty-five minutes later, a flower arrangement of epic proportions was delivered with a card for Maureen. The vase was filled predominantly with multicolored roses, which looked stunning in yellow and white with green fern as a backdrop. Maureen was delighted to sign for them and thought Jimmy had sent them to thank her for her work with Rebecca. She would reward him later, she promised herself.

But the flowers were not what they seemed to be. The green foam usually found at the bottom of the vase had been removed. In its place was a plastic explosive, tinted green. The thin wire connecting the detonator to the wireless receiver plugged into the C3 wound around one of the roses and was concealed by several thick sprigs of fern.

Maureen called Jimmy. "Thank you for the beautiful flowers. You shouldn't have," she said breathlessly.

"What flowers?"

Just then, the light caught the wire at just the right angle. She paused. "What's that wire?" she said aloud as the bomb detonated. She was killed instantly, along with the two admin workers, biker girlfriends, who did the filing, accounts receivable, and other office work.

The top half of the building was destroyed, with debris flung over five hundred meters and smashed windows on eight of the surrounding buildings. The floor, walls above it, and the roof collapsed onto the public area and ground floor below. Michael, the bar manager, and two gang members who were waiting for a meeting with Jimmy died within moments. Mallory, who was due back at that time, had been held up and was running half an hour late, which saved his life.

The gas line ruptured, and within minutes a second explosion destroyed all that remained of the main structure. That started a fire that took the fire brigade three hours to bring under control, causing extensive damage to the adjoining shops and restaurants.

If the bomb had detonated thirty minutes later, it would have spelled an end to the war. Jimmy's meeting with a restaurant owner who wanted permission to open a further establishment ran over time. They had been haggling over how much he could afford to pay for the privilege and protection, so Jimmy and Gordy avoided the first attempt on their lives.

****

In the months prior, after the Apaches set up camp in Perth, they had been stealthily checking out Jimmy's operation, as they intended to take over when they had a firm base and sufficient *foot soldiers*. All they had been waiting for was enough intelligence so they could hit hard with simultaneous attacks on businesses and high-ranking personnel. Had things stayed as they were, the takeover would have started with the assassination of Jimmy and Gordy in a combined ambush. However, fate, in the guise of Nicky Pantella, stepped in, and with the subsequent murder of the three leaders, they moved their agenda forward under the guidance of the Eastern States bosses and imported gang members.

The Grave's clubhouse, a converted warehouse in the Wangara commercial area, rarely had fewer than six people in it at any time, and during meetings or social functions, as many as fifty. It was a large concrete structure with a roller door entry, formerly a trucking depot. It was surrounded by an eight-foot-tall brick fence and electric solid steel gates with intercom access, much like a fortified gold reserve. CCTV cameras guarded the entrance, and the gang felt it was secure enough to withstand anything. The building was attacked by the Apaches within minutes of the bomb being detonated in the city.

****

Having a home base in the USA, where guns, ammunition, and all manner of war-making hardware were far more readily available than in Australia, the Apaches were always going to be a formidable force and a worthy opponent. Unlike Jimmy's local gang, who had no such resources other than purchased illegal firearms. Mallory's empire was run on a more vicious and personal reputation, with individual threats of violence and, in extreme cases, murder. They were well funded from years of running an extremely profitable drug trade but did not have the armaments of their American counterparts. There was considerable income from the associated add-on businesses, such as ownership of clubs, bars, illegal extortion of businesses, prostitutes, and gambling ventures, and made many millions of dollars every year. Some venues were intended to run at a loss so as to be able to launder the phenomenal amounts of cash, but such was Jimmy's *luck*. Even some of those couldn't help but make a profit.

The Apaches had imported a considerable amount of weaponry and explosives for the battles they knew would be coming with the Grave and other gangs in each state in Australia because their mission was to completely take over nationwide. With a population of only some thirty million, Australia was seen to be easy pickings. Senior gang members in the west had been to the USA for training in operations like mercenary camps. The Apaches were no ordinary biker gang; they were well trained and prepared for a war where the financial rewards where astronomical, as was the war chest of fighting funds at their disposal.

Earlier in the week before the roses were delivered to Maureen, a Mack semi-trailer truck had been stolen from a large roadhouse stop at Badgingarra, some fifty kilometers outside the Perth metro area. The cab was stealthily disconnected from its trailer, which was full of refrigerated chickens for a large takeaway food chain, while the driver was having breakfast at the roadhouse. The Apaches were not interested in the cargo, only the prime mover.

That the cab had been stolen was the story the driver told his bosses when he discovered the theft, but the truth was that he had been paid five thousand dollars in cash to turn a blind eye and not rush his early morning meal. As it was three mountainous bikers of Maori descent carrying baseball bats who visited him, he wisely chose to take the money and stay out of the hospital or the cemetery, which were his only other options.

The white nondescript prime mover was only distinctive by the extremely sturdy steel bull bar on the front of it. It was the sort of bar that could hit a steer at a hundred kilometers an hour and not be dented. The Apaches thought it would make an ideal battering ram and had been on the lookout for such a truck.

Shortly after the explosion at the Lantern Bar in the city, the Mack truck burst through the gates at the clubhouse without warning. It rolled over the steel, smashing and damaging them as if they were made of paper. The truck screeched through the carpark, dragging a tattered gate panel under the wheels, and, with a noise resembling a sonic boom, crashed down the steel roller door, ripping it from its runners in the wall and tossing it aside inside the building.

Once through the doorway, the cab steered off to the right to make way for the second vehicle, following immediately behind. The yellow people mover van, with near-black window tinting, followed through the carnage and veered to the left. In a highly orchestrated and precision-rehearsed move, six men jumped out of the vehicles through the side doors, wearing gloves, masks, dark-blue overalls, and rubber boots. Each was armed with a .45 automatic pistol and a silenced submachine gun.

They fanned out, shooting everyone they saw without warning. Within seconds seven men and one woman lay dead, including one biker who ran into a toilet, trying to hide, but a hail of bullets ripped through the locked door.

Ninety seconds was all they needed to murder everyone in attendance, then the attackers splashed petrol from cans they brought with them, and within moments flames spread through the building. The six gunmen and the truck driver jumped into the Toyota and backed the vehicle out of the clubrooms. They were gone from the area before the fire alarm could be raised, changing out of the overalls back into nondescript clothes while on the road. They deposited their weapons into a large khaki carry-all bag and, only nine minutes later, entered the Gnangara Pine Plantation.

The Toyota drove through a gate, which had the lock cut off earlier by a fellow Apache, and headed a kilometer into the trees along an access track. As one, they stepped from the vehicle at a clearing, carrying the bag with the weapons with them but leaving the overalls, masks, and gloves inside. One of the men doused the van with petrol and set fire to it. By the time the fuel tank exploded, ensuring there would be no evidence to recover, they were three kilometers away, riding trail bikes that had been left there for them.

****

Later, the same day, two tattoo parlors, a gymnasium, an agency that supplied doormen and bouncers for numerous clubs and bars, two sex shops, and another bar called Rockets were firebombed. Multiple Molotov cocktails were thrown through broken windows of the Grave's controlled establishments in an extended attack that lasted well into the night. On the first day of the war, thirty-six people were killed, and a further thirty were wounded. Jimmy's reputation took a battering, and his business interests were severely damaged.

Though incapable of any meaningful sincere feelings or affection, two of the only three people in the world he cared about were now dead. He was alone without family, save for Gordy. Though down, he was far from out, and he put into place the retaliatory plans he and Gordy designed months before. Though his wife had been murdered, the only emotion he felt at the end of the day was pure, vengeful anger.

The Northbridge War of the Roses had begun, and there could be only one winner so far as Mallory was concerned. Jimmy Mallory had to hit back just as hard, or he would lose the respect of the various criminal elements and police officers on his payroll. He didn't want anyone to believe it would be the end of his era and the beginning of an Apache dawn.

He and Gordy had drawn up a hit list, and his men responded within twenty-four hours with devastating results, which showed everyone, including the Apaches, Jimmy was not one easily defeated. Over the next two days, a further seventeen men were shot dead in homes or businesses on both sides. As the violence escalated, the police swooped in on whoever they could to try to bring a speedy conclusion to the war.

While many, particularly some high-ranking police officers, despised Mallory, at least he was the devil they knew rather than an unknown NZ invader, with US backing, who most believed could evolve into a worse scenario if they took ascendancy.

Chapter 11

Separated, Again

At the morning meeting with the commissioner, Felix and Sam reviewed the Apaches' attacks on the Grave, the deaths, and damage to property and acknowledged the serious death toll, which was climbing by the hour.

"This bloodbath was exactly what I wanted you two to avoid by working together on this. I will not have these bikers going to war in our city," the commissioner said accusingly.

Sam stayed silent, as this was Felix's case, and he was the senior officer. Once the gangs got involved with the latest vigilante murder, it inferred that the previous killings were all somehow gangland related. Felix defended himself with an angry note in his voice. "Sir, I'm sorry, but it was inevitable. Our intelligence, such as it is, tells us that Jimmy Mallory initially thought the death of his brother was an attack by the Apache Gang. Why he thought that, we will never know. But once he did, he retaliated by killing three of their hierarchy. We haven't found the bodies, and we are reliably informed we never will, as they have been dumped at sea. No one in either gang is willing to talk to us, so what we are getting is hearsay and from informants, and sadly, what they are giving us is scant."

"Go on, Felix," the commissioner said when he paused for a breath.

"We don't know who killed Desmond Mallory or why, and we don't know why the same gun was used in previous vigilante killings. We are as much in the dark as we were before. Our best guess right now is that for some reason, the vigilante got rid of the gun, and someone else acquired it. If not that, then it is suggestive that the killer is someone who works in the drug business and, for reasons known only to them, has been killing other criminals. But as Des wasn't part of Jimmy's business, so far as we know, it blows that theory out of the water. We presume it was this second person who killed Mallory for some unknown reason. By all accounts, Des wasn't a saint, but he was not part of Mallory's crime gang. We've heard rumblings of insane jealousy if anyone went near his wife, and we have heard a murmur or two that he was violent toward her if he drank. We know that night, he drank a lot, so it is possible, though Rebecca Mallory denies it, that if he hurt her outside the club and the vigilante witnessed that assault, he may have followed the cab to their home. The problem with that theory is that not only does she deny he hit her, but the cab driver also was not aware they were being followed; traffic was light that time of the morning, and the cabbie didn't witness an assault."

That had been a scenario Sam and Felix discussed at great length, but while feasible, they felt it unlikely on several fronts. Past behavior of the vigilante had been to intervene in an assault, not follow the offender home. They further felt if they had been tailed, the cab driver would have noticed at that time of night because traffic was light, especially around the back streets of Redcliffe, where the Mallorys lived.

Felix went on, "Possibly, Rebecca Mallory is sexually involved with someone else, and that person killed Des. Of course, she denies that. It's all ifs and maybes, as we have no evidence or definite leads, just hearsay and supposition. We also know that Des didn't mind a fight himself; so possibly, he made enemies, and this had nothing to do with Jimmy. But again, the use of the gun and silencer muddies the waters. With regards to the wife, she either is involved, or she isn't. If she isn't, she didn't hear a thing, which suggests the use of a silencer or simply that Mrs. Mallory was just too drunk and fell asleep, as she asserts. It's possible, as in the previous murders where the gun was used, that the lack of witnesses could suggest a silencer was used then, too. That would take us back to it being an underworld murder. So we are just going around and around in circles."

Felix referred to his notes before going on. "So the possibilities are; one, the vigilante killed Desmond Mallory. Though why he was targeted in his home, we don't know, or even how the killer knew where he lived. Two, Rebecca killed him or was romantically involved with whoever did so they could be together when the dust settles. Three, it's gang-related, and the use of the gun is because the vigilante got rid of it. Four, it is someone in Mallory's life that had it in for him. Meanwhile, now Jimmy will hit back against the Apaches, and it's very likely to be open warfare. I'm afraid that means a lot more killings to come."

The commissioner sat with his fingers bridged in front of his face. "The situation is a nightmare. The press are having a field day, and we look like a bunch of idiots."

Felix and Sam stayed silent, as there was nothing they could add. Eventually, he turned to Sam. "Time to split you two up again, I think. Sam, I want you and your team to concentrate on the vigilante angle and pull out all the stops. Also, look into the wife and whether she was having an affair or not. If so, who with, and did she and this man in her life have her husband knocked off? As far as possible, though, keep away from any gang angle. Top priority, Sergeant; if you can solve this mystery, maybe we can get the gangs to sit down and make peace."

"Yes, sir. I will do my best," Sam replied, not at all happy with his assignment, though he dared not voice his disgust.

"Meanwhile, Felix, I want you to come down hard on both of the gangs and their operations. Arrest as many as you can, for whatever reasons, and get them off the streets as soon as possible. I want total disruption to their organizations. Because a bomb has been used, we can invoke anti-terrorist criteria, which gives us a lot more power to seize and arrest without warrants. Do you get me?"

"I get you, Commissioner," Felix answered with a grim smile.

"I will get the legal eagles to fight any bail applications to get these bastards locked up for as long as possible in hopes it will quieten things down. I want raids on houses, businesses, and clubrooms. Let's teach these bikers we are the law here, not them. Do I make myself clear, Felix?"

"Yes, sir."

"I'm going to see the premier and attorney general and try to get rewards posted for information leading to arrests, etcetera. I also want you to push for immunity for any gang member who rolls on the others and get them into witness protection. Maybe some of them will be worried that they might be killed next in an all-out war. I want you both to continue to meet me every morning at nine for a briefing on both investigations, and if either of you needs any help or resources, let me know."

They agreed, thanked him, and left, fully aware they were now very much under the microscope. Outside his office, they shook hands and wished each other luck. As they walked toward the exit, Felix said, "Sam, your instincts have always been pretty good. What does your gut tell you here? Forget what you can prove. What do you think?"

Sam paused for a while, gathering the various threads he possessed before answering, "I keep going back to the psych evaluation we have of the vigilante and why he does what he does. We think he is someone who has suffered or been exposed to a severe violent act on the streets at night. So he was probably a victim himself or someone he cared for was, and this is his way of striking back at whoever hurt him or his family. The problem, of course, is that over the last twelve months alone, we have hundreds, if not thousands, of victims of crime that it could be. The killings are random, and as you know, we get reports of multiple crimes every single night. Sure, there have been fewer since he started whittling the number of offenders down, but it's a Pandora's Box of previous cases. So I think he is just out there, not necessarily looking for people to shoot, but then again, maybe he is searching for crimes in progress. He is likely to, let's say, come across them when they do as if he is hunting for prey. When he discovers something going down, he strikes with ruthless, almost militant, efficiency. I think somehow he made a mistake about Des Mallory, or he knows something about him we don't, and it's a vigilante killing for that reason. The gang stuff is a consequence of that, but it wasn't part of the plan."

Felix listened and nodded. Having worked with Sam for years, he liked the way he looked at situations and went on his instincts. It was his gut that helped capture the killer in the Domin8 case, and that wasn't the first time his abilities had served him well.

Sam continued, "I'm going to get my team to look closer at the fatalities or serious assaults we have had in Northbridge over the last two or three years. We are going to go through the victims with a fine-tooth comb to see if anyone jumps off the page at me. Even though they have been looked into before, maybe we missed something. I will also have a closer look at Rebecca and see if there is something there, but my gut feeling is that will be a waste of time. Now that Maureen is dead, Rebecca may be more helpful, but the use of the same gun as the vigilante killings makes that improbable unless we have joined in with a movie production, and the first five killings were setting up a scenario where Des's murder could be blamed on the vigilante. But that's just too farfetched for my money. The simplest, most rational solution is generally the right one, as you know, Felix."

"Makes good sense, Sam. Keep me posted, will you? I'm going to have my hands full with raids on the biker members now. They made a mistake and used explosives, so as the commissioner says, we can use the anti-terrorism laws, giving us much greater powers to search, seize, and arrest. More importantly, we can hold in custody without charge indefinitely."

They said farewell to each other at the elevators, and Sam went back to his office morosely; he still had very mixed feelings about the case. If his thinking was correct, he had an awful sensation in the pit of his stomach that the killer was going to be someone he could empathize with. He thought it likely it was someone who Sam wouldn't want to lock away for years where, sooner or later, he would be stabbed by some biker in retaliation for Desmond Mallory.

As a police officer, he could not condone members of the public shooting offenders in the street, even though sometimes he would like to clean up the garbage he came across himself. If people were allowed to take the law into their own hands, it would lead to chaos and anarchy, as it now had with the biker war. But Sam knew he was going to feel sorry for the guy when he found him. Despite the lack of evidence, sooner or later, the mystery man would make more mistakes, as he had with murdering Desmond Mallory. If he hadn't killed Jimmy's brother, he could have disappeared into the sunset if he stopped and would never have been taken to account.

Three days later, Sam saw something that everyone else had overlooked, and instantly he understood who the killer was. His earlier instinct had been correct, and now he thought he knew the man's identity. Sam did not want to arrest him, but how could he not? Sam had been going through the reams of files of serious assault victims when one name rang a bell, but he couldn't remember why. For some reason, the name Pantella was familiar, and it kept nagging away at him. The victim had been an eighteen-year-old out with his friends for his first legal visit to a nightclub. As so often happened, there had been a fight outside the club, and a group had surrounded him, kicking him repeatedly. Unfortunately, on this occasion, it resulted in death after the particularly ferocious attack.

Just after three o'clock in the morning, he experienced an epiphany. Sam suddenly sat up in bed and inadvertently yanked the bed covers off his girlfriend. She had stayed over that night, and they had shared some frantic lovemaking. When he sat up, he exposed her naked body to the chilly, air-conditioned night air.

"Sammy!" Natalia moaned and tugged the quilt back over her, snuggling again underneath; she always felt the cold more than he did.

"Sorry, love," he said and slipped out of bed and walked naked to the lounge area of his tenth-story apartment, which looked out over the city. He sat on the couch, not seeing the cityscape, and thought about the killer and what a bloody idiot he had been. Nicholas Pantella was going to be jailed because he picked the wrong victim and changed his MO. Sam couldn't avoid arresting him, even if he wanted to, because his name was already on the witness statement for taking Des and Rebecca home in his cab. It would be too much of a coincidence for the vigilante not to be the cab driver.

With the realization came understanding. A cab driver sees a lot of violence happening in the streets late at night and probably came across his victims while driving around doing his job. There was no doubt that with what happened to his brother some months before, Nicholas Pantella would have been bitter with the justice system and angry, giving him ample motive, at least in his own mind.

Sam closed his eyes and shook his head sadly as he recalled the details of the brutal and senseless killing of Simon Pantella. He recalled it had been a fight that went too far. What made it worse was the hopelessly inadequate sentence given to the perpetrators who fatally beat Pantella in an orgy of violence. Sam hadn't been involved in the case, but everyone in the force talked about the senselessness of it at that time.

Sam knew he had no choice; he had to gather evidence and arrest the cab driver. That was his job. There was a gang war going on because of Pantella's actions, and stopping that war had to take precedence, yet he would hate himself for doing it. The man had suffered, no doubt, and when Jimmy Mallory heard he had killed Des, Pantella's life wouldn't be worth living.

Sometimes Sam loved his work, and sometimes he hated it. This was one of those times when it was the latter. He knew, without a shadow of a doubt, that by arresting and putting him in jail, Sam was handing him a death sentence. Yes, he could request protective custody, which sounded fine in theory, but with the bounty that would be placed on his head, sooner or later, someone would find a way to get to him. A prisoner could not possibly be watched twenty-four hours a day.

On the other side of the coin, even if Sam accepted the first four victims were all killed while in the act of killing or seriously wounding another person, the same could not be said of Desmond Mallory. There was no doubt that was a case of cold-blooded murder. That made it hard for Sam to find any mitigating circumstances in that case. Perhaps before anything, a return interview with the wife was in order to confirm or deny whether she was subjected to domestic violence that night. Maybe if the cab driver saw Mallory assault her—and Sam suspected he must have—he would have had some justification to murder him, if only in his mind. Either way, Sam needed evidence. There was always the very slim chance it could be a coincidence.

****

Later that morning, Sam knocked on the door of Rebecca Mallory's home. Maureen had died in the bomb blast, so he thought he might get more out of Rebecca without the woman he thought of as The Queen Bitch listening. *What a nasty piece of work Maureen Mallory was*, he thought while waiting for Rebecca to open the door.

After a couple of minutes, the door opened, and Sam did a double-take. She was wearing a grubby housecoat, her hair was messy, and she didn't have any makeup on. It was evident to Sam she had only just gotten out of bed, and she looked as if she would go back there any minute. He held up his ID and reminded her of his name in response to the vacant stare she gave him.

Rebecca begrudgingly opened the door wider to let him in. Sam followed her inside and closed the door behind him. Together they walked through to the family area, where he saw the kitchen was untidy, with dishes piled up in the sink, and there was a dusty and musty odor in the air. She turned on the coffee pod machine but still had not said a word. Sam sat on a stool at the breakfast bar and waited for her to face him, which she seemed intent on not doing quickly. She got two cups out of the sink and rinsed them under the tap until the water ran hot, then plunked them down on the counter without drying them off first.

"I've got no milk, so it will have to be black. I ran out yesterday and haven't been bothered to go to the shops. Jesus, I have to get myself sorted out, don't I?" she said, and Sam suddenly felt sorry for her. With all that had gone on, he had to remind himself she was a victim, having found her husband's dead body in their hallway in a puddle of blood, shot dead.

"Black is fine, Rebecca, thank you very much. Listen, if you like, I can get someone from victim support to come around and help out a bit. They can tidy up and do some shopping for you. Maybe even washing, things like that. They understand how tough it is when you lose someone to a violent crime and that it takes time to get back on your feet."

Rebecca still had her back to him, and he saw her shoulders shake as she cried. She didn't reply for over a minute until she finally sniffed loudly and said, "Yeah, that would be good, thanks. Fuck, I need some help, don't I? You must think I'm a real slob, but I'm not, usually."

"I don't think anything of the sort, Rebecca. I understand how tough this is for you. Give yourself a break. I will get support to contact you this afternoon, okay?" Sam looked at her face as she approached and noted how puffy and bloodshot her eyes were. She looked like she was only just holding on to sanity.

"Thanks, I appreciate it," Rebecca replied softly as

she put a cup of black coffee in front of him, spilling some as she did, but made no move to wipe it up. Sam saw a dishcloth on the sink, so he reached over and grabbed it, cleaning up the spill from the stone benchtop.

"What did you want from me? Not just to offer domestic help, I'm sure," she said with a sneer that didn't suit her.

Sam took a sip before putting the mug down and said, "Rebecca, I have to ask you some pretty tough questions, so I thought I would come alone so it's off the record. It's just me talking to you about Des, is that okay? If you don't feel up to it, that's fine, but I need your help to understand a couple of things if you think you can."

"Yeah, ask away. Since Maureen was killed, I decided to try to distance myself from the Mallory family; in fact, I might go back to Melbourne and get away from these horrible people for good. If I can find the motivation, that is."

"Thanks, Rebecca. I think getting away would be the best possible thing you could do, especially now there's this war going on. If you want my advice, I would pack a bag, lock up the house, and take off for a month or two today. You can always come back later and sort the mess out, and by then, hopefully, all the shit will be over, one way or another."

Momentarily she brightened up, as the idea clearly had merit. Sam took another sip of coffee, which he thought was quite possibly the worst he had ever tasted. Rebecca responded with more emotion in her voice. "You know what? I think I will, right after the funeral. I will head off back home; spend some time with my mum and dad. Thanks for the suggestion."

They looked at each other over the tops of their coffee cups until Sam broke the silence when his cup was empty. "Rebecca, once again, this is pretty much off the record, okay? So anything you tell me is not going to come up and bite you on the behind. It's for my understanding and background more than anything you can help with, directly."

"Go on, this sounds interesting."

"Well, I've heard a couple of things about your relationship with Des. He was violent toward you, especially when he had been drinking. That's true, isn't it?"

She nodded and suddenly looked scared. "But Des never meant it, and he was always so sorry afterward. If Jimmy finds out I've told you, he will have me killed. Maureen told me that."

Sam nodded and gave her a friendly, consoling smile. "I'm not going to tell anyone, don't worry. Des drank a lot on that night, didn't he? And he hit you; that's why you didn't hear anything. Or if you did, you were so scared you couldn't intervene. I'm guessing it started outside the club when you left, then in the cab. That's why you said the driver was nice. Then it got worse when you got home. That's what happened, wasn't it?"

Rebecca looked down at her feet. She didn't nod; she didn't need to say anything; it was obvious. Sam now knew why the vigilante shot Des: to save her from being hurt badly by a drunk and out-of-control Desmond Mallory. Maybe Pantella thought Mallory might kill her in a drunken rage, so once again, he acted to save someone from being severely hurt or possibly killed.

"What happened in the cab, Rebecca? What exactly did you mean by the driver was nice to you?" She paused a long time, but just as Sam was about to repeat the question, she said in a tearful voice, "Des hit me, and the driver asked me if I was all right, so Des threatened to hurt him too. Des liked nothing more than a good fistfight, and he was in the mood that night, that's for sure." She stopped long enough to wipe the tears from her eyes.

"If the driver had said one more thing, it would have been horrible. Des never backed down in his life. So I told him I was fine, that Des was my husband, and to please take us home. Then Des hit me again, really hard, because I had the nerve to interfere. He told the driver it was his fault that I got hurt and that he was going to hurt me a lot more once we got home. Des told the driver he could either take us home, and I would get hurt, or he would beat him up and catch another cab, and I would get hurt even worse. So he took us home. Why wouldn't he? Des paid, and he drove off." She was openly sobbing as she remembered the details of that night.

"What happened after that, Rebecca?" Sam asked gently and recoiled as she started screaming at him.

"He did what he always did when he was pissed, all right? He punched and kicked me, pulled my hair, and ripped my clothes off. Then he threw me on the bed, and if it weren't for the fucking doorbell, nothing would have stopped him from raping me."

She paused. When she started again, her voice was quieter. "It would have been worse for me if the doorbell hadn't rung because Des was so drunk he wouldn't be able to come quickly, and then he would have gotten even angrier and blamed me. Then, boy, he really would have gone to town on me. Are you satisfied now? Des was a fucking prick when he was drinking; he got mean, really mean to me, and hurt me."

Sam nodded, his heart sinking. He understood it all now. "And the gunshots, did you hear them?" he asked.

"I didn't know they were gunshots; I swear. I heard some noises and a thud, but I thought it was one of the neighbors complaining or something after I'd screamed, and Des was in a fight with him. I didn't dare go out and investigate. He would have killed me for trying to interfere, especially after what happened in the cab. I stayed in bed, and I just fell asleep. When I woke up and plucked up the courage to leave the bedroom, that's when I found Des dead. I didn't lie about that. If I'd told you the truth before, Maureen would have told Jimmy. Then Jimmy would have killed me for badmouthing his brother. That's what they're like; they are horrid fucking people, and I wish I'd never fallen for Des. But I was young and stupid, and I pretty much did it to spite my parents. I wish to God I never had. But look, you have to understand, most of the time, Des was a good man and a good husband. It was only when he drank he got mean to me."

There was just one more thing Sam had to ask her, but he thought he knew what the answer would be. "What about the affair you were having, Rebecca?"

"The affair? What fucking affair? Jesus Christ, Des beat me up if he thought I looked at someone. He would have put me in a grave or buried me at sea, more like if he thought I actually fucked them. I wouldn't have dared to do anything with anyone, even if I wanted to, not that I ever did. If someone says I did, they are lying, and they didn't know Des very well at all. I've watched him beat men senseless who he thought were trying to pick me up. That was the thing about him; he liked me to dress like a slut, and for men to look at me and want me because it made him feel like a big man. But looking too hard, touching, and especially trying anything with me, he would explode in a temper that knew no limits. Everyone knew that, and everyone was scared of him when he was in a jealous rage."

Sam understood. He had seen similar stories in domestic violence cases many times. "Okay, Rebecca, thanks very much for telling me the truth. If you want my advice, don't wait for the funeral. Get out now. Just disappear for a while; things are going to get ugly around here, and who knows, Jilly Mallory may not survive."

"I'll think about it. Can you please go now?" Rebecca pleaded.

Silently Sam stood up and left quietly, leaving her crying in the kitchen. He felt very sorry for her and hated himself even more for what he had to do next.

Chapter 12

Two's Company, Three's a Joy

After gently making love after they woke in the early hours of the morning following the night at Alan Chan's, Nicky and Didi showered together. They took turns washing each other slowly, enjoying each other's bodies. Nicky was fascinated with the wonderfully colored tattoos adorning her skin up close. He could clearly understand why some people called it body art, as every different tattoo on her was indeed a work of art, highly ornate with beautiful bold, striking colors.

She had bleeding roses, the snake on her thigh, the lucky golden koi, a kingfisher, an Australian flag with the Southern Cross, an exquisite peacock, two white doves building a nest, a sparkling unicorn, and more. He couldn't help but ask why she had so many, and she looked momentarily sad when she answered after a pause. "Marcus was a tattoo artist, and I loved him, and he said he wanted to make me even more beautiful than I already was. Not that I've ever seen myself as beautiful before or after him. That was one of the many lies he told me. Every day when I look in the mirror since he left me, I'm reminded of him and the lies he told. I'm so glad you like them, Nicky." Then she gave a small smile that was more of a grin. "At least I didn't let him put his name on me."

"Well, the only good thing I can say about him is that he had good taste, Didi, and by that, I mean that you are beautiful. He didn't lie about that."

"Thank you, kind sir. You're not so bad yourself."

Nicky and Didi hugged under the stream of water flowing from the showerhead and kissed deeply. The kissing led to touching, which led to moaning, and still wet, they made it back to bed and made love again, slowly and deeply. Didi bit his shoulder and dug her nails into his back as she climaxed. With precise timing, Nicky finished at the same moment, deep inside the greatest love of his life.

Reluctantly, the morning lovemaking had to end. Didi and Nicky dressed and got into the coupe, which started straight away, which was never a given; sometimes, it took two or three attempts. *Maybe the gods are smiling on me now,* he thought. In the back of his mind, he worried that he had to tell Didi about the men he had killed at some point, and maybe then the gods would stop smiling.

The early morning traffic was light on the drive back to Didi's, and Nicky played a few tracks from what he thought was arguably the best James Hendry album ever, *Goodbye Sunrise.* They both started singing along with tracks like "Love Lies," "Saturday Night Downtown," and "Screaming Jets." His hand caressed Didi's upper thigh, and he looked into her eyes every chance he got.

As planned, they made it back to North Beach before Siobhan woke up. It was to be the first time he shared the crunchy nut cornflake breakfast with them. They were going to go out for the day into the city and to Kings Park. It was a special day for Siobhan, but it was just as much a treat for the adults to be together as a family for a day's outing.

For Nicky, it was his first day out with a woman he loved and a child he adored as if she were his own. Didi felt that her life could not get any better than to have a man she loved and someone who not only accepted her daughter but loved her as he so clearly did, and Siobhan felt complete for the first time with a mummy and daddy to spend the day with. Most of Siobhan's friends at school had two parents, and in her world, she always missed not having a father and could not understand why she couldn't have one. The weather promised to be a beautiful day, and she had been looking forward to it with mounting excitement.

While Didi got breakfast ready, Nicky crept into Siobhan's room to watch her sleep and was stunned to find her not hugging Mr. Banshee as she always had every night before. Nicky looked around the room and spotted him; he was sitting crookedly on a bookshelf in the corner. Instead, she hugged the fluffy yellow rabbit he had bought for her on the first night they met. Seeing her cuddle it brought a gasp as his breath caught in his chest and brought tears to the corners of his eyes, making him blink quickly to clear them.

He crept back out and grabbed Didi's hand with a finger over his lips to shush her. He led her back to the bedroom to show her. She raised a hand over her mouth in genuine shock and happy surprise; her little girl had moved on from the rat of a father to Nicky in no time at all and of her own free will, and it was a beautiful thing. In Didi's opinion, this was an event of epic proportions. She had never said a bad word to Siobhan about her natural father because she always hoped he would want to be a part of their life at some point, in some way. For Siobhan's sake, she hoped he would want to come back, if not to be with Didi, then so he could spend some time with his daughter so that she could grow up knowing who her father was.

It wasn't about the money for support. Marcus had never given her one cent toward bringing their daughter up, and she was fine with that. Didi had been genuinely alone emotionally and financially, and she didn't want anything from him except to acknowledge he had fathered a child. She'd always hoped that he could love Siobhan for who she was and perhaps even take some responsibility for the situation he helped create.

Above everything else, she wanted her daughter to be happy. Didi knew that a large part of Siobhan's future happiness had been jeopardized by not having a father figure in her life. Didi realized how much Siobhan missed the daddy she never really knew, and instead, she loved Mr. Banshee to death. Ever since Siobhan became old enough to make her feelings known, she was protective of Mr. Banshee. He was the one tangible thing she could hold on to that represented her father. She clung to the hope that one day, her daddy would want her and would come to see her. When he did, Siobhan didn't want the doll to be out of her sight, so she could show him when he came back to her that she had kept him and loved him.

Now Siobhan had abandoned Mr. Banshee to the bookshelf and instead cuddled a toy from the only man to have shown her any interest and kindness. Her heart swelled with pride and love for the man who had taken their world and shaken it upside down.

Siobhan woke up at that moment and saw them

both there. Her face lit up with a broad smile, and she sat up and held her arms wide open for a cuddle. Nicky held back, letting her mummy go first.

He said, "Good morning, princess. Did you sleep well? I told you I would bring your mummy back safe and sound." He smiled at her as she looked at him over Didi's shoulder.

"Are we still going to Kings Park?" she asked.

"We sure are," he answered as Didi hugged her daughter. "And as a surprise, I borrowed a special seat for you to sit on in the car, so you can see out the window better while you wear your seat belt."

"Yippppeeeeeeeee! Can we get ice cream?"

"Only if you eat all of your breakfast," Didi said while Nicky nodded and winked at her, making the thumbs-up sign so Didi couldn't see behind her back.

"Well, only if you don't give me too much. I only have a little tummy, and Nicky promised me ice cream."

They laughed at her, and then the three of them went through to the dining area for breakfast. Siobhan carried the rabbit, her new appendage, and they all kept as quiet as possible so that they wouldn't wake Bree and Caroline. They enjoyed their crunchy nut cornflakes, served with orange juice, and black coffee for Nicky, and chatted away, making plans for later, each enjoying the family happiness that was so unfamiliar to them.

After breakfast, Nicky cleaned up while Didi dressed Siobhan. Suddenly, she ran into the kitchen carrying two different dresses, one in each little hand, and cried out, "Nicky, you have to decide which one I wear. Mummy likes this one, but I like the yellow one.

It's the same color as Buggy."

Her eyes pleaded with Nicky to choose the right one for her, and he realized Buggy was the name she had come up with for the rabbit. *A child's homage to Bugs Bunny, perhaps?* He wondered.

"Hmm," Nicky said and tried to look thoughtful when he felt like giggling. "They both look pretty, don't they?" The choice was simple, and at that moment, Nicky knew there wouldn't be much he would ever be able to deny Siobhan. He also realized she was learning how to wrap him around her little finger.

"I like the yellow one, too. But I may not be able to tell you and Mr. Buggy apart if you wear the same color."

She stomped her foot down and raised her eyes at him exaggeratingly, saying in a comical, huffy voice, "Nicky, he's a rabbit, and I'm a *girl*."

Nicky smiled as she ran off back to her room to a laughing Didi, who had heard the exchange. Siobhan yelled out, "See, I told you Nicky would like the yellow one, Mummy."

****

Nicky couldn't recall ever having such a good day. The weather was perfect; sunny and warm but not too hot, and he and Siobhan bonded more than he thought possible. They played rolling down the side of a hill, laughing and giggling until they were both dizzy, and Nicky had to stop, or he would have been sick from vertigo.

They played chasing games, hide and seek, and they went on every swing, slide, and rocking horse in the park at least five times. When they weren't playing, they were walking in the botanic gardens, admiring the view across the Swan River, taking the treetop walk, and dodging the water fountains which squirted water out of holes in the ground at odd times.

Nicky chased a giggling Siobhan with wet hands, threatening to tickle her after he dipped them in the water. Watching with tears in her eyes, Didi had to pinch herself while thinking, *Is this real? Is this not just a dream that I will wake up from? Is this really happening? Have I found love and the perfect man?*

They ate hamburgers and chips for lunch, followed by the promised ice cream, which they ate while sitting on a bench looking out over the city. Each time Siobhan looked at Nicky, he had a dab of strawberry ice cream on the tip of his nose, which she found hilarious.

Later while walking through a nature bush trail, they came across a patch of bright-yellow buttercups, and Nicky knelt and picked one. He crooked a finger at Siobhan for her to come to him. "I bet you, Miss Muffat, that I can tell if you like butter or not."

Her eyes widened as she wondered how on earth he could know that. Nicky held the delicate little flower under her chin, and the bright yellow reflected on her skin.

"Yep," he said. "You do like butter, don't you?" She nodded back, clearly impressed. He then held the flower under his chin.

"Can you see yellow reflected on my chin?" She nodded at the display of magic while Didi stifled a laugh with her hand over her mouth. "See, that's why these magical flowers are called buttercups, Vonnie. If they shine yellow light on you, that means you love butter, but if it doesn't, that person thinks butter is yucky. It only works with these flowers."

"Wow, can I keep it and show my friends at school?" Her eyes were wide with wonder. Nicky tucked the stem around her ear. It looked pretty against her black hair.

"Sure, you can, princess, but I think it might have wilted by then, and it probably won't work. But you can try." Siobhan reached her arms around his neck and hugged him tightly, which was all the thanks Nicky needed.

In the early evening, just before it was time to head back home, Nicky and Didi were sitting on a bench, watching Siobhan feed the ducks and swans in the lake when Nicky took Didi's hand in his and stood up. She went to stand up too, but he stopped her by shaking his head. Instead, he faced her and got down on one knee. Her heart fluttered as he looked into her eyes and said, "Didi, I've been alone for so long now, and I never thought I would meet someone like you. I love you. Will you marry me?"

"Oh, yes. In a heartbeat."

Nicky hugged her tightly as she cried tears of joy.

Siobhan came running, concerned, and said, "Mummy, what's wrong? Why are you crying?"

"I'm crying because I'm so happy, baby. Nicky has asked me to marry him so we will always be together, the three of us, as a family."

She looked confused for just a moment until understanding dawned in her eyes. "So will you be my daddy?"

"I will, but only if you want me to be, princess."

"*Yipppeeeeee!*" she replied, clapping her hands together.

"I think that's a yes," Didi said.

Chapter 13

Retaliation

The organized crime underbelly of Perth had been quiet for a long time before the War of the Roses. Jimmy Mallory had brought all of the local pushers under his umbrella, and there were only minor skirmishes. People in the know, especially from older generations, often talked about the crime wars of the past with nostalgia, as if they were good things and were needed periodically to clean out the bad blood. They spoke about territory wars that happened in the sixties and again in the seventies, followed by the big one in the eighties. It seemed like there was a turf war every decade for people to romanticize about after it was all over.

Jimmy and the Devil's Grave had ruled with an iron fist for ten years or more, and no one dared to challenge him other than occasionally misguided fools who thought they could muscle in. Those dumb enough to take Jimmy on usually ended up disemboweled and floating in the Swan River, as Jimmy always punished miscreants publicly to deter others from taking their chances at toppling him. Things had run smoothly for such a long time some mistakenly thought Mallory had turned soft. But Jimmy never forgot his roots when he fought to get to the top of the heap, and his brutality was only matched by his cunning. Within twenty-four hours of the bomb blast killing his wife, four Apache members were gunned down in separate incidents in a hail of bullets and shotgun pellets.

Two were riding their motorbikes on the freeway when a black four-door sedan pulled up alongside them. Shotguns extended through open side windows, and if the sudden wave of gunfire didn't kill the men, coming off motorbikes at a hundred kilometers an hour did. The driver of the car timed it to perfection, killing the men just before the next off-ramp at Leederville. They were gone from the area within minutes, while behind them, multiple cars collided trying to avoid the fallen bikers.

Another gang member was receiving a tattoo on his chest and was laid back in the parlor chair when two men entered. They motioned for the artist to move aside, and the moment he did, the Apache was hit with four shotgun blasts. The artist hadn't moved quite quickly enough and caught some of the stray pellets in his left leg, side, and arm. He was shaken up and suffered blood loss but was not seriously hurt. Despite intense questioning by police, he could not identify the murderers as they were wearing masks of different superheroes, or at least that was what he told the police, though Felix Milanski doubted that was the truth.

The fourth victim was picking up that week's protection money from a Japanese restaurant and karaoke bar on the second floor above a laundry in Cannington. On entering, he came face-to-face with two of the Grave members holding sawn-off .22 rifles, modified to fire continuously. They were shot seventeen times, but one bullet missed, passed through the window, and hit a sixty-year-old woman across the street in a hairdressing salon.

With two innocent bystanders wounded in the crossfire, the police and public were enraged. The biggest tactical squad in Perth's history swung into action with twenty-two searches conducted in one day, resulting in numerous firearms confiscated, drugs seized, and forty-eight arrests made.

Jimmy's paid informers knew the protagonists had gone too far with the bombing and shootings and chose not to pass on advance notices of the impending police raids, as they would have in the past. Those calls would have permitted Jimmy to get any illegal weapons or drugs out of the building before the raid. Mallory and the Grave were the hardest hit by the police swoops simply because they were entrenched and had multiple businesses that were easy targets. Jimmy grudgingly gave respect to the police for responding as they had. Several Apaches were arrested, too, and were housed in a separate jail in solitary confinement.

The task force hoped they had broken the back of the gangs, which would give them some breathing space and halt the killings for a while. But that night, the Apaches' clubhouse in Dianella burned to the ground from a hail of firebombs thrown through the windows with four members inside. When those inside tried to flee, they were shot by a sniper who lay on the rooftop of a building two hundred meters away. The remaining key members on both sides went into hiding, so what followed became more like a strategy, or chess game, played between two equally matched players trying to pick each other off one by one.

When the search warrant was carried out on Jimmy's new headquarters in a bar called The Crew,

Gordy and Jimmy were present, and both were armed. Neither could be arrested, as they had previously secured permits to carry them from a friendly head of the licensing section. Each license had cost twenty-five thousand dollars and showed Jimmy's foresight in knowing that they could carry guns without fear of prosecution and confiscation if they became targets in the future.

The Apaches hadn't been established in Western Australia long enough to amass many political and police contacts. They also didn't have Jimmy's subtlety in cultivating such *friends in high places.* Because Mallory himself wasn't a biker but merely controlled them, in the past, he was seen to be a *colorful figure with underworld connections*, while all the Apaches were fully badged members. Without the political clout to provide intelligence and warnings, their weapons were scattered in lock-up sheds and garages throughout the metropolitan area, readily accessible for planned executions but useless as a means of defense from an immediate attack.

For the first time since the Apaches planned the takeover, some of the gang members were worried it was not going to be as successful as they were assured it would. Jimmy was a worthwhile opponent and had the tenure, connections, and money to wait them out and then pick them off at his leisure, one member at a time. The heads of the gang in Sydney made the decision to bring in a specialist, and the call went out to America for a professional hitman to be brought to Perth to find and kill Jimmy Mallory and his second in command, Gordy.

Three days later, an assassin known only as The

Renegade arrived at Perth airport. His identity was a closely guarded secret and not shared with the local Apaches, so they could not inform on him if they were caught and went into witness protection. He disembarked from a Qantas plane, sailed through customs and immigration checks, and took a cab to the Sheraton Hotel. He had booked a suite for two weeks under the same alias he traveled under, which was by no means his only one. He thought two weeks should be enough time for him to track down Jimmy and Gordy and complete his mission, though he hoped to have the job done long before then.

The man was in his late forties and did not resemble a biker in any way. The Renegade wasn't one and never had been. He was a contractor, brought in for specialized jobs. He was tall, though not overly so that he attracted unwanted attention and graying at the temples. He was fit-looking and handsome and wore expensive suits with Italian shoes or casual designer clothing. He knew he would fit right in at the Sheraton without raising suspicion because he resembled a businessman, not a killer for hire.

At eight o'clock the next morning, he sent a text to a mobile phone number from the disposable phone he had purchased at the airport, stating the agreed code word and that he had arrived and was ready for the pickup. A text returned within minutes with his instructions. At ten o'clock, he took a cab to the Perth Train Station in the city and walked around, trying to look casual, but all the while alert and looking for police or anyone who appeared to be watching for him. When he was sure it was safe, he went to the lockers and opened up number 14 with the key that had been left for him in an envelope at the reception desk of his hotel.

He removed the suitcase from the locker, crossed the enormous open space of the station hall, and climbed into the same cab he had arrived in. He asked the cabbie to show him some of the city before returning to the hotel and spent the trip watching through the window to make sure he wasn't being followed. Back in his room, he opened the case and took out a red manila folder containing information of locations and pictures of the two targets he had come to kill. Below the envelope was a large, detailed map of the Perth metropolitan area with an expanded diagram of Northbridge. Known haunts of Jimmy Mallory were marked in red.

Under the paperwork were his weapons. He removed the shoulder holster holding the Walther PPK automatic pistol, his preferred weapon of choice, a silencer, two magazines, and a spare box of ammunition. The Renegade checked the mechanisms and condition of the firing pin by dry firing. Satisfied, he loaded one of the magazines into the handle of the gun and put his shoulder holster on. He crossed to the mirror and put his jacket on, making sure the gun couldn't be detected. The size of the Walther made it the ideal concealed weapon, with more than enough stopping power. The Walther used a .32 bullet but had a muzzle velocity of much larger calibers. The Renegade was satisfied. The holster was almost invisible, made easier because his entire wardrobe of suit jackets was tailored to hide the bulge under his armpit.

He took out a smaller attaché-style case from inside the larger and opened it. Inside it was an Israeli engineered, disassembled sniper's rifle with a silencer. The telescopic sight and twelve hollow point magnum rounds would be accurate over long distances. It fitted perfectly into cut-outs made in the high-density sponge and would only take seconds to assemble and load when the need arose. In the meanwhile, he would keep the case locked up in the hotel safe. There was always a possibility, no matter how slim, that his room could be the target of a thief. He had become as successful as he had by being careful.

The Renegade tidied up and ordered a mug of fresh percolated black coffee and Danish pastries from room service. When it arrived, he sat at the desk provided, overlooking the city and Swan River, although he had no interest in the view. He sipped his coffee and read the contents of the file from start to end three times until it was all committed to memory. When he felt he knew everything, he studied the pictures and memorized the two faces of his targets. His memory was near photographic, which made him very good at what he did.

The Renegade was devoid of emotion and felt nothing when he killed. He performed his task with no conscience or scruples. He did what he did for money, as he liked the finer things in life and didn't want to work too hard to earn them. Good food and wine while traveling to exotic locations and being paid well to kill people gave him the lifestyle he had always craved for minimal effort. He owned a home in Malibu on the beach and a summer cabin in the Bahamas. He only did twelve jobs a year, which took an average of between seven and ten days per kill. The rest of the time, he lived an enviable lifestyle.

The fee for each hit was one hundred thousand US dollars, plus all reasonable expenses paid in cash. Therefore, he would net two hundred thousand dollars for this trip to Australia. He guaranteed success to his employers, no matter how long the job took; there was no such thing as failure in his vocabulary. He would kill his targets, or he would die trying.

It was because of his uncompromising attention to detail and past successes the Apaches used him exclusively. While his demands were rigid, he never let them down, no matter how complex, or risked himself in carrying out the task. Two hundred thousand dollars was seen as chicken feed compared to the drug profits they would inherit once Jimmy and Gordy were eliminated, so it was seen to be good business.

The Renegade studied the map and marked the locations with likely spots the two men could be found, such as businesses they owned, as well as potential places with a good sightline, where he could shoot them using the sniper's rifle. He would give himself four full days to check everything out and then make his plan for the hit. When the coffee pot was empty, he picked up the attaché case and left the room, intending to have a look around the Northbridge area and check out some of the bars and clubs to get a feel for the locations for himself.

He would first visit the cemetery where the memorial ceremony would be held for Jimmy's wife, Maureen, whenever that would be. The remains of her body were at the coroner's office, according to his notes. If he could find a place to use the rifle, and the date was acceptable, the funeral would be his preference. Make the hit and get out. He was sure the police would be in attendance, but he doubted they would be looking for a sniper. The funeral would be his first choice to kill from a distance and be out of the area before the cops knew what had happened.

****

Jimmy Mallory glanced at the display on his mobile phone and saw it was from a number he knew well. It was one of his informers within the police, so he answered with a noncommittal, "Yeah?"

Without preamble, the voice said, "Merry Christmas, Mr. Mallory."

Jimmy told the caller he had the wrong number and hung up. Phones could easily be bugged, and Mallory knew his was monitored continuously by the cops, so each of his people on the take had different codes.

He could use a burner phone and sometimes did, usually around the time a large shipment of drugs was coming in. But with electronic surveillance being what it was, he felt it was better to be safe than sorry. Let them tap his phone. The pigs wouldn't make head or tail of the codes his people used. Merry Christmas, Mr. Mallory was not only acknowledgment of an excellent Australian film but also code for: *meet me in the usual place and time; I have information to share*. It also amused Jimmy to use his famous Merry Christmas tag with his favorite informer.

Jimmy waited fifteen minutes, and then he and Gordy left The Crew through the rear door and climbed into a Mercedes with dark tinted windows. Gordy told the driver, Rocco Marcone, where to go, and a few minutes later, they parked near the Jade Tea Pot Chinese restaurant. It was too early for diners, and inside, one man sat at a rear table eating spring rolls.

Slowly, he dipped them in a creamy sweet and sour sauce.

Rocco waited outside to stop anyone from entering while Gordy and Jimmy warily walked in, sat down with the man, and ordered a pot of green tea. They smiled at each other, then Gordy got up, drew his gun discreetly, and left to check the rear of the restaurant and restrooms. He also made sure the windows and back door were locked, so there would be no unpleasant surprises. Once he found it to be secure, he returned and sat with Jimmy and nodded imperceptibly to him. Jimmy stood and went out to the restroom. Once there, he folded his arms and leaned casually against the old chipped sink. He didn't have long to wait for the man who had been eating spring rolls to come and talk to him. Everyone knew not to keep Jimmy waiting.

Mick Connors was not a police officer, but he worked in data entry for the Major Crime Investigation Unit. His job was to enter information and correlate details from the investigating officers for the many concurrent cases going on. This vital work ensured that evidence from one team was quickly available for the rest of the squad to read and allowed for easy cross-referencing.

Mick occasionally came up with useful titbits of information, and Jimmy was smart enough to know that things that seemed like titbits to some could be whole meals to others. While his temper and the sadistic, violent streak were well known, some would even say legendary, so was his reputation for generosity to people who supplied him with the vital information he needed to stay on top.

"Hi, Mick, how's the family and little Derek?" He

smiled as the short furtive man entered.

Among Jimmy's strengths were his memory and ability to make people think he loved them yet hated everyone else. He always remembered people's names and any relevant information about their families. He found, over the years, that being able to make his associates feel special held him in good stead. He always asked after the family by their names and gained respect by doing so.

Derek, Mick's son, was autistic and suffered from a range of allergies, which meant he was almost permanently ill, suffering one ailment or another. The household medical bills would cripple any average family with a regular income, and Jimmy knew they suffered, though Mick never complained. Mick and his wife Vicky loved their little Derek with an incredible passion and worked tirelessly to make his life as happy as they could, and occasional gifts from Jimmy were always welcome. The way Mick saw it, the police provided him with a job, and that was all. He felt no guilt whatsoever for divulging secrets if it helped his family.

"He's not been so bad just lately, Mr. Mallory, sir. Thanks for asking. I was sorry for your loss recently and for your troubles that followed. You've always been good to me, Mr. Mallory, and I do hope you solve your problems soon."

"Thank you, Mick, that's kind of you. They can't keep a good man down, and it won't be long before I am back on top. Just you wait and see. Now, Mickey boy, what do you have for me?"

"Well, Mr. Mallory, something quite strange, really, and I'm not sure how useful it will be, but it surely is a bit weird. It's also quite dangerous, me bringing it to you with everything that's going on; I'm sure you understand, Mr. Mallory, sir."

"Don't I always appreciate what you bring me, Mick, my son? And don't I always make sure you have a Merry Christmas?" Jimmy held his arms wide apart as if he intended to hug the man.

"You do, Mr. Mallory, sir, and God bless you for it. The thing is, I noticed something unusual about the ballistics report on your brother's murder. The officers in the squad have been sworn to secrecy about it, and that in itself makes it interesting. They are trying to keep a lid on it and threatened suspension for anyone leaking it. They won't say why, so it must be something vital if they are trying to stop it from leaking. That's why I mentioned it was dangerous for me to tell you about it. The word in the squad is that it must not get back to you."

"Go on. Mickey, I love it so far."

"The ballistics report says it was the same weapon used by the vigilante in his previous four murders and on your brother."

Jimmy stared at Mick, trying to comprehend exactly the meaning of what he just said, which could sometimes be a challenge with Mick. "Mick, just let me get my head around this for a minute. You're saying the prick that's out there knocking off people on the streets for being a bit naughty is the same man who shot Des?" He could hardly hide his skepticism in his voice.

"Well, not exactly that, Mr. Mallory, no, but it's the same gun that was used. So possibly it's the same man for all five killings, or if not, the vigilante did the first four, and he knows who did your brother because

205

he used his gun to do it if you see what I mean? The key is the gun; either the same man did your brother, or he had passed on the weapon after his four kills, and the person he gave it to used it to kill Des."

"Now, Mick, you listen to me, my friend." Jimmy put his arm around his neck and held him close. "When I leave here, Gordy is going to come in and give you two grand in folding. That's to thank you for what you've told me today. But, Mickey boy, there is twenty grand in it for you for any info that identifies this vigilante for me. You get that info to me straight away. Got me, Mick?"

The cash register inside Mick's brain went ticking into overdrive. Twenty thousand dollars in cash would make a massive difference to Derek's life, maybe even a little holiday away for the family, to somewhere nice, in the sunshine. That would be just the ticket. "You can count on me, Mr. Mallory," he replied. "If there is any information I can get for you, you will be the first to know. That's a promise."

"Good man, Mickey. Have a nice Christmas, eh?"

Jimmy walked back into the restaurant and sat down. He sipped the green tea poured for him and then leaned close to Gordy and whispered. Gordy nodded, then stood up and went out the back to deliver the cash to Mick Connors from the wad of Jimmy's money he always carried for such an occasion. When Gordy came back, they waited in silence for Mick to leave the restaurant, and then Jimmy told him the information Mick had provided.

Gordy nodded, quietly processing the info, and started thinking about how they could use their resources to catch the do-gooder who was wandering on their streets and dared to murder his boss's brother.

"Gordy, I never bothered mentioning it because I didn't believe it, but I do need to ask you something."

"Sure, Boss. Fire away?"

"Rebecca told Maureen, God rest her soul, that at the party, Des was jealous of you touching up his wife." He held up his hand to halt Gordy protesting and then carried on, "Mate, I don't give a flying fuck if you were banging the bitch or not. That's not why I'm asking you, so tell me straight. I know Desi had a temper, and I know he was insanely jealous. Did he get shitty on the night?"

"Boss, you know me. I'd never do anything like that. I was talking to her, having a laugh and a joke. She's a good chick. But that's all. I know better than to have touched her up. Des had gone off to play pool and left her all alone, and she was getting antsy, so I spent some time with her till he got back. End of story. Yeah, now that you mention it, I reckon he was shitty about it by the time he returned, and he was half pissed by then. You've got my word; there was nothing for him to be shitty about."

"That's about how I imagined it. What do we know about this so-called vigilante, mate?"

"Not much except what I read in the papers. He hasn't affected our business, so he hasn't been our concern so far. It seems like if he comes across some prick beating someone up, he shoots them dead. So far, his victims have all been doing some pretty nasty things. I think one bloke was doing a break-in, but he had beaten the owner and would have died if not for the Samaritan, from what I gather."

"Hmm, that was what I thought too. So let's say on

the night Des left Mimi's Bar in a shitty mood with Rebecca because of you, and suppose he belts her once or twice because that was his way with her. And then let's say this vigilante saw it happen, followed them home, and—bang, bang—Desi's dead. Am I making sense here?"

"Yeah." Gordy nodded slowly. "I can see it might have happened that way. As you say, Des had a temper, and I had heard it whispered that he liked to hit her when he was in the mood, and he did seem to be in the mood that night."

"Well, let's take it one step further. Who would be out and about on the streets in the middle of the night when those four others were killed and be available to see Des belt his bitch? In fact, how did they get home? They caught a cab, didn't they? We need to have a good talk with the cabbie that took them home, I think, don't you, Gordy? I think that could be very entertaining. I want you to go to work and find me this fucking cab driver. Start with Rebecca. Fuck the shit out of her and give her a slapping. I don't care what you do to her, but let's see if we can get our hands on the driver. Get me?"

Gordy nodded, already thinking what he would like to do to Beck. She had a killer body, and he had fancied her for years. Now Des was out of the way, and he had Jimmy's permission to fuck her. He would look forward to that.

Chapter 14

The Kitty Palace

Didi took two phone calls from her boss, Marty, the manager of the Kitty Palace Gentlemen's Club, within three hours of each other. The first came in before three in the afternoon on the day following the family fun day at Kings Park. She took the call while she and Nicky were enjoying a coffee, holding hands, and admiring the ring they had just bought that sat on Didi's left hand. They were killing time until they had to pick up Siobhan when she finished school. Neither had ever been engaged before. Although Didi came closest when she had been living with Marcus, but they hadn't been formally engaged to be married.

They sat opposite each other, sharing a large portion of pineapple cheesecake. Nicky was drinking his usual black coffee, and she had a caramel latte when she heard her phone ring and felt the vibration in her purse. Reluctantly, she let go, as she needed both hands to delve inside the depths of her handbag chaos. Finding the phone, she saw Marty's name on the screen, apologized to Nicky, and answered it.

"Hi, Marty." Didi tucked her left hand back into Nicky's while she held the phone with her right, and he noticed her face change to a worried look while she listened.

"Okay, thanks for letting me know," she said and hung up after three minutes of listening to Marty's voice. Once she tucked the phone back in the bag, she sighed and said, "No work for me tonight, it seems. The cops have raided the place and are searching it from top to bottom."

"Wow, why? Did he say?"

Didi bit her lip and thought for a while before answering him. "It's all to do with this biker war. The girls have been talking the last few days. Some of them have even quit because they think it's too dangerous to work somewhere that's owned by, well, let's call them shady characters."

Nicky sat up straight, a concerned look on his face, and squeezed her hand a little tighter. "I had no idea your place was owned by them, although, I suppose now I think about it, I'm not entirely shocked."

"We rarely see the owners of the club, and Marty is a good guy who really cares for his girls, as he calls us. He's been the manager there for forever, but the owners are—shall we say—well, I suppose you would call them underworld. I don't get involved. I just do my job, and it pays well. But I have seen some unsavory people going up the back stairs sometimes. Biker types, you know?"

Nicky nodded. He had been working the streets long enough to know a huge chunk of Northbridge was either owned, partnered with, or protected by bikers. That was just the way it was.

"Well, since Jimmy Mallory's brother was killed, there's been a war going on, and biker-owned establishments are under attack from other gangs, and the police are trying to stop the war." Nicky's face dropped further as he realized that he was the root cause of the war by killing Desmond Mallory. "The cops are there now, tearing the place apart: looking for drugs, guns, or evidence of anything illegal, and they have told Marty not to open up tonight, at the very least." She looked up at him and smiled conspiratorially. "Can you take tonight off, too? Maybe we could go to the movies or something?"

Nicky knew the time had arrived that he had to tell her about his alter-ego life and admit the killings. "Yeah, that's a great idea," he said after thinking about it. "Let's do that. I've not taken a sick day in years, but first, it's time I told you something, something bad. You might not like me so much when I tell you." He gazed sadly into her eyes.

"You're scaring me, Nicky. What is it?" Her face looked frantic as all her fears she'd kept buried resurfaced.

Nicky had been dreading this moment. He knew he should have done it before, but he had got so wrapped up in the relationship with Didi and Siobhan he'd pushed it aside mentally. Also, as he had decided to stop killing, Nicky thought he might have been able to avoid telling her altogether on those occasions when he had thought about it. Now it was time, he decided, for better or worse, she had to know. Nicky didn't want any secrets between them, primarily as what he'd done had caused such unimaginable consequences.

"We've never talked about that night since, but let me ask you a serious question; please take your time and tell me the truth. The night we met those two men who were going to rape you. Suppose *the vigilante* had saved you, and he shot dead those lowlife scumbags

211

like he's been doing to others. What would you have thought? Before you answer, consider this, one of those men may never walk the same again; I smashed his knee to pieces, and the other guy may never have kids because of where I kicked him so hard. Oh, and let's not forget his broken nose, so he may have some disfigurement for the rest of his life."

She stared at him, eyes wide open, scared, yet thoughtful. "They were going to rape me, and they didn't care if they hurt me, Nicky. Who knows, maybe they would have even killed me so that I couldn't identify them. You saved me from suffering for the rest of my life just because they wanted sex with me and didn't care if I said no. If I had a gun that night, I would have shot them myself."

"So if I had killed them and just left them dead in the alley and taken you home, you would have been fine with that?"

"Yes, I would." She squeezed his hand, showing her sincerity.

He took a deep breath and thought, *okay, here goes*. Then he began. "Since Simon was murdered, and I call it murder despite the judge being so lenient on his killers, there have been a few other people I have saved by killing people that were attacking them."

She snatched her hand away from his and covered her open mouth. "You mean you are *the vigilante*. You, Nicky?"

He stared back; the pain etched on his face was vivid. He nodded.

"But you're a good man, Nicky. You wouldn't do something like that unless you thought you had to. You are the kindest, gentlest man I've ever known. It's not like you to kill people and not care."

"I was like that, Didi, but I'm not that man anymore. Since I met you and fell in love with you and Siobhan, you've given me my life back. Before you, I was just this empty shell driving a cab at night and sleeping by day. I had no life, nothing to live for, and I didn't care about anything or anyone. I had shut up shop and was killing time until I died. I started taking a gun to work with me because I hoped one day to come across those bastards who killed Simon and trust me, I would have gladly shot them if I had. Then one night, I saw a man beating a woman to death with a beer bottle in a park, and I shot him. My intention at the time was to stop him, not necessarily kill him. I mean, I didn't plan it; it was like fate, I suppose. In that one moment, I knew if I didn't do something, she would have died a horrible death or been turned into a vegetable, so I intervened."

"Oh, Nicky." She shook her head sadly.

"And I didn't care if I got caught. I saw something terrible was happening, and no one else was there to help. Like when Simon was killed, no one helped him. Maybe a hundred people were on the street then, but not one of them intervened. If I hadn't shot him, she would be dead now, and the man would have gotten off because he was drunk and had an unfortunate life to that point like it was society's fault or something. And she didn't deserve that. So I had the gun with me, and I shot him because I could. Then I just went back to my empty life."

"Oh my God, Nicky." She still had her hand over her mouth and her eyes wide.

"Time passed. The police didn't come knocking,

and the papers seemed to say good riddance to the man I killed. He was a habitual violent criminal, so everyone seemed to say he was no loss. I kept driving my cab, I never looked for trouble, but you know what this city is like in the middle of the night when all the lowlife riffraff walks the streets. It's a jungle. One night I witnessed someone being robbed after he'd been knocked unconscious. The victim was on the ground, bleeding badly and in serious trouble. The attacker was just about to kick him in the face, probably repeatedly, even though he was unconscious. I thought the bastard was going to murder him, just like Simon had been. So I shot him. I didn't lose any sleep then either; just one less scumbag walking the streets so far as I was concerned, and one more decent person I had saved by being there."

Didi was speechless; she didn't know how to react or what to say.

"There were another couple of occasions, too. I didn't do it for the publicity, even though I got plenty of it, and all of it good. I didn't care, honestly. I was going through the motions of being alive but not living if you know what I mean. And it wasn't like I was out there looking for bad guys to kill, but if I came across a situation where I thought someone's life was in danger, I did something about it. During this time, I met you because you were a victim, too, but there was no time to get the gun out at that time. But I did have my torch. I waded in to help, intent on hurting them because I was just so sick and tired of the violent drunken people on our streets and no one doing anything about it." Nicky lowered his gaze and almost whispered, "God help me, Didi, I wanted to kill those two, but I didn't because you were watching."

She didn't reply, still too shocked, and Nicky carried on: "Then I started taking you home, and slowly, even though I dared not admit it to myself, I was falling for you, hoping like hell you would fall for me because for the first time in a long, long time I was starting to wake up and feel alive again. All because of you, Didi. Suddenly life was worth living; you gave me purpose.

"So one night, I was waiting for you, but I was early and parked up the street from the club. This big drunk guy gets into the cab and starts beating up his wife in the back seat. When I asked if she was okay, he threatened to beat me up, too, and he meant it. He had this kind of look in his eye like if I gave him any excuse, he would beat me to a pulp. Then he hit her, hard, again just because I'd asked if she was all right. She screamed, and he said it was my fault he hurt her because I interfered. I hated him and his arrogance. He thought he owned her, and he could do that to her. Even if she was his wife, it didn't give him the right to beat her up. He told me he was going to hurt her even worse once he got her home, *real bad*, he said, and it would be more than usual because I'd interfered. While I was driving, I had this mental image of him punching and kicking her over and over again just because he thought he owned her, and in my mind, all I could see were those men kicking Simon to death."

"That was Jimmy Mallory's brother?" Didi asked incredulously.

He nodded. "Yes, it was, though I didn't know that at the time. To me, he was just another lowlife wife-beater who would one day end up killing her. I was enraged, Didi, and scared for what he intended to do to her behind closed doors. I mean, how many times do you hear of domestic violence where the wife ends up being killed? So anyway, I took them home, parked the car, walked back to the house, and rang the doorbell. When he opened it, he looked ready to murder whoever had disturbed him, and I knew I was right to do what I did. I shot him. Then I left. Maybe she is still alive today because I did what I did. I don't know."

"The night you shot Desmond Mallory was the same night we made love on the beach. How could you make love to me after murdering someone?"

"Boy, Didi, when you put it like that…" He shook his head. "All I can say is this: before we made love that night, I was a dead man walking. Mum and Dad had died. I gave up my life to raise Simon, which, don't get me wrong, I gladly did, but then he was so senselessly murdered life seemed pointless. Then for the longest time, I was nothing, Didi, just nothing. Everything in my life was blackness, and I lived on remote control. And then we made love that night, and suddenly I was alive again, and I knew I was in love. I had something to look forward to and someone to love. Even better, it was two people to care for because of Siobhan. I could have a family and a baby if you fell for me, and I believed you had. In an instant, it seemed, everything changed for me because you wanted me. We've talked many times about your favorite song, *Memories,* but Didi, that night when we made love on the beach, you saved my life. I put the gun away when I got home that night, and it's never come out since, and it won't. I am not that man anymore; I am your man if you will still have me. I love you, Didi."

****

She looked into his pain-filled eyes and saw the love he had for her and the sincerity. She felt confused. It was too much to take in, but one thing struck her amid the overwhelming information he had just shared like a beacon on an inky-black night. He had been honest with her. That honesty was more important to her than anything else. Men had always lied to her, used her, abused her, left her, all while lying. But Nicky, who she loved with every fiber of her being, had told her the painful truth. Nicky had risked losing her by being truthful, and that fact staggered her. He had a choice; he could have lied to keep her or been truthful and risk losing her. She knew then he made the right choice.

At that moment, she knew everything would be okay. Yes, Nicky had killed people, but why had he done so? To save others from hurt or even death, just like he had risked his life to save her from the two rapists. She loved him; it was that simple, and he was a good man, if not a great man. She took his hand back in hers and licked her lips slowly. "So what movie shall we go see tonight?"

Nicky had been holding his breath, and he let it out in a rush. "I love you, Didi."

Didi smiled and said, "Damn, I wanted to say it first. We better go; there's a certain little girl we're going to be late for if we dillydally anymore. I'm glad you told me the truth, hon. That means more to me than anything else. I trust that you did what you did for the right reasons, and I will stand by you for that, but only because you were honest with me."

The rest of the evening passed with the beautiful

normalcy Nicky had come to love. Eating together, bathing Siobhan, reading her stories complete with crazy voices, playing with her, and listening to her giggle. His favorite part of the evening was when he was kissing Siobhan good night, and she told him that she loved him, and he replied that he loved her too. Again, he asked permission to take Mummy out that night, and she wasn't perturbed at all.

Nicky called the owner of the cab and apologized for the late notice, but he felt he was coming down with a bad headache that seemed like it might turn into a migraine, so it was probably best he canceled his shift. Nicky knew Darryl was shocked. Of all the people he had ever employed, Nicky had never taken a night off for sickness, so Darryl would believe he must be genuinely unwell.

When asked if she wouldn't mind babysitting Siobhan, Caroline said, "Cut it out, Didi. You stay home for five years other than work and then want to go out for two nights in one week? What's going on with you, guys? Anyone would think you were engaged or something. Of course, I don't mind, especially with no work for me tonight. You guys go out and have fun. What are you going to see?"

Didi hugged her best friend. "Not sure yet, but any night out with Nicky is a good one."

Bree and Caroline had been thrilled with the announcement of the engagement made to them by a very excited bride-to-be. To some, it might seem to be too quick, but they had seen the enormous change come over Didi for the four months she had known Nicky. The feelings the couple had for each other was evident, so the friends did not doubt at all that it was real, and the pair would be one of those happily-ever-after couples. They also knew no one deserved it more than Didi because of all she had been through with Marcus.

They went to see *Jurassic World* and were in transit when Didi's phone rang for the second time that day. Again, it was Marty, calling to let her know the cops had gone, and while they had a lot of mess to clean up, the Kitty Palace would be open for business, as usual, the next night. The best news was that Didi would no longer be dancing. She was to start as a bar staff on her next shift. She thanked Marty over and over, promising she would be eternally grateful to him. Nicky smiled at her news; his life was complete and content, at long last.

Nicky turned his phone off because he didn't want Darryl to be able to reach him later if he hadn't been able to fill his shift. Because his phone was switched off, he didn't get the message from Detective Sgt. Sam Collins to call him in the morning until much later.

****

Sam had been to Nicky's home twice during the day and found he wasn't there. He then contacted Nicky's employer and been informed he was taking the night off sick, so he returned to Nicky's home a third time in the evening. Still, there was no luck. He left a message for him to call him about a serious matter as early as possible in the morning, and he left a business card in his mailbox with the same message written on the back.

Nicky and Didi had a fantastic night at the movies, not knowing the police had attempted to contact him. But even if he had, Nicky wouldn't have worried; he would have thought it was just a routine follow-up.

They had coffee at Didi's home after the movies and giggled like naughty school children. They decided he should spend the night, the first man to ever do so since Marcus. They made love, trying to be quiet, which only caused them to giggle more. Trying to muffle their sounds made it even funnier. Meanwhile, in the other bedroom, Caroline smiled as she heard them. Her best friend was so happy, and she couldn't think of anyone who deserved that more than Didi.

Sam reported his failed attempt to interview the cab driver for a follow-up and that it was going to be rescheduled for the following day. The information was entered into the database as per standard operating procedures. The entry, left by Sam, was read by Mick Connors. He had been reading every single entry on the case, looking for anything useful so he could earn his reward. Once he saw it was a reinterview of the cab driver who took Des home, he put two and two together and thought it was worth reporting on to his good friend, Mr. Mallory. The night before, he and his wife Vicky had been dreaming about how they could spend the money promised if he could get the right information. It looked like their run of rotten luck might just have changed.

On his lunch break, he phoned Jimmy using his code, "Merry Christmas, Mr. Mallory," and that he was seeing a movie at five that evening. The reply was, "Yes," Jimmy had seen it too and enjoyed it immensely. Jimmy and Gordy went through the usual routine at the Golden Teapot of checking to make sure the place was secure. When Jimmy and Mick were finally in the men's room together, Mick excitedly shared his news.

"The cab driver was to be reinterviewed by the head of the investigation sometime today; there must be some connection there, Mr. Mallory, sir. It seems he has a girlfriend and spent the night there or something; that's a bit sketchy. He wasn't home for the interview anyway, so he's been asked to go in tomorrow."

"Did you bring me his home address, Mick?"

"I'm sorry, Mr. Mallory, sir, I didn't. I can only add to the database and read current information going in, but I don't have access to historical data. The information should be there tomorrow to log once the interview has been conducted, and notes are left for me to post on it. If you give me a day or two, I will dig around some more and find it for you, sir; you can rely on me, Mr. Mallory."

"You do that, Mickey boy, and I promise you'll have a very Merry Christmas indeed, my son."

Chapter 15

The Renegade

Michael Winterbourne came from a privileged Mormon family. He went to a private school in rural Utah, then onto The University of Utah in Salt Lake City, where he studied to be a dentist like his father before him. But by the seventeenth month of study, he was so bored he began to experiment with drugs and gambling.

Michael had always been a loner, with few male friends, though most girls thought he was handsome and mysterious in the reserved way he carried himself and the general air of disdain Michael bestowed on people he didn't want to get to know. With all good intentions and belief that he controlled the drugs and not they him, he started with soft party drugs and grass but soon graduated to tablets and cocaine as a preference.

He loved playing no-limit Texas holdem poker, especially when high, which increased the buzz he felt. He became a regular at several legal and illegal gaming establishments. Things went well for a while. Michael was an intelligent man and played well. But soon, his grades started to slip as his nights got longer playing cards and using cocaine and uppers to help stay awake. One night he was invited by Cindi, a girl he sometimes dated, to a party at one of the frat houses. There, in the games room beside the swimming pool, he was introduced to crack cocaine. From that point, he began a downward spiral of paranoia, temper outbursts, and very poor decision-making while holding low pocket pairs at the poker table.

When he discovered Michael's grades, his father threatened to cut his son's allowance off if he didn't improve immediately. But Michael gambled more often, believing his unlucky run was due to end soon, and it was the only way he could think of to repay a debt. He owed a large sum of money to his drug dealer, Richie. The dealer knew Michael came from a wealthy family and had willingly staked him to feed his habit and grow his dependence, but his patience was fast running out. In recent times Richie recognized he was receiving what he knew to be bullshit reasons why the now hopeless addict couldn't, or wouldn't, pay what he owed.

Over the years, Richie had heard all the excuses imaginable for nonpayment of drug debts from junkies. During a quiet chat, conducted with a very sharp knife held to Mike's throat, and two of his strong-arm goons holding his arms, Michael was given three days to pay, or Richie would cut out one of his eyes. One month later, if still unpaid, he would lose the other.

The threat was a watershed moment for Michael when he realized his privileged life to date didn't count for anything in the game in which he now played. He made one last attempt to win back his losses by playing poker that Friday night. He staked his buy-in using a marker, given in good faith by the illegal casino owner, Louie, because he too knew Michael came from a well-heeled family and should, he thought, be good for the money if he lost.

In the last game of poker he ever played, Michael lost when he bet all-in with a queen-high flush, certain he had the best hand. Unfortunately, the man who called his bet held a full house of fours over sevens. When the grinning man opposite him turned over his winning hand, Michael's heart sank, and he knew he was in serious trouble.

For once, Michael didn't use cocaine to escape his dilemma. He realized he owed twenty thousand dollars in gambling debts and six thousand for drugs and didn't have a cent to his name to pay either. Michael phoned his father, Bruce Winterbourne the second, and begged for a loan of thirty thousand dollars. That would settle his debts, save his eyesight, and give him a small stake to start winning again at poker, he believed. Michael knew he would start to win soon; it was only a matter of time, so he could ultimately pay his father back and get on top. It was just that he had suffered the worst run of bad luck and bad cards imaginable, which he tried to explain over the telephone.

His father was a good man, a hardworking, loyal husband, and a fine upstanding Mormon. Unfortunately, when Michael asked for the loan, Bruce had no idea as to the severe mess his son had found himself in. Gambling was a sin, Bruce told his son, and he refused to help and told him it was time for him to stand on his own two feet and face up to his responsibilities. Michael should solve his own problems and stop using his family as a crutch because he alone had caused the problems through stupidity. He droned on to Michael that it was just like he himself had been at the same age, not that he had gotten into gambling and alcohol, but he had been on the *wrong side of the tracks once or twice,* so he knew what he was talking about.

No amount of begging and pleading from the errant son would change his father's mind. He scoffed at the suggestion his son would have an eye cut out over a paltry six thousand dollars, and the only advice he gave Michael was for him to "Grow up." As good a father as he was in some ways, they had never been close, and at that moment, in a blinding flash of understanding, Michael realized he hated his father with a cold, heartless passion that knew no depths.

Michael hung up the payphone receiver so hard it broke into two pieces and cut his hand. Knowing he was in deep trouble, he came up with a plan, and later that night, he went to his dealer's condo apartment and waited for his henchmen to leave, which they did just after midnight. As Richie opened the door to his knock, Mike pushed him inside and stabbed him to death with a sharp, long-bladed kitchen carving knife stolen from the student common room. After Michael washed the blood off his gloved hands and arms, he ransacked the apartment and came up with just over five thousand dollars in cash and a stash of cocaine and other drug paraphernalia.

At nine the next morning, he gave the five thousand dollars to Louie, the owner of the casino, as part payment in good faith and was given precisely one week to come up with the rest. Nonpayment of debt of that magnitude could not be permitted, Louie explained in a fatherly way. Louie never raised his voice, but that only made him sound more menacing. Louie placed an arm around Mike's shoulder. "If you don't come up with the money within the time I've given you, you will be killed, son," he said in his silky soft voice and shrugged. "It's just business," he further explained. "After all, if we don't stamp down on people who owe us money, it would lead to anarchy. Surely you can see that, can't you?"

Michael had to agree; he could see the common sense, but it was the next thing Louie said which gave him an idea of how he could get out of debt. Still, with a conciliatory arm around him, Louie explained further. "Just because we will fit you with concrete boots and drop you in the middle of the lake, the debt won't go away. We will then go and see your father and give him one week to pay, with the same result if he doesn't pony up. And then your mother would be next. Trust me, son, that money will get paid, one way or another, with compounding interest. This isn't a charity; you can see that, can't you?"

Michel promised to come up with a solution within the week and left to make plans around the spark of an idea he had brewing. Michael knew a lot of students left their car keys under floor mats or hidden on the sun visor of their cars in the student's car park, and often there was a lot of borrowing going on. Carrying a fuel can full of petrol later that night, he stole an old Chevy Nova belonging to one of the jocks who was away with the football team and made the two-hour drive to his parents' house.

Once there, Michael used his keys to silently enter, climbed the grand staircase, and, using the chloroform he stole from the lab at the university, made sure his parents wouldn't wake up while he carried out the next phase. He accomplished his task easily, as they had stopped using the same bedroom years before. His father snored so loudly every night; his wife had refused to sleep in the same room with him and often joked she would move farther down the street.

When they were taken care of, he went into the basement and pulled and pushed the flexible connection to the home heating system until he could hear gas leaking from it. Some years before, Michael watched a repairman service the heater and saw how, when the thermostat kicked in, there was a spark that was created to light the pilot light, which in turn ignited the gas in the boiler. His idea was that if he could flood the basement with gas for when the thermostat next switched on, the house would explode. At least that was what he hoped. Michael had to be careful he left no evidence that showed the pipe had been tampered with, so he could not hit it with a hammer or a heavy tool. He had to make it look like normal wear and tear, and that took fifteen minutes of worrying at the joint.

Michael closed the basement door behind him, climbed the stairs, and gave his parents another dose of chloroform to be sure they wouldn't wake anytime soon, then locked up and left. He jogged back to the car, which he had parked at a convenient spot half a mile away, on a hill, so he could watch the house without anyone seeing him. He had a knife with him and would not have hesitated to kill anyone he came across. He would have made their death look like a mugging gone wrong if he had been confronted by a jogger or dog walker, as unlikely as that was at that time of night.

After twenty minutes of watching nervously from

the Nova, he suddenly saw the burst of flames blow out of the windows and then heard the boom. He thought the house would be engulfed in fire in very little time, so he started the engine and drove away. Like a lot of elegant homes in the area, the Winterbourne home was predominately built with timber. Michael's planning had been perfect; the thermostat sparked and lit the gas boiler in a basement saturated with gas. The explosion wasn't catastrophic, but it was enough to start the fire that would destroy the house and kill the two drugged, sleeping inhabitants. Their smoke inhalation would hide his use of chloroform, he hoped, if the medical examiner bothered to check, which he doubted.

Michael drove back to Salt Lake City under the speed limit so as not to attract the attention of a highway patrol cop. He took the car to an industrial area that had long since been disused and wiped it down anywhere he could have touched to remove fingerprints. He changed into a completely fresh set of exercise clothes for the jog back and put the old ones on the seat. Then Michael set fire to the vehicle using the gasoline in the can as an accelerant. Michael thought when the burned-out wreck was discovered, it would appear to have been stolen and torched by joyriders. No one would ever know he had been the driver and made the ride to his parents' house in it.

He made it back to his dorm and stealthily got inside his room without anyone seeing him. He then climbed into bed and was asleep within minutes. Michael did not spare a thought for having committed three murders. It was a matter of life or death, and choosing between his parents' deaths or his own life had been an easy choice. When he thought about

Richie, the drug supplier, just before he fell asleep, Michael decided he was just a dealer who threatened to cut his eyes out, so was no real loss to society. It was all his father's doing anyway. If only he had agreed to help out, the killings wouldn't have happened. It wasn't like his parents couldn't afford it; they were rich, and so he rationalized it was their fault, not his.

The police interviewed him, as expected. Two officers made the drive to tell him about the destruction of the family home and the death of both parents. They had died in their sleep from smoke inhalation and therefore didn't suffer, he was informed. The fire appeared to have been caused by a leaking gas line, the early investigation showed. As a standard procedure, they asked him questions about his whereabouts and asked to see his car. He explained that a few days before, he had it serviced and had hardly used it since. Detective Hampton compared the current reading on the odometer to what was on the invoice. He noted it had only traveled sixteen miles and could not have been used to drive to the family home and back. Asked what his movements were the night before, Michael told them he was alone studying for an upcoming exam on wisdom teeth. No, he was sorry, but no one could substantiate it. He spent the night alone.

The officers performed their due diligence and, as he was the sole inheritor to the estate, established that Michael did have an important upcoming exam, which his lecturer explained was vital for him to pass. As far as possible, the officers checked out that he hadn't rented a car to make the drive, and as it took several days for the theft of the student's vehicle to be reported, they didn't attach the significance to the investigation.

The two officers' hearts weren't really into conducting a full investigation because it appeared the deaths were an accident. They were asking just routine questions which might be needed for the coroner's report. So far as they could see, Michael had no motive to murder his parents and no opportunity because it hadn't come to light. Michael acted suitably upset when the police delivered the tragic news, further allaying any suspicions he was anything but a grieving son who lost both parents in a horrifying accident.

Forensics didn't turn up anything suspicious. It seemed like a regrettable gas leak from a worn connection caused the fire. The boiler hadn't been checked by a maintenance call out for three years, and while the wear could be described as unusual, it was by no means unique. There were no signs of a break-in and no other suspicious circumstances to cause the investigators to believe anything untoward had triggered the fire. The medical examiner had a further six bodies waiting to be examined from an outbreak of food poisoning from spoiled meat used at a hamburger takeaway shop, so was too busy to have more than a cursory look at the two victims. The coroner would later confirm he was satisfied and ruled Michael's parents died in an accident.

While waiting for official confirmation, Michael sold Richie's stolen drugs around campus to recover as much money as possible. He raised just over three thousand dollars and went to Louie and asked for more time to pay the balance. He explained that he would be inheriting his parents' estate, but it would take some time until probate came through and he could access the money. He offered what he considered to be a fair and reasonable interest rate if he could get an extension to pay the balance.

Louie sat with his fingers tented in front of his face and studied the young man who sat before him and considered his options. Louie was no one's fool, and he realized the boy had murdered his parents to get the inheritance to pay his debts. That was good, and it was bad. It was good because, unlike others, Michael hadn't tried to weasel his way out of paying what he owed. He took his debt as a responsibility and was looking for a way to pay it, albeit late. But it was bad because if the cops arrested him for murder, he wouldn't receive the inheritance and therefore wouldn't be able to pay Louie. With both parents dead, Louie could not approach them if he executed Michael for nonpayment, so that was bad too. It was good, though, because Michael hadn't displayed a hint of conscience. People who could kill in cold blood and not be bothered by it were, in Louie's opinion, quite rare and sometimes useful. But it was also bad because Louie knew if he upset Michael, he could just as quickly be murdered. The key, Louie felt, in trying to control a murderous man who had no conscience was to reason with him and make him realize Louie was doing him the greatest service in the world by not punishing him further. The silence dragged on before Louie made a decision that would forever alter both of their lives.

"Mikey, you're a good kid, and I like you. But business is business; you can see that, can't you? You came to me and borrowed money. Now you can't pay it back in the time I gave you, and that is bad for my reputation and bad for business. I can't have others thinking I'm an easy touch. *Comprende*?" The man who would become known as The Renegade nodded, knowing there was nothing he could say that would affect a change in Louie's attitude. He would allow him to work out a payment plan—or he wouldn't. If he didn't, Michael would have to come up with a plan B, which he was confident he could do. He still had two days left of his original deadline.

"How do I know the cops won't arrest you for bumping off your oldies and freeze the estate, so you get nothing? What happens to the money you owe me then? And don't tell me it won't happen because I won't believe you. The fact is it might, despite what they have told you right now. Sometimes the cops lie to get you into a false sense of security. The simple fact is, Mikey, you owe me, and you can't pay. Am I right, or am I right?"

"Just because I can't pay right now doesn't mean I won't pay and with interest when I can," Michael replied, keeping his voice low and calm.

"True, and that's why I like you, Mikey. You've got some balls on you, and you got some style too. I tell you what, how about a proposition? I give you a way that gives you time to repay, without interest, so the debt stays as it is until probate. If you're arrested, I forget the whole business and write off the debt forever. Interested?"

Michael may have had poor grades, but he was an intelligent young man, and he knew instantly what Louie wanted. "Who do you want me to kill?" he asked, his face deadpan.

That day was the beginning of his new career. Michael was never charged for his parents' murder and eventually inherited the estate. Michael had to agree.

Louie had been right; it took months for the insurance and bank to settle.

Louie dined one night in February at a well-known restaurant with over twenty business acquaintances. During dessert, his partner was shot dead in his home. The police investigation assumed the murder was committed by an intruder, using an untraceable Smith and Wesson .38 revolver, which had been left at the scene, wiped clean of prints. The home had been ransacked, and the wall safe emptied, so robbery, they believed, was the motive.

Seven months later, after probate made him wealthy in his own right, Louie asked him to do a job for an associate of his who headed up a biker gang which ran drug distribution in Salt Lake City. Michael wasn't interested until Louie pointed out the benefits to his lifestyle of becoming an assassin for profit but that he would do well to keep his identity secret if he chose the route. Drug dealers were notorious for entering witness protection programs when facing overly long prison sentences as a way of reducing jail time.

Michael had loved western movies as a child and came up with The Renegade as a code name, plus the idea was appealing because the biker gang that wanted the job done was the Apaches. With Louie's help and contacts, things were set in motion for his new career. Michael and Louie had become good friends over the months, and Michael never touched cocaine or played Texas holdem again.

Soon The Renegade's reputation grew with his list of kills, and he became known as one of the most professional hitmen available. His price increased with his reputation, and he became choosy with which jobs he accepted or declined. When he gave a guarantee, he never failed and never made an excuse. No target or situation was deemed to be too hard. The only variable was how long it took and the price he would charge, and on that point, he would not be rushed or pushed. If he accepted a job, it was up to him when he did it. That was a given unless there were exceptional circumstances, such as an upcoming trial date where the target would give evidence. Rushing would always cost more because Michael knew people only truly appreciated a service if they paid for it.

The family home was rebuilt by the insurance company, but Michael didn't move back. Instead, he sold and bought something more in keeping with his lifestyle since he had dropped out of university and become a professional killer. He never married but was rarely without female company because while he liked women and enjoyed sex, he was incapable of feeling any emotion for them. Love, compassion, and other such feelings were alien to him.

Michael Winterbourne, aka The Renegade, was hunting Jimmy and Gordy in Perth, Western Australia. He would not stop and would not fail. He would kill them: of that, there was no doubt in his mind.

Chapter 16

The Interview Process (3)

Nicky phoned Detective Sgt. Sam Collins just after nine the next morning and apologized for missing him the evening before. He was unconcerned, believing the call was a formality, and explained that he had a bad headache and spent the night at his fiancée's. He hadn't gone to work and had his phone turned off, so he only just got the message.

Sam asked if Nicky could call into the station that morning as there were some further questions he had to be asked and a recorded statement taken as a follow-up to his earlier interview. They agreed to ten thirty, and true to his word, Nicky arrived punctually. Sam was summoned to the reception desk and escorted Nicky through to one of the interview rooms. Sam offered Nicky a coffee, which he declined, and explained he had to get some sleep before he had to work later that night.

Sam nodded in understanding and began. "Mr. Pantella, I'm going to keep this informal, just for the moment. This interview is not being recorded, and a witnessing officer is not accompanying me for corroboration. There is no one watching through an observation window, so it's just you and I having a little chat, okay?"

Suddenly, Nicky felt inexplicably worried, and butterflies began to gnaw in his stomach. Cautiously, he nodded, too scared he might give away his nerves if he spoke out loud.

"There's a lot of people, including many police officers I know, who think The Vigilante has done this city a service by cleaning up some riffraff and helped reduce the violent crime rate. Until quite recently, people felt safer at night walking the inner-city streets, which is a good thing. But of course, the police cannot possibly share that opinion officially. You understand that, don't you?"

Nicky nodded again, uncomfortable with the direction things were heading, and wondered where he had gone wrong. *The time has come to pay the piper*, he thought and was further saddened to think that just when he retired to settle down with Didi, someone he loved more than life itself, he was about to be arrested for five murders. Nicky's heart pounded in his chest, and he felt dizzy. He wanted to scream with anger and frustration but forced himself to stay calm and listen. He knew his only hope was to deny everything because he couldn't possibly have left evidence at any of the scenes.

"I know your employers keep records of your pickups, and if we dug deep enough, I'm pretty sure we could place you in the areas where five people were shot dead while they were in the act of committing violent crimes. Also, most people are not aware that satellite navigation systems can store past information, and when needed, we can plot someone's exact times and movements by downloading the memory. Did you know that, Mr. Pantella?"

He held up his hand to stop Nicky from denying it. "Shush, for a moment. That was a rhetorical question. Save your breath for now. We are speaking hypothetically. It's just a chat: no accusations, no need for alibis or excuses, not for the moment anyway."

Nicky settled back in the chair, depressed and feeling as if he would vomit.

"So the smart person," Sam continued, "and I'm sure you are very smart, Mr. Pantella, would deny everything and let us try to prove otherwise. They would think, quite rightly, that even if we could put you in the areas, at approximately the times of the crimes, what would it actually prove? You are a cab driver, so it's circumstantial if taken by itself. We know you took Desmond Mallory home, and he was murdered there, so it's not as if you tried to hide that fact. Without a confession, your lawyer would say that lots of other cab drivers were probably in those areas, too. So realistically, by itself, it's not enough. Do you see what I mean? That is, of course, if we made that accusation and assuming you denied it, which you would, wouldn't you?"

Sam looked pointedly at Nicky, whose skin was crawling and the hair on the back of his neck standing on end. Nicky nodded, still not daring to speak, knowing the tone and timbre of his voice would give him away. "We could then point out that we are aware of the tragic loss of your brother, and furthermore, we know of the ludicrously short sentence the offenders received. We could argue this gave you the ideal motive to take out your anger on other violent offenders you came across while driving your cab at night. We police must try to satisfy three aspects in any investigation:

those being means, motive, and opportunity. While it's open to interpretation, it could be argued that we can show you had two of them. You have the motive, and you had the opportunity. But then, of course, we have the means to prove."

Nicky had found his voice. "Go on."

"I've looked up your various firearms licenses, and if our victims had been shot with any one of the rifles in your possession, we would be forced to arrest you; we would have no choice. And let me tell you in all seriousness, Mr. Pantella, that would give me no pleasure whatsoever. But the law is the law, even if justice is sometimes sadly lacking, as I know you have found in your own experience."

"My brother was going to be a doctor. He'd been accepted into university. He was worth more than that pack of dogs all put together."

"Mr. Pantella, you wouldn't find one police officer who wouldn't agree with that statement. However, we represent the law, as unpalatable as that is sometimes. You see, no matter what the justification, we cannot permit people to take the law into their own hands and shoot offenders on the streets. If we allowed that, it would be mayhem out there, wouldn't it?"

Nicky shrugged as if to silently ask how bad it would be if everyone was armed and shot violent criminals. "Maybe this vigilante, whoever he is," Nicky stressed, "felt he had nothing left to live for. Maybe he lost his parents in a car crash and gave up his life, a good life in the army, to raise the brother he loved, only for him to be murdered by a pack of animals. But maybe that person now does have something to live for. Maybe he has fallen in love and has already lost his desire for any further revenge killings."

"That would be a wonderful thing if he had, but we have two problems. First and foremost is the gun. We can't find any trace of you owning a nine-millimeter pistol, meaning it is an illegal firearm. Worse, it is fitted with a silencer. We can't have illegal guns out there in the public domain now, can we? It could fall into anyone's hands, another criminal, a child even; stranger things have happened. What would you say if I told you we were currently searching your house as we speak, and in such a search as this, we use metal detectors to search in roof spaces, under floors, and inside walls?"

Nicky's heart suddenly thumped in his chest. If they were searching inside his home, he was gone. *But surely the cop is bluffing; don't they have to show me a search warrant?* "Search away. You won't find anything," he said, trying to sound more confident than he felt.

Sam smiled. "Good answer, Nick. You almost fooled me. We are *not* searching for a weapon in your house, not *yet*. I said this is informal for the time being. I just wanted to see your reaction. It's funny, but people come up with all sorts of weird and wonderful ways to hide things that they think are safe. Sometimes, the more elaborate a hiding place, the easier it is to find. You know we've gotten pretty good over the years at finding things people don't want found. Think about that, Mr. Pantella, and imagine what a metal detector might turn up in your home."

"Well, hypothetically, if this man has retired, and he wanted to get rid of the gun, what would you suggest he do with it?" Nicky had the vaguest hope that the policeman was trying to offer him a lifeline, but he had no idea.

"Well, that is the question, and the problem, isn't it? If The Vigilante got rid of it in such a way that it just vanished, the case would stay open. And you never know, one day he may get caught by some other means because the case was ongoing. Perhaps he could find some way of getting it to someone who might be on his side, who could get rid of the weapon in a way that ends the case. Let's come back to that in a minute because the gun is only one of two of this man's problems. The other one is far more serious and dangerous."

"What's that?" Nicky asked, leaning forward.

"I see I've got your interest now. Jimmy Mallory, the last victim's brother: that's the problem. Mallory is a cruel, murdering animal. A smart one, yes, but make no mistake; he is a drug-dealing murderer in the worst possible way. This man maims or kills people for looking at him the wrong way. He is a sadistic head of a drug-dealing empire who has no conscience or morals, and he won't rest until he has caught up with the man who has killed his brother, who happens to be The Vigilante's fifth victim. The mistake our vigilante made was that he used the same gun on all five victims, and his last victim was Jimmy Mallory's brother. Do you see the problem?" Sam paused and let the question sink in until he saw the dawning horror slowly appear on Nicky's face.

"You *do* see what I mean, don't you? Mallory initially thought it was a gangland hit on his brother, so he murdered three members of a rival gang who he believed were responsible in retaliation. His misguided revenge has gone on to create a war between two powerful and particularly vicious biker gangs trying to get exclusive control of the illegal drug trade in Perth. Quite frankly, I don't give a tinker's cuss if they want to kill each other; good riddance. But there is always a cost with a gang war, and that cost is innocent bystanders. But regardless of that, sooner or later, Mallory is going to find out it was a *vigilante* killing, not a gang takeover of his territory. How? He will find out because all of the bullets came from the same gun. You see, a man like Jimmy has cops on the take, who he pays for information, and sooner or later, there will be a leak. That's one of the reasons he isn't in jail; corrupt cops tip him off. So it's only a matter of time before someone gives him a copy of the ballistics report linking all those deaths together. When he learns that, I wouldn't want to be in, hypothetically speaking, your shoes or the shoes of this person you've fallen in love with."

Nicky turned ashen gray. The thought he had put Didi in danger terrified him far more than any fear for his safety.

"Here's the dilemma facing me, Mr. Pantella. If I place you under arrest and put you in jail, word will get to Mallory, and he will have you killed within days. He must, you see, to save face because then he can negotiate a peace with the Apaches. You would not be safe in prison, there are too many of his gang members there, and there will already be a bounty on your head. So I'd be sending you to your death if I do that, and if I find that gun officially and link it to you, I must arrest you."

Nicky couldn't contain himself; he would not put Didi in danger. "I will do anything you say. I don't care for myself, or at least I didn't up till meeting and falling in love with Didi. But I can't let anything happen to her because of my stupidity. Arrest me. I will give you the gun. At least then he will get me and not her."

Sam shook his head with sadness. He took no pleasure in this conversation whatsoever. Sam liked this simple man, who had been through so much tragedy, and now faced certain death yet would face it willingly to protect his love.

"Do not say another word. You're fortunate I'm a bit hard of hearing today, maybe due to a touch of hay fever or maybe a head cold. If I thought you said you could produce the gun, well, then I'd have to arrest you, wouldn't I? I would have no other choice. Let's think out loud for a minute or two and look at some of the things this hypothetical person could do. Firstly, he could take his girl and go on holiday for a month or so, maybe less, because there is a war going on now, and you never know, Jimmy Mallory could get knocked off his pedestal and murdered. That would solve the vigilante's problem nicely. Another thing this person could do, hypothetically speaking, would be to get rid of the gun. Remember we mentioned that before? Of course, I can't be a party to getting rid of the evidence, but let's say you knew a friendly policeman. You could get the gun to him on the QT and rely on him to get rid of it in such a way that the case stayed closed. Who knows? There might be a way of linking it to someone else involved in the gang war going on, or perhaps there was some other way of getting Jimmy Mallory to think it was someone else: possibly another mass murderer? One thing he should not do is hand himself in. While we might know who he is, we can't prove it without the gun, yet we must keep Mallory out of the loop, and that's the tricky part."

Sam took one of his cards out of his wallet and, leaning forward in his chair, handed it to Nicky. In a conspiratorial and quiet voice, he murmured, "If it were me, I would buy one of those cheap, disposable mobile phones, and then I would send their friendly policeman a text message about where they could find that gun. I would also make sure there was not a single fingerprint or piece of DNA evidence anywhere on it or in it. Every bullet, every dismantled piece of that gun has to be cleaned and wrapped up in something. I would let it soak in bleach for a while, just in case forensics was to check it for DNA. Then I would destroy the phone and dump it in the ocean or somewhere it could never be found. Lastly, I would grab my girl and go away for a few days or even weeks. I would review the situation and see if there was a way to find out which way the wind was blowing with Jimmy Mallory. Your friendly policeman may be able to help there. Think about it, but don't think too long, will you? There is only so long I can hold back a search warrant. Meanwhile, I will put into our log that I interviewed you and think you don't have anything further to offer us. Hopefully, that should get back to Mallory and keep him at bay, at least for a while, but I wouldn't count on it."

He stood up and held out his hand to shake. "Thanks for coming in, Mr. Pantella. I'm glad to hear you believe The Vigilante has resigned. But you do understand that this is the last of these informal chats that we can have, don't you? If there is a next time, I will have to read you your rights."

"Yes, I do. I can't thank you enough. I promise it

will never happen again. I want you to know it wasn't for the glory or anything like that; I spent months in, well, kind of like a daze, not caring if I lived or died. I never went and sought those people out. At the time, I thought I was saving lives, not taking them."

"I get that, Nick, I honestly do, and that's the only reason why I'm not searching your house for that gun right now. You've had a bad run, and I figure the justice system owes you a favor, but this is it. You only get this one chance. Make sure you make the most of it." He turned and opened the door, letting Nicky walk out ahead of him.

Chapter 17

Gordon "*Gordy*" Russell

When Gordon "*Gordy*" Russell attended Hollowood High School, he was on the outer sphere of the *in* people. While not disliked by them, he wasn't overly liked either. If push came to shove, he could hold his own in a fight, but he was too tall for his build and always looked gangly and clumsy, though his reach held him in good stead. Later in life, he filled out and put muscle on his frame through extensive gym work. Then, if his steel-gray eyes looked at someone the wrong way, it would instill fear into their hearts. But when he was at school, he was simply skinny, gangly Gordy. He didn't belong to any of the significant gangs or groups of friends with a common interest, not because he didn't want to, but because he wasn't invited. If he had been asked to join the book club, chess club, or anything, he would have jumped at the chance. Deep down, he was a lonely boy who wanted to feel like he belonged somewhere, anywhere.

He was a good enough student—neither overly intelligent nor dumb—so he wasn't picked on for being a teacher's pet, but the tougher guys didn't want him as part of their group either. He got by with okay grades and was careful never to excel because kids who were thought to be *too smart* got the crap kicked out of them after school in the bike sheds or on the oval. He was used to being in the background, not holding his arm up to answer the teacher's questions, but able to complete test papers and receive a reasonable pass level. His reports each year would say that he could do better if he tried. Not that teachers thought of him as lazy; he just didn't seem to apply himself as well as he could.

Gordy had been back at school ten days after the summer break and was in the end cubicle of the boy's toilet between classes when he heard a group of boys enter from the far end. In such a situation, he always kept quiet and lifted his feet off the floor, hoping he wasn't noticed for fear of toilet rolls, water, or rubbish being thrown over the door. He recognized two of the voices belonging to Billy Wellingham and Scott Sayers: two tough kids who generally had a couple of others in tow, and that day was no exception. Gordy heard them open up the windows and light up cigarettes.

Gordy had never smoked, and the pungent smell hit his nostrils, and he struggled not to sneeze. He was quite sure that if they heard him, they would have beaten him up, accusing him of listening in to their conversation, when really, all he was doing was using the facilities. He froze further as he heard Wellingham say, "That bastard Mallory has dissed me for the last time. We are going to get him tonight, right?"

There were murmurings of approval from the others, and one of the others joined in. "Yeah, Mallory is too big for his boots and needs to be taught a fucking lesson."

"What about his old man, though?" Another joined in, but Gordy wasn't sure who the voice belonged to. "I heard a rumor that if his kids get hurt, he goes after whoever does the hurting."

"Fuckin' let him. So long as we stick together, we can take them both. Some old codger ain't going to frighten me. Let's make sure the prick toes the line and learns who runs this fucking school," Wellingham muttered.

"Right," Sayers agreed, then it sounded to Gordy he rammed a fist into his palm. "He always walks home down Jolimont Street. We need to get there ahead of him, so let's all leave school a few minutes early. We'll wait out of sight in that laneway where that lemon tree is, on the corner. When he draws level, we jump him and beat the shit out of him. Boys, I don't want to see him in school for a month, right?" Wellingham sniggered.

The gang readily agreed on the level of pain they were going to inflict on the unsuspecting Jimmy Mallory, how many teeth they wanted to knock out, and how many ribs they wanted to break. Gordy was sickened by the thought of such a ferocious ambush. While Mallory was no friend of Gordy's, he had never been an enemy either. True, he was a tough kid, one of the toughest by reputation, but he wasn't a bully. If you didn't upset him, generally, Mallory left you alone. What Gordy knew of him was that he seemed to do his business fairly, and fairness was something Gordy hadn't seen a lot of at school.

Eventually, they finished their cigarettes and left the toilet. Gordy finished with a sigh of relief and went hunting through the school for Jimmy Mallory. He found him leaning against the wall near the lunch shop, thumbs hooked into the belt of his jeans, looking cool and aloof as he usually did. Jimmy was with one of his mates: a tearaway called Roger Brixton. As he approached, Jimmy looked Gordy over, seemingly sizing up any potential threat, and dismissed it, but Roger took up a fighting stance. Roger stood side-on, feet apart, weight balanced on the balls of his feet, with both fists raised. He wanted people to think he was a kickboxer, or karate exponent, though he had no training whatsoever. He figured that, as he watched Bruce Lee on TV every chance that came along, he knew what to do.

Gordy stopped a few feet away, arms by his sides, and said, "Jimmy, can I have a word, please? I have some information that I think you will want to hear."

"Oh, for fuck's sake, Rog." Mallory laughed. "Settle the fuck down, will you? It's only Gordon good on ya."

Gordon good on ya was a character in a TV ad that had run some years before. After that, anyone named Gordon suddenly acquired "Good on ya" as a nickname, unfortunately for Gordy. He couldn't stand the ad or the name but laughed along rather than appearing to be upset, as that would be sure to make any teasing worse.

"What's up, Gordy?" Jimmy asked warily.

"Jimmy, I was taking a dump in the toilet when a bunch of guys came in and started talking about how they are going to lie in wait for you on your way home tonight and put you in the hospital. It was Billy Wellingham and Scott Sayers, I know them for sure, but there were a couple of others though I couldn't tell you their names. Sounded like four or five in total."

Jimmy raised his eyes but didn't look perturbed, which impressed Gordy. "Why would you be telling me this then, mate?" he asked, still wary.

"Cos four or five on one, especially when he has no idea they are lying in wait for him, is a shitty thing to do. You never did me any harm, Jimmy, so I thought you should at least know. Maybe you can go home another way or something."

Jimmy thought about it for a minute before standing up straight. He held his hand out to a stunned Gordy. He took the proffered hand and shook it firmly, the way his father had taught him, like a man.

"Well, Gordy, I never forget a favor or a friend, and you've shown me that you are a good friend who done me a service, and I'm in your debt. I won't go a different way home. If they want a piece of me, they can have it, but at least I know it's coming, and I will hurt as many as I can. Thanks for telling me, and maybe one day I can return the favor to you, mate."

"Don't worry, Jimmy, man, I'll go with you. I fancy a good scrap," Roger said.

"Cheers, Rog. See you around, Gordy, and thanks again."

"They will be in the alley on Jolimont Street, Jimmy, behind the lemon tree." Gordy started to walk away but after four paces turned back and added, "Jimmy, if you could do with a hand, I'd like to help."

Mallory looked him up and down. It was as if, for the first time, he saw Gordy in a different light. "Man, I could always use the help, and you'd be welcome, but you know you might get hurt, don't you? Sayers and Wellingham are pretty mean, and they don't usually take prisoners."

"My grandad was in the Great War, and he always told me that some principles are worth fighting for and getting hurt for. So where shall we meet?" Jimmy and Gordy's friendship was forged that day and would last for many years. While other men came and went through Jimmy's orbit, none hung around as Gordy did. He was always loyal, always faithful, and would willingly go into battle alongside his best friend.

The three boys took on the five members of the Wellingham/Sayers gang that night, and Roger's kickboxing skills didn't help him much. He was knocked out early on in the fight but was able to hold up one of the attackers for a while by planting several karate chops to the face and one decent knee to his opponents' stomach.

Jimmy and his new friend fought side by side in a vicious brawl. Once it became apparent that it was a fight and not an ambush, two of their opponents lost heart and ran after receiving a few blows. As his opponent felled Roger, Billy Wellingham went down after Mallory delivered a savage left hook to his nose followed by a cheek-breaking kick in the face. He lost all further interest in fighting. It then became a two-on-two fight, and with those odds, there could only be one result as Mallory fought relentlessly with the energy of three men.

Gordy's long arms and superior reach kept his opponent away with the boxing style jabs that his father had taught him to use, though he was tiring quickly. Jimmy head-butted Scott Sayers, breaking his nose when he got too close, then followed it up with a flurry of punches that knocked him to the ground. Sayers stayed down and rolled into a ball to avoid any bones being broken from further kicks.

Jimmy turned and saw Gordy toe to toe with the

last attacker exchanging blows. While he could no doubt have won his fight on those terms, Mallory saw Gordy was getting hurt. If his opponent got inside, it could easily go the other way with his long arms a hindrance if it got to grappling. Jimmy saw blood dripping from his new friend's nose and mouth and came up behind his opponent. With a brutal rabbit punch to his left kidney, he ended the fight and possibly caused severe internal bleeding to Martin Fassbender.

Leaving the three boys battered and writhing on the ground, the victors helped Roger to his feet and, with one on each side of him, led him away. They realized there was always the chance a neighbor had phoned the police, so didn't want to hang around. They took Roger back to Jimmy's house, where his long-suffering mother bathed their wounds and gave them lemonade. When he felt better, Roger left, leaving Gordy behind because Jimmy said he wanted him to meet his dad. Jimmy's father arrived on time at six and saw the signs of violence and demanded to know the details while scanning the boys' faces and bodies, noting their marks and bruises.

When Jimmy finished telling the story, he said in his strong Liverpool accent, "You're a real good lad, Gordy, and this family owes you a debt. We never forget our debts, do we, Jimmy?"

"No, Dad. That's exactly what I told him before he volunteered to fight with me."

"Aye. Well, lad, I want you to come to tea with us on Sunday evening. Betty will cook us a roast. You, Jimmy, and I will play some darts and have a couple of beers. Do you like a beer, Gordy?"

At his age, Gordy had never tasted beer, but

Jimmy's dad was such an imposing character he didn't have the nerve to admit it. "I'd love to have a beer with you, Mr. Mallory. Thank you."

From that day forward, Jimmy and Gordy were best friends and did everything together, including being expelled from school. They started work as laborers at the brickworks together, and finally, they entered into a life of crime together.

****

Gordy knocked on Rebecca's door with a smile on his face. Gordy wanted to make sure he got any information from Beck before enjoying himself. Rebecca gave a thin smile when she opened the door and invited him in, offering him a drink as she did.

"Yeah, Beck, I will have a beer if there is one going." He checked out her ass as she led him inside and noted the outline of her panties through the skirt she wore. He licked his lips with anticipation. He sat on the couch, and when she brought his drink, he patted the seat alongside him for her to sit.

"So, Beck, how are you doing?"

"Not so bad now, thanks, Gordy, but I was down for a while there. The cops sent some home help from victim support services, and they cleaned the place up for me. That helped me feel a bit better about myself. I'd let the house go a bit, and that seemed to make things worse. It's time I brightened myself up a bit, so you are looking at the new me."

"There was nothing wrong with the old you, Beck. I always fancied you."

She blushed and recognized the hunger in his eyes. "Thanks, Gordy. You always knew how to make a girl feel good."

"Give me a chance, and I could make you feel *real* good, Beck."

She stared back and had conflicting thoughts at once. She had always *liked* Gordy; he wasn't as mean or as cruel as the rest of Jimmy's gang and had always been kind to her. She also had to admit she hadn't had any good sex for a long, long time. With Des, more recently, it had been his way or the highway. Her job was to satisfy him, and if she got any enjoyment herself, that was a bonus. It hadn't always been like that, though. In their early days, Des used to be a kind and considerate lover. But once the drunken beatings started, no matter how sorry he was or how hard he tried to make up to her following, during sex, he became more demanding and less considerate. Rebecca was conflicted, though, because she had decided to get away from the Mallory influence and try to find a normal life again back in Melbourne. If she did anything with Gordy, he might want more from her and get angry when he couldn't have it when she left. It was a dilemma, especially when she remembered what the friendly policeman, Sam, had warned her about when he told her to get away.

But, she worried, *what if Gordy has been told by Jimmy to hurt me, and I decline his advances, too?* With that thought, she became petrified that the purpose of today's visit by Gordy was more than just a friendly hello and to make sure she was coping. Perhaps it was to make sure she didn't talk to anyone ever again. As scared as Rebecca felt, she stayed calm enough to realize it would be in her best interests to have Gordy as a friend rather than an enemy. She sighed inwardly while smiling outwardly. It wouldn't be the first time

253

she had sex and acted as if she enjoyed it, and she doubted it would be the last. It made sense to have an ally in Gordy, and clearly, he liked her. She needed to play on that and pretend she liked him a lot more than she did.

Rebecca placed a hand on his upper thigh and felt the muscle underneath. *He is a very fit and healthy man*, she thought. *If I were going to have sex to save myself, I could do far worse.* "Well, Gordy, I haven't felt good in a long time, and I've always liked you if you want to know the truth. But with Des…" She let the silence hang for him to reach his own conclusion as to what she meant and, at the same time, squeezed his thigh harder. "I always wondered why you never married, Gordy. You would be a catch for any woman."

Gordy reached across and started to unbutton her shirt while watching her face. She slowly licked her bottom lip and gazed back, feeling the stirring of excitement in her lower tummy. He cupped her breast in his big hand, totally engulfing it. Her chest was by no means small, and she remembered the adage about big hands and hoped it was true.

He massaged her breast through her bra, and they both felt her nipple stiffen. She moved her hand higher up his thigh and felt him already hard for her. She realized that, in Gordy's case, that old saying was true. "I have to do some business first, Beck, for Jimmy. If we get that out the way, the rest is our time. He wants me to ask you about the cab driver. He thinks he might be the one who shot Des. What do *you* think?" He let go of her breast but left her shirt gaping open so he could see her purple see-through bra.

She stopped squeezing him and sat back on the

couch, letting her shirt stay wide open. Her skirt had ridden up, and she left it that way, trying to look as sexy as she could. Rebecca now knew why Gordy had come calling. She had to make this believable, or she understood he could hurt her, and no cab driver was worth that. Even if the cabbie saved her from a bad beating and rape, she had to look after herself first.

"Gordy, all I can tell you is what I told Maureen. Des was angry with me because he thought you were making a pass at me when he went off to play pool. When Des drank and got jealous, it was always me who suffered, and that night was no exception. As soon as we got outside the bar, he hit me twice in the stomach and dragged me to the cab rank. Then he threw me onto the back seat, making sure I bashed my head on the doorframe. I yelled and was crying, and the cab driver asked if I was okay. Des threatened him if he didn't take us home, but he just stared at me, so I had to assure him I was fine and to please take us home. Des thought that my speaking up undermined him, so he hit me again and blamed the cabbie for interfering. The cabbie didn't say another word, and when we got home, Des paid him but spat on the money first. Then Des dragged me inside. Once the door closed behind us, he started on me again, kicking and punching, and I might have screamed. I'm not too sure because I was in so much pain, but he ripped my dress, hit me a few times, and threw me on the bed. He was getting undressed when the doorbell rang. Des swore and went to answer it but shut the bedroom door first. All I heard was a funny kind of noise and a thud. I thought it was a neighbor complaining about me screaming, and Des and he were fighting. I knew better than to interfere; that would have only made him angrier at me, and then I fell asleep. That's all I can tell you, Gordy, honestly."

He took his time thinking, looking at her. Rebecca thought he was distracted with thoughts of the sex he would be having with her soon. "The thing is," he said quietly, "we've found out Des was killed with the same gun as that vigilante used in those other shootings, so Jimmy thinks the cab driver is a likely candidate."

"Well, I will tell you one thing; the guy wasn't scared of Des, and most men would be. People tended to take notice of Des when he was pissed off, yet the cabbie just stared back at him." She nodded in agreement. "You know what? The more I think about it, the more I think, yeah, it could be, Gordy. It was probably enough time for him to park somewhere and walk back. It was raining, so no one would have seen him at that hour."

"Take your top off, Beck."

She stood slowly, unbuttoned her cuffs and took the shirt off, tossing it to one side, and stood meekly waiting for her next instruction. Rebecca suddenly felt incredibly turned on and liked that he was telling her what to do.

"Now, the skirt," he said, his voice sounding croaky.

Rebecca wished she had worn matching underwear rather than the plain pale-green, unsexy cotton panties she had on. She unzipped, pushed her skirt down, and stepped out of it. *I have to make this good so he doesn't hurt me,* but she realized she was enjoying it and decided it wouldn't take much acting.

Gordy took her hard, aggressively, and used her body for his pleasure, yet she loved every moment of it.

Unlike Des, Gordy didn't hurt her and took his time but did it ruthlessly. When she cried out, it was because she was enjoying an earth-shaking, toe-curling orgasm as he raced toward his climax. Her knees were on the floor, and her body bent over the couch. He was behind her, holding her hips so tightly that the next day, she had ten little bruises to help remember the best sex she'd had in years.

Before he left, he demanded, and she willingly agreed to a blow job. While performing, she changed her mind about going to Melbourne. Perhaps there was good reason to hang around, after all, she wondered. Gordy made her feel special, and she had come twice. With Des, one orgasm was rare, and she could tell Gordy liked her. *Maybe things are looking up*; she wondered as she performed as well as she knew how. Gordy was some catch, and she let him know how much she enjoyed him by not taking him out of her mouth when he came.

****

Gordy left Rebecca's house with a smile on his face. He had always known she would be a hot fuck, and she had been. He could easily see himself going back for more, many times more, now that he had Jimmy's permission. Gordy had never seen himself as the kind of guy to settle down, but that was generally because the type of women he met in the past precluded that option. He mainly slept with women at the clubs who had great looks, tight bodies and were good in bed, but they rarely had too much going on between the ears. He was sure there were exceptions to that rule, but then he would be dealing with the stigma of dating a woman who let other men gawp and fondle her. No, it was

257

better to have fun and stay single. But Rebecca was different. Now that she was alone again, maybe she deserved some serious attention. He had always liked her and didn't appreciate the way Des treated her. But the dickhead she married was Jimmy's brother, and no matter what, Gordy loved and respected Jimmy. If you could trust someone to watch your back no matter what, if you trusted them implicitly with your money, your wife, your possessions, and your life, and that wasn't love, then what was?

Rebecca happened to be married to Jimmy's brother, but so far as Gordy was concerned, Beck could have been married to anyone, and he would have respected that union. Although he could kill, hurt, or mutilate enemies without hesitation, he thought of himself as a moral man with scruples. Those scruples included not touching another man's wife, even if it was handed to him on a plate. Not that it had ever been on a plate with Beck, and that in itself was something else to appreciate about her. She respected her marriage vows. Even if that respect was based on fear, it was still *"r-e-s-p-e-c-t."*

So while she had been Des's wife, he could only look on from the sidelines and admire her from afar. But now Des was gone, and Jimmy didn't care what he did with her. Sure, when Jimmy said that, he didn't mean for him to start living with her. He meant for Gordy to fuck her, hurt her, or even kill her if he needed to, to find out about the taxi driver, which he had done. So far as he was concerned, that gave him a license to see her again if he wanted. She didn't know any more than she had told him. Gordy was convinced of that. She didn't try to lie to him, and he had liked her for that too. There seemed no point in hurting her when she was so willing to tell him everything she knew. *Yes,* he thought while driving back, *there is a lot to like about her.*

He used his mobile phone's Bluetooth connection to call Jimmy and tell him what Beck had told him. Jimmy listened and asked pertinent questions but did not ask if he had fucked her; Jimmy didn't seem to care. Gordy ended the call as he pulled into an empty spot in front of the bar he used as an office for his own business interests. He grinned as he realized he was already looking forward to the next time he could be with Beck.

If he hadn't been distracted, Gordy would have driven carefully around the block, looking for signs of danger before parking. Had he done so, he would have noticed the two burly men sitting in a car on the other side of the road and would have been on high alert. But he remembered how she had tasted earlier as he got out of the car, his back to the men, only ten meters away. The two Apache members couldn't believe their luck as they watched Gordy arrive as if he didn't have a care in the world. They got out of their car simultaneously, both holding 12-gauge pump-action shotguns. Like synchronized swimmers moving in time with each other, they raised and fired at once.

Gordy didn't have a chance to react and pull the gun from his shoulder holster. His last thought was to phone Beck and ask her out to dinner, somewhere beautiful, later that night. The first blast got him in the back, high up, and the second disintegrated his shoulder blade, which spun him around so he could see the two men as they shot him repeatedly, advancing across the road. The force pushed him back against his car while hundreds of pellets broke windows and blew holes in the car's body. It was over in seconds. Gordy fell to the road, bleeding profusely and twitching, shot at close range eight times: four from each attacker. Their stolen car sped away within moments and got lost in the late afternoon traffic. People who heard the shots ran for cover, and when asked later by police for a description, all they could say was that they were big men, burly, and couldn't provide many more details than that.

Chapter 18

Things Unraveling

The women who worked at the Kitty Palace could not believe the change that had come over Didi. Instead of the mousey, timid thing who wore a permanent sad look, there was now a confident-looking woman strutting around who looked taller, somehow. She wore an engagement ring that sparkled in the crystal downlights of the bar area and smiled at everyone she came in contact with. The biggest change, to the other girls' shock and horror, was she flirted openly with the customers rather than treat them with barely concealed disdain.

The dancers watched her from afar at the way she laughed and joked with the male patrons at the bar and shook their heads; she was a different person suddenly. Didi proudly showed off the engagement ring to anyone who asked and told them about the wonderful man in her life who drove a taxi on the night shift and loved James Hendry songs.

The tip jar had never been so full, and Marty was delighted with his decision to allow her to switch roles. She was happier, and so were the regular customers. He asked her about her beau during one of her breaks after Marty went out of his way to tell her how pleased he was with her, and he listened to her tell him how fantastic Nicky was. She mentioned the tragedies that had befallen him and that had molded him into the man he was. She told them about the attempted rape after leaving the club four months earlier, and that was how they met when he saved her from a fate worse than death. Marty responded that he would like to meet him and that if he wanted to come into the club sometime, he wouldn't have to pay for drinks.

Didi laughed and said, "No way, Jose. I don't want him in here, where all the other girls might tempt him away from me." She was joking and told Marty what Nicky had said to her when she asked if he would come in and see her dance.

"Didi, you've got yourself a one in a thousand," he replied with a genuine smile of affection.

Didi lightly punched his arm and corrected him, "Nicky is one in a million."

With everyone talking about Didi and the new man in her life, it wasn't surprising that word filtered to someone who put two and two together and came up with four. Mark, one of the security doormen, wondered if Didi's guy wasn't the same cab driver that Jimmy Mallory was looking for. He decided to report his suspicion because there was a substantial reward for information, and he needed the money to maintain his drug habit. However, Gordy had been shot dead earlier, and while Mark Bronsky would have gone to see Jimmy or phoned him to report his suspicions straight away, he decided to wait. Everyone knew how violent Mallory could get when he was angry, and no one wanted to be within a mile of him until he calmed down over the loss of his best friend. It was one of those times where Jimmy, quite literally, might shoot the messenger.

****

The last echo of the final shotgun blast had barely died in the city streets when Dan, the bar manager of *The Crew Bar and Grill,* grabbed the baseball bat he kept behind the bar and looked out the window of the entrance door to see a car speeding away from across the street. He couldn't see who had been shot but recognized Gordy's car parked in front of the building. With dawning horror, he noticed the smashed windows and blood splatter on what was left of the glass of the vehicle.

Dan raced out to see if he could help, hoping that Gordy would only be wounded, as he had always liked Jimmy's right-hand man. He rounded the car, but one look was enough to see Gordy was dead. His body was broken and battered, with large chunks blown away by shotgun blasts and an ever-widening pool of blood growing around him. There was nothing Dan could do to help, so he went back inside to call the police. He was one of five people who called in the same report, and the air was split with the sound of sirens within minutes.

Meanwhile, Dan plucked up the courage to call Jimmy. Without preamble, when Mallory answered the phone, he said, "Jimmy, it's Dan at *The Crew.* They got Gordy. He's been shot dead out the front. Police are on their way." There was total silence that dragged on until Dan finally asked, "Are you there, Jimmy? Did you hear me?"

"Yeah, I heard you, Dan. Thanks for letting me know."

Jimmy sounded broken and depressed, and Dan

hung up the phone gently, wondering what he should do. Open the bar as usual or close it for the night? If he chose wrong, he would have to face the consequences. Then he realized the street would be cordoned off while forensics did their thing, so he may as well phone the staff and tell them not to come to work. He grabbed a piece of paper and a marking pen and wrote: *Closed until further notice*. He hung it on the door with sticking tape and then went into the office to phone the staff.

****

For the first time in his life, Jimmy Mallory shed tears for the loss of a true friend. He hadn't cried for Maureen when she was blown up in the bomb blast, yet he did for Gordy. His relationship with Maureen had been more of a marriage of convenience, business, and friendship with benefits, although it hadn't always been that way. With the passing of time and the opportunities for him to sleep with any one of hundreds of women who threw themselves at him, Maureen became more of a partner who took care of the administrative side of the business. The affection was still there, and they hadn't stopped having sex, but over time, they had slipped into a comfortable relationship that didn't demand he had to be faithful to her.

Maureen had enjoyed their lifestyle and the privileges that being married to a crime lord with unlimited wealth brought, and she knowingly turned a blind eye to his philandering. Partly that was because she didn't want to face the consequences if she angered him in a confrontation; she knew how fierce his temper could be. Unlike his late brother, Jimmy had never hit Maureen, but she liked to think she had never given him cause to.

Jimmy was driving his BMW on the freeway when Dan called. The long silence was caused by him pulling across traffic into the breakdown lane and stopping the car, which was not easy at that time of day. Once parked and the phone call ended, he punched the steering wheel repeatedly and broke down in a mixture of genuine grief and surprise that he could feel such an emotion.

Eventually, he composed himself and thought about his situation. He was far from stupid and realized that taking out his anger, wrongfully, on the Apaches had been a mistake. Because of that error in judgment, he had lost everything: his wife, best friend, and soon, his business empire. He could not possibly come back after this blow, and he doubted he could muster the support from what remained of the Grave. In the final analysis, he asked himself, *did he even want to come back?*

Jimmy had amassed a fortune of over thirty-five million dollars, which was sitting in a bank account in the Cayman Islands. He owned nightclubs and bars, along with various properties in Perth and along the Eastern Seaboard. Jimmy knew he could leave and enjoy the rest of his life; he had earned the right to do that. He would never have to worry about the criminal life he had led again. The safe at his house held nearly a million dollars in cash, which would be more than enough to make a getaway.

Suddenly, the image of his father appeared, shaking his head. He had died of a self-inflicted gunshot wound to his head before he could succumb to lung cancer. He could no longer bear to see his body wither and waste away under the violent onslaught of a fight he could not possibly win. Such was the man his father was, and Jimmy knew that, had he been alive, he would have kicked his son's ass for thinking of running away from a fight. But the question was, did he want to fight anymore?

With cars and trucks whizzing by on the freeway, Jimmy slowly refocused, and his mind became more lucid. Pragmatism told him that, yes, he had lost the battle with the Apaches, especially true that he was now without Gordy. He had suffered severe loss of face in his ranks, and the cops were raiding everything of his within sight. That alone was ruining the legitimate businesses.

Jimmy decided that he could live with everything being over so long as he walked away from it all on his terms. That meant that he would tell the Apaches he quit on one condition. Jimmy would stop all hostilities toward them and give them everything willingly because the single most important thing to him was getting even with the *fucking cab driver* and avenging the death of his only brother. He knew by doing so, his father would rest in his grave.

Jimmy would focus all of his attention on finding and demanding retribution from the man who had shot and killed Des: the guy who had started the whole damn war that had taken away his wife, best friend, and business empire. His mind made up, Jimmy started the car, wiped the last of his tears away from his now-determined face, and pulled back into the traffic flow. He decided his next move would be made later that night.

****

Felix's team worked all night with nothing to show for it. They had the street cordoned off, and forensics had performed all their tests for no return. Every witness and worker in surrounding businesses were interviewed, and the best description they could come up with was two big guys who could have been Caucasian, Samoan, Sri Lankan, or Indian. They were driving a pale-blue sedan, but it could have been a wagon that either did or didn't have alloy wheels. One man said it was an SUV and stated that he should know; he had worked as a used car salesman for seven months. Another bystander thought it was: "One of those big Japanese cars," but couldn't hazard a guess as to which one. The two men were wearing anything from denim jackets to white shirts and leather colors. Hair color was stated as being blonde, black, brown, or gray hair of varying lengths and styles. One woman said she was sure one of them was bald. Felix knew eyewitness testimony was notoriously unreliable for many reasons, fear of reprisal being one of them.

The only consistent thing that everyone agreed with was the speed that events unfolded. The first thing people became aware of was the gunshots. Then, when they looked to see what was happening, they saw two men shooting a third. At that point, most ran or dived for cover, so the next thing they heard was a car speeding away. Some witnesses were in shock and required counseling; others were so scared of retribution they said they couldn't remember anything more specific, though police suspected they did.

Felix tried unsuccessfully to track Jimmy Mallory down at any of his known haunts and businesses, but he didn't return phone calls. Felix wondered if he had been killed himself or if he was in hiding. He supposed time would tell.

****

Mick Connors felt miserable. It was as if he had been given a beautiful Christmas present only to have it snatched away as if it was for someone else. He clenched his fists, stared at the computer screen, and wondered for the thousandth time in his life, *why me?*

He finished reading the report entered by Detective Sgt. Collins regarding his follow-up interview with Nicholas Pantella. He had written that he believed that Mr. Pantella had nothing further to add that could assist the investigation and that, in his opinion, he had nothing to do with the shooting of Desmond Mallory. Nor had he witnessed anyone who could have committed the murder due to the inclement weather on the night. Worse news followed. Mick read that on two of the previous murders, Mr. Pantella had furnished alibis so could not be the vigilante. The alibis needed to be substantiated, which would be attended to in due time, but Detective Collins' opinion was that Nicholas Pantella was not involved or make a credible witness, as he had seen nothing that would add to the investigation.

Mick wondered if he should tell Mr. Mallory this new development. In his heart, he knew, if he didn't, and Jimmy did anything to hurt the driver, Mick would not be able to live with the guilt that he had caused it. Essentially, Mick was a good man but had always considered himself unlucky. He often thought of himself in the same light as a song lyric he'd once heard, "*I ask for nothing in life, and gain even less.*" He could no more willingly stand by and let an innocent man get hurt so that he could make some money than he could become the Pope. He looked at his watch and noted it was too late in the day to send a message to meet Jimmy. He dared not text anything not coded that could be interpreted by possible listeners, so it would have to wait for the next day to tell him.

Later, as he was driving home rehearsing what he would say to his wife to explain why they couldn't book a holiday, he heard the news on the radio about Gordon Russell being shot dead. Like most people who came into contact with Gordy, Mick quite liked him. He was a big, hulking giant of a man but a gentle one. Mick was quite sure that, if push came to shove, Gordy could crush someone's windpipe in his hands, but mostly he was quiet, polite, and thoughtful. By the time he pulled into his driveway, he felt sad for the loss of a quiet-spoken man he barely knew. Later Mick read that Gordy had been credited with more than twenty murders if the papers were to be believed. While reading the sensational story, he shook his head and thought, *you just never know about people; he seemed so nice.*

****

Nicky spent the day worrying. Not for himself, but for Didi and Siobhan and the danger he had inadvertently put them in. Nicky would cut off his right arm before he saw them get hurt, and he was terrified that they might be. In the light of what the detective had told him, he looked at his situation from every possible angle. No matter how many ways he thought about it, he could see no way out that didn't involve running away or giving himself up.

The first thing he knew he must take care of was

the gun. It had to go, but how? He could somehow get it to the cop, but how did he know it wasn't some elaborate trap to get him to produce the weapon so he could then be arrested? He had seen enough TV shows to know the police could be devious when they were in pursuit. Sam had seemed honest and willing to give Nicky a pardon as long as he stopped the killing, but could he be trusted? He took the gun from its hiding place and, within seconds, had it dismantled. He grabbed the shells, silencer, and the magazine and dumped them all into a bowl of bleach. No matter what else he did, the cop's suggestion of bleach to destroy or degrade any DNA trace was a good one, and he was grateful for the tip.

Wearing black kitchen latex gloves, he took each shell from the bleach, wiped them down carefully, and packed them back in a small plastic bag. He did the same with the magazines, silencer, and the gun itself, reassembling it with practiced ease. He could have done it blindfolded as he had during his army training. From the kitchen drawer, he took a large ziplock plastic bag, wiped it thoroughly to ensure there were none of his fingerprints on it, and sealed the gun in it. He then slipped everything into a large, padded postbag, which he had picked up from the city post office after he left the police station earlier. Nicky stuffed the envelope into his backpack with a jacket folded up and placed on top. He would think about what to do with it while at work later that night, but a commercial skip bin seemed like a good idea.

Nicky called Didi and said he was sorry, but he wouldn't be there for dinner that night. He told her he felt a headache coming on, probably a touch of stress after the police interview, and that he needed to sleep before working that night. Nicky promised to be there to pick her up from work as per usual and that he loved her. She offered to come over and give him a scalp massage, but she didn't own a car, and as tempted as he was to accept, he begged off. He needed to think about how he could get out of the deep hole he had dug for himself, and he didn't want her at his house in case Mallory turned up. In preparation that it happened, Nicky had loaded his rifles and hid them strategically throughout the house; he had no compunction about shooting the man dead if he had to. He just didn't want Didi to get caught in any crossfire.

Nicky knew that when he was with Didi, she distracted him from being able to pursue a rational thinking process. She was wonderful, but not what he needed at that moment. Didi pointed out there was a certain little girl who would miss her bedtime story, and his heart melted so much he nearly changed his mind. He didn't, though; it was more important to find a way out, and if he kept putting it off, the chance to plan any future together could be taken away from him.

He slept for a while, fitfully, and when he was eating a dinner of macaroni and cheese warmed up from the freezer later, he saw the breaking news bulletin of the latest killing in the city on TV. He watched avidly as the segment outlined who the victim was, the state of the gang war that was raging for control of the Northbridge drug trade, and the victim's relationship with Mallory. When the interview with the head of the investigation, Detective Insp. Felix Milanski, from the organized crime squad, appeared, the inkling of an idea took shape. Nicky stretched the concept into a plan and thought it through from every angle. He knew he had a chance; it could work if he was lucky and all the stars aligned. Nicky dashed into Simon's room, which had barely been touched since he'd died, other than cursory dusting and cleaning. Nicky fired up Simon's old study computer and impatiently waited for it to boot up. *Maybe, just maybe, there is a way out of this mess,* he fervently hoped.

Nicky's plan began with putting people together. The man he had shot was Des, who was married to Rebecca. Des was Jimmy's brother. Gordon Russell was best friends with Jimmy and had been murdered in the bloody gang war that Nicky had unknowingly started. Could Nicky make it look like Russell had shot Des? Nicky thought he could, and with Sam Collins appearing to want to help, he felt he had a better than even chance of getting rid of the gun, throwing suspicion away from himself, and getting Jimmy Mallory off his back.

Once the computer booted up, he searched for the two names which were careering through his brain: Jimmy Mallory and Gordon Russell. Numerous pages eventually loaded, including an excellent article from a journalist named Jeremy Myers, who was later found floating in the Swan River. Jeremy had been strangled by someone using the belt of his trousers. His pants were removed, and the police believed his death occurred in the middle of a gay hookup that had gone wrong. People in the know knew that was incorrect. Jimmy Mallory would never allow anyone to expose him in the press without repercussions, so he had taken steps to murder the journalist and ruin his reputation in retaliation.

As Nicky's plan crystallized, he was dumbstruck with how good it *could* be. He grabbed a pencil and writing pad and, after a couple of false starts, began writing a note. Finally, Nicky had what he thought sounded right. Still wearing his gloves, he typed the letter out on the computer, printed it, and read it, making sure that he used a fresh sheet of paper from the middle of the ream to avoid previous fingerprints. Once he was satisfied, he folded it, went back to his backpack, and slipped the note inside the padded bag with the gun before sealing it up permanently.

He grabbed a black marker pen from the kitchen drawer and wrote on the front, using his left hand so the writing could not later be identified as his own:

INSPECTOR FELIX MILANSKI
POLICE DEPARTMENT
CURTIN HOUSE
60 BEAUFORT STREET PERTH 6000
****

Nicky left the house carrying his backpack nervously, knowing he was close to getting rid of the one thing that could incriminate him. He continually looked over his shoulder, scared he was being watched by police, or worse, one of Mallory's gang. In his car, Nicky frantically checked vehicles behind him and alongside at traffic light stops. After he picked up the cab and began his shift, he waited until it got dark and then drove carefully to the largest post office in the city. He parked in a nearby taxi rank, where three other cars were ahead of him, far away from any likely CCTV cameras.

He said hi to the other drivers and asked if they could keep an eye on his cab as he had an errand to run.

They agreed, and Nicky locked it and entered an alley where he put on his jacket and pulled the hood up to obscure his hair and face. He slipped his gloves on once more and took the parcel from the backpack, then wiped it over with a cloth from his pocket to ensure he had not left prints. Nicky tucked it under his jacket and hid the backpack behind a bin, then left the alley from a different exit and walked unhurriedly across the road to the post office. He deposited the package into the parcel slot and walked away while keeping his head bent low to hide his face from any CCTV cameras.

Nicky smiled with relief and took a different route back to the cab via another alleyway, where he removed the jacket. He threw it into a rubbish skip bin, hoping a homeless person would find it, as it was a good jacket. Whistling an appropriate tune, *I'm Still Standing*, he went back to the cab and drove away, feeling the weight of the world had been lifted from his shoulders. Now he could turn his thoughts to trying to get Didi to leave town with him for a few days.

****

The Renegade was furious and wanted to punch the wall when he saw the news broadcast of Gordon Russell's shooting. "Fuck those fucking fuckers," he screamed at the TV, which was a favorite saying whenever something didn't go his way. Not only had the useless Apaches cost him a hundred thousand dollars by reducing his targets from two to one, but they had probably forced Jimmy Mallory underground. That would make it more difficult for him to complete the job they had hired him to do. What were they thinking? Killing Russell was a short-term gain for a long-term loss. While he had been researching, plotting, and planning for the perfect dual killing, they had ruined everything. Why bring him from the USA if they were going to go after the targets themselves? It made no sense at all.

Winterbourne spent time musing what Mallory was likely to do next. As far as he could reason, there was only one solution left, but he needed a car, and it would be best if he cabbed it to the airport to hire one. There was less chance of being remembered there than a small branch, and stealing a car was not something he wanted to do because no matter how well he planned, something could always go wrong, and if he were found in a stolen vehicle, it would be over.

He changed into more appropriate clothing, black jeans, a T-shirt, soft-soled shoes, and a light black jacket, which would hide the shoulder holster. He then opened the hidden compartment in his suitcase and selected one of six credit cards with the matching international driver's license. He debated whether to take the sniper's rifle with him, just in case and decided he would. While he expected the Walther would be enough, if things went wrong and he had to move fast, it would be good to have it with him. Best to take it with him and get rid of it if required than to leave it behind because the hotel had his passport number, and he didn't want to blow that identity unless necessary.

Forty-five minutes later, he left the airport car park in an almost new Toyota sedan. The car came equipped with a navigation unit, but he wouldn't use it because he didn't want to leave a footprint of where he had driven in the GPS memory. He would use the maps on his disposable phone to find the house he was looking for. Winterbourne stopped at a busy supermarket and bought two bags of snack food and a few drinks. He hoped that would be enough, but if not, it was back to the drawing board. His instincts told him that everything would be over by then, one way or the other. He had studied the plans of Mallory's house and knew that Jimmy had an excellent alarm system with camera surveillance overlooking the front and rear of the home. The roof of the two-story building was clay tiles, and that would be his way inside.

He left the vehicle in a shopping center car park three streets from Mallory's house, removed the bags from the back, and walked with confidence as if he lived in the area. He strolled to Jimmy's house, deliberately approaching from the side farthest from the triple garage so he could study the building and look for any sign of occupancy. As Michael drew level, he noted there were no lights shining from the windows, and the envelopes and junk mail sticking out the letterbox confirmed his first thought; Mallory was in hiding.

The Renegade looked around carefully and saw no one else watching the house. He walked up the grass verge by the driveway, moving from tree to tree, and then to the side of the garage. Silently, he climbed onto a garbage bin and pulled himself up onto the roof. He stopped momentarily and looked around carefully, staying completely still as he listened for any sign that he had been seen or heard.

From the apex of the garage roof, it was a straightforward climb on top of the second story. Winterbourne circled the building, creeping on the clay tiles, to the rear of the house. By moonlight, he kicked the tiles until he found one that moved, then knelt and slid it upward, followed by the one alongside it. Once he made a start, it was simple to move others until he had a hole in the roof large enough. He lowered himself carefully through the gap, using the torch function on his phone to see the ceiling joists to step onto. Inside the cavity, he pushed and pulled the tiles back into place so that in the morning, a nosy neighbor looking up wouldn't notice the hole and call the police. He did a three hundred and sixty-degree search by torch as he recalled the details of the house floor plan. Upstairs contained four bedrooms and three bathrooms. By tracking the air conditioning ducting, he estimated where the main hallway at the top of the stairs was located, which theoretically shouldn't have a motion sensor for the alarm.

Traditionally, there were two schools of thought when designing home security systems in the situation he was facing. The first was to put an infra-red detector in the hall and ignore individual bedrooms, using the theory that if someone broke in via a bedroom when the intruder came into the hallway, they would be detected. The second plan, and the one that cost more money to install, was to leave the hall but put detectors in each room. The Renegade thought with all of Mallory's capital and natural paranoia, he would opt to protect each room and ignore the hall because the alarm would be triggered much quicker to an intruder that way.

Carrying his bags, Michael climbed over the silver ducting, not caring if he damaged it until he arrived at a spot he thought should be correct. From his pocket, he took a camera attachment on a flexible rod for the phone and plugged in the cable. The Renegade lifted the insulation batts out of the way and used a pen from his jacket pocket to punch a hole through the plasterboard ceiling. Once the hole was big enough, he poked the camera lens end through the hole and looked around three hundred and sixty degrees watching the phone screen. He focused sharply on the image as he inspected the junction of the ceiling and walls, just under the cornice looking for a motion detector.

His first assumption was correct; there wasn't a sensor in the hallway between bedrooms: only in the bedrooms themselves. He moved the camera away from the ceiling and lowered the angle of viewing to look at the doorways. If they had been left open, the detectors within those bedrooms might pick him up, which would make it dangerous to drop from the roof there. His luck held as all the doors were closed.

Winterbourne cleared the insulation batts away and held onto the roof beams to steady himself. Braced carefully, with one foot on a joist, he kicked a hole in the ceiling with the other foot. When the section of the plasterboard dropped, he listened intently, silenced gun in hand, in case there was a dog or housekeeper not mentioned in the file who decided to investigate the noise. The house and neighbors stayed silent.

He dropped his bags down and lowered himself onto the floor below. Gun still in hand, he made sure any bedroom doors were secure. As there were no windows in the hallway, he turned on the light, then made himself comfortable sitting on the plush, carpeted floor with his back against the wall, gun on one side of him, and the snacks and drinks on the other. The Renegade settled down to wait.

His theory was that sooner or later, Jimmy Mallory would come home because he would have things in the house that he would want to take with him if he was going to run. Quite possibly, he had a safe with cash and passports, which he would need if he intended to leave the country. Even if he was going to stay and fight the Apaches, it was still more than reasonable to assume he would come home for clothes or anything else stashed here sooner or later. Once Mallory returned, he would turn off the alarm, allowing The Renegade to creep down the stairs and kill him and anyone else with him. Michael had developed patience over the years; he could wait. As he stretched out, The Renegade allowed himself to drift into a dreamless sleep.

Chapter 19

Waving the White Flag

Wayne Norton had lost both legs in a high-speed motorbike accident while trying to outrun a police ambush when he had been with the Sydney chapter of the Apaches. He had two kilos of heroin concealed in the pannier bags, which he knew carried fifteen years in jail if he was caught with it in his possession. His bike skidded at a hundred and forty kilometers an hour at a roadblock, and he careered into a car they had used to block the road. Norton was arrested and charged when he awoke from extensive surgery, including the amputations. Norton stayed in the hospital for the next few months recovering while the court case built against him.

In the eventual proceedings, the Apaches used their best lawyer, a Queen's Counsel, who outperformed the public prosecutor, who could never rise to the same lofty rank as his opponent. Reginald Montgomery QC used his expertise so that not only was Norton found not guilty but was awarded three million dollars in damages because, in the absence of a warrant, the police chase was deemed to be illegal. As the chase was illegal, he argued, then anything found on Wayne's person or property was inadmissible. The newspapers mocked the police and then the system that could allow a drug trafficker to escape jail time when he was caught with that amount of cocaine. One headline summed it up with poor taste when it decreed, *Drug Dealer Walks Free Without Legs*, which referred to the loss of both of Wayne's legs in the accident.

In the following years, Norton stayed with the Apaches but took no part in their criminal activities. He became a virtual member of the board or adviser rather than a foot soldier. He had traveled to Perth with the initial push westward to help plan the eventual takeover as he was known for his pragmatic planning skills. In the process, he fell in love with the city and stayed. He bought a ground-floor apartment with a rear view of the river, complete with a parking spot where he could quickly negotiate his wheelchair in and out of the car and inside the apartment. He chose not to have artificial limbs and didn't mind his new nickname, Stumpy, because everyone had a nickname in the Apaches.

He kept in contact with the bikers and socialized with them regularly. He was content with his role and enjoyed his comfortable lifestyle. Through the club, there was no shortage of women to party with and who found sex with a legless man fun and challenging. Apaches traditionally shared their women; they had to accept that came with the territory, and for some women, that was the attraction.

Wayne Norton was contemplating going to bed after his favorite show, *Anarchy in the UK*, finished on TV when he was surprised by a knock on his door. When he opened it, he was even more surprised to see Jimmy Mallory pointing a .357 magnum pistol directly at his face. They stared at each other for a minute or so before Wayne realized he wasn't about to get shot. He shrugged and grumbled, "If you're going to shoot, shoot for fuck's sake. Or come in and have a drink with me. I don't get as many visitors as I'd like these days."

"You're alone?" Jimmy asked.

"Alone and legless. You're safe here, Jimmy."

Jimmy put his gun back into the holster under his armpit and followed the man in the wheelchair inside, closing the front door behind him. He watched Norton like a hawk to make sure he didn't grab a hidden gun from somewhere.

"Grab a seat anywhere you like. Coffee, beer, scotch? Oh, relax, Jimmy. I don't have any weapons here. The cops would love to find me with an illegal gun so they could lock me up. Even if I did, I'm not part of the war between you and the boys, though, of course, I know all about it. I have no active part in the business anymore."

"I know that, Wayne. I just wanted to talk to you; I hope you don't mind?" He sat on a chair near the dining table, back to the wall, so he could see any threat coming.

"Me, mind a gun in my face at eleven o'clock at night? Hell no, it reminds me of the old days. Plus, as I said, I don't get as many visitors as I'd like, so you're welcome here anytime. You have my word on that, and that's something I don't give lightly. What is it you think I can do for you, Jimmy?"

"It's a wise man who knows when he is beaten, Wayne, and I'm beaten. With my best friend and right-hand man, Gordy, shot today and my wife and brother both killed recently, I've realized that all I have left is a crumbling business that I don't enjoy anymore. I've had a good run, made plenty of money, and I certainly have no desire to die for it. It's got nothing to do with cowardice, you understand. I'm just drained and ready to quit. I'm offering to sign everything over to you guys."

"You'll forgive me, Jimmy, if I'm skeptical?" Norton poured two large bourbons and passed one to Jimmy.

"Yeah, I get that. But I want to finish one thing, which has nothing to do with business. I need a couple of days, and then you have my word. I will leave the state and the country, and you will never see me again having sold you all I own."

"You're assuming I have any control or influence over things, which I don't, but let's pretend for a moment that I did. The first question to ask is, why should I believe you? How do I know you aren't using the time to bring in more troops?" Wayne put a second drink on the table in front of Mallory, sipping from one himself, after Jimmy drained his.

"It's a fair question. All I can say is that I'm through, and you've won. Now, if you know anything about me at all, you would know I wouldn't admit that if I didn't mean it. I would fight back and keep fighting, but I'm done with it all. I'm proposing that we make an appointment for three days from now at your lawyer's offices. I own four bars and two clubs freehold probably worth around ten million or more on the market. I will sign them all over to any nominee you like for two million in cash, which can be my traveling money. I've got assets and funds overseas, so three days from now, I'm gone, without another shot being fired. You guys have control of my businesses, legally, for a paltry two million dollars. And I will tell the

Grave to join with the Apaches, or walk away if that is their choice. I believe they will willingly join if their safety is assured. That should show my intentions are straight. What do you think?"

Wayne nodded thoughtfully. He picked up his mobile phone and tapped it against his chin. "If I can broker this deal, here is what I know they will demand. One, you phone your managers and tell them you are out, with new owners taking over immediately. By tomorrow morning, you will tell them a representative will be with them to go over the books, etc. Two, that representative will stay in attendance until contracts are signed on Friday. Three, you are not to go anywhere near them. You can reassure them that the new owners have no intention of making any staff changes if the books are right, and if they are making money, the new owners will want to maintain the status quo. They will be owners, not operators. Of course, we want all your contacts on the importation end and the correct introductions made. Similarly, we need the distribution specifics and people on board."

"I can do that, no problem." He sipped the bourbon again.

"The other thing they will ask is why the three days? What do you intend to do that's so important?" He stared pointedly, waiting.

Jimmy knew nothing would satisfy Wayne but the truth. "All of this mess started when my brother, Des, was killed on my birthday. He was shot dead inside his own house. I made the mistake of blaming the Apaches, thinking it was a move against me. I was wrong; I regret that decision, and I'm sorry I retaliated. Then things went from bad to worse. Now it's an all-out war between us, and the cops are raiding everything in sight. It's not good for business, for me, or you, and it has to stop. I apologize to your people for making the wrong assumption when I did." He held his hands open to show openness and honesty. "I got three of yours, and you killed my wife and Gordy, and then there are all the other casualties in between. I think we're even. I leave, give you everything for some chump change money I can use for walking around until I get clear, and you can get on with business. The cops will be happy. They can scale back on the raids, and life can get back to normal. But I have to have enough time to get even with the prick that killed my brother. I know who he is. I just need to find him and make him pay."

"What if you don't find him in time?"

"I will. But if I don't, then I'm gone anyway. When I give my word to anyone, I never break it. Saturday morning, whether I've got the bastard or not, I fly out, never to return." With that, he drank the last of the alcohol in one gulp.

"Grab yourself a beer out of the fridge or another bourbon, then go in the other room and watch some TV while I make some calls. Let's see if we can't sort this out. If I can, you will ring your managers on loudspeaker while I listen in and tell them the score. Agreed?"

An hour and a half later, the deal was brokered, and officially the *War of the Roses* was ended. Jimmy called his people, including what was left of the Grave, informing. He assured them there would be no reprisals and that all staff would keep their jobs in the merger. When he left Wayne's, Jimmy felt hollow. While it was over, the battle had ended with a whimper and not a bang, which was not his usual style. But all he wanted was to get even with the cab driver and move on.

He was still wary and decided not to trust the truce completely, so he went to the Hyatt and checked in for two nights. He always kept an overnight bag with spare clothes in the boot of his car for emergencies. Once inside his room, he collapsed on the king-sized bed and slept for ten hours.

****

Meanwhile, at Mallory's house, The Renegade also slept. No one within the Apaches thought to make the call and cancel his contract. Had they done so, they would have paid him anyway; that was the rule, which was fair to both sides. But if they made the call, he could have gone back to his hotel and slept comfortably in bed rather than on the carpeted floor.

Chapter 20

Information Received

Jimmy Mallory was woken up by his mobile phone ringtone, sung by the Liverpool Football Club fans, in memory of his father. He groggily picked it up and answered, "Yeah?"

"Mr. Mallory, it's Mark Walls. I do security at the Kitty Palace. You probably don't know me, but I've worked here for about two years."

Jimmy always remembered his staff. "Yes, I remember, Mark. What do you want?"

"Well, Mr. Mallory, I just wanted to pass on my sympathies for your brother, wife, and Gordy. He was a good bloke, and he will be missed. Plus, I have a bit of information I believe will interest you, that I'm told you will pay handsomely for, regarding a certain cab driver."

Jimmy sat up straight in bed, completely awake. "Go on, I'm listening."

"One of the girls who has been here a long time just got engaged to a guy she says drives cabs at night. He saved her from being raped. He almost killed the two guys who attacked her, and they started dating. Well, it just seemed to me that maybe it's the same cabbie you were looking for: for murdering your brother, God rest his soul."

"Why would you think he's the one, Mark?"

"Well, me and her had quite a long chat, as given the chance, she doesn't shut up about him, Didi, that is. She's a nice girl, and I'm happy for her 'cos she's had it pretty tough. But just in passing, I asked her about him, the general description and the fact that he's Australian. That seemed to fit with what Gordy told me about the guy you were looking for. I thought the main reason it may be him is that it took guts for him to wade in and fight off two guys that were raping her with only a flashlight as a weapon. Mr. Mallory, I'm not saying it is him. It just seemed like a huge coincidence if it wasn't, that's all."

"I like initiative, and you're right, it's worth checking out. I've sold the club, and part of the deal is I don't go there anymore, so I can't talk to this Didi there. So here's what I'd like you to do, my son. She starts at nine tonight, I assume. I will be parked around the corner and will message you my whereabouts when I get there. Make sure you are on the door and, when she arrives, ask her to go with you to meet me and bring her to my car. I will give you a couple of grand for your trouble, and if it turns out it is the right cabbie, I will get a large bonus to you as a Christmas present. How does that sound?"

"No trouble at all, Mr. Mallory. I will bring her to you, don't you worry."

"Oh, I'm not worried, Mark; I know you won't let me down." The implied threat hung in the air until he ended the phone call and lay back in bed. He was in no hurry to leave. He had nothing but time to kill until nine o'clock that night. He fancied a swim later, and a massage to relieve the tension, but other than that, he had no other plans.

Jimmy had some thinking to do. The information from Mark was a lead, but that was all it was, and he didn't have time to spare, so he couldn't afford to put all his eggs in one basket. If it turned out the cabbie wasn't the killer, he had to accept there were hundreds of drivers working at night. Even though brave Australian ones may be rare, that probably still left twenty or thirty other possibilities, and they were not good odds so far as he was concerned. Jimmy needed to talk to his once friendly cops whom he had paid a fortune to over the years. They had all run for cover, understandably so when hostilities broke out, but it was time to make some phone calls, tell them the war was over and a truce reached. Ultimately, he was leaving. They could help him in identifying the driver, or he could send a letter to the Corruption and Crime Authority detailing payments he had made to them over the years. He had a journal in the safe at his home, and he could send copies of it if needed. He didn't like to turn on them, but nobody forced them to take the money in good times, and now he needed help in the bad. Then there was Mick Connors. He hadn't heard from him for a while. *Time to rattle his cage*, he decided.

****

Sam Collins answered a call on his cell phone while he was in the canteen around lunchtime. "Sam, it's Felix. I've had a parcel delivered you will want to come and see. The bomb squad has been and gone, giving us the all-clear after x-raying it, as the fear was it could have been dangerous by the weight of it."

"Okay, I'm intrigued. What is it?" Sam asked.

"It's a gun, and if the accompanying note is to be believed, it's the one that was used to kill your vigilante victims, including Desmond Mallory."

"I'm coming now." He leaped to his feet and took off at a run. On the way to the Organized Crime Squad offices, Sam smiled while wondering what Nick Pantella was playing at by sending the gun to Felix. It was a good thing he had taken Sam's advice to get rid of it, so it would now be tough to mount a case against him, but he wondered why he had chosen the manner he had. What on earth could the note say? He knocked on Felix's door and, without waiting for a reply, entered.

"Come in, Sam, grab a seat." Sam nodded and sat where he was directed. "Well, it looks like the Organized Crime Squad may have solved your case for you, Sam. No, no, it's okay, don't thank me." He grinned, which was rare indeed. Felix was not known for smiling at work. "Once forensics and ballistics finish with the gun and confirm things, we will know for sure, but at the moment, it seems pretty clear." He pointed at the desktop. Inside of a ziplock bag sat a gun, silencer, and magazines.

"Thanks for solving my case for me, Felix. You must let me know what exactly you did so I can once more learn from the master. What makes you think this is the weapon?"

"Obviously, you mean in addition to our superior police work ethic, dedication, and sheer brilliance?" he replied, smiling broadly.

This is spooky, Sam mused. His mood was so unlike the Felix Sam had known for years, who tended to be serious all of the time. He spoke aloud,

"Naturally, Felix, that goes without saying. So apart from the superior police work, dedication, and sheer brilliance, what leads you to believe that this is the weapon in question?"

"Well, since you ask, this is a note that came with it." He held up a single sheet of typed paper, which was slotted inside of a plastic sleeve to help preserve any fingerprints that may have been on it.

THIS GUN BELONGED TO GORDON RUSSELL. HE MADE ME KEEP IT FOR HIM, SO JIMMY NEVER SAW IT IN HIS POSSESSION. HE TOLD ME HE USED IT TO KILL JIMMY'S BROTHER SO HE COULD BE WITH HIS WIFE. HE KILLED OTHERS WITH IT FOR FUN. NOW HE IS DEAD I WANT RID OF IT SO I DON'T GET THE BLAME.

Oh my, you clever bastard, Nicky, Sam thought. *Not only has he got rid of the gun, but he's also come up with a plausible explanation and a scapegoat for the killings.* Nicky had crafted a tale that would divert attention from him so that even if Nicky were charged sometime in the future, the note would create sufficient doubt in any jury's mind, and that would be enough to stop a guilty verdict. It was a masterstroke, and Gordon Russell could hardly deny it; he was dead. Sam had to hand it to Nicky; he had done very, very well.

"What do you think, Felix? Does it sound genuine?" Sam asked, trying hard to keep the admiration from his voice.

"Well, it begs the question if it's not genuine, why send it to us? Let's workshop it a minute. Do you think it likely that Russell wanted Rebecca Mallory? We always thought her having an affair was a possibility, remember. If he did, everything else makes sense and falls into place. It's the kind of gun he would have, especially with the silencer, and from what I hear, taking potshots at thugs on the street may well be something he did for fun. It could also have been a motive to scare violent thugs from Northbridge if it was affecting trade at the Mallory-owned bars and clubs, and of course he couldn't use the weapon he has registered in his name; he wasn't *that* stupid. So, for my money, if there is any possibility he had the hots for her and ballistics match the gun to the killings, it's pretty open and shut. But of course, Sam, it's your investigation, so it's not for me to say. One thing I will say is that our illustrious commissioner will be over the moon, and you will probably be the *Golden-Haired Boy*, again, for saving his bacon."

"Well, you know me, Felix. I'm always happy to help a commissioner. Listen, when I went back and reinterviewed Rebecca after Maureen was killed, she told me that she wasn't having an affair with anyone. Further, Rebecca said that even if she wanted to, she was so scared of Des that she wouldn't have done it. She also told me that Des was extremely jealous on the night because of the attention Gordy was paying her while he was off playing pool. I believed her; she was scared shitless of her husband, so I don't think her and Russell were at it. But the note says he did it so he could *be* with her; it doesn't say they were already having an affair. Maybe he just fancied her from afar and didn't like the abuse she was getting from Des. If that were the case, he would have needed to do something on the quiet, so Jimmy didn't know. It does all click into place, doesn't it?"

Milanski nodded, watching Sam closely. He noted

his eagerness but also that Sam seemed to be looking for his validation. That wasn't like the Sam of old, who normally voiced his opinions and *damned the torpedoes*. He shrugged and nodded at Sam for him to continue. *Something is going on here,* Felix thought, but he couldn't figure out what. Some sixth sense told him Sam wasn't being entirely truthful.

"With regards to the earlier killings," Sam went on, "Gordy would be out and about at those times in Northbridge. He had a reputation for being a bit of a night owl, I've heard. It's plausible he was the vigilante and that he might have found it fun. Who can say? So I guess he had means, motive, and opportunity. With him now dead, we can't check his alibi, even if he had one."

"Hmm. Gordy had a license to carry a firearm, as does Jimmy. So Russell couldn't use his own gun as *The Vigilante*, assuming he is our man. If Russell intended to kill Des to clear the field, let's face it; with his connections, it would be easy for him to buy it illegally. He and Jimmy were as thick as thieves, and Jimmy would have been round at his place all the time, so again, it makes sense that he might find someone to hold the weapon for him until such times as he wanted to use it."

The brilliance of Pantella's plan is breathtaking, Sam thought. Nicky had sent the Glock to a superior officer in a different division, so if the note was accepted as genuine, as surely it would be, it wouldn't be left to Sam to stop the investigation. He would probably be ordered to drop the case whether he wanted to or not. Nicky would get away clean, and while Sam had spent his adult life trying to catch criminals, Pantella was one murderer he was happy to give a second chance to.

"Do you think this could help put an end to the war, Felix?" he asked.

"It will certainly help as far as Jimmy is concerned. Gordy, being gunned down in the street, must have affected him, but we can't find him to talk about it. It's a worry that he might be planning more reprisals, but my feeling is he may lose interest now. I'm going to get this down to ballistics and ask them to rush it through, then to forensics to see if we can lift any prints and DNA off it. As it was Desmond Mallory's murder that started all of this, and Gordy seems to have done it, with him dead, we can hopefully broker a deal between the two gangs and have an end to the killings. By tomorrow we should know, and you might be out of a job, Sam. But it won't be a black mark for you for not catching him, because the killer is dead."

"I can live with that. Just so long as the murders stop, I'm happy. Do you want me to do any more to help put this to bed? Reinterview Rebecca again, maybe?"

"Let me think about it, Sam. To be honest, I can't see much point. If the gun is the one that was used, then we have everything tied up neatly. Realistically, what more can she tell us that we don't already know? I think she is probably blameless herself anyway. I'm hoping that when we meet in the morning in the commissioner's office, we will have ballistics at least. Forensics could be another day or two, but so long as this is the murder weapon, I see no reason to disbelieve the note that came with it, because what other explanation is there, Sam?" He raised his eyebrows and stared pointedly, wanting to give his old partner a chance to tell him whatever it was he was keeping secret.

Sam didn't rise to the bait. "Okay, I will go back over the notes and make sure I've not missed anything. Can you give me a call as soon as you know for sure?" Sam asked.

"No problem." They shook hands, and Sam left, grinning so Felix couldn't see his glee.

After Sam closed the door, Felix couldn't shake the feeling that something was going on. He didn't know what it was, but he didn't like the feeling of secrecy from his former protégé one little bit.

****

Nicky didn't want Didi to worry, but he did want to get her away for a few days until his plan came to fruition so she would be safe. He proposed a few days down south in the forest region and argued it would be the perfect getaway for the three of them.

"Nicky, I've only just started a new job, and I can't ask for time off and leave them in the lurch. Plus, there are all sorts of things going on at work at the moment, so it's best I keep quiet for a while."

"What sort of things?" he asked suspiciously.

"I don't know, but there are rumors going around about the man who was shot on the streets yesterday. They say he was Jimmy Mallory's right-hand man, and no one knows what Mallory will do in retaliation. I've seen Gordon Russell in the club a few times, but I've never spoken to him."

Nicky knew Didi never read newspapers and didn't like the news on TV while Siobhan was awake, because it seemed it was all bad things happening in the world. Consequently, if people didn't tell her about things, she had no idea what was going on in the world, which was an almost childlike trait Nicky adored about her. "Baby, it's because of all this violence I want us to get away for a bit; let everything blow over." He grabbed her hand across the table where they were sitting having coffee. "I'm worried about you, love."

She smiled a dazzling smile at him and said, "I can't tell you how wonderful it is that you worry about me. It's a lovely feeling, and I'm still getting used to it." She fanned herself with her free hand to cool her blushing face.

"Well, that's my job, to worry about you and Siobhan. With all this stuff going on, people getting shot, firebombs and stuff, not to mention the fact that you work in one of the places owned by these bikers, I'm terrified that every time I drop you off there that it's going to be the last time that I see you."

Didi saw the concern etched into his face and suddenly felt distraught. "Oh my God. I had no idea, Nicky. Really? I'm so sorry. I don't want you to worry, but I have only just started this job, which Marty gave me as a favor. I don't want to let them down, but I don't want you to worry either."

"Baby, could you at least try? Talk to your boss; blame me even. Tell him how worried I am and that I've asked you to take just a few days off. He may understand, you never know; he may even be concerned himself."

Didi knew Nicky was not the sort of person to try to talk someone into doing something they wouldn't want to do. She nodded and said, "For you, my love, anything." She crossed to the wall phone next to the breakfast bar and sat on a stool while she dialed

Marty's phone number.

She is so gorgeous, Nicky thought, and exaggeratedly mouthed the words "*I love you,*" when she glanced back at him.

Didi smiled, then her face turned serious when she heard Marty answer. "Oh, hi, Marty. It's Didi. I'm sorry to call you, but can I talk to you about something?" After a silence, she continued, "Marty, with all of the fire-bombings and shootings going on, especially yesterday with that man being killed in the street, Nicky is seriously worried for my safety. Yes, I agree, Marty, it is nice to have someone worry for me for a change, and, let me tell you, I'm not used to that. I know it's short notice, but would it be all right if I took two or three nights off? Just so things can calm down a bit, hopefully. Pretty please?"

This time the silence was much longer as Marty was talking. Didi's face was at first seriously intent as she listened, which made Nicky worry, but then she smiled and looked relieved.

"Thanks for telling me that, Marty. That sounds good, and I will see you tonight as normal. Bye for now." She hung up the handset and turned to Nicky, with a grin on her face. "Well, I'm glad I made that call, love. It seems like all the fighting is over now. Marty is going to have a meeting with all the staff tonight to pass on information given to him by Jimmy Mallory. It seems that he has surrendered to the other gang. His best friend being killed was the straw that broke the camel's back. He has sold all his business interests to new owners and is leaving the state in a couple of days. The war is over as of last night."

"Really? Wow, what will that mean for you and the

other staff?"

"Well, Marty says no one is losing their jobs. The club is making good money, so the new owners want him to stay on as manager. One of them is there now going over things with him. So there is no need to worry about me anymore, Nicky, but I still loved the fact that you did."

She stood, seductively, and walked to him and sat on his lap; legs astride his thighs, facing him. She placed her hands on his shoulders. He hardened immediately as she softly ground herself against him. "I really do love that you worry about me, Nicky. You deserve a reward for that."

She kissed him deeply, and his hands went to her sides, slowly lifting her T-shirt so he could feel her bare skin, which never failed to excite him. His thumbs rested on the sides of her bra as they kissed. He then brought them around to cup her breasts in his palms. Then they traced their way down and underneath her bottom while standing up at the same time.

Nicky carried her like that, with her legs wrapped around him and her hands on his shoulders. They kissed each other through to the bedroom, where he kicked the door closed behind him. She slid her legs back down to the floor so he could undress her. Nicky took his time, kissing every piece of skin he uncovered. There was no hurry; they had all the time in the world.

Chapter 21

Come into my Parlor

Sam answered his phone later in the day when he saw Felix's name on the display. He was very keen to hear the latest. "Hi, Boss," he answered laconically, trying to hide his enthusiasm.

"I'm not your boss, so stop calling me that. However, if I were, I'd make you get a haircut, you longhaired, layabout hotshot."

Sam realized for Felix to mention his hair, he must indeed be overdue for a trim; he had been so busy it had slipped his mind. He smiled at Felix's observational skills; they had not dimmed in the time since they had worked together. Sam knew there wasn't much that escaped his eagle eye. "If you've got some good news for me," he said, "I will be able to find time for a haircut. Come to think of it; I might even be able to have some time to make love to my girlfriend. She's been missing it, Felix, with me working so much overtime." Sam knew the jibe would rile Felix, who was notoriously straitlaced. Sam never missed an opportunity to mess with him.

"A bit of abstinence might do you some good, lad. Talking of sex, how is your mate, Dave Barndon these days?" Dave was the man who had been at the center of the sex and murder case that became known as the

Domin8 case.

Sam remembered at the time Felix couldn't understand how a married fifty-year-old car dealer could have had so many affairs with women he met from the internet. Felix had wavered between dismay, anger, shock, horror, and disgust at his exploits.

"Dave is doing all right. I saw him about a month ago. He and Shannon seem happy together now, but it was touch and go for a while. His health will never be the same again; his nerves are not the best, and he lost the sight of one eye."

"I didn't know he lost the eye. I thought they saved it with only partial vision loss?"

"So did the doctors at the time, but he woke up one morning blind when the retina detached, and the specialist couldn't save it. So, Felix, what's the news?"

"Well, it's interesting, Sam. We're hearing from different sources that Jimmy has surrendered to the Apaches and is leaving town in three days. The war is over; it seems. Once he lost his mate Gordy, he apparently realized he was screwed and now wants to escape with his life. He has agreed to sell them his businesses and is leaving our shores, never to return, if he can be believed. The bastard has probably got enough money to laze on the beach at the Costa del Sol for the rest of his life, while the rest of us slave away." The bitterness in his voice was obvious to Sam.

"Hmmm. That's good, I guess, but troubling, too. Why three days, Felix? If he wanted to quit, why wouldn't he just leave? Sounds odd to me."

"You see? There you go again. I come up with a perfectly good scenario which everyone is happy with, everyone but you. What is it with you picking holes in my cases?"

Sam could tell Felix wasn't angry; he was interested but kidding along, and his mood was far too jovial. He was the most honest cop Sam had ever known, so possibly, it meant Felix had doubts too. "Look, if it's over, I'm delighted. I just wonder why three days? What does he expect to do in that time, why not run immediately? And also, why would the Apaches agree to that? He must have a good enough reason for them to accept it. Forgive me, Felix, but it just doesn't sound right." As he asked the questions, the answer became crystal clear, but he dare not say a word for fear Felix may see through his deception. Mallory obviously wanted the time to catch up with and kill the man who shot his brother, and he thought three days were enough, which also meant he must have a good idea who did it.

"Well, for a start," Felix answered, slowly, as if he hadn't realized the implication before, "if he is selling his business interests, contracts need to be drawn up. You can't do that sort of stuff at the drop of a hat. Plus, I suppose he has other things to get done if he is never coming back. He's not returning calls, is not at any of his businesses, and he's not been to his house. He could be on that boat of his for all I know."

"What boat's that?"

"Big thing called *The Intrepid*. He keeps it at the marina in Nedlands. Anyway, let's talk about your case. Ballistics have matched the gun, and there is no doubt this is the weapon used in all the vigilante killings."

"Great news, though I'm out of a job. Any fingerprints?"

"Nothing. They think it's been washed in bleach. I

wonder how Russell knew to do that. It's been so thoroughly cleaned you can bet there won't be any DNA. As it stands right now, as far as I am concerned, the case is closed, and I'm sure the commissioner will agree with that assessment tomorrow morning. He won't want you to do your usual trick of coming up with reasons to keep a case open when everyone else wants it closed, Sam. We need to stay on high alert until we know Mallory has left the city, but assuming he does, it's all finished. We will keep chipping away at the individuals who performed the actual murders, but as we all know, unless people talk, which they won't, it's doubtful we will make any further arrests."

"Maybe sometime down the track, you can get one of them to roll on the others to save his neck on something else, you never know. Can you get Mallory for anything before he does a runner?" Sam asked.

"You mean we do an Al Capone on him for tax fraud? I doubt it. At least we didn't have any innocent fatalities, just a couple of minor woundings, and scumbags killing other scumbags. It could have been a lot worse. Fancy a beer on your way home?"

Usually, Sam would have agreed without hesitation, but he had to try to get in touch with Nick Pantella and warn him. *That shouldn't take too long*, he thought. "Well, I was going to get my hair cut, but you talked me out of it: you smooth talker. See you there in a while."

After he hung up, he looked up Nicky's number and dialed it, but the call went unanswered and switched through to his message bank. "Nick, it's Sam. Hats off to you. Your plan has worked beautifully; the case is closed now. That person we spoke about is leaving town soon but says he has a job to do before he leaves, and I'm worried about what that might be, so you must be very, very careful. I hope you've taken my advice and gone away for a while. Ring me when you get a chance, please, so we can talk about it."

That's that, Sam mused. There wasn't too much more he could do. He could hardly put Nick Pantella into protective custody, and with Jimmy Mallory leaving, Pantella should be able to watch himself for a couple of days. If not, as harsh as it sounded, Sam decided Pantella had made his bed, and now he had to lie in it. Sam stood up and left the office to go and have a much-needed beer with his old boss.

****

Mick Connors called Jimmy Mallory, wondering if because of everything that had happened, he would answer, but he did.

"Mick, old son, I was just thinking about you and wondering why you hadn't come through for me. I worried I might not have paid you enough over the years."

"Mr. Mallory, sir, how can you possibly think that? I will always be indebted to you. The fact is I only found something out late yesterday, but when I heard about poor Gordy, I thought you might not be in the mood to take a call from me. Then, today, the place has been all of a flap. Even my lunch break got canceled, and I've only snuck out now to call you, so I'm hoping they won't notice I'm gone. They've asked me to work back late tonight too, so I'm doing my best, honestly, Mr. Mallory."

"All right, all right. Calm down, Mickey boy, I'm just pulling your leg. Now, what have you got for me?"

Jimmy asked.

"His name is Nicholas Pantella and lives at 18 Deveraux Street in South Perth. But, Mr. Mallory, the senior investigator reinterviewed him and has noted that he is satisfied he is not a witness to anything that could be helpful. He also has alibis for two of the previous vigilante murders, so the feeling is that he is not the killer, nor would he be a decent witness."

"Is that so, Mick, is that so?" Mallory said thoughtfully. *What the hell does that mean? It all made perfect sense before, but now the cops are discounting him. Maybe he is a terrific liar,* he wondered. *There's something to think about there. Would he be such a good liar with a gun in his mouth?* That was the question Jimmy pondered. He still had the planned meeting with this cabbie's girlfriend later. He would question her closely, very closely maybe even have some fun with her. "You may have heard I'm selling up and leaving town, Mick, and that's true I am, but I'm here until Saturday. I will send you a little Christmas present before I head off. Of course, if you see anything else before then, let me know, and it will be a much bigger gift under the tree for you. Get my drift, old son?"

"Thanks, Mr. Mallory, sir. I'm sure going to miss you."

****

Dinner had been fun, as usual. They ate Siobhan's favorite meal: fish fingers, canned spaghetti, which she called sketty, and fried eggs. The five talked happily, kidding around before discussing possible locations for the upcoming wedding ceremony. The reception was a given, so far as Nicky was concerned. It would be at

Allan Chan's, as he couldn't bear the thought of breaking Allan's heart by having it elsewhere.

Once dinner was finished, Nicky, as had become his habit, did the dishes and tidied the kitchen while Didi bathed Siobhan. When he glanced at his phone, Nicky noticed a missed call from Sam Collins and listened to the request to call him back. He chose to do that after he dropped Didi off at work because he didn't want her to overhear, and he had a story to read his *princess*. He'd found a beautifully bound compendium of William the Bear stories earlier in the week, and he read a second one involving bees, honey, and a pesky rabbit to the giggling delight of Siobhan at her bedtime. Didi took up her usual spot, leaning against the doorframe, smiling contentedly, and laughing along.

Once Nicky finished reading the story, he said good night to Siobhan and kissed her forehead. She reached up her arms to hug him and whispered that she loved him; he smiled and whispered he loved her too. Then they left, turning the light off, and as always, Didi threw her arms around him in the passage and hugged him tightly.

****

They met at the bar they had gone to for years, but it had recently changed its format to having skimpily clad barmaids in an attempt to boost their flagging customer base. This change was much to Felix's disgust and Sam's delight, who had never objected to looking at attractive women showing off their bodies. It seemed to Sam that trade had lifted considerably, and the bar was busy, which made it difficult to hear each other speak. That only served to annoy Felix more.

They didn't have a lot to talk over that hadn't been

discussed on the phone earlier, and with sexy-looking bar staff wearing next to nothing, Sam found himself easily distracted. His love life was waning, and he felt it was time to break up with his current girlfriend, who was too *clingy* for him. Sam rarely stayed with one for too long, though he acknowledged it was probably because he hadn't yet met the right one. He had married a childhood sweetheart in his younger days and was in no hurry to repeat his mistake. As he was fond of saying to Felix, he was always on the lookout for a new ex-girlfriend.

Felix's phone buzzed and vibrated on the bar top, and he snatched it up, disgusted with his younger companion. He thought it was high time Sam settled down. The display showed the number was withheld, and he covered up one ear while trying to listen with the other. "Milanski," he barked, using his gruffest voice.

He suddenly sat bolt upright as he heard the voice announce, "Jimmy Mallory, returning your call."

"Hang on a second; it's too noisy in here. Let me go outside," he replied, then barged his way through the crowd of people ogling the barmaids.

Once he reached a quiet spot, Felix said, "Thanks for returning the call, Mr. Mallory. We have some news about the killer of your brother and wondered if you'd like to pop into the station or let me know where and when we can catch up with you so that we can have a chat about it."

"I won't have time for that shit. I'm leaving town and have a million things to do. Why can't we do it on the phone?"

Felix closed his eyes and shook his head. Mallory

was one arrogant son of a bitch whom he would love to slap some manners into. "Well, the fact is that we have recovered the weapon used and now know who shot your brother, but we don't give out that sort of information over the phone."

"Look, you rang me and asked me to return the call, and that I've done, as busy as I am. So if you don't want to talk to me, why ask me to ring back?"

"There is no need for that attitude, Mr. Mallory. As I've explained, we don't give out the names of murder suspects over the phone, but if you'd like to make an appointment at any time and place that suits you, I'd be happy to pass on the information I have."

"Well, it ain't gonna happen, so if that's all. I'll be going."

Felix had held his temper long enough. "Look, you lowlife piece of shit, who do you think you're talking to? For your information, the killer is someone you know very fucking well. Now, if you don't care who shot dead your brother, well, then that reinforces what we all think of you."

"I already know who did it." His voice oozed menace, and Felix suddenly understood how Mallory could instill fear in people. "I promise you he will be dead by midnight," he continued, "now leave me alone and fuck off."

Before Felix could respond, the phone went dead, and it took Felix three minutes to calm down enough to go back inside the bar to finish his beer. His mood was black, and he decided he was going to go home to his wife and leave Sam to stare at the almost nude women. He reentered the noisy bar, tilted his head close to Sam's, and said, "That was Mallory on the phone. He won't meet up for a talk about who we believe murdered his brother and got abusive, so I lost my temper and told him to fuck off."

"Really? Well, good for you. What did he say to that?"

"He told me he already knew who killed his brother and that the culprit would be dead by midnight. Then he hung up on me, the bastard."

Sam stared back at Felix, wondering what that meant. He suddenly realized it could only mean Mallory had discovered Nick Pantella was the killer and was going to get his revenge. *Shit. What can I do without giving the game away?* he asked himself, and the idea came to him immediately. He hated himself for it, but he had to get Felix to help without telling him why.

"Shame you didn't tell him it was his best mate, Gordy, who did the deed. Here's what I reckon, Felix. I think Mallory believes the taxi driver shot Des, and he is going to grab him tonight." Sam slapped the bar top for emphasis. "That's why he wanted three days; so he could track down Nick Pantella and murder him."

"Why would he think that, Sam?" Felix asked, a wary glint in his gaze.

"Who else would he think it was? It's the only person that would make sense. He would have enough cops on the take to feed him information, and we've interviewed the driver twice. That alone might make him stick out, especially if he knew about the same gun used for *the Vigilante* killings. We have to do something, Felix."

"Really, what do you think we ought to do, bearing in mind it's now after seven o'clock?"

"Well, I tried to phone him just before I came here, and he didn't answer. I'm going to check out the cabbie's house and try to find him, but if that's not successful, where would Jimmy take Pantella if he did grab him?"

Felix shook his head, seemingly deep in thought. "We're told he is forbidden to go to any of his businesses; that's part of the deal with the Apaches. So there are only two options I can think of: one, his house, and two, his boat. If you're right, he could dump the body at sea, so the boat is a strong possibility. It's more likely the house, though, because if he left it empty, the body could stay there forever. So long as he pays the bills, no one is going to enter it. But I can't get a stakeout authorized this late, let alone a search warrant without evidence."

"Well, there's only one thing for it. We have to do it ourselves. Do you want to stake out the house or the boat, Boss?"

Chapter 22

Endgame

The Renegade believed he possessed eternal patience under normal circumstances, but he was bored beyond belief. He decided enough was enough, and it was time to move. Winterbourne knew that meant coming back to the house later, but for now, he had to do something or go mad. He had cleaned the Walther and reassembled it twice, the second time with his eyes closed, and was too bored to do it for the third time. His phone was dead, and he had cursed himself repeatedly for not bringing a charger with him. Sitting in the upstairs hallway was like being in prison, without the obligatory hour for exercise.

He had discovered the utility hole for the ceiling had a pull-down ladder, so leaving and coming back later the same way presented no problem. *Perhaps*, he thought, *I could go back to the hotel, have a shower and a decent meal, bring my phone back to life, and come back later tonight.* He would bring his charger next time so that the phone wouldn't die again. He had several strategic and thought-provoking games downloaded, which helped pass the time and keep his mind active, but to play them, he needed power.

There was a possibility he could miss Mallory, but it was almost eight, and he intended to return by eleven at the latest, so if Mallory did come back, there was every chance he would stay for the night and still be in attendance when Winterbourne returned. Either way, he could not sit around any longer. The only potential problem he could see was the hole he had kicked in the ceiling, which was obvious there had been an intruder if Mallory saw it. Jimmy was no idiot, but, Michael reasoned, there was minimal risk, as the master bedroom was on the ground floor, so he would have no reason venture upstairs assuming he was alone. The risk was acceptable and worth taking to save his sanity, The Renegade decided, and with that, he gathered up his things. He left the bags of food and drinks that were leftover in the roof space and climbed back onto the roof, carrying only the rifle case.

He decided to take the rifle with him because if Mallory was in attendance when he returned, he could set up the hit from one of the trees, which had excellent views through the main windows. If he were offered a clean shot, it would save the problem of getting back inside the house without being heard, so it seemed to be the right decision.

Once the roof tiles were secured back in place, he climbed down onto the garage roof, then onto the ground, careful not to make any noise. He reached the end of the driveway when a man stepped out from behind a tree with a gun pointed at him. "Well, well, well, what do we have here?" he asked, showing a wry smile, his tall frame highlighted by the streetlamp behind him.

Without hesitation, The Renegade threw the rifle case at the stranger, hoping he would flinch, which would gain enough time to draw his pistol. While the case was in the air, The Renegade reached for the Walther; he knew he had to kill the interferer who had the unmistakable look of a policeman.

In the thirty years Felix Milanski had been on the job, he had arrested hundreds of criminals in many different situations, but he had never shot anyone. On ten previous occasions, an offender had thrown something to put Felix off balance and gain enough time to run away. Sometimes, the ruse worked, human reflexes being what they were, but not this time. The rifle case was heavy and unwieldy, an awkward item to throw with any pace or accuracy. It would have hit Felix's chest had he not seen it coming and calmly stepped to his left-hand side. The case missed him and clattered on the driveway safely, while Felix's gun didn't waver.

Felix thought he was dealing with a burglar, not an assassin, so he said, "Don't be stupid. You're under arrest," when he saw the unmistakable movement the man made to reach under his jacket to his left armpit. Felix knew that could only mean one thing, but his shocked brain couldn't accept he was about to be in a gunfight, which delayed him from pulling the trigger for a split second, though that was enough. In his younger, fitter, more agile, and alert days, Felix would have got off a shot quicker, but he couldn't believe what was happening; *the burglar is reaching for a gun!* His brain shouted.

He had trained for such scenarios at the police firing range, but this was real life, and in an instant, he realized he had to shoot or be shot himself. The Renegade had practiced to draw, aim, and fire a thousand times and was quick, especially against someone who wasn't expecting it. Within moments the gun was in his hand, outside his jacket, swinging through its arc to find its target. Unlike Felix, he would not hesitate to pull the trigger.

For Felix, time slowed down as if he were in a dream state. He could not mentally process what was happening. By the time his brain sent the signal to his trigger finger, both guns had fired at the same time.

****

Nicky Pantella kissed Didi passionately and lovingly in the front seat of the cab. He had parked on the opposite side of the road from the Kitty Palace, but thirty meters away. The rain had stopped, but the cold made the windows fog up from their collective excessive body heat.

"You're getting me all worked up, and I have to go to work," Didi said breathlessly.

"Same here," he replied, feeling his erection throbbing. "We could always go to my place, and both be late for work, for an hour."

She looked into his eyes, seeing the love and desire there for her, and asked, "Will you always want me like you do right now, Nicky?"

"Even when you're ninety." And they both giggled at that mental image.

"I've never been as happy as I am right now, Nicky, with you in my life. Please never leave me."

"I'm never leaving you, Didi. Don't you know that by now?"

She smiled nervously. "I know you love me, but sometimes I think that I don't deserve to be this happy. And then I worry that such happiness can't last. It never has. Not for me, anyway."

313

He hugged her tightly, trying to dispel her fears by sheer willpower. "We have all the time in the world, babe, and I'm never leaving you unless I'm in a pine box. Even then, I will come back and haunt you from the grave."

She wiped the tear from her eye and hugged him back before pulling away and staring at him. "If you died, Nicky, so would I. I couldn't live without you in my life. I better go. See you at four, lover." She tried to smile but couldn't. For some reason she couldn't put her finger on, she felt incredibly sad.

"I'll be here, babe, with a coffee. Hey, I was thinking, how about we go back to the beach tonight and watch the sun come up? Maybe even skinny-dip again?"

"Oh my God, Nicky, I love you so much it hurts. That's a great idea, but don't you think it will be too cold?" With that, she opened the door and stepped out in one practiced, fluid motion, ready to face a night of leering drunken men asking her for a blow job or at the very least a date when she finished work.

Nicky watched her walk down the street then cross the road when a break came in the traffic. It was a busy night in town, even though the weather wasn't perfect. Lots and lots of people were out for dinner, drinks, or the veiled promise of a hookup that lured them into the city. As she crossed the road, her tiny skirt lifted momentarily in the breeze to show him her leg almost to her panties, and he smiled to himself, still not believing his luck to have snared such a beautiful woman who adored him back.

Time to make that call to Sam Collins, he thought and absentmindedly tapped on the return phone number displayed on the screen and waited for it to answer. He had now lost sight of her and patiently listened to the rings on the phone before it answered, "Sam Collins."

"Nicky Pantella. Sorry, it took a while to get back to you. I didn't want Didi overhearing our conversation, for obvious reasons."

"That's okay; I'm glad you are both safe. Look, something's come up, and you need to be very—and Nick, I do mean very—careful, for the next two days. Your plan has worked a treat; the police heat is off of you to the point where I think the case will be officially closed tomorrow morning. So you are home free, but, and this is a big but. Are you listening?"

"I'm here. All ears."

"Jimmy Mallory has told a senior officer, the one you sent the gun to, in fact, that the killer of his brother will be dead before midnight tonight. He wouldn't accept that we knew who the killer was and that it was someone close to him. He must know something or thinks he knows something, and you need to watch your step, bud. As we speak, his house is being staked out by a colleague, and I'm on my way to his boat, unofficially, of course, as really, we don't have any reason to do it through channels."

"His boat? Why there?"

"He's agreed to peace with the Apaches and promised to sell all of his business interests to them. Part of the deal is he cannot go near the bars and clubs, so that only leaves his house and his boat if he were to grab you and take you somewhere to kill you."

"Me? How can he know anything about me?"

"Maybe he doesn't. We don't know anything for sure, but if he has informers in the department, it wouldn't be difficult to find out that you were interviewed as the last person to see Desmond Mallory alive. He may also know the same gun was used in earlier killings, so he may have connected the dots. When he spoke to my colleague, he sounded pretty sure of himself. That's the same colleague who is staking out his house, by the way. My advice to you is grab your girl and get out of dodge now and don't come back till I tell you that you can, which will likely be next week."

"Fuck it. Okay, I will. I just dropped Didi off at work at the Kitty Palace. I will go in and get her out."

"You're kidding me? She works at the *Kitty Palace?* The same Palace that is owned by Jimmy Mallory, are you for real?"

"Oh my God, I didn't think. I'm going to go get her now." Not waiting for a response, he hung up the call and jumped out of the car, locking it by remote as he dashed across the street, terrified for the first time in his life. He ran all the way, in through the doorway and up the narrow stairs to the glass cubicle containing one of the girls selling entry tickets.

"Fifteen dollars, thanks; you're lucky, the first show starts in ten," she said with a bored tone in her voice.

"I'm here to see Didi. I'm her fiancé. There's a family emergency I need to tell her about. Can you please get her for me?"

"Didi, so you're the one, are you?" She looked him up and down, as if liking what she saw and thinking that she could have gone for him herself.

"She's not turned up yet. You can wait for her if you like. It's not like her to be late, so I don't think she will be too far away."

"No, you're mistaken. I just dropped Didi off just down the street. Please check for me." His voice was starting to fray, nerves rattled. This could not be happening, he thought.

"Look, man, you might be her fiancé, and you may have dropped her off down the street, but I've been on the door since eight thirty, and I'm telling you she hasn't come up these stairs. Maybe she decided to grab a coffee before work. If you don't believe me, check with Mark. He's the security guy on the door downstairs. He will tell you."

He looked at her blankly. "There was no guard on the door downstairs."

"Well, there was. Maybe the pair of them have gone off for a coffee together before Didi's shift starts."

Nicky's skin crawled with fear, and without another word, he dashed back down the stairs. He stopped suddenly when he saw the back of a security guard standing there. The man had most definitely not been there before.

"Where's Didi?" Nicky demanded without any preamble.

The man, who was a lot bigger and burlier than Nicky, turned and took up a wary stance. He was used to drunken freaks who wanted to hassle the girls, but he thought it was a bit early in the night for trouble.

"Who wants to know?" His eyes seemed furtive, looking from side to side, assessing the perceived threat, but Nicky thought he also looked guilty.

"I'm her fiancé. I just dropped her off down the street, and the girl up there tells me she didn't arrive. There's a family emergency I need to talk to her about."

Nicky saw the guy's eyes light up, and with a sinking heart, he knew that this man knew not only where Didi was but who Nicky was and who would want them both.

The guard's mind raced as dollar signs flashed in his brain. What might it be worth to Jimmy for him to hand over the very man he wanted to use Didi to draw out? The night could be very profitable, indeed.

"The big boss wanted her to work at one of the other clubs tonight and took her away, but he didn't tell me which one. Want me to call him and ask?"

So this is how it ends, Nicky thought with a plummeting heart. *No, not if I can help it; it won't.* Nicky had no choice. He had to save Didi, and he knew he could possibly die trying. But the one thing Nicky was sure of was that she was worth dying for. His mind raced; was there any other way he could save her that didn't involve him capitulating? No, there wasn't that he could see. The only hope he could see would be to bargain for her life with his own.

"Yeah, give him a call. Tell him I need to see Didi. I'm Nick."

The guard took out his mobile phone while warily watching Nicky; he called Jimmy's mobile number.

****

"Yeah," Jimmy Mallory answered, as the Bluetooth in the BMW showed who the call was from.

"Boss, it's Mark again. I have Didi's fiancé here asking after her. He says it's a family emergency and needs to see her."

Well, now, Jimmy thought, *that's a bit of luck and will save me a whole heap of time.*

"Mark, he's the cab driver, yes?"

"Yes, Boss."

"Put him on."

Mark handed the phone to Nicky, smirking. "Speak," Jimmy demanded as if he were talking to a dog.

"You've got my fiancée, Didi, and I want her back."

"Who the fuck do you think you're talking to?"

"I'm talking to a man who I will spend the rest of my life hunting down to kill if he doesn't let Didi go. End of story."

"So you're the one who killed my brother?"

"No, but I am the one who will kill you if you harm her."

Just for a moment, Jimmy wavered. That hadn't been the response he was expecting. The guy sounded cold and full of bravado when he should be scared. *He said he didn't kill Des, and the cop told me it was someone close to me. Could that be true?* He wondered. Maureen told him that Rebecca had said the cab driver wasn't scared of Des when he got angry. She was right; this guy didn't sound afraid at all. Was it possible the cops had been telling the truth when they had said that the killer was someone he knew? He had no choice. He had to proceed as if this was the guy. After all, what would it matter if he wasn't?

"You're lying, and all that's going to get you is your girlfriend killed, very, very slowly, after I fuck her a couple of times."

Nicky knew that the type of man Mallory was, there was only one thing he might respect; someone as tough as he was. Nicky dared not show his fear, no matter what. "Listen to me, you lowlife. I lost everything worth living for a long time ago. Until she came along, I had nothing. Now she is the one good thing in my miserable life. If you touch her, no matter where you go, what you do, or how well you hide, I will find you. You will spend the rest of your life looking over your shoulder, and one day, I promise you, I will be there."

"Oh, for fuck's sake. Stop with the amateur dramatics. What movies have you been watching? Just stop it now, you fuckwit, and listen to me. I've been threatened and attacked by better men than you before I've had my breakfast on three days out of seven. I'm not scared of them, and I'm not scared of you now, so grow up. You might have killed some defenseless men by shooting them; yes, I know you are *The Vigilante,* too, so don't bother denying it. But I've killed far more men with my bare hands than you've had fares in a month. Don't be thinking I would be scared by some fucking taxi driver, so save your breath. I've stared bikers down who don't give a shit about life, and they fear me. Are you ready to talk sensibly now, or shall I hang up and have some fun with your girl?"

Nicky sighed, knowing all was lost. "Let her go, and you can do what you like to me." Internally, Nicky was becoming more and more flustered; his nerves were frayed paper thin. He had to save Didi any way he could.

"Listen, sonny, whether I let her go or not is up to you. I tell you what. I will give you a sporting chance, and that's more than you gave my brother."

"Your brother was a scumbag who liked to beat up women, and he deserved all he got."

"So you admit it, then? You did kill him?"

"If you let Didi go, you can have me, and I'll tell you whatever you want to know."

"I already told you, old son. I will give her and you a sporting chance. Here's the deal. You get one only opportunity, okay?"

"I'm listening."

"You know the Yacht Squadron Marina in Nedlands?"

"Yeah, that's where I keep my boat, too."

"Keep joking, smartass. I can hear your girlfriend moving around in the boot of my car. Maybe she will enjoy your jokes, too. Should I let her out and ask her?"

"Yes, I know the Flying Yacht Squadron in Nedlands. I'm a cab driver, for fuck's sake, and it's my job to know where rich wankers like you keep their boats. Go on."

"Oh, I like you. We're going to have some fun tonight, Nicky boy. When you enter the car park, go to the far right-hand side and through the gate marked F, which is one of the walkways to the boats. It will be propped open for you. Be a love and close it after you, won't you? My boat is *The Intrepid*; it's the tenth one along on the right-hand side. You won't miss it; it's the biggest. Your girlfriend and I will be having cocktails on the flybridge; she may or may not have her clothes on, depending on how long you take to get there. I will have a clear view of your arrival, and of course, I can make sure you're not followed too. Now, let's see. I will be there in around ten minutes. You should be there within twenty-five. If you get delayed by, oh, I don't know, the police maybe? I will throw the ropes and go shark fishing, using bits of your girlfriend for bait. Are we clear?"

"I understand." Nicky ended the call and then deliberately dropped the phone on the ground. As the security guard bent to pick it up angrily, Nicky brought his knee up into the guard's face, hard. It was the perfect shot; it broke his nose and rendered him unconscious. The big man fell like a stone to the ground, spraying blood.

Nicky sprinted back to the cab, dialing Sam's number on the way.

****

The man known as The Renegade was bleeding badly and knew he was in trouble. His left arm hung uselessly; the bullet had shattered the bone in his upper arm. His only consolation was that the cop wasn't moving, so he was probably dead. He knew he didn't have long; the sound of the gunshots would bring the neighbors out, for sure, so he had to move. It was probably only the steady rain that had started ten minutes before that obscured him from people looking through windows.

He put his gun back in his holster, limped over to the cop, and looked down at him. His chest was a mass of blood. There was no way he could survive such a wound, and The Renegade's need was greater. He knelt and undid Felix's belt. With a series of yanks, he pulled it through the pants loops until it was free, and the cop groaned as he moved. *So he isn't yet dead,* The Renegade thought. He slapped the groaning man's face a couple of times.

"Where can I find Mallory? Tell me that, and I will call you an ambulance." That was a lie, but if everything was to end, and it looked like it would now, it would at least end with the job completed, and his reputation would stay untarnished. So long as he finished the hit they had paid him for, the Apache hierarchy would use their best endeavors and lawyers to get him out on bail if he was arrested. After that, he would leave this rotten, unlucky country, never to return. He slapped the cop's face another couple of times and watched his eyes flutter open.

"Why?" he moaned.

"I'm going to kill Mallory. Now, where do I find him, old man?"

"The boat…Nedlands, Flying Yacht Squadron. He's there." With that, his eyes closed.

The Renegade stood and looked around. He saw house lights had switched on all up and down the street and knew if he was going, he had to go immediately. He wrapped the belt around his arm two or three times using his teeth to help pull it tight as a tourniquet, then ran over to the gun case, trying not to jar his wounded arm, picked it up, and half ran, half walked, away.

By the time he got back to his car, the shock had worn off and the pain set in, but he could not afford the luxury of giving in to it. He had not become one of America's highest-paid assassins because he gave up. He spent a few minutes getting the belt adjusted just right, and the blood flow stopped adequately, and then he tucked his useless hand inside his jacket pocket so it didn't move when he did and bring more pain. The Renegade started the car and programmed the marina into his phone GPS, thanking his lucky stars that he had rented an automatic car. He wiped the sweat from his eyes, gritted his teeth, and pulled away from the car park, heading toward Nedlands and finally, Jimmy Mallory.

Stephen B King

****

"Sam, it's Nicky," he said as he ran. "Mallory has Didi, and he is taking her to the boat. I'm going now; he says he will shoot her if I call the cops. You mustn't interfere. It's me he wants, and he can have me as soon as I get her clear."

"Nick, don't be stupid. He won't let either of you go. You know that."

"I don't care for myself, only her. She deserves better. I have to try; please don't interfere." Before Sam could say another word, he hung up as he reached the cab.

Nicky gunned the engine, yanked the gear shift, and floored the accelerator. The car lurched and swerved into the traffic and clipped the car parked in front of him. He overcorrected and hit another vehicle on the other side of the road. But it was as if he didn't realize what he'd done, or if he did, he didn't care. His tires screeched for purchase as he sped away, heading out of Northbridge toward Didi: the only woman in the entire world who mattered.

****

Sam tried to call Felix, but it rang out without answer and went to his message service. He groaned but didn't leave one. It was clear Sam was on his own. He scanned the marina from side to side. At that time of night, the gates were all closed, and without an electronic access card, he wasn't getting into the boat pen area that way. Sam had hoped to get to the boat before Jimmy arrived and have the element of surprise, and thanks to Nicky's phone call, he had to assume he had been successful.

The rain had reduced to a drizzle, but it was still a

cold night, and the breeze was stiff. Sam looked around and tried to decide what to do. The fencing was tall and had strands of razor wire protecting the boats from people climbing over, so that was out. He ran to the fence and looked across the marina to where he could see the outline of *The Intrepid* in the distance, and then he had an idea.

He raced back to his car and from the glove box took a plastic ziplock evidence bag and put his gun inside it. Then as an afterthought, Sam turned the volume off on his mobile phone and tucked that inside too. It would need protection from the water, and he could ill afford for Felix to return his call at just the wrong time. Sam knew he had to hurry because he didn't know how long he had before Mallory would arrive. He started the car, drove to the parklands alongside the marina, and stopped close to the riverbank. Sam stripped off his jacket, shoes, and pants, tossing them inside the car. Then, clutching the evidence bag, he ran across the grass to the edge of the Swan River and walked into the water.

It had not been a warm day, and the water was cold as it seeped through, instantly chilling him to the bone. Undeterred, he kept going, wading through what felt like a combination of sludge, sand, and weeds until it was too deep to walk. He dived forward, being very careful not to drop the bag containing the gun, and the coldness took his breath away.

Sam swam slowly out into the river beyond the fence line and rock breakwater. He was aiming for the shape of *The Intrepid*, four hundred meters away, swimming slowly as the cold gnawed away at his strength, his spirit, and his soul. He was barely a hundred meters away when he saw the deck lights go on *The Intrepid* and realized with a sinking heart he was too late to get to the boat ahead of Mallory. He trod water, shivering as he tried to think of an alternate plan.

Sam Collins, for all of his physical fitness, was not a great swimmer. That and the coldness of a dark unfriendly river and insistent current were stealing his energy slowly and relentlessly. He suddenly felt incredibly tired and realized he needed to move while he still could. As quietly as possible, the plastic bag clenched between his chattering teeth, he aimed for a boat, one pen closer to shore using his breaststroke. Agonizingly slowly, Sam worked his way toward the nearest vessel, which seemed to take forever. The current was not helping his cause as it relentlessly tugged him backward. *The tide must be going out,* he thought, *just my luck. Why couldn't it be coming in and help me?*

Exhausted and cold, Sam made it to the rear of the boat, put his gun on top of the marlin board, and stopped to get his breath back. With shivering, trembling fingers, he undid the clasp to lower the ladder into the water as he did not have the strength to climb up unaided. Praying it wouldn't squeak and give his position away, Sam slowly lowered the ladder until it was in place. He knew it would be a mistake to rush and make too much noise, so one millimeter at a time, he climbed onto the marlin board and lay across the stern of the boat.

God, I'm so fucking cold, he thought. He couldn't remember ever being so chilled in his life and had to struggle not to let his teeth chatter. Out of the water, he took his socks off and let them float away. Nothing said policeman approaching like squelching socks on a fiberglass deck, he thought. He had to stifle a laugh at the humor of the situation, even as cold as he was. He wished for a towel or something to dry himself with, but a quick scan of the boat deck showed no such luxury visible. *Perhaps you'd like an electric heater, too?* He wondered, then told himself to stop being a girl and get on with it.

He took the gun and his phone out of the plastic bag, looked at it in the moonlight, and clicked off the safety. Reaching over the door on the stern of the boat, which led out onto the marlin board, he undid the bolt latch, again hoping for non-squeaky hinges, and opened it outward.

He was two boats away from Jimmy Mallory's *Intrepid*. They were arranged two craft to each pen, with a walkway between Mallory's and the vessel alongside the one Sam was on. With a sinking heart, Sam realized his mistake; he had changed course and chosen a boat that was closer to shore. Jimmy would be looking toward the gate, waiting for Nicky to arrive and make sure he hadn't been followed. He would be on high alert, meaning Sam dare not move until Nicky came to provide a distraction, but even then, if Sam stood up, he would be seen quickly, as Mallory would be facing his way.

Cautiously, he found a way to kneel on the marlin board so he could peer over the top to watch the other boat. There was a light breeze, chilling him even more, which he had not thought would have been possible. That, too, he realized, was another problem he had not foreseen. The other boat was about twenty meters away, but more like thirty to target, where he could see

Mallory on the flybridge with a woman alongside him. Assuming he got a clear shot when the time came, thirty meters was a long way with a handgun in ideal conditions, and it was far from ideal conditions.

Despite what people thought when they watched TV, hitting a target at that distance with a pistol was a difficult shot in the best of conditions. A kill shot would be almost impossible under normal circumstances, but Sam was shivering, and his hands were shaking. He knew he probably couldn't hit the boat, let alone one man on it. Sam seriously doubted he could succeed, yet the only hope Nicky and Didi had was for Sam to make an almost impossible shot.

Sam was okay on the police shooting range but was not by anyone's definition a marksman. He scored enough to keep his rating and permission to carry a firearm, and that was all. Knowingly shooting to kill someone was not an easy thing to do, and he knew that from experience. During the Domin8 case, Sam had shot and killed a man at a similar range by emptying his entire magazine at a sniper hidden in a tree but had only hit the man twice. Sam had achieved that feat when a hostage wasn't standing alongside the target, and he hadn't been shivering at the time.

The death had upset him for a while, and he received counseling afterward as protocol demanded, but he felt that he hadn't suffered any long-term effects. The man had beat his wife to death and hid in a tree to shoot Dave Barndon, so it was reasonably easy to justify his action. The internal investigation unit cleared him almost instantly. The thing was that out of nine shots Sam fired in rapid succession, he hit the sniper only twice, which had caused him to fall from the tree he was hiding in. Mooney broke his hip, tearing his femoral artery, and had bled to death quickly. It could be argued that the shots Sam fired didn't kill him at all, and had Clinton Mooney's foot not caught in a branch as he fell, he wouldn't have died. That thought did give Sam some comfort in his darker moments.

Sam reasoned, based on that experience, shooting Jimmy Mallory in his condition at that distance was next to impossible. Hitting the target was a foolish attempt at best and just plain stupid at worst. There was nothing for it; he had to get closer, which meant getting back in the water. Inwardly, he groaned at the thought. Before slipping back in the river, fearing he might not be successful, he knew he had to tell Felix what was happening, not knowing that at that precise moment, Felix was lying motionless and unconscious, shot by The Renegade. With cold fingers and making numerous mistakes, which he had to go back to fix, Sam sent a text message to Felix:

—Mallory is on the boat with the g/friend of the cab driver. The cabbie is in transit to save her. I am in the water, trying to get close to the boat. Send help urgently.—

Not waiting for a response, he turned the phone off, resealed the phone and gun back in the bag, and zipped it closed. Squirming carefully, hating what was to come next, he very slowly and quietly slipped back into the almost icy dark water.

With relief, he found that, as his body temperature was already so low, the water felt warmer than before, and for a short while, he felt better. He put the bag between his teeth so he could use both hands to pull himself along the stern of the boat slowly.

Once there, he peered around the corner and saw Mallory still on the flybridge, sitting in the skipper's chair, facing his way and looking down the walkway toward the gate. At his side, in the other seat, sat a woman. She seemed to be sitting quietly. Her arms had been tied behind her back, Sam realized.

Sam slipped below the surface after taking a deep breath and kicked off, heading for the floating concrete walkway, hands reaching out ahead of him as, when underwater, he couldn't see a thing. When he touched a combination of slimy seaweed and sharp barnacles on the thick concrete pile going down, anchoring the walkway to the river floor, he recoiled in horror. Sam jolted upward, banging his head on the underside of the sidewalk. He saw stars and could now add a pulsing headache to his list of discomforts. He could not remember if he had ever had a more miserable time in his life before that night.

Chapter 23

All the Time in the World?

Nicky was frantic as he drove toward the marina. He couldn't stop thinking about just how cruel life could be. Didi, who had never hurt a soul in her life and who had the most incredibly beautiful daughter by a man who dumped her, was now in the hands of a murderer who would kill her without a moment's hesitation, and it was all his fault.

Everyone knew Jimmy Mallory was a sadistic thug, while Didi was the purest, gentlest soul anyone could imagine. She was so meek and timid, so kind and caring. Nicky ached for Didi and wanted to save her more than anything in the world. Life was cruel, too, when he viewed his own existence. Both of his parents lost to a drunk driver and then raising Simon to help him grow into a wonderful young man, who was taken away by a gang of thrill-seekers who thought it would be fun to kick him to death. After that fateful night, he had gone off the rails. He accepted that, and he had taken lives he shouldn't have. It was Didi, with her kind and gentle nature, who showed him that life could be so much better with her than alone. She had never said a word since he told her about his vigilante alter ego. She never passed judgment and didn't hold his actions against him. She didn't have to; it was her honest,

331

loving, and caring spirit that showed him he had been wrong. By forgiving and wanting to be with him, she had given him something to live for.

He supposed, thinking back as he drove, that he could have used the gun to reason with the people rather than kill them or fire warning shots to scare them off. Nicky knew that he would never know now what that outcome would have achieved with that approach. But one thing was for sure; if he had let those people kill, hurt, or maim the victims they had been hurting and walked away himself, then Didi would be safe at work now and not held captive.

But on the other side of the coin, if he had been the type of person who ignored people being hurt and walked away rather than intervene, he never would have met Didi in the first place. She would have been stripped of her dignity, along with her clothes, and brutally raped in that alley. Nicky would have ignored her plight like so many others seemed to when faced with the choice between saving someone and risking themselves or walking away. If he lost Didi, he would have less than nothing, and Nicky would not be able to live knowing that he had been the one responsible for her death at Mallory's hands. Nicky knew that if Jimmy Mallory had made a mistake, it was not realizing that Nicky would die gladly if he could save Didi. He had nothing left to lose without her.

He turned off Stirling Highway, getting ever closer to the yacht club, and tried to think of any plan that would bring a different outcome, but he couldn't see one. The confrontation would be the end of the line, one way or another. He lifted his hand off the steering wheel and held it out; it wasn't shaking. Nicky had accepted his fate. His only consolation was that he would be back with his parents and Simon. The single variable was whether he could save Didi first.

****

Jasmine and Brendon Hamilton lived opposite Jimmy Mallory's house. They had been terrified of him by reputation but in later TV interviews admitted that he was nothing if not an extremely personable, kind, and generous neighbor. Whenever he'd held parties at his house, and he often did, he not only warned the people living around him but invited them to attend. As his reputation preceded him, if you were asked, unless you had an overseas trip planned at that time, you went rather than risk offending Jimmy's feelings.

Jasmine knew that going to one of Jimmy's parties was like going to a Hollywood movie star's house. While they always started very faux-posh, with women elegant and dressed to kill, by midnight, everything changed. By then, they were likely to be half-naked, snorting cocaine, and having sex with other attendees, or any of the drop-dead gorgeous hostesses, in any one of the five bedrooms, the swimming pool, the spa, or anywhere the mood took them.

Jasmine forbade them from going again after the last party. Two young women wanted to take them upstairs to one of the bedrooms and have a foursome. Her drunk husband, to Jasmine's horror, immediately agreed. While she never dared admit it to a living soul afterward, when she finally calmed down and stopped yelling at her husband for "encouraging those bimbos," she regretted her decision. Her remorse scared her, and she felt if they went to another one of his parties, next time she might agree. It had been a secret fantasy of

Jasmine's for years to experience another woman. The thought of being with two stunningly beautiful, sexy women, with her husband's permission, made her tremble when she permitted herself to fantasize. She rationalized that some fantasies are best left that way, and if they took that step, what effect would it have on their marriage?

Jasmine and Brendon were playing cribbage when they heard two gunshots from across the road. They had been drinking red wine and were gearing up to make love later, which they tried to do once a week. The wine would inevitably lead to the type of lovemaking during which, while closing her eyes, she would sometimes imagine it to be one of those women going down on her instead of Brendon, though she would never admit that fantasy to him. After all their years of marriage, they had developed the wonderful familiarity of each other's bodies that only comes from years of knowing what turned each other on and off, but occasionally, Jasmine let her mind wander.

When people hear what sounds like gunshots, they wonder if it is a car backfiring or someone had dropped something loudly. Sometimes they wonder *what* it was, not wanting to think it was the sound of a gun. But as they lived opposite a known gangster, Jasmine and Brendon instantly knew what they'd heard because they half expected to hear it sooner or later. They dived to the floor simultaneously and huddled under the table, hugging each other, waiting for more shots, the cards, crib board, and matchsticks scattered all around them.

When no more shots came, Jasmine urged her husband to go and see what was happening. She could imagine herself at the bridge club having the best gossip of the week: a gunfight at Jimmy Mallory's house. After some bickering, Brendon crawled to the front windows and slowly, almost comically, raised himself to a height where he could pull the curtains to one side and peer over the sill.

Brendon saw one man scurrying away, carrying a case, and another person lying on the driveway. He believed there was no danger to them as the shooter was escaping. More importantly, the man lying in the driveway seemed to have been shot and could need medical help. He jumped up and ran to the phone, dialed the emergency number, and yelled at the operator that a man had been shot and needed police and ambulance assistance immediately. He gave the address and then hung up. Meanwhile, Jasmine was still lying under the table, shouting questions at him to find out what was going on. He ignored her and raced into the kitchen to grab their first aid kit, then ran out the front door to see if he could aid the wounded man.

Brendon had been in the merchant navy in his younger days and had had some basic medical training, but he had never seen a gunshot wound. He knelt by Felix's side, saw all of the blood on his chest and around his body, and thought that there was no point; surely no one could survive such trauma. Brendon ripped open a large gauze pack, pulled the man's shirt open, and pressed it over the wound with one hand. He felt the man's neck with the other for a pulse. It was there but very faint. He thought quickly. A gunshot wound to the chest must mean a collapsed lung at the very least. Therefore, he would be having trouble breathing. He looked up as Jasmine arrived and screamed at what she saw.

"Jas, stop it, right now. We don't have time for that. Go and get a blanket; we have to try to keep him warm." She stood stock-still, just staring. "Jas, now, move." Then he took a deep breath and, using one hand to open the man's mouth, pinched his nostrils together while keeping the pressure on the wound to slow the bleeding with the other hand. He remembered his first aid training from years before and began the kiss of life.

The pulse was there, still faint, when the ambulance arrived and relieved Brendon, who was physically, mentally, and emotionally exhausted. The first police car arrived shortly afterward and questioned the couple and other neighbors who had come to watch. Once the police knew who owned the house, they first thought it was a criminal underworld shooting and hypothesized the person running away would be Mallory carrying a suitcase. But the lack of a car was confusing; if it was Mallory, why run away? Why not drive?

A search through the victim's pockets turned up Felix's police ID which was radioed in for the Major Crime Squad to attend.

****

Felix's phone was locked with a four-digit security code, but a feature of the phone was that incoming text messages were displayed on the screen and could be read without using the code. When Sam sent his text, it stayed displayed on the screen.

A uniformed officer, with outstanding initiative, accompanied Felix inside the ambulance to the hospital. His name was Paul Raymond. Paul was the youngest of three brothers who were all police officers of varying ranks. Paul heard a message tone coming from Felix's jacket pocket and removed the phone, looking at the screen. When he read the message, he realized the wounded man had been on a stakeout, perhaps waiting for Mallory to return. He radioed in his discovery and advised dispatch of a hostage situation and that an officer needed assistance at Mallory's boat, though he didn't know where that was. Within minutes the location was discovered, and the Tactical Response Group was sent to the Nedlands Marina. They had been on high alert ever since the gang war started and responded immediately.

****

Sam tried to slow the tremors that were wrenching through his entire body when he heard Nick Pantella's voice call out, "I'm here, Mallory. Now let her go."

"Listen, asshole, in my hand is a .357 magnum, and it's pointed at your girlfriend's head. You don't give the orders here. I do. Now step onto the boat and cast off the ropes. We're going for a little ride."

Nicky stood on the concrete walkway, looking around. Sam thought he was trying to decide how best to handle the situation he faced. "A few years ago, I was in the army," Sam heard him shout, "and I was pretty good too. I know more about weapons than you ever will. Sure, you could kill Didi, but I'm not dumb. If I step on that boat, you will kill her and me both, so why would I do as you say?"

Sam watched as Mallory pulled Didi to her feet and held the gun to her head. She cried out in anguish and fear. The unmistakable sound of a trigger being pulled back echoed across the marina.

Sam took the opportunity to gently but purposefully kick across the gulf between the two boats

337

and come up against the marlin board of *The Intrepid*. He felt a trickle of blood run down his face from the gash on his head, from hitting the barnacles under the walkway.

"Mallory! Isn't your beef with me? Don't you want to deal with me over the death of that useless wife-beating dickhead of a brother of yours? That pistol is one of the finest handguns ever made, but even if you were the best shot in the world, you couldn't hit me with it at this range. And this is a pretty big marina. I'd say there are a few people on their boats right now. Some maybe even listening to this conversation, but they are certainly going to come running the moment you shoot. You can kill me, I don't care, but I do care for Didi, so let her go, and I will come to you."

Sam was shivering horribly. He tried and failed to pull the ziplock bag open. It was too wet, so he tried to pry it open with his teeth. Finally, after what seemed like an eternity, it opened, and Sam took his gun out of the bag and clicked off the safety catch.

Mallory was framed clearly in the moonlight, ten meters away, standing on the flybridge. Sam aimed, waiting for the moment when he thought it safe to fire. He couldn't take a chance of hitting Didi, and he knew if he missed, Mallory would know where he was and would shoot back. Mallory could kill Sam in the water, then the girl and Nicky would come running. He wouldn't be able to help himself, then Mallory would kill him too. He would sail away and come ashore somewhere farther up or down the coast. With his money, he could hide for years. Sam dare not miss, but if he hit Mallory while his gun was pointing at Didi's head, Jimmy could pull the trigger involuntarily, and she could die. It was an impossible situation, so Sam waited for an opening.

Mallory suddenly hit Didi a brutal blow on the head with his pistol. Blood squirted out as she stumbled, and he pushed her away. She hit the railing and tumbled over the side of the flybridge. Her legs disappeared over the edge, and Sam heard the splash as she hit the water. Mallory brought the gun round in a two-handed stance to take a shot at Nicky, who, as Sam had predicted, immediately ran toward the boat. He would be in range within seconds. Sam fired, trying desperately to stop his shaking hands, but the bullet ricocheted off the chrome rail across the front of the bridge, missing Mallory by inches. He fired again and again, but each bullet missed its mark. Mallory turned toward him at the stern, a shocked look on his face, and fired three shots in return. The second one hit Sam in the shoulder.

Sam felt like a sledgehammer hit him. He spun violently in the water, causing the gun in his hand to fly away and sink. Mallory turned back to Nicky, who was now within range. All Nicky could see was the spot where Didi had entered the water. He had to save her; he had no other thought in mind.

****

The Tactical Response Group van screeched to a halt in the marina car park. The headlights shone on a man standing at the fence with what looked like a rifle resting through one of the holes in the chain links. He seemed to be aiming through a telescopic sight, yet one of his arms hung uselessly at his side. The officers poured out of the sliding doors on both sides, shouting at him to drop his weapon. As one, they saw it kick in recoil as it fired, yet a silencer muffled the sound of the single gunshot.

Unhesitating, three men opened fire with their Heckler and Koch machine guns, and The Renegade fell against the fence, his body hit multiple times with nine-millimeter bullets. He fell, dead, as the rifle hung at a forty-five-degree angle, stuck in the fencing.

****

Nicky didn't see Mallory's head disintegrate from the bullet fired from The Renegade's sniper rifle. From his peripheral vision, he was aware of a body tumbling from the flybridge to fall on the bow and the sound of gunshots from behind him but only vaguely. Mallory landed half on the contained life raft and half on the fiberglass deck, breaking his back, but he was already dead.

The expanding ripples showed where Didi had entered the water, and Nicky dived full length through the air. Taking a deep breath, he entered the cold, deep dark water, desperate to find the love of his life. He missed her on the first pass; she must have sunk too quickly, he realized frantically. Nicky surfaced, praying he would see her, then got his bearings and duck-dived straight back down again, hoping for some light: any light.

The TRG officers heard the shouting and splashing, shot the lock on the gate leading to the walkway, and ran to where Nicky flailed in the water. Six officers arrived to see a hysterical man in the water pleading: "Help me for God's sake. She fell in the water here; please help get some light so I can find her." Then he dived down again.

Five powerful mag light flashlight beams shone

into the water, lighting the river water down to the weed and rocks below. Nicky saw Didi's white top billowing in the water as she floated face down a meter above the bottom.

He reached her just as Marvin, a member of the TRG and a powerful swimmer, joined him. Together they held her and kicked for the surface. With her lifeless body between them, they swam back to the walkway, where Didi was grabbed and pulled onto the concrete surface. Another TRG member began CPR. Nicky and Marvin were pulled up, and Nicky fell at Didi's side, grabbed her hand, and began talking to her, telling her, "Wake up, baby. Please, please, baby, wake up."

Meanwhile, the other officers, still not clear what the situation was, fanned out and scoured the area, guns held at the ready. They found Jimmy Mallory's body on the deck, while another officer, Justin, scanned the water around the boat with his torch and saw Sam's body floating face up twelve meters behind the stern.

"There's another one in the water!" Justin screamed and without a thought, dived from the back of the boat and swam out to grab him. He reached Sam and pulled his body to a recovery position using his wounded shoulder. When Justin grabbed it firmly, Sam groaned. He woke from the shock and unconscious state he had been in while drifting away from the boat. "He's alive!" Justin shouted and then kicked back to the walkway and help.

Epilogue

Before the ambulance could take Sam away, he insisted on speaking to Nicky and refused all arguments to the contrary. No amount of pleading by paramedics would stop him; he was insistent. He was wrapped from head to foot in heat-retaining blankets and had an injection of morphine for his shattered shoulder. A paramedic brought Nicky from Didi's ambulance to see Sam. He wriggled his right hand outside the blankets and waved the paramedic away so he could talk to Nicky in private. He was still shivering and in a quiet, shaky voice, asked, "How's your girl?"

Nicky's eyes were red, bloodshot from worry and tears. He wore a blanket himself, as he too was cold and shivering, though he barely felt it. "They think she will be all right, thank God. The concussion seems to be the worst of it. She's awake now. Thank you, Sam, thank you so much. You saved our lives."

Sam put his hand on Nicky's arm and squeezed it as best he could. "Yes, thank God for that. You're a brave man, Nick, very brave, and you two deserve a happy life together. So what I'm about to tell you is important." Sam shook his arm to make sure Nicky paid attention, then continued. "Remember this, Nick, no matter what, deny, deny, deny. Do you understand me?"

Nick looked at him quizzically. "Not really, no."

"Nick, the case is closed now. They have the man they think was *the vigilante* and who they think killed Desmond Mallory. Now that Jimmy Mallory is dead, there is no need to tell them any differently, okay? You've been through enough, so keep quiet and deny everything. Mallory thought you could tell him who killed his brother because he didn't want to believe it was his best mate, and that's all you know. Do you understand me, Nick? You need to look after your girl now. You deserve a life together. Go and find it. Just never, ever, tell them what really happened."

Nicky nodded. "I understand. You saved both our lives tonight, shooting when you did. I can never thank you enough for what you've done for Didi and me. Thank you, Sam."

"You deserved a break, and you're welcome. Just don't fuck these last little bits up when you make your statement, and make sure Didi knows to say the same thing, okay? Now get out of here, be with her."

****

Sam Collins recovered the use of his arm but only after an operation to repair his shattered shoulder and several weeks of extensive physiotherapy. The .357 magnum bullet caused a lot of damage. He discovered he had developed a phobia of water and had continual nightmares for weeks afterward. In time, with help, Sam fully recovered, though any time he came close to the Swan River, he shuddered with fear.

He was questioned at length why he and Felix had taken it upon themselves to perform two unauthorized stakeouts, and Sam explained there had been no time to do otherwise after the phone conversation with Mallory. Internal affairs had to agree that both officers had shown outstanding ingenuity, bravery, and dedication at significant personal risk to ensure the safety of two potential hostages.

Sam received his second commendation for bravery, and the FBI uncovered The Renegade's various identities, which connected him to twenty-seven murders for hire. Once more, Sam became the poster boy for the WA Police Department due to the extensive publicity of a vigilante halted, Mallory being killed, a hitman dead, and a gang war over. He received a promotion to detective inspector as the media strongly inferred Sam had achieved these feats single-handedly while he did his best to show he was only one part of a much larger team.

****

Three months later, Sam received a wedding invitation in the mail, and he knew he could not decline. The accompanying note explained that Didi and Nicky had waited for him to recover so he could attend, though Sam knew this from Nicky's hospital visits. The pair had visited regularly and kept him informed of the police interviews, though as Sam had predicted, the investigators appeared to want to tie up loose ends rather than look for any evidence that would lead to a new direction.

Sam knew who he would take as his plus one. He had broken up with his girlfriend and was enjoying being single again. She hadn't liked the spotlight placed on him and became jealous of the women who suddenly saw him as a hero and wanted to get to know him. As the invitations for him to attend charity events, parties, and gala performances seemed never-ending, she could see a future littered with other women vying for his attention, and it was evident that Sam was not ready to settle down. Possibly with his fame, he never would be, and she broke up with him while they could still talk civilly to each other.

Sam arrived at the church with his arm fresh out of the sling and had to admit he had never seen a more beautiful bride than Didi. Her daughter, Siobhan, a tiny version of Didi herself, glowed as the flower girl, clutching a yellow stuffed rabbit in one hand and a posy of flowers in the other. She stole the show and everyone's hearts. Siobhan hardly left Nicky's side, who looked handsome and fit, dressed in a black tuxedo and bow tie, while Didi looked radiant in traditional white. Later at the reception, held at Alan Chan's Chinese restaurant, the three danced together to the bridal waltz. Siobhan held in one of Nicky's arms while the other held Didi, and there was not a dry eye as the guests watched the trio dance hugging each other, their overwhelming love for each other evident.

Didi's friend, Caroline, dragged Sam up on the full dance floor when the formalities had ended, as the DJ played a selection of dance songs. To the resounding rhythm and lyrics of *Sacrifice*, he held her while her eyes bored into his and let it be known, silently, that he could ask her out if not that night, then any night he chose. Sam promised he would call her.

From the side of the dance floor, at one of the eight-seater tables, a still convalescing Felix Milanski, Sam's plus one, shook his head and wondered, not for the first time, when his younger friend and colleague would ever settle down and marry. *It's not fair*, he thought. *Sam can't stay happy for the rest of his life; he has to become miserable sooner or later, just like everyone else.*

There was little doubt that Felix's life had been saved that night by the kiss of life performed on him for over fifteen minutes by Brendon Hamilton. His workmates, knowing his strict moral code, teased him and asked if he remembered being kissed that long by a married man. Felix's belief that marriage vows were made for life was well known by those who worked with him, which fueled more joke-taking at his expense.

After the shooting, which almost took his life, Felix and his wife planned for his retirement in earnest. They had already bought a caravan that would take them on the six-month trip around Australia when they joined the *Grey Nomad Brigade.* Then he could fish, relax, and stay away from criminals permanently. Though, at times, he worried he would get bored. He had only eighteen months left to serve, time enough, he thought to turn his back on what seemed to him to be a never-ending tide of crime. He often worried that for each one he locked away, three took his place.

It was an extended embrace between Sam, Nicky, and Didi when the reception ended, and they took their leave for their honeymoon. The happy couple thanked him again in whispered tones while Sam assured them that their much-deserved happiness made it all worthwhile.

Felix and Sam returned to their table and came face-to-face with Alan Chan. He held two crystal glasses, half-filled with a deep and dark amber liquid and ice. "These very special, single malt drinks for you. My way to say thank you for saving Nicky and Miss Didi." He handed them the glasses and bowed deeply.

"Why, thank you," Sam replied, genuinely pleased,

while Felix nodded, gladly taking his glass. Allan held up his hand and backed away, leaving the two alone at the table. It was quiet now that almost everyone else had gone.

Felix stared over the top of his glass at Sam for long minutes.

"What, Felix? What are you staring at?"

"I know what you did, Sam. I want you to know that. Don't deny it, because I know you too well. I know what you did and why. I agree with you; you made the right choice; they deserve the break you gave them."

Sam stared back and slowly nodded. He should have known he could never pull the wool over his old boss' eagle eye. He didn't reply; some things were best left unsaid. Instead, he raised his glass as a silent toast, and they drank to Nicky and Didi's future health and happiness.

Author's Note

As with *Domin8*, this book was originally self-published because of an issue with my former publisher, who helped me with *Forever Night* and then was bought out. It's all water under the bridge now, but back then, this was titled: *The Vigilante Taxi*. Like *Domin8*, I was never entirely happy with it but didn't know enough to see how I could do better. *Taxi* was the third book I'd written, and my editor, Alex, to be fair to her, struggled to sort the manuscript out. She is American, and I am Australian, and that cultural difference didn't help.

Now I've written thirteen books and have a fantastic publisher: *The Wild Rose Press* of NY, and I have an equally amazing editor, Melanie Billings. Mel tirelessly has taught me to be a better writer (bless you, Mel), and when I picked up *Taxi* to read three years after releasing it, I was disappointed and determined I could now tell the story of Didi and Nicky much better. It's a fact that the more you write, the better you get at the craft—that is most definitely true for me.

The Vigilante and the Dancer, as it's now titled, I felt was always a good story and deserved better from me in telling it, and so I have spent many months rewriting it. I am now delighted with the changes—loads of them throughout its hundred-odd thousand-word length, and I hope, dear reader, you are too.

Northbridge exists here in my home city, though all the establishments mentioned are fictitious. The area is the hub of nightlife entertainment of Perth, Western Australia, and includes our very own Chinatown. Is there violence on the streets at night? Yep, you bet. Is it as bad as I've portrayed? Well, sometimes, sadly, yes, it is. As an author trying to tell a tale, naturally, I have exaggerated some things and embellished others for the benefit of the story. There is, without doubt, a drug underworld in all cities, and sadly Perth is not immune from its evil clutches. I did extensive research and met with several *colorful shady characters,* none of whom I will name who helped me understand the criminal element.

I'd like to think that the positives in this story far outweigh the negatives. I believe we deserve, and can all find love and happiness, no matter if we are a car dealer, a single parent lap dancer, or a taxi driver who has suffered more tragedy than any one person should have to.

Yes, I can sleep better at night, believing that.
SBK

A word about the author...

I was born in the UK, what seems like an epoch ago, and moved to Australia at age sixteen. I was a long-haired rock guitarist and poet/songwriter before real life got in the way, and I gave it all up for love.

I've always felt I had tales to tell and won short story competitions and published poetry in my wilder, younger days. More recently, I've written and published thirteen novels. While they have mainly been police procedural thrillers, mainly focusing on serial killers, they all have a love theme running through them.

I believe love and family are everything. Anything else you gain in life is a bonus.

I live in Perth, in Western Australia, and am fiercely patriotic and parochial. My wife is amazing in that she not only puts up with living with a writer but encourages it. I've been blessed with five children, and I adore them all.

http://stephen-b-king.com

Lightning Source UK Ltd.
Milton Keynes UK
UKHW022109281222
414549UK00018B/183

9 781509 243440